D I A N A.

BY

SUSAN WARNER,

AUTHOR OF

'THE WIDE, WIDE WORLD,' 'QUEECHY,' ETC. ETC.

LONDON:

JAMES NISBET & CO., 21 BERNERS STREET.

MDCCCLXXVII.

Copyright.]

'Know well, my soul, God's hand controls
    Whate'er thou fearest ;
Round Him in calmest music rolls
    Whate'er thou hearest.

'What to thee is shadow, to Him is day,
    And the end He knoweth ;
And not on a blinded, aimless way
    The spirit goeth.'

WHITTIER.

CONTENTS.

———◆———

CONTENTS.

DIANA.

———◆———

CHAPTER I.

THE SEWING SOCIETY.

I AM thinking of a little brown house, somewhere in the wilds of New England. I wish I could make my readers see it as it was, one June afternoon some years ago. Not for anything very remarkable about it; there are thousands of such houses scattered among our hills and valleys; nevertheless one understands any life story the better for knowing amid what sort of scenes it was unfolded. Moreover, such a place is one of the pleasant things in the world to look at, as I judge. This was a small house, with its gable end to the road, and a lean-to at the back, over which the long roof sloped down picturesquely. It was weather-painted; that was all; of a soft, dark grey now, that harmonized well enough with the gayer colours of meadows and trees. And two superb elms, of New England's own, stood beside it and hung over it, enfolding and sheltering the little old house, as it were, with their arms of strength and beauty. Those trees would have dignified anything. One of them, of the more rare weeping variety, drooped over the door of the lean-to, shading it protectingly, and hiding with its long pendant branches the hard and stiff lines of the building. So the green draped the grey; until, in the soft mingling of hues, the light play of sunshine and shadow,

A

it seemed as if the smartness of paint upon the old weather-boarding would have been an intrusion, and not an advantage. In front of the house was a little space given to flowers; at least there were some irregular patches and borders, where balsams and hollyhocks and pinks and marigolds made a spot of light colouring; with one or two luxuriantly-growing blush roses, untrained and wandering, bearing a wealth of sweetness on their long, swaying branches. There was that spot of colour; all around and beyond lay meadows, orchards, and cultivated fields; till at no great distance the ground became broken, and rose into a wilderness of hills, mounting higher and higher. In spots these also showed cultivation; for the most part they were covered with green woods in the depth of June foliage. The soft, varied hilly outline filled the whole circuit of the horizon; within the nearer circuit of the hills the little grey house sat alone, with only one single exception. At the edge of the meadow land, half hid behind the spur of a hill, stood another grey farm-house; it might have been half a mile off. People accustomed to a more densely populated country would call the situation lonesome; solitary it was. But nature had shaken down her hand full of treasures over the place. Art had never so much as looked that way. However, we can do without art on a June afternoon.

The door of the lean-to looked towards the road, and so made a kind of front door to the kitchen which was within. The door-sill was raised a single step above the rough old grey stone which did duty before it; and sitting on the door-step, in the shadow and sunlight which came through the elm branches and fell over her, this June afternoon, was the person whose life story I am going to try to tell. She sat there as one at home, and in the leisure of one who had done her work, with arms crossed upon her bosom, and an air of almost languid quiet upon her face. The afternoon was quiet-inspiring. Genial warm sunshine filled the fields and grew hazy in the depth of the hills; the long hanging elm branches were still; sunlight and shadow beneath slept in each other's arms; soft breaths of air, too faint to move the elms, came nevertheless with reminders and suggestions of all sorts of sweetness; from the leaf-buds of the woods, from the fresh turf of the meadows, from a thousand hidden flowers and ferns at work in their secret laboratories, distilling a thousand perfumes, mingled and untraceable. Now and then the breath of the roses was quite distinguishable; and from fields farther off the delicious scent of new hay. It was just the time of day when the birds do not sing; and the watcher at the door seemed to be in their condition.

She was a young woman, full grown, but young. Her dress was the common print working dress of a farmer's daughter, with a spot or two of wet upon her apron showing that she had been busy, as her dress suggested. Her sleeves were still rolled up above her elbows, leaving the crossed arms full in view. And if there is character in faces, so there is in arms; and everybody knows there is in hands. These arms were after the model of the typical woman's arm; not chubby and round and fat, but moulded with beautiful contour, showing muscular form and power, with the blue veins here and there marking the clear delicate skin. Only look at the arm, without even seeing the face, and you would feel there was nervous energy and power of will; no weak, flabby, undecided action would ever come of it. The wrist was tapering enough, and the hand perfectly shaped, like the arm; not quite so white. The face, —you could not read it at once, possibly not till it had seen a few more years. It was very reposeful this afternoon. Yet the brow and the head bore tokens of the power you would expect; they were very fine; and the eyes under the straight brow were full and beautiful, a deep blue-grey, changing and darkening at times. But the mouth and lower part of the face was as sweet and mobile as three years old; playing as innocently and readily upon every occasion; nothing had fixed those lovely lines. The combination made it a singular face, and of course very handsome. But it looked very unconscious of that fact.

Within the kitchen another woman was stepping about actively, and now and then cast an unsatisfied look at the doorway. Finally came to a stop in the middle of the floor to speak.

'What are you sittin' there for, Diana?'

'Nothing, that I know of.'

'If I was sittin' there for nothin', seems to me I'd get up and go somewheres else.'

'Where?' said the beauty languidly.

'Anywhere. Goodness! it makes me feel as if nothin' would ever get done, to see you sittin' there so.'

'It's all done, mother.'

'What?'

'Everything.'

'Have you got out the pink china?'

'Yes.'

'Is your cake made?'

'Yes, mother; you saw me do it.'

'I didn't see you bakin' it, though.'

'Well, it is done.'

'Did it raise light and puffy?'

'Beautiful.'

'And didn't get burned?'

'Only the least bit, in the corner. No harm.'

'Have you cut the cheese and shivered the beef?'

'All done.'

'Then I think you had better go and dress yourself.'

'There's plenty of time. Nobody can be here for two hours yet.'

'I wouldn't sit and do nothin', if I was you.'

'Why not, mother? when there is really nothing to do.'

'I don't believe in no such minutes, for my part. They never come to me. Look at what I've done to-day, now. There was first the lighting the fire and getting breakfast. Then I washed up, and righted the kitchen, and set on the dinner. Then I churned and brought the butter and worked *that*. Then there was the dairy things. Then I've been in the garden and picked four quarts of ifs-and-ons for pickles; got 'em all down in brine, too. Then I made out my bread, and made biscuits for tea, and got dinner, and eat it, and cleared it away, and boiled a ham.'

'Not since dinner, mother?'

'Took it out, and that; and got all my pots and kettles put

away; and picked over all that lot o' berries. I think I'd make preserves of 'em, Diana; when folks come to sewing meeting for the missionaries they needn't have all creation to eat, seems to me. They don't sew no better for it. *I* believe in fasting, once in a while.'

'What for?'

'What for? Why, to keep down people's stomach; take off slice of their pride.'

'Mother! do you think eating and people's pride have anything to do with each other?'

'I guess I do! I tell you, fasting is as good as whipping to take down a child's stomach; let 'em get real thin and empty, and they'll come down and be as meek as Moses. Folks ain't different from children.'

'You never tried that with me, mother,' said Diana, half laughing.

'Your father always let you have your own way. I could ha' managed *you*, I guess; but your father and you was too much at once. Come, Diana—do get up and go off and get dressed, or something.'

But she sat still, letting the soft June air woo her, and the scents of flower and field hold some subtle communion with her. There was a certain hidden harmony between her and them; and yet they stirred her somehow uneasily.

'I wonder,' she said after a few minutes' silence, 'what a nobleman's park is like?'

The mother stood still again in the middle of the kitchen.

'A park!'

'Yes. It must be something beautiful; and yet I cannot think how it could be prettier than this.'

'Than what?' said her mother impatiently.

'Just all this. All this country; and the hayfields, and the cornfields, and the hills.'

'A park!' her mother repeated. 'I saw a "park" once, when I was down to New York; you wouldn't want to see it twice. A homely little mite of a green yard, with a big white house in the middle of it; and homely enough *that* was too. It might do very well for the city folks; but the land knows I'd be sorry enough to live there. What's putting parks in your head?'

But the daughter did not answer, and the mother stood still and looked at her, with perhaps an inscrutable bit of pride and delight behind her hard features. It never came out.

'Diana, do you calculate to be ready for the sewin' meetin'?'

'Yes, mother.'

'Since they must come, we may as well make 'em welcome; and they won't think it, if you meet 'em in your kitchen dress. Is the new minister comin', do you s'pose?'

'I don't know if anybody has told him.'

'Somebody had ought to. It won't be much of a meetin' without the minister; and it 'ud give him a good chance to get acquainted. Mr. Hardenburgh used to like to come.'

'The new man doesn't look much like Mr. Hardenburgh.'

'It'll be a savin' in biscuits, if he ain't.'

'I used to like to see Mr. Hardenburgh eat, mother.'

'I hain't no objection—when I don't have the biscuits to make. Diana, you baked a pan o' those biscuits too brown. Now you must look out, when you put 'em in to warm up, or they'll be more'n crisp.'

'Everybody else has them cold, mother.'

'They won't at my house. It's just to save trouble; and there ain't a lazy hair in me, you ought to know by this time.'

'But I thought you were for taking down people's pride, and keeping the sewing society low; and here are hot biscuits and all sorts of things,' said Diana, getting up from her seat at last.

'The cream'll be in the little red pitcher—so mind you don't go and take the green one. And do be off, child, and fix yourself; for it'll be a while yet before I'm ready, and there'll be nobody to see folks when they come.'

Diana went off slowly up-stairs to her own room. There were but two, one on each side of the little landing-place at the head of the stair; and she and her mother divided the floor between them. Diana's room was not what one would have expected from the promise of all the rest of the house. That was simple enough, as the dwelling of a small farmer would be, and much like the other farm-houses of the region. But Diana's room, a little one it was, had one side filled with bookshelves; and on the bookshelves was a dark array of solid and ponderous volumes. A table under the front window held one or two that were apparently in present use; the rest of the room displayed the more usual fittings and surroundings of a maiden's life. Only in their essentials, however; no luxury was there. The little chest of drawers, covered with a white cloth, held a brush and comb, and supported a tiny looking-glass; small paraphernalia of vanity. No essences or perfumes or powders; no curling sticks or crimping pins; no rats or cats, cushions or frames, or skeletons of any sort, were there for the help of the rustic beauty; and neither did she need them. So you would have said if you had seen her when her toilette was done. The soft outlines of her figure were neither helped nor hidden by any artificial contrivances. Her abundant dark hair was in smooth bands and a luxuriant coil at the back of her head—woman's natural crown; and she looked nature-crowned when she had finished her work. Just because nature had done so much for her and she had let nature alone; and because, furthermore, Diana did not know or at least did not think about her beauty. When she was in order, and it did not take long, she placed herself at the table under the window before noticed, and opening a book that lay ready, forgot I dare say all about the sewing meeting; till the slow grating of wheels at the gate brought her back to present realities, and she went downstairs.

There was a little old green waggon before the house, with an old horse and two women, one of whom had got down and was tying the horse's head to the fence.

'Are you afraid he will run away?' said the voice of Diana gaily from the garden.

'Massy! no; but he might hitch round somewheres, you know, and get himself into trouble. Thank ye—I am allays thankful and glad when I get safe out o' this waggin.'

So spoke the elder lady, descending with Diana's help and a great deal of circumlocution from her perch in the vehicle. And then they went into the bright parlour, where windows

and doors stood open, and chairs had been brought in, ready
to accommodate all who might come.

'It's kind o' sultry,' said the same lady, wiping her face.
'I declare these ellums o' yourn do cast an elegant shadder.
It allays sort o' hampers me to drive, and I don't feel free till
I can let the reins fall; that's how I come to be so heated.
Dear me, you do excel in notions!' she exclaimed, as Diana
presented some glasses of cool water with raspberry vinegar.
'Ain't that wonderful coolin'!'

'Will the minister come to the meeting, Diana?' asked the
other woman.

'He'd come, if he knowed he could get anything like this,'
said the other, smacking her lips and sipping her glass slowly.
And then came in her hostess.

If Mrs. Starling was hard-favoured, it cannot be denied that
she had a certain style about her. Some ugly people do.
Country style, no doubt; but these things are relative; and in
a smart black silk, with sheer muslin neckerchief and a close-
fitting little cap, her natural self-possession and self-assertion
were very well set off. Very different from Diana's calm grace
and simplicity; the mother and daughter were alike in nothing
beyond the fact that each had character. Perhaps that is a
common fact in such a region and neighbourhood; for many
of the ladies who now came thronging into the meeting looked
as if they might justly lay claim to so much praise. The room
filled up; thimbles and housewives came out of pockets; work
was produced from baskets and bags; and tongues went like
mill-clappers. They put the June afternoon out of countenance. Mrs. Barry, the good lady who had arrived first, took
out her knitting, and in a corner went over to her neighbour
all the incidents of her drive, the weather, the getting out of
the waggon, the elm-tree shadow, and the raspberry vinegar.
Mrs. Carpenter, a well-to-do farmer's wife, gave the details of
her dairy misfortunes and success to *her* companion on the next
seat. Mrs. Flandin discussed missions. Mrs. Bell told how the
family of Mr. Hardenburgh had got away on their journey to
their new place of abode.

'I always liked Mr. Hardenburgh,' said Mrs. Carpenter.

'He had a real good wife,' remarked Miss Gunn, the store-keeper's sister, 'and that goes a great way. Mrs. Hardenburgh was a right-down good woman.'

'But you was speakin' o' *Mr.* Hardenburgh, the dominie,' said Mrs. Salter. 'He was a man as there warn't much harm in, I've always said. 'Tain't a man's fault if he can't make his sermons interestin', I s'pose.'

'Mr. Hardenburgh preached real good sermons, now, always seemed to *me*,' rejoined Mrs. Carpenter. 'He meant right; that's what he did.'

'That's *so!* ' chimed in Mrs. Mansfield, a rich farmer in her own person.

'There was an owl up in one of our elm-trees one night,' began Mrs. Starling—

'Du tell! so nigh 's that!' said Mrs. Barry from her corner.

'—And I took up Josiah's gun and *meant to* shoot him; but I didn't.'

'He was awful tiresome—there!' exclaimed Mrs. Boddington. 'What's the use of pretendin' he warn't? Nobody couldn't mind what his sermons was about; I don't believe as he knew himself. Now, a minister had ought to know what he means, whether any one else does or not, and I like a minister that makes *me* know what he means.'

'Why, Mrs. Boddington,' said Mrs. Flandin, 'I didn't know as you cared anything about religion, one way or another.'

'I've got to go to church, Mrs. Flandin; and I'd a little rayther be kep' awake while I'm there without pinching my fingers. I'd prefer it.'

'Why has anybody *got* to go to church that doesn't want to go?' inquired Diana. But that was like a shell let off in the midst of the sewing circle.

'Hear that, now!' said Mrs. Boddington. 'Ain't that a rouser?' Mrs. Boddington was a sort of a cousin, and liked the fun; she lived in the one farm-house in sight of Mrs. Starling's.

'She don't mean it,' said Mrs. Mansfield.

'Trust Di Starling for meaning whatever she says,' returned the other. 'You and I mayn't understand it, but that's all one, you know.'

'But what *do* she mean?' said Mrs. Salter.

'Yes, what's the use o' havin' a church, ef folks ain't goin' to it?' said Mrs. Carpenter.

'No,' said Diana, laughing; 'I only asked why any one *must* go, if he don't want to. Where's the *must?*'

'When we had good Mr. Hardenburgh, for example,' chimed in Mrs. Boddington, 'who was as loggy as he could be; good old soul! and put us all to sleep, or to wishin' we could. My! hain't I eaten quarts o' dill in the course o' the summer, trying to keep myself respectably awake and considerin' o' what was goin' on! Di says, why *must* any one eat all that dill that don't want to?'

'Cloves is better,' suggested Miss Gunn.

Some laughed at this; others looked portentously grave.

'It's just one o' Di's nonsense speeches,' said her mother; 'what they mean I'm sure I don't know. She reads too many books to be just like other folks.'

'But the books were written by other folks, mother.'

'La! some sort, child. Not our sort, I guess.'

'Hain't Di never learned her catechism?' inquired Mrs. Flandin.

'Is there anything about going to church in it?' asked the girl.

'There's most all sorts o' good things in it,' answered vaguely Mrs. Flandin, who was afraid of committing herself. 'I thought Di might ha' learned there something about such a thing as we call *duty.*'

'That's so,' said Mrs. Mansfield.

'Just what I am asking about,' said Di. 'That's the thing. Why *is* it duty to go to church when one don't want to go?'

'Well, I'm sure it was time we had a new minister,' said Mrs. Salter; 'and I'm glad he's come. If he's no better than old Mr. Hardenburgh, it 'ill take us a spell to find it out; and that'll be so much gained. He don't *look* like him any way.'

'He *is* different, ain't he?' assented Mrs. Boddington. 'If we wanted a change, we've got it. How did you all like his sermon last Sabbath?'

'He was very quiet—' said Mrs. Flandin.

'I like that,' said Diana. 'When a man roars at me, I never can tell what he is saying.'

'He seemed to kind o' know his own mind,' said Mrs Salter.

'I thought he'd got an astonishin' knowledge o' things in the town, for the time he's had,' said Mrs. Mansfield.

'I wisht he had a family,' remarked Miss Gunn ; 'that's all I've got agin him. I think a minister had allays ought to have a family.'

'He will,—let him alone a while,' said Mrs. Boddington. 'Time enough. Who have we got in town that would do for him ? '

The fruitful topic of debate and discussion here started, lasted the ladies for some time. Talk and business got full under weigh. Scissors and speeches, clipping and chattering, knitting and the interminable yarn of small talk. The affairs, sickness and health, of every family in the neighbourhood, with a large discussion of character and prospects by the way ; going back to former history and antecedents, and forward to future probable consequences and results. Nuts of society ; sweet confections of conversation ; of various and changing flavour ; suiting all palates, and warranted never to cloy. Then there were farm prospects and doings also, with household matters ; very interesting to the good ladies, who all had life interest in them ; and the hours moved on prosperously. Here a rocking-chair tipped gently back and forward, in harmony with the quiet business enjoyment of its occupant ; and there a pair of heels, stretched out to the farthest limit of their corresponding members, with toes squarely elevated in the air, testified to the restful condition of another individual of the party. See a pair of toes in the air and the heels as nearly as possible straight under them, one tucked up on the other, and you may be sure the person they belong to feels comfortable—physically. And Mrs. Starling in a corner, in her quiet state and black silk gown, was as contented as an old hen that sees all her chickens prosperously scratching for themselves. And the June afternoon breathed in at the window and upon all those busy talkers ; and nobody knew that it was June. So things went, until Diana left them to put the finishing touches of readiness to the tea-table. Her going was noticed by some of the assembly, and taken as a preparatory note of the coming entertainment; always sure to be worth having and coming for in Mrs. Starling's house. Needles and tongues took a fresh stir.

'Mis' Starling, are we goin' to hev the minister?' somebody asked.

'I don't know as anybody has told him, Mis' Mansfield.'

'Won't seem like a meetin', ef we *don't* hev him.'

'He's gone down to Elmfield,' said Miss Gunn. 'He went down along in the forenoon some time. Gone to see his cousin, I s'pose.'

'They've got their young soldier home to Elmfield,' said Miss Barry. 'I spect they're dreadful sot up about it.'

'They don't want *that*,' said Mrs. Boddington. 'The Knowltons always did carry their heads pretty well up, in the best o' times; and now Evan's got home, I s'pose there'll be no holding 'em in. There ain't, I guess, by the looks.'

'What'll he do now? stay to hum and help his gran'ther?'

'La! no. He's home just for a visit. He's got through his education at the Military Academy, and now he's an officer; out in the world; but he'll have to go somewhere and do his work.'

'I wonder what work they do hev to do?' said Mrs. Salter; 'there ain't nobody to fight now, is there?'

'Fight the Injuns,' said Mrs. Boddington; 'or the Mexicans; or the English maybe; anything that comes handy.'

'But we hain't no quarrel with the English, nor nobody, hev we? I thought we was done fightin' for the present,' said Miss Barry in a disturbed tone of voice.

'Well, suppos'n we be,' said Mrs. Boddington; 'somebody might give us a slap, you know, when we don't expect it, and it's best to be ready; and so, Evan Knowlton 'll be one o' them that has to stand somewhere with his musket to his shoulder, and look after a lot o' powder behind him all the while.'

'Du tell! if it takes four years to learn 'em to du that,' said Miss Babbage, the doctor's sister.

'The Knowltons is a very fine family,' remarked Miss Gunn.

'If the outside made it,' said Mrs. Boddington. 'Don't they cut a shine when they come into meetin', though! They *think* they do.'

'It takes all the boys' attention off everything,' said Mrs. Flandin, who was an elderly lady herself.

'And the girls'—added Mrs. Starling. But what more might have been said was cut short by Miss Barry's crying out that here was the minister coming.

CHAPTER II.

THE NEW MINISTER.

THE little stir and buzz which went round the assembly at this news was delightful. Not one but moved excitedly on her seat, and then settled herself for an unwonted good time. For the new minister was undiscovered ground; an unexamined possession; unexplored treasure. One Sunday and two sermons had done no more than whet the appetite of the curious. Nobody had made up his mind, or her mind, on the subject, in regard to any of its points. So there were eyes enough that from Mrs. Starling's windows watched the minister as he dismounted and tied his horse to the fence, and then opened the little gate and came up to the house. Diana had returned to the room to bid the company out to supper; but finding all heads turned one way, and necks craned over, and eyes on the stretch, she paused and waited for a more auspicious moment. And then came a step in the passage, and the door opened.

Mr. Hardenburgh, each lady remembered, used to make the circuit of the company, giving every one a several clasp of the hand and an individual word of civility. Here was a change! The new minister came into the midst of them and stood still, with a bright look and a cheery 'Good afternoon!' It was full of good cheer and genial greeting; but what lady could respond to it? The greeting was not given to *her*. The silence was absolute; though eyes said they had heard, and were listening.

'I have been down at Elmfield,' the new-comer went on, not at all disturbed by his reception; 'and some one informed me I should find a large circle of friends if I came here; so I came. And I find I was told truly.'

14

'I guess we'd 'most given you up,' said the mistress of the house, coming out of her corner now.

'I don't know what reason you had to expect me! Nobody asked me to come.'

'We're real glad to see you. Take a chair,' said Mrs. Starling, setting one for his acceptance as she spoke.

'Mr. Hardenburgh allays used to come to our little meetins,' said Mrs Mansfield.

'Thank you!—And you expect me to do all that Mr. Hardenburgh did?'

There was such a quaint air of good-fellowship and simplicity in the new minister's manner, that the little assembly began to stir anew with gratification and amusement. But nobody was forward to answer. In fact, they were a trifle shy of him. The late Mr. Hardenburgh had been heavy and slow; kind, of course, but stiff; you knew just what he would do and how he would speak beforehand. There was a delightful freshness and uncertainty about this man. Nothing imposing, either; a rather small, slight figure; with a face that might or might not be called handsome, according to the fancy of the speaker, but that all would agree was wonderfully attractive and winning. A fine broad brow; an eye very sweet; with a build of the jaw and lines of the mouth speaking both strength and the absolutest calm of the mental nature.

'I was afraid I should be late,' he went on, looking at his watch,—'but the roads are good. How far do you call it from Elmfield?'

'All of five miles,' said Mrs Starling.

'Yes; and one hill to cross. Well! I came pretty well. The long June afternoon favoured me.'

'Mr. Hardenburgh used to drive a buggy,' remarked Miss Barry.

'Yes. Is that one of the things you would like me to do as he did?'

'Well, none of our ministers ever went such a venturesome way before,' said the timid little old lady.

'As I do? But if I had been in a buggy, Miss Barry, this afternoon, I am afraid you would have got through supper and been near breaking up before I could have joined your society.'

'How long was you comin', then?' she asked, looking startled.

'And there's another thing, Mr. Masters,' said Mrs. Mansfield; 'why *do* the days be so much longer in summer than in winter? I asked Mr. Hardenburgh once, but I couldn't make out nothin' from what he told me.'

Sly looks and suppressed laughter went round the room, for some of Mrs. Mansfield's neighbours were better informed than she in all that lay above the level of practical farming; but Mr. Masters quite gravely assured her he would make it all clear the first time he had a quiet chance at her house.

'And will you walk out to supper, friends?' said Mrs. Starling. 'Here's Di been standin' waitin' to call us, this half hour.'

The supper was laid on a long table in the lean-to, which was used as a kitchen; but now the fire was out, and the tea-kettle had been boiled and was kept boiling in some unknown region. Doors and windows stood open, letting the sweet air pass through; and if the floor was bare and the chairs were wooden, both one and the other were bright with cleanliness; and the long board was bright in another way. Yet the word is not misapplied. Such piles of snowy bread and golden cake, such delicate cheeses and puffy biscuits, and such transparencies of rich-coloured preserves, were an undoubted adornment to Mrs. Starling's deal table, and might have been to any table in the world. The deal was covered, however, with white cloths. At the upper end the hostess took her place behind a regiment of cups and saucers, officered by great tin pots which held the tea and coffee. Diana waited.

Everybody had come expecting a good supper and primed for enjoyment; and now the enjoyment began. Mrs. Starling might smile grimly to herself as she saw her crab-apples and jellies disappear, and the piles of biscuits go down and get heaped up again by Diana's care. Nobody was at leisure enough to mark her.

'Eat when you can, Mr. Masters,' said Mrs. Boddington;

'you won't get hot biscuits anywhere in Pleasant Valley but here.'

'Why not?' said Mr. Masters.

'It ain't the fashion—that's all.'

'I s'pose you've seen the fashions to-day down at Elmfield, Mr. Masters,' said Mrs. Salter. 'They don't think as we hev no fashions, up here in the mountains.'

'Their fashions is ridiculous!' said Mrs. Flandin. 'Do you think it's becomin', Mr. Masters, for Christian women to go and make sights of themselves?'

''In what way, Mrs. Flandin?'

'Why, goodness! you've seen 'em. Describin's impossible. Euphemie Knowlton, she came into church last Sabbath three yards in extent, ef she was a foot. It beat me, how she was goin' to get in. Why, there warn't room for but three of 'em in the slip, and it took 'em somethin' like half an hour to get fixed in their places. I declare I was ashamed, and I had to look, for all.'

'So had I,' assented Miss Carpenter. 'I couldn't fairly keep my eyes off of 'em.'

'And I'm certain she couldn't go agin the wind, with her bonnet; it stuck just right up from her face, and ended in a pint, and she had a hull garden in the brim of it. I think ministers had ought to preach about such doin's.'

'And you don't know what ministers are good for if they don't?' said Mr. Masters.

'Did you ever see a minister that could get the better of 'em?' said Mrs. Boddington. ''Cos, if you did, I would like to go and sit under his preachin' a spell, and see what he could do for me.'

'Does that express the mind of Pleasant Valley generally?' asked the minister, and gravely this time.

'La! we ain't worse than other folks,' said Mrs. Salter. ''There's no harm in dressin' one's self smart now and then, is there? And we want to know how, to be sure.'

'I hope you don't think Euphemie Knowlton knows how? 'Tain't a quarter as becomin' as the way we dress in Pleasant Valley. There ain't the least bit of prettiness or gracefulness

B

in a woman's bein' three yards round ; anyhow we don't think
so when it's nature.' So Mrs. Salter.

'What do you think o' lettin' your hair down over the
shoulders, as if you were goin' to comb it?' said Mrs. Boddington; 'and goin' to church so?'

'But how ever *did* she make it stand out as it did?' asked
Miss Carpenter. 'It was just like spun glass, nothin' smooth
or quiet about it. Such a yellow mop I never did see. And
it warn't a child neither. Who is she anyhow?'

'Not she. It is a grown woman,' said Mrs. Flandin ; and
she looked like a wild savage. 'Don't the minister agree with
me, that it ain't becomin' for Christian women to do such
things?'

It was with a smile and a sigh that the minister answered,
'Where are you going to draw the line, Mrs. Flandin?'

'Well! with what's decent and comfortable.'

'And pretty?'

'La! yes,' said Mrs. Salter. 'Do let us be as nice as we kin.'

'I think people had ought to make themselves as nice-
lookin' as they can,' echoed one of the younger ladies of the
party ; and there was a general chorus of agreeing voices.

'Well!' said the minister; 'then comes the question, what
is nice-looking? I dare say the young lady with the flowing
tresses thought she was about right.'

'She thought she was the only one,' said Mrs. Boddington.

A subject was started now which was fruitful enough to
keep all tongues busy ; and whether biscuits or opinions had
the most lively circulation for some time thereafter it would be
hard to say. Old and young, upon this matter of town and
country fashions, and fashion in general, 'gave tongue' in
concert ; proving that Pleasant Valley knew what was what as
well as any place in the land ; that it was doubtful what right
Boston or New York had to dictate to it ; at the same time the
means of getting at the earliest the mind of Boston or New
York was eagerly discussed, and the pretensions of Elmfield to
any advantage in that matter as earnestly denied. The minister
sat silent, with an imperturbable face that did him credit. At
last there was a rush of demands upon him for his judgment.

He declared that so much had been said upon the subject, he must have time to think it over; and he promised to give them some at least of his thoughts before long in a sermon.

With this promise, highly satisfied, the assembly broke up. Mrs. Starling declared afterwards to her daughter, that, if there had been any more fashions to talk about they would never have got done supper. But now bonnets were put on, and work put up, and one after another family party went off in its particular farm waggon or buggy. It was but just sundown; the golden glory of the sky was giving a mellow illumination to all the land, as one after another the horses were unhitched, the travellers mounted into their vehicles, and the wheels went softly rolling off over the smooth road. The minister stood by the gate, helping the ladies to untie and mount, giving pleasant words along with pleasant help, and receiving many expressions of pleasure in return.

'Dear me, Mr. Masters!' said Miss Barry, the last one, 'ain't you afraid you'll catch cold, standing there with no hat on?'

'Cold always attacks the weakest part, Miss Barry. My head is safe.'

'Well, I declare!' said Miss Barry. 'I never heerd that afore.'

And as she drove off in her little green waggon, the minister and Diana, who had come down to the gate to see the last one off, indulged in a harmless laugh. Then they both stood still by the fence a moment, resting; the hush was so sweet. The golden glory was fading; the last creak of Miss Barry's wheels was getting out of hearing; the air was perfumed with the scents which the dew called forth.

'Isn't it delicious?' said the minister, leaning on the little gate, and pushing his hair back from his forehead.

'The stillness is pleasant,' said Diana.

'Yet you must have enough of that?'

'Yes—sometimes,' said the girl. She was a little shy of speaking her thoughts to the minister; indeed, she was not accustomed to speak them to anybody, not knowing where they could meet entertainment. She wondered Mr. Masters did not go like the rest; however, it was pleasant enough to stand there talking to him.

'What do you do for books here?' he went on.

'O, I have all my father's books,' said Diana. 'My father was a minister, Mr. Masters; and when he died his books came to me.'

'A theological library!' said Mr. Masters.

'Yes. I suppose you would call it so.'

'Have you it *here?*'

'O yes. I have it in my room up-stairs. All one end of the room full.'

'Do you read these books?'

'Yes. They are all I have to read. I have not read the whole of them.'

'No, I suppose not. Do you not find this reading rather heavy?'

'I don't know. Some of the books are rather heavy; I do not read those much.'

'You must let me look at your library some day, Miss Diana. It would be certain to have charms for me; and I'll exchange with you. Perhaps I have books that you would not find heavy.'

Diana's full grey eyes turned on the minister with a gleam of gratitude and pleasure. Her words were not needed to say that she would like that kind of barter.

'So your father was a clergyman?' Mr. Masters went on.

'Yes. Not here, though. That was when I was quite little. We lived a good way from here; and I remember very well a great many things about all that time, till father died, and then mother came back here.'

'Came *back*,—then your mother is at home in Pleasant Valley?'

'O, we're both at home here—I was so little when we came; but mother's father lived where Nick Boddington does, and owned all this valley—I don't mean Pleasant Valley; but all this hollow; a good large farm it was; and when he died he left mother a nice piece of it, with this old house.'

'Mr. Boddington,—is he then a relation of yours?'

'No, not exactly; he's the son of grandpa's second wife; we're really no relations, but we call each other cousin.

Grandpa left the most of his land to his wife; but mother's got enough to manage, and nice land.'

'It's a beautiful place!' said the minister. 'There is a waggon coming; I wonder if any of our friends have forgotten something? That is—yes, that *is* farmer Babbage's team; isn't it? What is the matter?'

For something unusual in the arrangements of the vehicle, or the occupants of it, was dimly yet surely to be discerned through the distance and the light, which was now turning brown rather than grey. Nothing could be seen clearly, and yet it came as no waggon load had gone from that door that evening. The minister took his hand from the gate, and Diana stepped forward, as the horses stopped in front of the lean-to; and a voice called out:

'Who's there to help? Hollo! Lend a hand.'

The minister sprang down the road, followed by Diana. 'What do you want help for?' he asked.

'There's been an accident—Jim Delamater's waggon—we found it overturned in the road; and here's Eliza, she hasn't spoke since. Have you got no more help?'

'Where's Jim?' asked Mrs. Starling, coming herself from the lean-to.

'Stayed with his team; about all he was up to. Now then,— can we get her in? Where's Josiah?'

But no more masculine help could be mustered than what was already on hand. Brains, however, can do much to supplement muscular force. The minister had a settee out from the house in two minutes and by the side of the waggon; with management and care, though with much difficulty, the unconscious girl was lifted down and laid on the settee; and by the aid of the women carried straight into the lean-to, the door of which was the nearest. There, by the same energetic ordering, well seconded by Diana, a mattress was brought and laid on the long table, which Mrs. Starling's diligence had already cleared since supper; and there they placed the girl, who was perfectly helpless and motionless in their hands.

'There is life yet,' said the minister, after an examination during which every one stood breathless around. 'Loose everything she has on, Miss Diana; and let us have some hartshorn, Mrs. Starling, if you have got any. Well, brandy, then, and cold water; and I'll go for the doctor.'

But Mr. Babbage represented that he must himself ' go on hum,' and would pass by the doctor's door; so if the minister would stay and help the women folks, it would be more advisable. Accordingly the farmer's waggon wheels were soon heard departing, and the little group in the lean-to kitchen were left alone. Too busy at first to think of it, they were trying eagerly every restorative and stimulant they could think of and command; but with little effect. A little, they thought; but consciousness had not returned to the injured girl, when they had done all they knew how to do, and tried everything within their reach. Hope began to fade towards despair; still they kept on with the use of their remedies. Mrs. Starling went and came between the room where they were and the stove, which stood in some outside shed, fetching bottles of hot water; I think, between whiles, she was washing up her cups and saucers; the other two, in the silence of her absences, could feel the strange, solemn contrasts which one must feel, and does, even in the midst of keener anxieties than those which beset the watchers there. The girl, a fair, rather pretty person, pleasant-tempered and generally liked, lay still and senseless on the table around which she and others a little while ago had been seated at supper. Very still the room was now, that had been full of voices; the smell of camphor and brandy was about; the table was wet in one great spot with the cold water which had been applied to the girl's face. And through the open door and windows came the stir of the sweet night air, and the sound of insects, and the gurgle of a brook that ran a few yards off; peaceful, free, glad, as if all were as it had been last night, or nature took no cognizance of human affairs. The minister had been very active and helpful; bringing wood and drawing water and making up the fire, as well as anybody, Mrs. Starling said afterwards; he had taken his part in the actual nursing, and better than anybody, Diana thought. Now the two stood silent and grave by the long table, while they still kept up the application of brandy to the face and heat to the extremities, and rubbing the hands and wrists of the patient.

'Did you know Miss Delamater well?' asked the minister.

'Yes—as I know nearly all the girls,' Diana answered.

'Do you think she is ready for the change—if she must make it?'

Diana hesitated. 'I never heard her speak on the subject,' she said. 'She wasn't a member of the church.'

Silence followed, and they were two grave faces still that bent over the table; but there was the difference between the shadow on a mountain lake where there is not a ripple, and the dark stir of troubled waters. Diana's eye every now and then glanced for an instant at the face of her companion; it was very grave, but the broad brow was as quiet as if all its questions were answered, and the mouth was sweet and at rest in its stillness. She wished he would speak again; there was something in him that provoked her curiosity. He did speak presently.

'This shows us what the meaning of life is,' he said.

'No,' said Diana, 'it doesn't—to me. It is just a puzzle, and as much a puzzle here as ever. I *don't* see what the use of life is, or what we all live for; I don't see what it amounts to.'

'What do you mean?' asked her companion, but not as if he were startled, and Diana went on.

'I shouldn't say so if people were always having a good time, and if they were just right and did just right. But they are not, Mr. Masters; you know they are not; even the best of them, that I see; and things like *this* are always happening, one way or another. If it isn't here, it is somewhere else; and if it isn't one time, it is another; and it is all confusion. I don't see what it all comes to.'

'That is the thought of a moment of pain,' said the minister.

'No, it is not,' said Diana. 'I think it often. I think it all the while. Now this very afternoon I was sitting at the door here,—you know what sort of a day it has been, Mr. Masters?'

'I know. Perfect. Just June.'

'Well, I was looking at it, and feeling how lovely it was;

everything perfect; and somehow all that perfection took a kind of sharp edge and hurt me. I was thinking why nothing in the world was like it, or agreed with it; nothing in human life, I mean. This afternoon, when the company was here and all the talk going on—*that* was like nothing out of doors all the while; and *this* is not like it.'

There was a sigh, deep drawn, that came through the minister's lips; then he spoke cheerfully—' Ay, God's works have parted company somehow.'

' Parted—?' said Diana curiously.

' Yes. You remember surely that when he had made all things at first, he beheld them very good.'

' Well, they are not very good now; not all of them.'

' Whose fault is that?'

' I know,' said Diana, 'but that does not help me with my puzzle. Why does the world go on so? What is the use of my living, or anybody's? What does it amount to?'

' That's your lesson,' the minister answered, with a quick glance from his calm eyes. Not a bit of sentiment or of speculative rhapsody there; but downright, cool common sense, with just a little bit of authority. Diana did not know exactly how to meet it; and before she had arranged her words, they heard wheels again, and then the doctor came in.

The doctor approved of what had been done, and aided in renewed application of the same remedies. After a time, these seemed at last successful; the girl revived; and the doctor, after administering a little tea and weak brandy and water, ordered that she should be kept quiet where she was, the room be darkened when daylight came on, the windows kept open, and handkerchiefs wet with cold water be laid on her head. And then he took his departure; and Diana went to communicate to her mother the orders he had left.

' Keep her there!' echoed Mrs. Starling. ' In the lean-to! She'd be a deal better in her bed.'

' We must make her bed there, mother.'

' There! On the table, do you mean? Diana Starling, you are a baby!'

' She mustn't be stirred, mother, he says.'

'That's the very thing!' exclaimed Mrs. Starling. 'She had ought to ha' been carried into one of the bed-chambers at the first; and I said so; and the new minister, he would have it all his own way.'

'But she must have all the air she could, mother, you know.'

'Air!' said Mrs. Starling. 'Do you s'pose she would smother in one of the chambers, where many a one before her has laid, sick and well, and got along too? Air, indeed! The house ain't like a corked bottle, I guess.'

'Not much,' said Diana; 'but Mr. Masters said, and the doctor says, that she cannot have too much air.'

'O well! Eggs can't be beat too much, neither; but it don't follow you're to stand beating 'em for ever. I've no patience. Where am I going to do my ironing? I should like the minister for to tell me;—or get meals, or anything else? I don't see what possessed Josiah to go and see his folks to-night of all nights.'

'We have not wanted him, mother, after all, that I see.'

'I have wanted him,' said Mrs. Starling. 'If he had been home I needn't to have had queer help, and missed knowing who was head of the house. Well, go along and fix it,—you and the minister.'

'But, mother, I want to get Eliza's things off, and to make her bed comfortably; and I can't do it without you.'

'Well, get rid of the minister then, and I'll come. Him and me is too many in one house.'

The minister would not leave the two women alone and go home, as Diana proposed to him; but he went to make his horse comfortable while they did the same for the sick girl. And then he took up his post just outside the door, in the moonlight which came fitfully through the elm branches; and he and Diana talked no more that night. He was watchful and helpful; for he kept up the fire in the stove, and once more brought wood when it was needed. Moonlight melted away at last into the dawn; cool clear outlines began to take place of the soft mystery of night shadows; then the warm glow from the east, behind the house, and the glint of the sunbeams on the tops of

the hills and on the racks of cloud lying along the horizon.
Diana still kept her place by the improvised bed, and the
minister kept his just outside the door. Mrs. Starling began to
prepare for breakfast; and finally Josiah, the man-of-all-work
on the little farm, came from his excursion and from the barn,
bringing the pails of milk. Then the minister fetched his horse,
and came in to shake hands with Diana. He would not stay for
breakfast. She watched him down to the gate, where he threw
himself on his grey steed and went off at a smooth gallop, swift
and steady, sitting as if he were more at home on a horse's back
than anywhere else. Diana looked after him.

'Certainly,' she thought, 'that is unlike all the other ministers
that ever came to Pleasant Valley.'

'He's off, is he?' said Mrs. Starling as her daughter came in.
'Now Diana, take notice; don't you go and take a fancy to this
new man; because I won't favour it, nor have anything of the
kind going on, I tell you beforehand.'

'There is very little danger of his taking a fancy to me,
mother.'

'I don't know about that. He might do worse. But
you couldn't; for I'll never have anything to say to you if
you do.'

'Why, mother?' inquired Diana in much surprise. 'I
should think you'd like him. I should think everybody would.
Why don't you like him?'

'He's too masterful for me. Mind what I tell you, Diana.'

'It's absurd, mother! Such a one as Mr. Masters never would
think of such a one as I am. He's a very cultivated man,
mother; and has been accustomed to very different society
from what he'll find here. I don't seem to him what I seem
to you.'

'I hope not!' said Mrs. Starling, 'for you seem to me a
goose. Cultivated! Who is cultivated, if you are not?
Weren't you a whole year at school in Boston? I guess my
gentleman hasn't been to a better place. And warn't you for
ever reading those musty old books, that make you out of
kilter for all *my* world? If you don't fit his neither, I'm sorry.
Society indeed! There's no better society than the folks of

Pleasant Valley. Don't you go and set yourself up; nor him neither.'

Diana knew better than to carry on the discussion.

Meanwhile the grey horse that bore the minister home kept up that long smooth gallop for a half mile or so, then slackened it to walk up a hill.

'That's a very remarkable girl,' the minister was saying to himself; 'with much more in her than she knows.'

The gallop began again in a few minutes, and was unbroken till he got home. It was but a piece of a home. Mr. Masters had rooms in the house of Mrs. Persimmon, a poor widow living among the hills. The rooms were neat; that was all that could be said for them; little and dark and low, with bits of windows, and with the simplest of furnishing. The sitting-room was cheerful with books, however—as cheerful as books can make a room; and the minister did not look uncheerful, but very grave. If his brow was neither wrinkled nor lined, the quiet eyes beneath it were deep with thought. Mr. Masters' morning was spent on this wise.

First of all, for a good half hour, his knees were bent, and his thoughts, whatever they were, gave him work to do. That work done, the minister threw himself on his bed and slept, as quietly as he did everything else, for an hour or two more. Then he rose, shaved and dressed, took such breakfast as Mrs. Persimmon could give him; mounted his grey again, and was off to a house at some distance where there was a sick child, and another house where there dwelt an infirm old man. Between these two the hours were spent till he rode home to dinner.

CHAPTER III.

HARNESSING PRINCE.

THE improvement of the sick girl was better than had been hoped; it was but a day or two before Mrs. Starling's heart's desire could be effected and her kitchen cleared. Eliza was moved to another room, and at the week's end was taken home.

It was the next day after this had been done, and Diana was sitting again in the elm shadow at the door of the lean-to. Not idly this time; for a pan of peas was in her lap, and her fingers were busy with shelling them. Still her eyes were very much more busy with the lovely light and shade on meadow and hill; her glances went up and down, from her pan to the sunny landscape. Mrs. Starling, bustling about as usual within the house and never looking out, presently hearing the gate latch, called out—' Who's that?'

' Joe Bartlett, mother,' Diana answered without moving.

It was not the gate that led to the flower patch and the front door. That was some distance off. Another little brown gate under the elm-tree opened directly in front of the lean-to door; and the patch between was all in fleckered sunlight and shadow, like the doorway where Diana sat.

The little gate opening now admitted a visitor who was in appearance the very typical Yankee of the story books. Long in the limbs, loose in the joints, angular, ungainly, he came up the walk with a movement that would tempt one to think he had not got accustomed to his inches, and did not yet know quite what to do with them all. He had a long face, red in colour; in expression a mixture of honest frankness, carelessness, and good humour.

' Mornin'!' said he as he came near. ' How's your folks this forenoon?'

23

'Quite well—all there are of us, Joe,' said Diana, shelling her peas as she looked up at him. 'How's your mother?'

'Well, she's pretty smart. Mother seems to be allays just about so. I never see the beat of her for keepin' along. You've had quite a spell o' nursin' folks, hain't you, down this way? Must ha' upset you quite considerable.'

'We didn't have the worst of the upsetting.'

'That's a fact. Well, she's gone, ain't she?'

'Who, Eliza Delamater? Yes; gone yesterday.'

'And you hain't nobody else on hand, have ye?'

'No. Why?'

'Mother's took a lonesome fit. She says it's quite a spell that you hain't ben down our way; and I guess that's so, ain't it?'

'I couldn't help it, Joe. I have had other things to do.'

'Well, don't you think to-day's a good sort for a visit?'

'To-day?' said Diana, shelling her peas very fast.

'You see, it's pretty silent down to our place. That is, when I ain't to hum; and I can't be there much o' the time, 'cept when I'm asleep in my bed. I'm off as soon as I've done the chores in the mornin'; and I can't get hum nohow sooner than to do up the chores in the evenin'; and the old lady has it pretty much her own way as to conversation the rest o' the time. She can talk to what she likes; but there ain't nothin' as can make a remark back to her.'

'It's too bad, Joe!'

'Fact!' said Joe seriously; all the rest had been said with a smile; 'but you know mother. Come! put on your bonnit and run down and set with her a spell. She's took a notion to have ye; and I know she'll be watchin' till you come.'

'Then I must go. I guess I can arrange it, Joe.'

'Well, I'll get along, then, where I had ought to be. Mis Starling cuttin' her hay?'

'Yes, this week and more.'

'It's turnin' out a handsome swath; but it had ought to be all down now. Well, good day! Hurry up, now, for down yonder.'

Diana brought in her pan of peas.

'Mother, where's Josiah Davis?'

'Where should he be? He's up in the hill lot, cuttin'
hay. That grass is all in flower; it had ought to been cut
a week ago; but Josiah always has one of his hands behind
him.'

'And he won't be in till noon. I must harness the waggon
myself.'

'If you can catch the horse,' said her mother. 'He's turned
out in the lot. It's a poor job, at this time o' day.'

'I'll try and make a good job of it,' said Diana. So she took
her sun-bonnet and went out to the barn. The old horse was not
far off, for the 'lot' in this case meant simply the small field
in which the barn and the barnyard were enclosed; but being
a wary old animal, with a good deal of experience of life, he
had come to know that a halter and a pan of corn generally
meant hard work near at hand, and was wont to be shy of
such allurements. Diana could sometimes do better than anybody else with old Prince; they were on good terms; and
Prince had sense enough to take notice that she never followed
the plough, and was therefore a safer venture than his other
flatterers. With the corn and the halter Diana now sought
the corner where Prince was standing whisking his tail in the
shade of a tree. But it was a warm morning; and seeing her
approach, Prince quietly walked off into the sun on the other
side of the tree, and went on to another shady resting-place
some distance away. Diana followed, speaking to him; but
Prince repeated his ungallant manœuvre; and from tree to tree
across the sunny field Diana trudged after him, until she was
hot and tired. Perhaps Prince's philosophy came in play at
last, warning him that this game could not go on for ever, and
would certainly end in his discomfiture some time; for, with
no apparent reason for his change of tactics, he stood still at
length under the tree farthest from the barn, and suffered himself to be made captive. Diana got the halter on, and, flushed
and excited with the chase, led him back over the lot and out
to the road, where Josiah had very culpably left the little
waggon standing in the shade of the elm, close by the lean-to
gate. Just as she got there, Diana saw a stranger who had his

hand on the gate, but who left it now and came forward to speak to her.

Diana stood by the thills of the waggon, horse in hand, but, to tell the truth, forgetting both. The stranger was unlike anything often seen in Pleasant Valley. He wore the dark-blue uniform of an army officer; there was a strip of gold down the seam of his pantaloons and a gold bar across his shoulders, and his cap was a soldier's cap. But it was not on his head just now; it had come off since he quitted the gate; and the step with which he drew near was the very contrast to Joe Bartlett's lounging pace; this was measured, clean, compact, and firm, withal as light and even as that of an antelope. His hair showed the regulation cut; and Diana saw with the same glance a pair of light, brilliant, hazel eyes and a finely trimmed mustache. *She* stood flushed and still, halter in hand, with her sun-bonnet pushed a little back for air. The stranger smiled just a little.

'May I ask how far I am from a place called Elmfield?'

'It is'—Diana's thoughts wandered,—'It is five miles.'

'I ought not to need to ask—but I have been so long away. —Do you know how or where I can get a horse, or any conveyance, to bring me there? I have ridden beyond this, and met with an accident.'

Diana hesitated. 'Is it Lieut. Knowlton?' she said.

'Ah, you know me?' said he. 'I forgot that Pleasant Valley knows me better than I know Pleasant Valley. I did not count on finding a friend here.' His eye glanced at the little brown house.

'Everybody knows Elmfield,' said Diana; 'and I guessed—'

'From my dress?' said Mr. Knowlton, following the direction of her look. 'This was accident too. But which of my friends ought I to know here, that I don't know? Pardon me,—but is this horse to be put to the waggon or taken away from it?'

'O, I was going to put him in.'

'Allow me'—said the young man, taking the halter from Diana's willing hands; 'but where is the harnessing gear?'

'O, that is in the barn!' exclaimed Diana. 'I will go and fetch it.'

'Pray no! Let me get it,' said her companion; and giving the end of the halter a turn round one of the thills, he had overtaken her before she had well taken half a dozen steps. They went together through the barnyard. Diana found the harness, and the young officer threw it over his shoulder with a smile at her which answered her deprecating words; a smile extremely pleasant and gentlemanly, if withal a little arch. Diana shrank back somewhat before the glance, which to her fancy showed the power of keen observation along with the habit of giving orders. They went back to the elm, and Mr. Knowlton harnessed the horse, Diana explaining in a word or two the necessity under which she · had been acting.

'And what about my dilemma?' said he presently, as his task was finished.

'There is no horse or waggon you could get anywhere, that I know of,' said Diana. 'The teams are apt to be in use just now. But I am going down to within a mile of Elmfield; and I was going to say, if you like, I can take you so far.'

'And who will do me such kindness?'

'Who? O—Diana Starling.'

'Is that a name I ought to know?' inquired Mr. Knowlton. 'I shall know it from this day; but how about before to-day? I have been gone from Pleasant Valley, at school and at the Military Academy, four, five,—ten years.'

'Mother came back here to live just ten years ago.'

'My conscience is clear!' he said, smiling. 'I was beginning to whip myself. Now are we ready?'

Not quite, for Diana went into the house for her gloves and a straw hat; she made no other change in her dress, having taken off her apron before she set out after Prince. She found her new friend standing with the reins in his hand, as if he were to drive and not she; and Diana was helped into her own waggon with a deferential courtesy which up to that time she had only read of in books; nor known much even so. It silenced her at first. She sat down as mute as a child; and

" Diana was helped into her own wagon with a deferential courtesy
which up to that time she had only read of in books."

Page 3.2

Mr. Knowlton handled Prince and the waggon and all in the style of one that knew how and had the right.

That drive, however, was not to be silent or stiff in any degree. Mr. Knowlton, for his part, had no shyness or hesitation belonging to him. He had seen the world and learnt its freedom. Diana was only a simple country girl, and had never seen the world; yet she was as little troubled with embarrassment of any sort. Partly this was, no doubt, because of her sound, healthy New England nature; the solid self-respect which does not need—nor use—to put itself in the balance with anything else to be assured of its own quality. But part belonged to Diana's own personality; in a simple, large nature, too simple and too large to feel small motives or to know petty issues. If her cheeks and brow were flushed at first, it was because the sun had been hot in the lot and Prince tiresome. She was as composedly herself as ever the young officer could be. But I think each of them was a little excited by the companionship of the other.

'Do you drive this old fellow yourself?' asked Mr. Knowlton, after a little. 'But I need not ask! Of course you do. There's no difficulty. And not much danger,' he added, with a tone so dry and comical that they both burst into a laugh.

'I assure you I am very glad to have Prince,' said Diana. 'He is so old now that they generally let him off from the farm work. He takes mother and me to church, and stands ready for anything I want most of the time.'

'Lucky for me, too,' said Mr. Knowlton. 'I am afraid you will find the sun very hot!'

'I? O no, I don't mind it at all,' said Diana. 'There's a nice air now. Where is your horse, Mr. Knowlton? you said you had an accident.'

'Yes. That was a quarter of a mile or so beyond your house.'

'And is your horse there?'

'Must be, I think. I shall send some people to remove him.'

'Why, is he *dead?*'

'I should not have left him else, Miss Starling.'

Diana did not choose to go on with a string of questions; and her companion hesitated.

C

'It's my own fault,' he said with a sort of displeased half laugh; 'a piece of boyish thoughtlessness that I've paid for. There was a nice red cow lying in the middle of the road'—

'Where?' said Diana, wondering.

'Just ahead of me; a few rods. She was lying quite quietly, taking her morning siesta in the sun; plunged in ruminative thoughts, I supposed; and the temptation was irresistible to go over without disturbing her.'

'*Over* her?' said Diana in a maze.

'Yes. I counted on what one should never count on—what I didn't know.'

'What was that?'

'Whether it would occur to her to get upon her legs just at that moment.'

'And she did?' inquired Diana.

'She did.'

'What did that do, Mr. Knowlton?'

'Threw my poor steed off *his* legs for ever!' And here, in despite of his vexation, which was real and apparent, the young man burst into a laugh. Diana had not got at his meaning.

'And where were you, Mr. Knowlton?'

'On his back. I shall never forgive myself for being such a boy. Don't you understand? The creature rose up just in time to be in the way of my leap, and we were thrown over—my horse and I.'

'Thrown! You were not hurt, Mr. Knowlton?'

'I deserved it, didn't I? But I was nothing the worse—except for losing my horse, and my self-complacency.'

'Was the horse killed?'

'No; not by the fall. But he was injured; so that I saw the best thing to do would be to put him out of life at once; so I did it. I had my pistols; I often ride with them, to be ready for any sport that may offer. I am very much ashamed to have to tell you this story of myself!'

There was so much of earnestness in the expression of the last sentence, it was said with such a deferential contrition, if I may so speak, that Diana's thoughts experienced a diversion from the subject that had occasioned them. The contrition

came more home than the fault. By common consent they
went off to other matters of talk. Diana explained and com-
mented on the history and features of Pleasant Valley, so far
at least as her companion's questions called for such explanation, and that was a good deal. Mr. Knowlton gave her details
of his own life and experience, which were much more interesting, she thought. The conversation ran freely; and again
and again eyes met eyes full in sympathy over some grave or
laughing point of intelligence.

And what is there in the meeting of eyes? What if the one
pair were sparkling and quick, and the brow over them bore
the fair lines of command? What though the other pair were
deep and thoughtful and sweet, and the brow one that promised passion and power? A thousand other eyes might have
looked on either one of them, and forgotten; these two looked
—and remembered. You cannot tell why; it is the old story;
the hidden, unreadable affinity making itself known to its
counterpart; the sign and countersign of nature. But it was
only nature that gave and took; not Diana and Mr. Knowlton.

Meanwhile Prince had an easy time; and the little waggon
went very gently over the smooth roads past one farm after
another.

'Prince *can* go faster than this,' Diana confided at last to
her companion.

'He doesn't want to, does he?'

Diana laughed, and knew in her heart she was of Prince's
mind.

However, even five miles will come to an end in time if you
keep going even slowly; and in time the little brown house of
Mrs. Bartlett appeared in the distance, and Prince drew the
waggon up before the door. Diana alighted, and Mr. Knowlton
drove on, promising to send the waggon back from Elmfield.

It was coming down, in more ways than one, to get out of
the waggon and go in to make her visit. Diana did not feel
just ready for it. She loosened the strings of her hat, walked
slowly up the path between the hollyhocks that led to the door,
and there stopped and turned to take a last look at Mr. Knowlton in the distance. Such a ride as she had had! Such an

entertainment! People in Pleasant Valley did not talk like
that; nor look like that. How much difference it makes, to
have education and to see the world! And a military education especially has a more liberalizing and adorning effect than
the course of life in the colleges; the manner of a soldier has
in it a charm which is wanting in the manner of a minister.
As for farmers, they have no manners at all. And the very
faces, thought Diana.

Well, she could not stand there on the door-step. She must
go in. She turned and lifted the latch of the door.

The little room within was empty. It was a tiny house; the
ground floor boasted only two rooms, and each of these was
small. The broad hearth of flagstones took up a third of the
floor of this one. A fire burned in the chimney, though the
day was so warm; and a straight-backed arm-chair, with a
faded cushion in it, stood by the chimney corner with a bunch
of knitting lying on the cushion. Diana tapped at an inner
door at her right, and then getting no answer, went across
the kitchen and opened another opposite the one that had
admitted her.

CHAPTER IV.

MOTHER BARTLETT.

THE little house, unpainted like many others, had no fenced enclosure on this side. A wide field stretched away from the back door, lying partly upon a hill-side; and several cattle were pasturing in it. Farm fields and meadows were all around, except where this one hill rose up behind the house. It was wooded at the top; below, the ranks of a cornfield sloped aspiringly up its base. A narrow footpath, which only the tread of feet kept free from weeds and grass, went off obliquely to a little enclosed garden, which lay beyond the corner of the house in some arbitrary and independent way, not adjoining it at all. It was a sweet bit of country, soft and mellow under the summer sun; still as grasshoppers and the tinkle of a cowbell could make it; and very far from most of the improvements of the nineteenth century. But the smell of the pasture and the fragrance that came from the fresh shades of the wood, and the freedom of the broad fields of pure ether, made it rich with some of nature's homely wealth; which is not by any means the worst there is. Diana knew the place very well; her eyes were looking now for the mistress of it. And not long. In the out-of-the-way lying garden she discerned her white cap; and at the gate met her bringing a head of lettuce in her hands.

'I knew you liked it, dear,' she said, 'and I had forgot all about it; and then it flashed on me, and I thought, Diana will like to have it for her dinner; and I guess it'll have time to cool. Just put it in a tin pail, dear, and hang it down in the well; and it'll be fresh.'

This was done, and Diana came in and took a seat by her old friend.

37

'You needn't do that for me, Mother Bartlett. I don't care what I have to eat.'

'Most folks like what is good,' said the old lady; 'suppos'n they know it.'

'Yes, and so do I, but'—

'I made a pot-pie for ye,' the old lady went on contentedly.

'And I suppose you have left nothing at all for me to do, as usual. It is too bad, Mother Bartlett.'

'You shall do all the rest,' said her friend; 'and now you may talk to me.'

She was a trim little old woman, not near so tall as her visitor; very wrinkled, but fresh-skinned, and with a quick grey eye. Her dress was a common working dress of some dark stuff; coarse, but tidy and nice-looking; her cap white and plain; she sat in her arm-chair, setting her little feet to the fire, and her fingers merrily clicking her needles together; a very comfortable vision. The kitchen and its furniture was as neat as a pin.

'I don't see how you manage, Mother Bartlett,' Diana went on, glancing around. 'You ought to have some one to live with you and help you. It looks as if you had half a dozen.'

'Not much,' said the old lady, laughing. 'A half dozen would soon make a muss, of one sort or another. There's nothin' like having nobody.'

'But you might be sick.'

'I might be;—but I ain't,' said Mrs. Bartlett, running one end of a knitting-needle under her cap and looking placidly at Diana.

'But you might want somebody.'

'When I do I send for 'em. I sent for you to-day, child; and here you are.'

'But you are quite well to-day?' said Diana a little anxiously.

'I am always well. Never better.'

'How old are you, Mother Bartlett?'

'Seventy-three years, child.'

'Well, I do think you oughtn't to be here alone. It don't seem right, and I don't think it is right.'

'What's to do, child? There ain't nary one to come and live with me. They're all gone but Joe. My Lord knows I'm an old woman seventy-three years of age.'

'What then, Mother Bartlett?' Diana asked curiously.

'He'll take care of me, my dear.'

'But then, we ought to take care of ourselves,' said Diana. 'Now if Joe would marry somebody '—

'Joe ain't lucky in that line,' said the old lady, laughing again. 'And may be what he might like, I mightn't. Before you go to wishin' for changes, you'd better know what they'll be. I'm content, child. There ain't a thing on earth I want that I haven't got. Now what's the news?'

Diana began and told her the whole story of the sewing meeting and the accident, and the nursing of the injured girl. Mrs. Bartlett had an intense interest in every particular; and what Diana failed to remember, her questions brought out.

'And how do you like the new minister?'

'Haven't you seen him yet?'

'Nay. He hain't been down my way yet. In good time he will. He's had sick folks to see arter, Joe told me; old Jemmy Claflin, and Joe Simmons' boy; and Mis' Atwood, and Eliza.'

'I think you'll like him,' said Diana slowly. 'He's not like any minister ever *I* saw.'

'What's the odds?'

'It isn't so easy to tell. He don't look like a minister, for one thing; nor he don't talk like one; not a bit.'

'Have we got a gay parson, then?' said the old lady, slightly raising her eyebrows.

'Gay? O no! not in the way you mean. In one way he *is* gay; he is very pleasant; not stiff or grum, like Mr. Hardenburgh; and he is amusing too, in a quiet way, but he *is* amusing; he is so cool and so quick. O no, he's not gay in the way you mean. I guess he's good.'

'Do *you* like him?' Mrs. Bartlett asked.

'Yes,' said Diana, thinking of the night of Eliza Delamater's accident. 'He is very queer.'

'I don't seem to make him out by your telling, child. I'll have to wait, I guess. I've got no sort of an idea of him, so

far. Now, dear, if you'll set the table—dinner's ready; and
then we'll have some reading.'

Diana drew out a small deal table to the middle of the floor,
and set on it the delf plates and cups and saucers, the little
saltcellar of the same ware, and the knives and forks that
were never near Sheffield; in fact, were never steel. But the
lettuce came out of the well crisp and fresh and cool; and Mrs.
Bartlett's pot-pie crust came out of the pot as spongy and light
as possible; and the loaf of ' seconds ' bread was sweet as it is
hard for bread to be that is not made near the mill; and if
you and I had been there, I promise you we would not have
minded the knives and forks, or the cups either. Mrs. Bartlett's
tea was not of corresponding quality, for it came from a
country store. However, the cream went far to mend even
that. The back door was open for the heat; and the hill-side
could be seen through the doorway and part of the soft green
meadow slope; and the grasshopper's song and the bell tinkle
were not bad music.

' And who was that came with you, dear? ' Mrs. Bartlett
asked as they sat at table.

' With me? Did you see me come? '

' Surely. I was in the garden. What should hinder me?
Who was it druv you, dear? '

' It was an accident. Young Mr. Knowlton had got into
some trouble with his horse, riding out our way, and came to
ask how he could get home. So I brought him.'

' That's Evan Knowlton! him they are making a soldier of? '

' He's made. He's done with his education. He is at home
now.'

' Ain't goin' to be a soldier after all? '

' O yes; he *is* a soldier; but he has got a leave, to be home
for awhile.'

' Well, what sort is he? I don't see what they wanted to
make a soldier of him for; his grand'ther would ha' been the
better o' his help on the farm, seems to me; and now he'll be
off to the ends o' the earth, and doin' nobody knows what.
It's the wisdom o' this world. But how has he turned out,
Die? '

' I don't know; well, I should think.'

' And his sisters at home would ha' been the better of him. By-and-by Mr. Bowdoin will die; and then who'll look after the farm, or the girls?'

' Still, mother, it's something more and something better to be educated, as he is, and to know the world and all sorts of things, as he does, than just to live on the farm here in the mountains, and raise corn and eat it, and nothing else. Isn't it?'

' Why should it be better, child?'

' It is nice to be educated,' said Diana softly. And she thought much more than she said.

' A man can get as much edication as he can hold, and live on a farm too. I've seen sich. Some folks can't do no better than hoe corn—like my Joe. But there ain't no necessity for that. But arter all, what does folks live for, Diana?'

' I never could make out, Mother Bartlett.'

The old lady looked at her thoughtfully and wistfully, but said no more. Diana cleared the table and washed the few dishes; and when all was straight again, took out a newspaper she had brought from home, and she and the old lady settled themselves for an afternoon of enjoyment. For it was that to both parties. At home Diana cared little about the paper; here it was quite another thing. Mrs. Bartlett wanted to hear all there was in it; public doings, foreign doings, city news, editor's gossip; and even the advertisements came in for their share of pleasure-giving. New inventions had an interest; tokens of the world's movements, or the world's wants, in other notices, were found suggestive of thought or provocative of wonder. Sitting with her feet put towards the fire, her knitting in her hands, the quick grey eyes studied Diana's face as she read, never needing to give their supervision to the fingers; and the coarse blue yarn stocking, which was doubtless destined for Joe, grew visibly in length while the eyes and thoughts of the knitter were busy elsewhere. The newspaper filled a good part of the afternoon; for the reading was often interrupted for talk which grew out of it. When at last it was done, and Mrs. Bartlett's eyes returned to the fire, there were a few minutes of stillness; then she said gently,

'Now, our other reading, dear?'

'You like this the best, Mother Bartlett, don't you?' said Diana, as she rose and brought from the inner room a large volume; *the* Book, as any one might know at a glance; carefully covered with a sewn cover of coarse cloth. 'Where shall I read now?'

The place indicated was the beginning of the Revelation, a favourite book with the old lady. And as she listened, the knitting grew slower; though, true to the instinctive habit of doing something, the fingers never ceased absolutely their work. But they moved slowly; and the old lady's eyes, no longer on the fire, went out of the open window, and gazed with a far-away gaze that went surely beyond the visible heaven; so wrapt and steady it was, Diana, sitting on a low seat at her feet, glanced up sometimes; but seeing that gaze, looked down and went on again with her reading and would not break the spell. At last, having read several chapters without a word of interruption, she stopped. The old lady's eyes came back to her knitting, which began to go a little faster.

'Do you like all this so much?' Diana asked. 'I know you do; but I can't see why you do. You can't understand it.'

'I guess I do,' said the old lady. 'I seem to, anyhow. It's queer if I don't.'

'But you can't make anything of all those horses?'

'Why, it's just what you've been readin' about all the afternoon.'

'In the newspaper?' cried Diana.

'It's many a year that I've been lookin' at it,' said the old lady; 'ever sen I heard it all explained by a good minister. I've been lookin' at it ever sen.' She spoke dreamily.

'It's all words and words to me,' said Diana.

'There's a blessin' belongs to studyin' them words, though. Those horses are the works and judgments of the Lord that are goin' on in all the earth, to prepare the way of his comin'.'

'Whose coming?'

'The Lord's comin',' said the old lady solemnly. 'The white *horse*, that's victory; that's goin' on conquering and to conquer; that's the truth and power of the Lord bringin' his kingdom. The red horse, that's war; ah, how that red horse has tramped round the world! he's left the marks of his hoofs on our own ground not long sen; and now you've been readin' to me about his goin's on elsewhere. The black horse, that's famine; and not downright starvation, the minister said, but just want; grindin' and pressin' people down. Ain't there enough o' that in the world? not just so bad in Pleasant Valley, but all over. And the pale horse—what is it the book calls him?—that's death; and he comes to Pleasant Valley as he comes everywhere. They've been goin', those four, ever sen the world was a world o' fallen men.'

'But what do they do to prepare the way for the Lord's coming?' said Diana.

'What do I know? *That*'ll be known when the book shall come to be read, I s'pose. I'm waitin'. I'll know by and by—

'Only I can seem to see so much as this,' the old lady went on after a pause. 'The Lord won't have folk to settle down accordin' to their will into a contented forgetfulness o' him; so he won't let there be peace till the King o' Peace comes. O, I'd be glad if he'd come!'

'But that will be the end of the world,' said Diana.

'Well,' said Mrs. Bartlett, 'it might be the end of the world for all I care, if it would bring Him. What do I live for?'

'You know I don't understand you, Mother Bartlett,' said Diana gently.

'Well, what do you live for, child?'

'I don't know,' said Diana slowly. 'Nothing. I help mother make butter and cheese; and I make my clothes, and do the housework. And next year it'll be the same thing; and the next year after that. It don't amount to anything.'

'And do you think the Lord made you—you pretty creatur!' —said the old lady, softly passing her hand down the side of Diana's face,—'for nothin' better than to make cheese and butter?'

Diana smiled and blushed brightly at her old friend, a lovely child's smile.

'I may come to be married, you know, one of these days!
But after all, *that* don't make any difference. It's the same
thing, married or not married. People all do the same things,
day after day, till they die.'

'If that was all'—said the old lady meditatively, looking
into the fire and knitting slowly.

'It *is* all; except that here and there there is somebody who
knows more and can do something better; I suppose life is
something more to them. But they are mostly men.'

'Edication's a fine thing,' Mrs. Bartlett went on in the
same manner; 'but there's two sorts. There's two sorts,
Diana. I hain't got much,—o' one kind; I never had no
chance to get it, so I've done without it. And now my life's
so near done, it don't seem much matter. But there's the
other sort, that ain't learned at no 'cademy. The Lord put me
into *his* school forty-four years ago—where he puts all his
children; and if they learn their lessons, he takes 'em up and
up,—some o' the lessons is hard to learn,—but he takes 'em up
and up; till life ain't a puzzle no longer, and they begin to
know the language o' heaven, where his courts be. And that's
edication that's worth havin',—when one's just goin' there, as
I be.'

'How do you get into that school, Mother Bartlett?' Diana
asked thoughtfully, and yet with her mind not all upon what
she was saying.

'You are in it, my dear. The good Lord sends his lessons
and his teachers to every one; but it's no use to most folks;
they won't take no notice.'

'What "teachers"?' said Diana, smiling.

'There's a host of them,' said Mrs. Bartlett; 'and of all
sorts. Why, I seem to be in the midst of 'em, Diana. The sun
is a teacher to me every day; and the clouds, and the air, and
the colours. The hill and the pasture abint the house,—I've
learned a heap of lessons from 'em. And I'm learnin' 'em all
the time, till I seem to be rich with what they're tellin' me.
So rich, some days I 'most wonder at myself. No doubt, to
hear all them voices, one must hear the voice o' the Word.
And then there's many other voices; but they don't come just

so to all. I could tell you some o' mine; but the ones that'll come to you'll be sure to be different; so you couldn't learn from *them*, child. And folks thinks I'm a lonesome old woman!'

'Well, how can they help it?' said Diana.

'It's nat'ral,' said Mrs. Bartlett.

'I can't help your seeming so to me.'

'That *ain't* nat'ral, for you had ought to know better. They think, folks does,—I know,—I'm a poor lone old woman, just going to die.'

'But isn't that nearly true?' said Diana gently.

There was a slight glad smile on the withered lips as Mrs. Bartlett turned towards her.

'You have the book there on your lap, dear. Just find the eleventh chapter of the Gospel of John, and read the twenty-fifth and twenty-sixth verses. And when you feel inclined to think that o' me agin, just wait till you know what they mean.'

Diana found and read:—

'"Jesus said unto her, I am the resurrection and the life: he that believeth in me, though he were dead, yet shall he live. And whosoever liveth and believeth in me, shall never die."'

CHAPTER V.

MAKING HAY.

JUNE had changed for July; but no heats ever withered the green of the Pleasant Valley hills, nor browned its pastures; and no droughts ever stopped the tinkling of its rills and brooks, which rolled down, every one of them, over gravelly pebbly beds to lose themselves in lake or river. Sun enough to cure the hay and ripen the grain, they had; and July was sweet with the perfume of hayfields, and lovely with brown hayricks, and musical with the whetting of scythes. Mrs. Starling's little farm had a good deal of grass land; and the haying was proportionally a busy season. For haymakers, according to the general tradition of the country, in common with reapers, are expected to eat more than ordinary men, or men in ordinary employments; and to furnish the meals for the day kept both Mrs. Starling and her daughter busy.

It was mid-afternoon, sunny, perfumed, still; the afternoon luncheon had gone out to the men, who were cutting then in the meadow which surrounded the house. Diana found her hands free; and had gone up to her room, not to rest, for she was not tired, but to get out of the atmosphere of the kitchen and breathe a few minutes without thinking of cheese and gingerbread. She had begun to change her dress; but leisure wooed her, and she took up a book and presently forgot even that care in the delight of getting into a region of *thought*. For Diana's book was not a novel; few such found their way to Pleasant Valley, and seldom one to Mrs. Starling's house. Her father's library was quite unexhausted still, its volumes took so long to read and needed so much thinking over; and now she was deep in a treatise more solid and less attractive than most young women are willing to read. It carried her out of the

46

round of daily duties and took her away from Pleasant Valley altogether, and so was a great refreshment. Besides, Diana liked thinking.

Once or twice a creak of a farm waggon was heard along the road; it was too well known a sound to awake her attention; then came a sound far less common—the sharp trot of a horse moving without wheels behind him. Diana started instantly and went to a window that commanded the road. The sound ceased, but she saw why; the rider had reined in his steed and was walking slowly past; the same rider she had expected to see, with the dark uniform and the soldier's cap. He looked hard at the place; could he be stopping? The next moment Diana had flown back to her own room, had dropped the dress which was half off, and was arraying herself in a fresh print; and she was down-stairs almost as soon as the visitor knocked. Diana opened the door. She knew Mrs. Starling was deep in supper preparations, mingled with provisions for the next day's lunches.

Uniforms have a great effect, to eyes unaccustomed to them. How Lieut. Knowlton came to be wearing his uniform in the country, so far away from any post, I don't know; perhaps he did. He *said*, that he had nothing else he liked for riding in. But a blue frock, with gold bars across the shoulders and military buttons, *is* more graceful than a frieze coat. And it was a gracious, graceful head that was bared at the sight of the door-opener.

'You see,' he said with a smile, 'I couldn't go by! The other day I was your pensioner, in kindness. Now I want to come in my own character, if you'll let me.'

'Is it different from the character I saw the other day?' said Diana, as she led the way into the parlour.

'You did not see my character the other day, did you?'

'I saw what you showed me!'

He laughed, and then laughed again; looking a little surprised, a good deal amused.

'I would give a great deal to know what you thought of me.'

'Why would you?' Diana said, quite quietly.

'That I might correct your mistakes, of course.'

'Suppose I made any mistakes,' said Diana, 'you could only tell me that you thought differently. I don't see that I should be much wiser.'

'I find I made a mistake about you!' he said, laughing again, but shaking his head. ' But every person is like a new language to those that see him for the first time; don't you think so? One has to learn the signs of the language by degrees, before one can read it off like a book.'

'I never thought about that,' said Diana. 'No; I think that is true of *some* people; not everybody. All the Pleasant Valley people seem to me to belong to one language. All except one, perhaps.'

' Who is the exception?' Mr. Knowlton asked quickly.

' I don't know whether you know him.'

' O, I know everybody here—or I used to.'

' I was thinking of somebody who didn't use to be here. He has only just come. I mean Mr. Masters.'

' The parson?'

' Yes.'

'I don't know him much. I suppose he belongs to the *parson* language, to carry on our figure. They all do.'

' He don't,' said Diana. 'That is what struck me in him. What are the signs of the "parson" language?'

' A black coat and a white neckcloth, to begin with.'

' He dresses in grey,' said Diana, laughing, ' or in white; and wears any sort of a cravat.'

' To go on,—Generally a grave face and a manner of great propriety; with a square way of arranging words.'

' Mr. Masters has no manner at all; and he is one of the most entertaining people I ever knew.'

' Jolly sort, eh?'

'No, I think not,' said Diana; ' I don't know exactly what you mean by jolly; he is never silly, and he does not laugh much particularly; but he can make other people laugh.'

' Well, another sign is, they put a religious varnish over common things. Do you recognise that?'

' I recognise that, for I have seen it; but it isn't true of Mr. Masters.'

'I give him up,' said young Knowlton. 'I am sure I shouldn't like him.'

'Why, do you *like* these common signs of the "parson language," as you call it, that you have been reckoning?'

The answer was a decided negative, accompanied with a laugh again; and then Diana's visitor turned the conversation to the country, and the place, and the elm trees; looked out of the window and observed that the haymakers were at work near the house, and finally said he must go out to look at them nearer—he had not made hay since he was a boy.

He went out, and Diana went back to her mother in the lean-to.

'Mother, young Mr. Knowlton is here.'

'Well, keep him out o' *my* way; that's all I ask.'

'Haven't you got through yet?'

'Through! There was but one single pan of ginger-bread left this noon; and there ain't more'n three loaves o' bread in the pantry. What's that among a tribe o' such grampuses? I've got to make biscuits for tea, Di; and I may as well get the pie-crust off my hands at the same time; it'll be so much done for to-morrow. I wish you'd pick over the berries. And then I'll find you something else to do. If I had six hands and two heads, I guess I could about get along.'

'But, mother, it won't do for nobody to be in the parlour.'

'I thought he was gone?'

'Only gone out into the field to see the haymakers.'

'Queer company!' said Mrs. Starling, leaving her bowl of dough, with floury hands, to peer out of a window. 'You may make your mind easy, Di; he won't come in again. I declare! he's got his coat off and he's gone at it himself; ain't that him?'

Diana looked and allowed that it was. Mr. Knowlton had got a rake in hand, his coat hung on the fence, and he was raking hay as busily as the best of them. Diana gave a little sigh, and turned to her pan of berries. This young officer was a new language to her, and she would have liked, she thought, to spell out a little more of its graceful peculiarities. The berries took a good while. Meantime Mrs. Starling's biscuit

D

went into the oven, and a sweet smell began to come there-
out. Mrs. Starling bustled about setting the table; with cold
pork and pickles, and cheese and berry pie, and piles of bread
brown and white. Clearly the haymakers were expected to
supper.

'Mother,' said Diana doubtfully, when she had washed her
hands from the berry stains, 'will you bring Mr. Knowlton out
here to tea, if he should possibly stay?'

'He's gone, child, this age.'

'No, he isn't.'

'He ain't out yonder any more.'

'But his horse stands by the fence under the elm.'

'I wish he was farther, then! Yes, of course he'll come
here, if he takes supper with *me* to-night. I don't think he
will. I don't know him, and I don't know as I want to.'

But this vaguely expressed hope was disappointed. The
young officer came in, a little while before supper; laughingly
asked Diana for some water to wash his hands; and followed
her out to the lean-to. There he was introduced to Mrs. Starling, and informed her he had been doing her work, begging
to know if that did not entitle him to some supper. I think
Mrs. Starling was a little sorry then that she had not made
preparations to receive him more elegantly; but it was too
late now; she only rushed a little nervously to fetch him a
finer white towel than those which usually did kitchen duty
for herself and Diana; and then the biscuits were baked, and
the farm hands came streaming in.

There were several of them, now in haying time, headed by
Josiah Davis, Mrs. Starling's ordinary stand-by. Heavy and
clumsy, warm from the hay-field, a little awkward at sight
of the company, they filed in and dropped into their several
seats round one end of the table; and Mrs. Starling could only
play all her hospitable arts around her guest, to make him
forget if possible his unwonted companions. She served him
assiduously with the best she had on the table; she would not
bring on any dainties extra; and the young officer took kindly
even to the pork and pickles, and declared the brown bread
was worth working for; and when Mrs. Starling let fall a word

of regretful apology, assured her that in the times when he was
a cadet he would have risked getting a good many marks for the
sake of such a meal.

'What are the marks for?' inquired Mrs. Starling curiously.

'Bad boys,' he told her; and then went off to a discussion
of her hay crop, and a dissertation on the delights of making
hay and the pleasure he had had from it that afternoon;
'·something he did not very often enjoy.'

'Can't you make hay anywheres?' Mrs. Starling asked a
little dryly.

He gravely assured her it would not be considered military.

'I don't know what military means,' said Mrs. Starling.
' *You* are military, ain't you?'

'Mean to be,' he answered seriously.

'Well, you are. Then, I should think, whatever you do
would be military.'

But at this giving of judgment, after a minute of, perhaps,
endeavour for self-control, Mr. Knowlton broke down and
laughed furiously. Mrs. Starling looked stern. Diana was in
a state of indecision, whether to laugh with her friend or
frown with her mother; but the infection of fun was too
much for her—the pretty lips gave way. Maybe that was
encouragement for the offender; for he did not show any
embarrassment or express any contrition.

'You do me too much honour,' he said as soon as he could
make his voice steady; 'you do me too much honour, Mrs.
Starling. I assure you, I have been most unmilitary this
afternoon; but really I am no better than a boy when the
temptation takes me; and the temptation of your meadow and
those long winrows was too much for me. I enjoyed it hugely.
I am coming again, may I?'

'You'll have to be quick about it, then,' said Mrs. Starling,
not much mollified; 'there ain't much more haying to do on
the home lot, I guess. Ain't you 'most done, Josiah?'

'How?' said that worthy from the other end of the table.
Mrs. Starling had raised her voice, but Josiah's wits always
wanted a knock at the door before they would come forth to
action.

'Hain't you 'most got through haying?'

'Not nigh.'

'Why, what's to do?' inquired the mistress, with a new interest.

'There's all this here lot to finish, and all of Savin hill.'

'Savin hill ain't but half in grass.'

'Jes' so. There ain't a lock of it cut, though.'

'If I was a man,' said Mrs. Starling, 'I believe I could get the better o' twenty acres o' hay in less time than you take for it. However, I ain't. Mr. Knowlton, do take one o' those cucumbers. I think there ain't a green pickle equal to a cucumber—when it's tender and sharp, as it had ought to be.'

'I am sure everything under your hands is as it ought to be,' said the young officer, taking the cucumber. 'I know these are. Your haymakers have a good time,' he added as the men rose, and there was a heavy clangour of boots and grating chairs at the lower end of the table.

'They calculate to have it,' said Mrs. Starling. 'And all through Pleasant Valley they do have it. There are no poor folks in the place, and there ain't many that calls themselves rich; they all expect to be comfortable; and I guess most of 'em be.'

'Just the state of society in which— There's a sweet little stream running through your meadow, Miss Diana,' said the young officer with a sudden change of subject. 'Where does it go to?'

'It makes a great many turns, through different farms, and then joins your river—the Yellow River—that runs round Elmfield.'

'That's a river; this brook is just what I like. I got tired with my labours this afternoon, and then I threw myself down by the side of the water to look at it. I lay there till I had almost forgotten what I was about.'

'Not in your shirt sleeves, just as you was?' inquired Mrs. Starling. The inquiry drew another laugh from her guest; and he then asked Diana where the brook came from. If it was pretty, followed up?

'Very pretty!' Diana said. 'As soon as you get among the hills and in the woods with it, it is as pretty as it can be; not a bit like what it is here; full of rocks and pools and waterfalls; lovely!'

'Any fish?'

'Beautiful trout.'

'Miss Diana, can you fish?'

'No. I never tried.'

'Well, trout fishing is not exactly a thing that comes by nature. I must go up that brook. I wish you would go and show me the way. When I see anything pretty, I always want some one to point it out to, or I can't half enjoy it.'

'I think it would be the other way,' said Diana. 'I should be the one to show the brook to you.'

'You see if I don't make you find more pretty things than you ever knew were there. Come! is it a bargain? I'll take my line and bring Mrs. Starling some trout.'

'When?' said Diana.

'Seems to me,' said Mrs. Starling, 'I could keep along a brook if I could once get hold of it.'

'Ah,' said Mr. Knowlton, laughing, 'you are a great deal cleverer than I am. You have no idea how fast I can lose myself. Miss Diana, the sooner the better, while this lovely weather lasts. Shall we say to-morrow?'

'I'll be ready,' said Diana.

'This weather ain't goin' to change in a hurry,' remarked Mrs. Starling.

But the remark did not seem to be to the purpose. The appointment was made for the following day at three o'clock; and Mr. Knowlton's visit having come to an end, he mounted and galloped away.

'Three o'clock!' said Mrs. Starling. 'Just the heat o' the day. And trout, indeed! Don't you be a silly fish yourself, Diana.'

'Mother!' said Diana. 'I couldn't help going, when he asked me.'

'You could ha' helped it if you'd wanted to, I s'pose.'

Which was no doubt true, and Diana made no response; for she wanted to go. She watched the golden promise of dawn the next morning; she watched the cloudless vault of the sky, and secretly rejoiced within herself that she would be ready.

CHAPTER VI.

MR. KNOWLTON'S FISH.

DOUBTLESS they were ready, those two, for the brook and the afternoon. The young officer came at half-past three; not in regimentals this time, but in an easy grey undress and straw hat. He came in a waggon, and he brought his fishing-rod and carried a basket. Diana had been ready ever since three. They lost no time; they went out into the meadow and struck the brook.

Now the brook, during its passage through the valley field, was remarkable for nothing but a rare infirmity of purpose, which would never let it keep one course for many rods together. It twisted and curled about, making many little meadow promontories on one side and the other; hurrying along with a soft, sweet gurgle that sounded fresh, even under the heat of the summer sun. It was a hot afternoon, as Mrs. Starling had said; and the two excursionists were fain to take it gently and to make as straight a course across the fields as keeping on one side of the brook left possible. They could not cross it. The stream was not large, yet quite too broad for a jump; and not deep, yet deep enough to cover its stony bed and leave no crossing stones. So sometimes along the border of the brook, where a fringe of long grass had been left by the mowers' scythes, rank and tangled; sometimes striking across from bend to bend over the meadow, where no kindly trees stood to shade them, the two went—on a hunt, as Mr. Knowlton said, after pretty things.

After a mile or more of this walking, the scenery changed. Mown fields, hot and fragrant, were left behind; almost suddenly they entered the hills, where the brook issued from

55

them; and then they began a slower tracking of its course back among the rocks and woods of a dell which soon grew close and wild. The sides of the dell became higher; the bed of the stream more steep and rough; the canopy of trees closed in overhead, and showed the blue through only in broken patches. The clothing of the hill-sides was elegant and exquisite; oaks, and firs, and hemlocks, with slender birches and maples, lining the ravine; and under them a free growth of ferns, and fresh beds of moss, and lovely lichens covered the rocks and dressed the ground. The stream rattled along at the bottom; foaming over the stones and leaping down the rocks; making the still, deep pools where the fish love to lie; and in its way executing a succession of cascades and tiny waterfalls that wanted no picturesque element except magnitude. And a good imagination can supply that.

And how went the afternoon? How goes it with those who have just received a new sense, or found a sudden doubling of that which they had before? Nay, it was a new sense, a new power of perception, able to discern what had eluded all their previous lives. The brook in the meadow had been to Diana's vision until now merely running water; whence had come those delicious amber hues where it rolled over the stones, and the deep olive shadows where the water was deeper? She had never seen them before. Now they were pointed out and seen to be rich and clear, a sort of dilution of sunlight, with a suggestion of sunlight's other riches of possibility. The rank unmown grass that fringed the stream, Diana had never seen it but as what the scythe had missed; now she was made to notice what an elegant fringe it was, and how the same sunlight glanced upon its curving stems and blades, and set off the deep brown stream. Diana's own eyes began to be quickened, and her tongue loosed. The lovely outline of the hills that encircled the valley had never looked just so rare and lovely as this afternoon when she pointed them out to her companion, and he scanned them and nodded in full assent. But when they got into the ravine, it was Diana's turn. Mosses, and old trees, and sharp turns of the gorge, and fords, where it was necessary to cross the brook and recross on stepping stones just lifting them above the water, here black enough,—Diana knew all these things, and with secret delight unfolded the knowledge of them to her companion as they went along. And still the bits of blue sky overhead had never seemed so unearthly blue; the drapery of oak and hemlock boughs had never been so graceful and bright; there was a presence in the old gorge that afternoon, which went with them and cleared their eyes from vapour and their minds from everything, it seemed, but a susceptibility to beauty and delight in its influence. Perhaps the young officer would have said that this presence was embodied in the unconscious eyes and fair calm brow which went beside him; I think he saw them more distinctly than anything else. Diana did not know it. Somehow she very rarely looked her companion in the face; and yet she knew very well how his face looked, too; so well, perhaps, that she did not need to refresh her memory. So they wandered on; and the fords were pleasant places, where she had to be helped over the stones. Not that Diana needed such help; her foot was fearless and true; she never had had help there before : was that what made it so pleasant? Certainly it did seem to her that it was a prettier way of going up the brook than alone and unaided.

'I am not getting much fish at this rate,' said young Knowlton at length with a light laugh.

'No,' said Diana. 'Why don't you stop and try here? Here looks like a good place. Right in that still, deep spot, I daresay there are trout.'

'What will you do in the meantime, if I stop and fish? It will be very stupid for you.'

'For me? O no. I shall sit here and look on. It will not be stupid. I will keep still, never fear.'   ·

'I don't want you to keep still; that would be very stupid for me.'

'You can't talk while you are fishing; it would scare the trout, you know.'

'I don't believe it.'

'I have always heard so.'

'I don't believe it will pay,' said Knowlton as he fitted his rod—'if I am to purchase trout at the expense of all that '—

All what? Diana wondered.

'Suppose we talk very softly—in whispers,' he went on, laughing. 'Do you suppose the trout are so observant as to mind it? If you sit here,—on this mossy stone, close by me, can't I enjoy two things at once?'

Diana made no objection to this arrangement. She took the place indicated, full of a breathless kind of pleasure which she did not stop to analyze; and watched in silence the progress of the fishing. In silence, for after Mr. Knowlton's arrangement had been carried into effect, he too subsided into stillness; whether engrossed with the business of his line, or satisfied, or with thoughts otherwise engaged, did not appear. But as presently and again a large trout, speckled and beautiful, was swung up out of the pool below, the two faces were turned towards each other, and the two pairs of eyes met with a smile of so much sympathy, that I rather think the temporary absence of words lost nothing to the growth of the understanding between them.

The place where they sat was lovely. Just there the bank was high, overhanging the brook. A projecting rock, brown and green and grey, with lichen and mosses of various kinds, held besides a delicate young silver birch, the roots of which found their way to nourishment somehow through fissures in the rock. Here sat Knowlton, with Diana beside him on a stone, just a little behind; while he sat on the brink to cast, or rather drop, his line into the little pool below where the trout were lurking. The opposite side of the stream was but a few yards off, thick with a lovely growth of young wood, with one great hemlock not far above towering up towards the sky. The view in that direction went up a vista of the ravine, so wood-fringed on both sides, with the stream leaping and tumbling down a steep rocky bed. Overhead the narrow line of blue sky.

'Four!' whispered Diana, as another spotted trout came up from the pool.

'I wonder how many there are down there?' said Knowlton as he unhooked the fish. 'It makes me hungry.'

'Catching the trout?' said Diana softly.

He nodded. 'Here comes another. I wish we could make a fire somewhere hereabouts and cook them.'

'Is that a good way?'

'The best in the world,' he said, adjusting his fly, and then looking with a smile at her. 'There is no way that fish taste so good. I used to do that, you see, in the hills round about the Academy; and I know all about it.'

'We could make a fire,' said Diana; 'but we have no grid-iron here.'

'I had no gridiron there. Couldn't have carried a gridiron in my pocket if I had one. Here's another '—

'You had not a gridiron, of course?'

'Nor a pocket either.'

'But did you eat the trout all alone? without bread, I mean, or anything?'

'No; we took bread and salt, and pepper and butter, and a few such things. There were generally a lot of us; or if only two or three we could manage that. The butter was the worst thing to accomplish—Here's another!'

'Such beauties!' said Diana. 'Well, Mr. Knowlton, if you get *too* hungry, we'll cook you one at home, you know.'

'Will you?' said he. 'I wish we had salt and bread here! I should like to show you how wood cookery goes, though. But I'll tell you! we'll get Mrs. Starling to let us have it out in the meadow—that won't be bad.'

Diana thought of her mother's utter astonishment and dis-approbation at such a proposal; and there was silence again for a few minutes, while the line hung motionless over the pool, and Diana's eyes watched it movelessly, and the liquid sweet-ness of the water's talk with the stones was heard,—as one hears things when the senses are strung to double keenness. Diana heard it, at least, and listened to something in it she had never perceived before; something not only sweet and liquid and musical, but in some odd sense admonitory. What did it say? Diana hardly questioned, but yet she heard,—'My peace never changes. My song never dies. Listen, or not listen, it is all the same. You may be in twenty moods in a year. In my depth of content I flow on for ever.'

A slight rustling of leaves, a slight crackling of stems or branches, brought the eyes of both watchers in another direction; and before they could hear a footfall, they saw, above them on the course of the brook, a figure of a man coming towards them, and Diana knew it was the minister. Swiftly and lightly he came swinging himself along, bounding over obstacles, with a sure foot and a strong hand; till presently he stood beside them. Just then Mr. Knowlton's line was swung up with another trout. Diana introduced the gentlemen to each other.

'Fishing?' said the minister.

'We have got all there are in this place, I'm thinking,' said Knowlton, shutting up his rod.

'You *had* not, two minutes ago,' said the other. 'What do you judge from? It doesn't do to be so easily discouraged as that.'

'Discouraged?' said Knowlton. 'Not exactly. Let us see. Four, five, six—seven—eight. Eight out of this little one pool, Mr. Masters. Do you think there are any more?'

'I always get all I can out of a thing,' said the minister. And his very cheery tone, as well as his very quiet manner, seemed to say he was in the habit of getting a good deal out of everything.

'I don't know about that,' answered the young officer in another tone. 'Doesn't always pay. To stay too long at one pool of a brook, for instance. The brook has other pools, I suppose.'

'I suppose it has,' said the minister, with a manner which would have puzzled any but one that knew him, to tell whether he were in jest or earnest. 'I suppose it has. But you may not find them. Or by the time you do, you may have lost your bait. Or you may be tired of fishing. Or it may be time to go home.'

'I am never tired,' said Knowlton, springing up; 'and I have got a guide that will not let me miss my way.'

'You are fortunate,' said the other. 'And I will not occupy your time. Good afternoon! I shall hope to see more of you.'

With a warm grasp of the young officer's hand, and lifting his hat to Diana, the minister went on his way. Diana looked after him, wondering why he had not shaken hands with her too. It was something she was a little sorry to miss.

'Who is that?' Knowlton asked.

'Mr. Masters? He's our minister.'

'What sort of a chap is he? Not like all the rest of them?'

'How are all the rest of them?' Diana asked.

'I declare, I don't know!' said Knowlton. 'If I was to tell the truth, I should say they puzzle all my wits. See 'em in one place—and hear 'em—and you would say they thought all the business of this world was of no account, nor the pleasure of it either. See 'em anywhere else, and they are just as much of this world as you are—or as I am, I mean. They change as fast as a chameleon. In the light that comes through a church window, now, they'll be blue enough, and make you think blue's the only wear—or black; but once outside, and they like the colour that comes through a glass of wine or anything else that's jolly. One thing or the other they don't mean—that's plain.'

'Which do you think they don't mean?' said Diana.

'Well, they're two or three hours in church, and the rest of the week outside. I believe what they say the rest of the time.'

'I don't think Mr. Masters is like that.'

'What *is* he like, then?'

'I think he means exactly what he says.'

'Exactly,' said the young officer, laughing; 'but which part of the time, you know?'

'All times. I think he means just the same thing always.'

'Must see more of him,' said Knowlton. 'You like him, then, Miss Starling?'

Diana did like him, and it was quite her way to say what she thought; yet she did not say it. She had an undefined, shadowy impression that the hearing would not be grateful to her companion. Her reply was a very inconclusive remark, that she had not seen much of Mr. Masters; and an inquiry where Mr. Knowlton meant to fish next.

So the brook had them without interruption the rest of the time. They crept up the ravine, under the hemlock branches and oak boughs; picking their way along the rocky banks; catching one or two more trout, and finding an unending supply of things to talk about; while the air grew more delicious as the day dipped towards evening, and the light flashed from the upper tree-tops more clear and sparkling as the rays came more slant; and the brook's running commentary on what was going on, like so many other commentaries, was heard and not heeded; until the shadows deepening in the dell warned them it was time to seek the lower grounds and open fields again. Which they did, much more swiftly than the ascent of the brook had been made; in great spirits on both sides, though with a thought on Diana's part how her mother would receive the fish and the young officer's proposition. Mrs. Starling was standing at the back door of the kitchen as they came up to it.

'I should think, Diana, you knew enough to remember that we don't take visitors in at this end of the house,' was her opening remark.

'How about fish?' inquired Mr. Knowlton, bringing forward his basket.

'What are you going to do with 'em?' asked Mrs. Starling, standing in the door as if she meant he should not come in.

'We are going to eat them—with your leave, ma'am, and by your help;—and first we are going to cook them.'

'Who?'

'Miss Starling and myself. I have promised to show her a thing. May I ask for the loan of a match?'

'A match!' echoed Mrs. Starling.

'Or two,' added Mr. Knowlton, with an indescribable twinkle in his eye; indescribable because there was nothing contrary to good breeding in it. All the more, Diana felt the sense of fun it expressed, and hastened to change the scene and put an end to the colloquy. She threw down her bonnet and went for a handful of sticks. Mr. Knowlton had got his match by this time. Mrs. Starling stood astonished and scornful.

'Will this be wood enough?' Diana asked.

Mr. Knowlton replied by taking the sticks out of her hand, and led the way into the meadow. Diana followed, very quiet and flushed. He had not said a word; yet the manner of that little action had a whole small volume in it. 'Nobody else ever cared whether I had sticks in my hand or not,' thought Diana; and she flushed more and more. She turned her face away from the bright west, which threw too much illumination on it; and looked down into the brook. The brook's song sounded now unheard.

It was on the border of the brook that Lieut. Knowlton made his fire. He was in a very jubilant sort of mood. The fire was made, and the fish were washed; and Diana stood by the column of smoke in the meadow and looked on, as still as a mouse. And Mrs. Starling stood in the door of the lean-to and looked on too, from a distance; and if she was still, it was because she had no one near just then to whom it was safe to open her mind. The beauty of the picture was all lost upon her: the shorn meadow, the soft column of ascending smoke coloured in dainty hues from the glowing western sky, the two figures moving about it.

'Now, Miss Diana,' said the young officer. 'If we had a little salt, and a dish—I am afraid to go and ask Mrs. Starling for them!'

Perhaps so was she; but Diana went, and got them without asking. She smiled at the dishing of the trout, it was so cleverly done; then she was requested to sprinkle salt on them herself; and then with a satisfied air, which somehow called up a flush in Diana's cheeks again, Mr. Knowlton marched off to the house with the dish in his hands. Mrs. Starling had given her farm labourers their supper, and was clearing away the relics from the board. She made no move of welcome or hospitable invitation; but Diana hastened to remove the traces of disorder, and set clean plates and cups, and bring fresh butter, and bread, and make fresh tea. How very pleasant, and how extremely unpleasant, it was altogether!

'Mother,' she said, when all was ready, 'won't you come and taste Mr. Knowlton's fish?'

'I guess I know how fish taste. I haven't eaten the trout of that brook all my life, without.'

'But you don't know my cookery,' said Mr. Knowlton; '*that's* something new.'

'I don't see the sense of doing things in an outlandish way, when you have no need to. Nor I don't see why men should cook, as long as there's women about.'

'What *is* outlandish?' inquired Mr. Knowlton.

'What you've been doing, I should say.'

'Come and try my cookery, Mrs. Starling; you will never say anything against men in that capacity again.'

'I never say anything against men anyhow; only against men cooking; and that ain't natural.'

'It comes quite natural to me,' said the young officer. 'Only taste my trout, Mrs. Starling, and you will be quite reconciled to me again.'

'I ain't quarrelling with nobody—fur's I know,' said Mrs. Starling; 'but I've had my supper.'

'Well, we haven't had ours,' said the young man; and he set himself not only to supply that deficiency in his own case, but to secure that Diana should enjoy and eat hers in spite of all hindrances. He saw that she was wofully annoyed by her mother's manner; it brought out his own more in contrast than perhaps otherwise would have been. He helped her, he coaxed her, he praised the trout, and the tea, and the bread, and the butter; he peppered and salted anew, when he thought it necessary, on her own plate; and he talked and told stories, and laughed and made her laugh, till even Mrs. Starling, moving about in the pantry, moved softly and set down the dishes carefully, that she too might hear. Diana sometimes knew that she did so; at other times was fain to forget everything but the glamour of the moment. Trout were disposed of at last, however, and the remainder was cold; bread and butter had done its duty; and Mr. Knowlton rose from table. His adieux were gay—quite unaffected by Mrs. Starling's determined holding aloof; and involuntarily Diana stood by the table where she could look out of the window, till she had seen him mount into his waggon and go off.

'Have you got through?' said Mrs. Starling.

'Supper?' said Diana, starting. 'Yes, mother.'

'Then perhaps I can have a chance now. Do you think there is anything in the world to do? or is it all done up, in the world you have got into?'

Diana began clearing away the relics of the trout supper, in silence and with all haste.

'That ain't all,' said Mrs. Starling. 'The house don't stand still for nobody, nor the world, nor things generally. The sponge has got to be set for the bread; and there's the beans, Diana; to-morrow's the day for the beans, and they ain't looked over yet, nor put in soak. And you'd better get out some codfish and put that on the stove. I don't know what to have for breakfast if I don't have that. You'd best go and get off your dress, first thing; that's my counsel to ye; and save washing *that* to-morrow.'

Diana went into no reasoning on that subject or any other; but she managed to do all that was demanded of her without changing her dress, and yet without damaging its fresh neatness. In silence, and in an uncomfortable mute antagonism which each one felt in every movement of the other. Odd it is, that when words for any reason are restrained, the feeling supposed to be kept back manifests itself in the turn of the shoulders and the set of the head, in the putting down of the foot or the raising of the hand, nay, in the harmless movements of pans and kettles. The work was done, however, punctually, as always in that house; though Diana's feeling of mingled resentment and shame grew as the evening wore on. She was glad when the last pan was lifted for the last time, the key turned in the lock of the door of the lean-to, and she and her mother moved into the other part of the house, preparatory to seeking their several rooms. But Mrs. Starling had not done her work yet.

'When's that young man comin' again?' she asked abruptly at the foot of the stairs, stopping to trim the wick of her candle, and looking into the light without winking.

E

'I don't know—' Diana faltered. 'I don't know that he is ever coming again.'

'Don't expect him either, don't you?'

'I think it would be odd if he didn't,' said Diana bravely, after a moment's hesitation.

'Odd! why?'

Diana hesitated longer this time, and the words did not come for her waiting.

'Why odd?' repeated Mrs. Starling sharply.

'When people seem to like a place—they are apt to come again,' said Diana, flushing a little.

'*Seem to*,' said Mrs. Starling. 'Now, Diana, I have just this one thing to say. Don't you go and give that young fellow *no* encouragement.'

'Encouragement, mother!' repeated Diana.

'Yes, encouragement. Don't you give him any. Mind my words. 'Cause, if you do, I won't!'

'But, mother!' said Diana, 'what is there to encourage? I could not help going to show the brook to him to-day.'

'You couldn't?' said Mrs. Starling, beginning to mount the stairs. 'Well, it is good to practise. Suppos'n he asked you to let him show you the Mississippi—or the Pacific Ocean; couldn't you help that?'

'Mother, I am ashamed!' said poor Diana. 'Just think. He is educated, and has every advantage, and is an officer in the United States army now; and what am I?'

'Worth three dozen of him,' said Mrs. Starling decidedly.

'He wouldn't think so, mother, nor anybody else but you.'

'Well, *I* think so, mind, and that's enough. I ain't a goin' to give you to him, not if he was fifty officers in the United States army. So keep my words, Diana, and mind what I say. I never will give you to him, nor to any other man that calls himself a soldier and looks down upon folks that are better than he is. I won't let you marry him; so don't you go and tell him you will.'

'He won't ask me, mother. You make me ashamed!' said Diana, with her cheeks burning; 'but I am sure he does not look down upon me.'

'Nobody shall marry you that sets himself up above me,' said Mrs. Starling as she closed her door. 'Mind!'.

And Diana went into her own room, and shut her door, and sat down to breathe. 'Suppose he should ask you to let him show you the Mississippi, or the Pacific?' And the hot flush rushed over her and she hid her face, as if even from herself. 'He will not. But what if he should?' Mrs. Starling had raised the question. Diana, in very maidenly shame, tried to beat it down and stamp the life out of it. But that was more than she could do.

CHAPTER VII.

BELLES AND BLACKBERRIES.

In the first flush of Diana's distress that night, it had seemed to her that the sight of Lieut. Knowlton in all time to come could but give her additional distress. How could she look at him? But the clear morning light found her nerves quiet again, and her cheeks cool; and a certain sweet self-respect, in which she held herself always, forbade any such flutter of vanity or stir even of fancy as could in any wise ruffle the simple dignity of this country girl's manner. She had no careful mother's training, or father's watch and safeguard; the artificial rules of propriety were still less known to her; but innate purity and modesty, and, as I said, the poise of a true New England self-respect, stood her in better stead. When Diana saw Mr. Knowlton the next time, she was conscious of no discomposure; and *he* was struck with the placid elegance of manner, formed in no school, which was the very outgrowth of the truth within her. His own manner grew unconsciously deferential. It is the most flattering homage a man can render a woman.

Mrs. Starling had delivered her mind, and thereafter she was content to be very civil to him. Further than that a true record cannot go. The young officer tried to ingratiate himself into her good graces; he was attentive and respectful, and made himself entertaining. And Mrs. Starling was entertained, and entertained him also on her part; and Diana watched for a word of favourable comment or better judgment of him when he was gone. None ever came; and Diana sometimes sighed when she and her mother had shut the doors, as that night,

68

upon each other. For to *her* mind the favourable comments rose unasked for.

He came very often, on one pretext or another. He began to be very much at home. His eye used to meet hers, as something he had been looking for and had just found; and the lingering clasp of his hand said the touch was pleasant. Generally their interviews were in the parlour of Diana's home; sometimes he contrived an occasion to get her to drive with him, or to walk; and Diana never found that she could refuse herself the pleasure, or need refuse it to him. The country was so thinly settled, and their excursions had as yet been in such lonely places, that no village eyes or tongues had been aroused.

So the depth of August came. The two were standing one moonlight night at the little front gate, lingering in the moonlight. Mr. Knowlton was going, and could not go.

'Have you heard anything about the Bear Hill party?' he asked suddenly.

'O yes; Miss Delamater came here a week ago to speak about it.'

'Are you going?'

'Mother said she would. So I suppose I shall.'

'Where is it? and what is it?'

'The place? Bear Hill is a very wild, stony, bare hill—at least one side of it is bare; the other side is covered with trees. And the bare side is covered with blackberry bushes, the largest you ever saw; and the berries are the largest. We always go there every summer, a number of us out of Pleasant Valley, to get blackberries.'

'How far is it?'

'Fifteen miles.'

'That's a good way to go a-blackberrying,' said the young man, smiling. 'People hereabouts must be very fond of that fruit.'

'We want them for a great many uses, you know; it isn't just to eat them. Mother makes jam and wine for the whole year, besides what we eat at once. And we go for the fun too, as well as for the berries.'

'So it is fun, is it?'

'I think so. We make a day of it; and everybody carries provisions; and we build a fire, and it is very pleasant.'

'I'll go,' said Mr. Knowlton. 'I have heard something about it at home. They wanted me to drive them, but I wanted to know what I was engaging myself to. Well, I'll be there, and I'll take care our waggon carries its stock of supplies too. Thursday, is it?'

'I believe so.'

'What time shall you go?'

'About eight o'clock—or half-past.'

'*Eight!*' said the young officer. 'I shall have to revive Academy habits. I am grown lazy.'

'The days are so warm, you know,' Diana explained; 'and we have to come home early. We always have dinner between twelve and one.'

'I see!' said the young man. 'I see the necessity, and feel the difficulty. Well, I'll be there.'

He grasped her hand again; they had shaken hands before he left the house, Diana remembered; and this time he held her fingers in a light clasp for some seconds after it was time to let them go. Then he turned and sprang upon his horse and went off at a gallop. Diana stood still at the gate where he had left her, looking down the road and listening to the diminishing sound of his horse's hoofs. The moonlight streamed tenderly down upon her and the elm trees; it filled the empty space where Knowlton's figure had been; it flickered where the elm branches stirred lightly and cast broken shadows upon the ground; it poured its floods of effulgence over the meadows and distant hills, in still, moveless peace and power of everlasting calm. It was one of the minutes of Diana's life that she never forgot afterwards; a point where her life had stood still—still as the moonlight, and almost as sweet in its broad restfulness. She lingered at the gate, and came slowly back again into the house.

'What are you going to take to Bear Hill, mother?' inquired Diana the next day.

'I don't know! I declare, I'm 'most tired of picnics; they cost more than they come to. If we could tackle up, now, and go off by ourselves, early some morning, and get what we want —there'd be some fun in that.'

'It's a very lonely place, mother.'

'That's what I·say, I'm tired o' livin' for ever in a crowd.'

'But you said you'd go?'

'Well, I'm goin'!'

'Then we must take something.'

'Well; I'm goin' to. I calculated to take something.'

'What?'

'Somethin' 'nother nobody else'll take—if I could contrive what that'd be.'

'Well, mother, I can tell you. Somebody'll be sure to carry cake, and pies, and cold ham, and cheese, and bread and butter, and cold chicken. All that's sure.'

'Exactly. I could have told you as much myself, Diana What I want to know is, somethin' nobody'll take.'

'Green corn to boil, mother?'

'Well!' said Mrs. Starling, musing, 'that *is* an idea. How'd you boil it?'

'Must take a pot—or borrow one.'

'Borrow! Not I, from any o' the Bear Hill folks. I couldn't eat corn out o' *their* kettles. It's a sight o' trouble anyhow, Diana.'

'Then, mother, suppose I make a chicken pie?'

'Do what you've a mind to, child. And there must be a lot o' coffee roasted. I declare, if I wasn't clean out o' blackberry wine, I'd cut the whole concern. There'll be churning just ready Thursday; and Josiah had ought to be sent off to mill, we're 'most out o' flour, and he can't go to-morrow, for he's got to see to the fence round the fresh pasture lot. And I want to clean the kitchen this week. There's no sitting still in this world, I do declare! I haven't set a stitch in those gowns o' mine since last Friday, neither; and Society comes here next week. And if I don't catch Josiah before he goes out to work in the morning and get the stove cleaned out—the flues are all choked up—it'll drive me out o' the house or out o' my mind, with the smoke; and Bear Hill won't come off then.'

Bear Hill did ' come off,' however. Early on the morning of
Thursday, Josiah might be seen loading up the little green
waggon with tin kettles and baskets, both empty and full.
Ears of corn went in too, for the ' idee ' had struck Mrs.
Starling favourably, and an iron pot found its way into
one corner. Breakfast was despatched in haste; the house
locked up and the key put under the door-stone for Josiah to
find at noon; and the two ladies mounted and drove away
while the morning light was yet fresh and cool, and the shadows
of the trees lay long in the meadow. August mornings and
evenings were seldom hotter than was agreeable in Pleasant
Valley.

For some miles the road lay through the region so de-
nominated. Then it entered the hills, and soon the way led
over them, up and down steep ascents and pitches, with a
green woodland on each side, and often a look-out over some
little meadow valley of level fields and cultivation bordered
and encircled by more hills. The drive was a silent one; Mrs.
Starling held the reins, and perhaps they gave her thoughts
employment enough; Diana was musing about another waggon-
ful, and wondering whereabouts it was. Till at a turn of the
road she discerned behind them, at some distance, a vehicle
coming along, and knew, with a jump of her heart, the colour
of the horse and the figure of the driver. Even so far off she
was sure of them, and turned her sun-bonnet to look straight
forward again, hoping that her mother might not by any
chance give a look back. She did not herself again; but
Diana's ears were watching all the while after that for the
sound of hoofs or wheels coming near; and her eyes served
her to see nothing but what was out of her field of vision.
The scenery grew by degrees rough and wild; cultivation and
civilisation seemed as they went on to fall into the rear. A
village, or hamlet, of miserable, dirty, uncomely houses and
people, was passed by; and at last, just as the morning was
wakening up into fervour, Mrs. Starling drew rein in a
desolate rough spot at the edge of the woodland. The
regular road had been left some time before, since when
only an uncertain wheel track had marked the way. Two or

three farm waggons already stood at the place of meeting; nobody was in them; the last comer was just hitching his horse to a tree.

'Here's Mis' Starling,' he called out. 'Good-day! good-day t'ye. Hold on, Mis' Starling—I'll fetch him up. Goin' to conquer all Bear Hill, ain't ye, with all them pails and kettles? Wall—blackberries ain't ripe but once in the year. I've left all my business to attend upon the women folks. What's blackberries good for, now, when you've got 'em?'

'Don't you like a blackberry pie, Mr. Selden?'

'Bless you!' said the farmer, 'I kin live without it; but my folks can't live 'thout comin' once a year to Bear Hill. It is a wonder to me why things warn't so ordered as that folks could get along 'thout eatin'. It'd save a sight o' trouble. Why, Mis' Starlin', we're workin' all the time to fill our stomachs; come to think of it, that's pretty much what life is fur. Now I'll warrant you, they'll have a spread by and by, that'll be worth all they'll get here to-day.'

'Who's come, Mr. Selden?'

'Wall, they ain't all here yet, I guess; my folks is up in the lot, hard to work, I s'pose. Mis' Seelye's gals is here; and Bill Howe and his wife; and the Delamaters; that's all, I guess. He's safe now, Mis' Starlin'.'

This last remark had reference to the horse, which Farmer Selden had been taking out of the shafts and tethering, after helping the ladies down. Mrs. Starling got out her pails and baskets destined for the berry-picking, and gave some of them to her daughter.

'They'll be all flocking together, up in the thickest part of the lot,' she whispered. 'Now, Diana, if you'll sheer off a little, kind o', and keep out o' sight, you'll have a ventur'; and we can stand a chance to get home early after dinner. I'll go along ahead and keep 'em from comin' where you are —if I can.'

Diana heard with tingling ears, for she heard at the same time the sound of the approaching waggon behind her. She did not look; she caught up her pail and basket and plunged into the wood path after her mother and Mr. Selden; but she had not gone three yards when she heard her name called.

'You are not going to desert us?' cried young Knowlton, coming up with her. 'We don't know a step of the way, nor where to find blackberries or anything. I have been piloting myself all the way by your waggon. Come back and let me make you friends with my sister.'

Blushing and hesitating, Diana had yet no choice. She followed Mr. Knowlton back to the clearing, and looked on, feeling partly pleased and partly uncomfortable, while he helped from their waggon the ladies he had driven to the picnic. The first one dismounted was a beautiful vision to Diana's eyes. A trim little figure, robed in a dress almost white, with small crimson clusters sprinkled over it, coral buckle and earrings, a wide Leghorn hat with red ribbons, and curly, luxuriant, long, floating waves of hair. She was so pretty, and her attire was so graceful, and had so jaunty a style about it, that Diana was struck somehow with a fresh though very undefined feeling of uneasiness. She turned to the other lady. Very pretty she was too; smaller even than the first one, with delicate, piquant features and a ready smile. Daintily she also was dressed in some stuff of deep green colour, which set her off as its encompassing foliage does a bunch of cherries. Her face looked out almost like one, it was so blooming, from the shadow of a green silk sun-bonnet; and her hands were cased in green kid gloves. Her eyes sought Diana.

'My sister, Mrs. Reverdy,' said young Knowlton eagerly, leading her forward. 'Miss Starling, Genevieve; you know who Miss Starling is.'

The little lady's answer was most gracious; she smiled winningly and grasped Diana's hand, and was delighted to know her. 'And we are so glad to meet you, for we are strangers here, you know. I never was at Bear Hill in my life; but they told us of wonderful blackberries here, and such multitudes of them; and we persuaded Evan to drive us—you know we don't often have him to do anything for us; so we came, but I don't know what we should have done if we had not met you. Gertrude and I thought we would come and see what a picnic on Bear Hill meant.' And she laughed again; smiles came very easily to her pretty face. And then she introduced Miss Masters. Knowlton stood by, looking on at them all.

'These elegant women!' thought Diana; 'what must I seem to him?' And truly her print gown was of homely quality and country wear; she did not take into the account a fine figure, which health and exercise had made free and supple in all its movements, and which the quiet poise of her character made graceful, whether in motion or rest. For grace is no gift of a dancing-master or result of the schools. It is the growth of the mind, more than of the body; the natural and almost necessary symbolization in outward lines of what is noble, simple, and free from self; and not almost but quite necessary, if the further conditions of a well-made and well-jointed figure and a free and unconstrained habit of life are not wanting. The conditions all met in Diana; the harmony of development was, as it always is, lovely to see.

But a shadow fell on her heart as she turned to lead the way through the wood to the blackberry field. For in the artistic elegance of the ladies beside her, she thought she recognised somewhat that belonged to Mr. Knowlton's sphere and not to her own—something that removed her from him and drew them near; she thought he could not fail to find it so. What then? She did not ask herself what then. Indeed, she had no leisure for difficult analysis of her thoughts.

'Dear me, how rough!' Mrs. Reverdy exclaimed. 'Really, Evan, I did not know what you were bringing us to. Is it much farther we have to go?'

'It is all rough,' said Diana. 'You ought to have thick shoes.'

'O, I have! I put on horridly thick ones,—look! Isn't that thick enough? But I never felt anything like these stones. Is the blackberry field full of them too? Really, Evan, I think I cannot get along if you don't give me your arm.'

'You have two arms, Mr. Knowlton—can't I have the other one?' cried Miss Masters dolefully.

'I have got trees on my other arm, Gatty—I don't see where

I should put you. Can't you help Miss Starling along, till we get out of the woods?'

'Isn't it very impertinent of him to call me Gatty?' said the little beauty, tossing her long locks and speaking in a half aside to Diana. 'Now he would like that I should return the compliment and call him Evan; but I won't. What do *you* do, when men call you by your Christian name?'

She was trying to read Diana as she spoke, eyeing her with sidelong glances, and as they went, laying her daintily gloved hand on Diana's arm to help herself along. Diana was astounded both at her confidence and at her request for counsel; but as to meet the request would be to return the confidence, she was silent. She was thinking, too, of the elegant little boot Mrs. Reverdy had displayed, and contrasting it with her own coarse shoes. And how very familiar these two were, that he should speak to her by her first name so!

'Miss Starling!' cried the other lady behind her,—'do you know we have been following your lead all the way we were coming this morning?'

'Mr. Knowlton said so,' Diana replied, half turning.

'Aren't you very much flattered?'

This time Diana turned quite, and faced the two.

'My mother was driving, Mrs. Reverdy.'

'Ah!' said the other with a very amused laugh. 'But you could have done it just as well, I suppose.'

What does she mean? thought Diana.

'Can you do anything?' inquired the gay lady on her arm. 'I am a useless creature; I can only fire a pistol, and leap a fence on horseback, and dance a polka. What can you do? I daresay you are worth a great deal more than me. Can you make butter and bread and pudding and pies and sweetmeats and pickles, and all that sort of thing? I daresay you can.'

'I can do that.'

'And all I am good for is to eat them! I can do that. Do you make cheeses too?'

'I can. My mother generally makes the cheese.'

'O, but I mean you. What do people do on a farm? women,

I mean. I know what the men do. You know all about it. Do you have to milk the cows and feed everything?—chickens and pigs, you know, and all that?'

'The men milk,' said Diana.

'And you have to do those other things? Isn't it horrid?'

'It is not horrid to feed the chickens. I never had anything to do with the pigs.'

'O, but Evan says you know how to harness horses.'

Does he? thought Diana.

'And you can cut wood?'

'Cut wood!' Diana repeated. 'Did anybody say I could do that.'

'I don't know—Yes, I think so. I forget. But you can, can't you?'

'I never tried, Miss Masters.'

'Do you know my cousin, Mr. Masters?—the minister, you know?'

'Yes, I know him a little.'

'Do you like him?'

'I like him,—yes, I don't know anything against him,' said Diana in great bewilderment.

'O, but I do. Don't you know he says it is wicked to do a great many things that we do? He thinks everybody is wicked who don't do just as he does. Now I don't think everybody is bound to be a minister. He thinks it is wicked to dance; and I don't care to live if I can't dance.'

'That is being very fond of it,' said Diana.

'Do you dance here, in the country?'

'Sometimes; not very often.'

'Isn't it very dull here in the winter, when you can't go after blackberries?'

Diana smiled. 'I never found it dull,' she said. Nevertheless, the contrast smote her more and more, between what Mr. Knowlton was accustomed to in his world, and the very plain, humdrum, uneventful, unadorned life she led in hers. And this elegant creature, whose very dress was a sort of revelation to Diana in its perfection of beauty, she seemed to the poor country girl to put at an immense distance from Mr. Knowlton

those who could not be charming and refined and exquisite in
the like manner.   Her gloves,—one hand rested on Diana's arm,
and pulled a little too ;—what gloves they were, for colour and
fit and make ! Her foot was a study. Her hat might have
been a fairy queen's hat. And the face under it, pretty and
gay and wilful and sweet, how could any man help being
fascinated by it?   Diana made up her mind that it was
impossible.

The rambling path through the woods brought the party out
at last upon a wild, barren hill-side, where stones and a rank
growth of blackberry bushes were all that was to be seen.
Only far off might be had the glimpse of other hills and of
patches of cultivation on them; the near landscape was all
barrenness and blackberries.

'But where are the rest of the people?' said Mrs. Reverdy
with her faint laugh. 'Are we alone? I don't see anybody.'

'They are gone on—they are picking,' Diana explained.

'Hid in this scrubby forest of bushes,' said her brother.

'Have we got to go into that forest too?'

'If you want to pick berries.'

'I think we'll sit here and let the rest do the picking,' said
Mrs. Reverdy, looking with charming merriment at Gertrude.
But Gertrude was not so minded.

'No, I'm going after berries,' she said. 'Only, I don't see
where they are. I see bushes, and that is all.'

'Just here they have been picked,' said Diana. 'Farther
on there are plenty.'

'Well, you lead and we'll follow,' said Mr. Knowlton. 'You
lead, Miss Starling, and we will keep close to you.'

Diana plunged into the blackberry bushes, and striking off
from the route she guessed the other pickers had taken, sought
a part of the wilderness lower down on the hill.   There was no
lack of blackberries very soon.   Every bush hung black with
them; great, fat, juicy beauties, just ready to fall with ripeness.   Blackberry stains spotted the whole party after they had
gone a few yards, merely by the unavoidable crushing up
against the bushes.   Diana went to work upon this rich harvest,
and occupied herself entirely with it; but berry-picking never

was so dreary to her. The very sound of the berries falling into her tin pail smote her with a sense of pain; she thought of the day's work before her with revulsion. However, it was before her, and her fingers flew among the bushes, from berry to berry, gathering them with a deft skilfulness her companions could not emulate. Diana knew how they were getting on, without using her eyes to find out; for all their experience was proclaimed aloud. How the ground was rough and the bushes thorny, how the berries blacked their lips and the prickles lacerated their fingers, and the stains of blackberry juice were spoiling gloves and dresses and all they had on.

'I never imagined,' said Mrs. Reverdy with a gay laugh, 'that picking blackberries was such a serious business. O dear! and it's only just eleven o'clock now. And I am *so* hungry!'

'Eat blackberries,' said Gertrude, who was doing it diligently.

'But I want to carry some home.'

'You can buy 'em. We come for fun,' was the cool answer.

'Fun,' said Mrs. Reverdy, with another echoing, softly echoing, laugh; 'it's the fun of being torn and stained and scratched, and having one's hat pulled off one's hair, and the hair off one's head.'

Diana heard it all, they were not far from her; and she heard, too, Mr. Knowlton's little remarks, half gallant, half mocking, but very familiar, she thought. No doubt, to his sister; but how to Miss Masters too? Yet they were; and also, she noticed, he kept in close attendance upon the latter young lady; picking into her basket, getting her out of her numerous entanglements with the blackberry branches, flattering and laughing at her; Gertrude was having what she would call a good time; why not? 'And why should I?' thought Diana to herself as she filled her pail. 'It is not in my line. What a goose I was, to fancy that this young man could take pleasure in being with me! He *did;* but then he was just amusing himself: it was not I; it was the country and the fishing, and so on. What a goose I have been!'

As fast as the blackberries dropped into the pail, so fell these reflections into Diana's heart; and when the one was full, so was the other.   And as she set down her pail and began upon a fresh empty one, so she did with her thoughts; they began all over again too.

'Miss Starling, it is twelve o'clock,' cried Mrs. Reverdy; 'where are all the rest of the people? Do you work all day without dinner? I expected to see a great picnic out under the trees here.'

'This is not the picnic place,' said Diana. 'We will go to it.'

She went back first to the waggons; put her berries in safe keeping, and got out some of the lunch supplies.   Mr. Knowlton loaded himself with a basket out of his waggon; and the procession formed again in Indian file, everybody carrying something, and the two ladies grumbling and laughing in concert. Diana headed the line, feeling very much alone, and wishing sadly it were all over and she at home.   How was she to play her part in the preparations at hand, where she had always been so welcome and so efficient?   All spring and life seemed to be taken out of her, for everything but the dull mechanical picking of berries.   However, strength comes with necessity, she found.

CHAPTER VIII.

THE NEW RICHES OF THE OLD WORLD.

THERE was quite a collection of people on Bear Hill to-day, as could be seen when they were all gathered together. The lunching place was high on the mountain, where there was a good outlook over the surrounding country; and here in the edge of the woods the blackberry pickers were scattered about, lying and sitting on the ground in groups and pairs, chatting and watching the preparations going on before their eyes. Pretty and wild the preparations were. Under a big tree just at the border of the clearing a fire was kindled; a stout spike driven into the trunk of the tree held a tea-kettle just over the blaze. Wreaths of blue and grey smoke curling up above the tea-kettle made their way through the tree branches into the upper air, taking hues and colours and irradiations from the sunlight in their way. The forest behind, the wilderness of blackberry bushes in front; the wide view over the hills and vales, without one spot of cultivation anywhere, or a trace of man's habitation; the scene was wild enough. The soft curling smoke, grey and embrowned, gave a curious touch of homeliness to it. From two fires it went, curling up as comfortably as if it had been there always. The second fire was lit for the purpose of boiling green corn, which two or three people were busy getting ready, stripping the green husks off. Other hands were unloading baskets and distributing bread and butter and cups, and unpacking ham and chickens. Meanwhile, till the fires should have done their work, most of the party were comfortably awaiting the moment of enjoyment, and taking some other moments, as it seemed, by the way. Mrs.

F

Carpenter in one place was surrounded by her large family of children; all come to pick blackberries, all heated with work and fun, and eager for the dinner. Miss Barry, quite tired out, was fanning herself with her sun-bonnet, and having a nice bit of chat with Miss Babbage, the schoolmaster's sister. Mrs. Mansfield and farmer Carpenter were happily discussing systems of agriculture. Mrs. Boddington was making a circle merry with her sharp speeches. Younger folks here and there were carrying on their own particular lines of skirmishing operations; but there were not many of these; the company had come for business quite as much as for play. Indeed, Miss Gunn's array of baskets and tin pails suggested that she was doing business on her brother's account as much as on her own; and that preserves and blackberry wine would be for sale by and by on the shelves of the store at the 'Corner.'

The little party that came up with Diana melted away as it met the rest. Mrs. Reverdy glided into the group gathered about Mrs. Boddington, and slid as easily into the desultory gossip that was going on. Diana had instantly joined herself to the little band of workers at the camp fire. Only one or two had cared to take the trouble and responsibility of the feast; it was just what Diana craved. As if cooking had been the great business of life, she went into it; making coffee, watching the corn, boiling the potatoes; looking at nothing else and trying to see nobody, and as far as possible contriving that nobody should see her. She hid behind the column of smoke, or sheltered herself at the farther side of the great trunk of a tree; from the fire, she said to herself. But her face took on a preternatural gravity at those times, whenever she knew it was safe. She thought she did not look at anybody; yet she knew that Miss Masters had joined none of the groups under the trees, and seemed instead to prefer a solitary post in front of them all, where her pretty figure and dainty appointments were displayed in full view. Was she looking at the landscape? Diana did not in the least believe it. But she tried to work without thinking; that vainest of all cheateries, where the conclusions of thought, independent of the processes, force themselves upon the mind and lay their full weight upon it. Only one does not stop anywhere to think about them, and the weight is distributed. It is like driving fast over thin ice; stay a minute in any one place, and you would break through. But that consciousness makes unpleasant driving.

The corn gave forth its sweet smell, and Diana dished it up. What was the use of taking so much trouble, she thought, as ear after ear, white and fair, came out of the pot? Yet Diana had enjoyed the notion of making this variety in the lunch. The coffee steamed forth its fragrance upon the air; and Diana poured it into prepared cups of cream and sugar which others brought and carried away; she was glad to stand by the fire if only she might. How the people drank coffee! Before the cups were once filled the first time, they began to come back for the second; and the second, Diana knew, would not satisfy some of the farmers and farmers' wives there. So pot after pot of the rich·beverage had to be made. It wearied her; but she would rather do that than anything else. And she had expected this picnic to be such a pleasant time! And it had turned out such a failure. Standing by her camp fire, where the ascending column of grey smoke veiled her from observation, Diana could look off and see the wide landscape of hill and valley spread out below and around. Not a house; not another wreath of smoke; not a cornfield; hollows of beauty with nothing but their own green growth and the sunshine in them; hill-tops fair and lovely, but without a fence that told of human ownership or a road that spoke of human sympathy. Was life like that, Diana wondered? Yet surely that landscape had never looked dreary to her before.

'Mrs. Starling will have another cup of coffee, Miss Diana.'

Diana started. What should bring Mr. Knowlton to wait upon her mother's cups of coffee? She sugared and creamed, and poured out in silence.

'May I come presently and have some?'

'Haven't you had any?'

'Just enough to make me want more. I never saw such good coffee in my life.'

'You are accustomed to West Point fare.'

'It's not that, though. I know a good thing when I see it.'

'When you taste it, I suppose,' said Diana; preparing his cup, however, she knew, with extra care.

'I assure you,' said Mr. Knowlton expressively, as he stirred it, 'I *have* appreciation for better things than coffee. I always want the best, in every kind; and I know the thing when I see it.'

'I make no doubt you can have it,' said Diana coolly, turning away.

'Hullo, Diany!' said Mr. Carpenter on the other side,— 'you're coming it strong to-day. Got no one to help ye? Shan't I fetch 'Lizy? she's big enough to do som'thin'. I vow I want another cup. You see, it's hard work, is picking blackberries. I ain't master here; and my wife, she keeps me hard at it. Can't dewolve the duty on no one, neither; she sees if I ain't got my pail filled by the time she's got her'n, and I tell you! I catch it. It makes me sweat, this kind of work; and that makes me kind o' dry. I'll be obleeged to you for another cup. You needn't to put no milk into it.'

'It's strong, Mr. Carpenter.'

'Want it, I tell you! working under orders this way makes a man feel kind o' feeble.'

'How do you think we women gèt along, Mr. Carpenter?' said Mrs. Boddington, coming up with her cup.

'How, Mis' Boddington?'

'Yes, I'm asking that. A little more, Diana; it's first-rate, and so's the corn. It takes you and your mother!—How do you think we women feel, under orders all the time?'

'Under orders!' said Mr. Carpenter.

'Yes, all the time. How d'you think we feel about it?'

'Must be uncommon powers of reaction,' said the farmer. 'My wife a'n't anywheres near killed yet.'

'Think any one'll ever get that piece of mantua-making under orders?' said Mrs. Boddington, looking towards the place where the frills and rufflings of Miss Masters' drapery stirred in the breeze, with the long light tresses of her unbound hair. The breeze was partly of her own making, as she stirred and turned and tossed her head in talking with Mr. Knowlton; the only one of the company whom she would talk with, indeed. The farmer took a good look at her.

'Wall,' said he,—'*I* should say it was best to do with that kind of article what you would do with the steam from your tea-kettle; let it go. 'Tain't no use to try to utilize everything, Mis' Boddington.'

'Evan Knowlton acts as if he thought differently.'

'Looks is enough, with some folks,' said the farmer; 'and she's a pretty enough creatur', take the outside of her. Had ought to be; for I guess that sort o' riggin' costs somethin'—don't it, Mis' Boddington?'

'Cost?' said the lady. 'Evan Knowlton is a fool if he lets himself be caught by such butterfly's wings. But men *are* fools when women are pretty; there's no use reasoning against nature.'

'Wall, Diany,' exclaimed Joe Bartlett, now drawing near with *his* coffee cup,—'how comes you have all the work and other folks all the fun?'

'Want some coffee, Joe?'

'Fact, I do; that is, supposin' you have got any.'

'Plenty, Joe. That's what I am here for. Hold your cup. Who are you picking for to-day?'

'Wall, *I* ain't here for fun,' said Joe; 'there's no mistake about that. I b'lieve in fun too; I do sartain; but I *don't* b'lieve in scratchin' it into you with blackberry brambles, nor no other. Thank'e, Diany; maybe this'll help me get along with the afternoon.'

'I never thought you would mind blackberry thorns, Joe.'

'No more I don't, come in the way o' business,' said Joe, sipping his coffee. 'Guess I kin stand a few knocks, let alone scratches, when I calculate to have 'em. But I don' know! my notion of pleasure's sun'thin' soft and easy like; ain't your'n? I expect to take scratches—bless you! but I don't call 'em fun. That's all I object to.'

'Then how came you here, Joe?'

'Wall,—' said Joe slowly,—'I've got an old mother hum.'

'And she wanted some berries?'

'She wanted a lot. What the women does with 'em all, beats me. Anyhow, the old lady'll have enough this time for all her wants.'

'How is she, Joe, to-day?'

'Days don't make no difference to my mother, Diany. You know that, don't ye? There don't nothin' come wrong to her. I vow, I b'lieve she kind o' likes it when things is contrairy. I never see her riled by no sort o' thing; and it's not uncommon for *me* to be as full's I kin hold; but she's just like a May mornin', whatever the weather is. There ain't no scarin' her, either; she'd jest as lieves die as live, I b'lieve, any day.'

'I daresay she would,' said Diana, feeling at the moment that it was not so very wonderful. Life in this world might be so dull as to be not worth living for.

'It's a puzzle to me,' Joe went on, 'which is right, her or the rest on us. Ef she is, we ain't. And her and the rest o' the world ain't agreed on nothin'. But it is hard to say she ain't right, for she's the happiest woman that ever I see.'

Diana assented absently.

'Wall,' said Joe, 'I'm a little happier for that 'ere cup o' coffee. I'll go at it agin now. Who's that 'ere little bundle o' muslin ruffles, Diany? she's a kind o' pretty creatur', too. She hain't sot down this hull noonspell. Who is it?'

'Miss Masters.'

'She ain't none o' the family o' our parson?'

'A cousin, I believe.'

'Cousin, eh,' said Joe. 'She hain't set down once. I guess she's afeard o' gettin' the starch out somewhere. The captain's sweet on her, ain't he? I see he tuk a deal o' care o' her eatin'.'

'Mr. Knowlton is not a captain yet, Joe; he is only a lieutenant.'

'Want to know,' said Joe. 'Wall, I kin tell ye, she likes him.'

And Joe strolled off, evidently bent on doing his best with the blackberry bushes. So must Diana; at least she must seem to do it. There was a lull with the coffee cups; lunch was getting done; here and there parties were handling their baskets and throwing their sun-bonnets on. The column of smoke had thinned now to a filmy veil of grey vapour, slowly ascending, through which Diana could look over to the round hill-tops, with their green leaves glittering in the sun; and farther still, to the blue, clear vault of ether, where there was neither shine nor shadow, but the changeless rest of heaven. Earth with its wildness of untrodden ways, its glitter and flutter; heaven,—how did that seem? Far off and inscrutable, though with an infinite depth of repose, an infinite power of purity. The human heart shrank before both.

'And I had thought to-day would be a day of pleasure,' Diana said to herself. 'If I could get into the waggon and go home—alone—and get the fire started and the afternoon work done ready for supper before mother comes!—They will not need me to pilot them home, at any rate.'

But things have to be faced, not run away from, in life; and trials take their time and cannot be lopped into easier length. Diana did what she could. She caught up her basket very quietly, carrying it and her sun-bonnet in one hand, and slipped away down the hill under cover of the trees till she was out of sight of everybody; then plunged into the forest of high bushes and lost herself. She began to pick vigorously; if she was found, anybody should see what she was there for. It was a thicket of thorns and fruit; the berries, large, purple, dewy with bloom, hung in quantities, almost in masses, around her. It was only needful sometimes to hold her basket underneath and give a touch to the fruit; and it dropped, fast and thick, into her hands. But she felt as if the cool soft berries hurt her fingers. She wondered whereabouts was pretty Miss Masters now, making believe pick, and with fingers at hand to supplement hers, and looks and words to make labour sweet, even if it were labour. 'But *she* will never do any work,' said Diana to herself; 'and he will be quite willing that she should not.' And then she noticed her own fingers; a little coarsened with honest usefulness they were—a little; and a little embrowned with careless exposure. Not white and pearly and delicate like those of that other hand. And Diana remembered that Mr. Knowlton's own were delicate and white; and she could understand, she thought, that a man would like in a woman he loved, all daintinesses and delicacies, even although they pertained to the ornamental rather than to the useful. It was the first time Diana had ever wished for white hands; she did wish for them now, or rather regret the want of them, with a sharp, sore point of regret. Even though it would have made no difference.

Picking and thinking and fancying herself safe, Diana made a plunge to get through an uncommonly tangled thicket of interlacing branches, and found herself no longer alone. Miss Gunn was three feet off, squatting on the ground to pick the more restfully; and on the other side of her was Diana's cousin, Nick Boddington.

'Hullo, Di!' was his salutation, 'where have you left my wife and the rest of the folks?'

'I don't know, Nick; I haven't left them at all.'

'What did you come here for, then?'

'What did you?'

'I declare! I came to have the better chance, me and Miss Gunn; I thought, where nobody was, I'd have it all to myself. I'll engage you are disappointed to find us—now, ain't you?'

'The field is big enough, cousin Nick.'

'Don't know about that. What is become of your fine people?'

'I haven't any fine people.'

'What's become o' them you *had*, then? You brought 'em here; have you deserted 'em?'

'I came to do work, Nick; and I'm doing it.'

'What did they come for? have you any guess? 'Tain't likely they come to pick blackberries.'

'I told Mis' Reverdy,' said Miss Gunn smotheredly from the depths of a blackberry bush and her sun-bonnet, 'that we'd have plenty for ourselves and Elmfield too to-morrow. I will, I guess.

'They'll want 'em, Miss Gunn,' said Mr. Boddington. 'They'll not carry home a pint, you may depend. Di, did they come after you, or you come after them, this morning?'

Diana answered something, she hardly knew what, and made

a plunge through the bushes in another direction. Anything to get out of *this* neighbourhood. She went on eagerly, through thicket after thicket, till she supposed she was safe. And as she stopped, Mr. Knowlton came round from the other side of the bush. The thrill of pain and pleasure that went through the girl gave no outward sign.

'Met again,' said the gentleman. 'What has become of you? I have lost sight of you since dinner.'

'One can't see far through these bushes,' said Diana.

'No. What a thicket it is! But at the same time, people can hear; and you never know who may be a few feet off. Does anybody ever come here, I wonder, when we are gone? or is this wild fruitful hill bearing its harvest for us alone?'

'Other parties come, I daresay,' said Diana.

She was picking diligently, and Mr. Knowlton set himself to help her. The berries were very big and ripe here; for a few minutes the two hands were silently busy gathering and dropping them into Diana's pail; then Mr. Knowlton took the burden of that into his own hand. Diana was not very willing, but he would have it.

'One would think blackberries were an important concern of life,' he said presently, 'by the way you work.'

'I am sure, you are working too,' said Diana.

'Ah, but I supposed you knew what it is all for. Now I have not the faintest idea. I know what *I* am after, of course; but what you are after is a puzzle to me.'

'Things are very often a puzzle to me,' said Diana vaguely, and having for some reason or other a good deal of difficulty in commanding herself.

'Aren't you tired?'

'No—I don't know,' said Diana. 'It does not signify.'

'I don't believe you care, any more than a soldier, what you find in your way. Do you know, you said something, up yonder at the camp fire, which has been running in my head ever since? I wish you would explain it.'

'I?' said Diana. 'I said something? What?'

'I told you what I wanted,—and you said you had no doubt I could get it.'

'I have no recollection of one thing or the other, Mr. Knowlton. I think you must have been speaking to somebody else at the time—not me. If you please, I will try the bushes that way; I think somebody has been in this place.'

'Don't you remember my telling you I always want the best of everything?' he said as he followed her; and Diana went too fast for him to hold the briary branches out of her way.

'There are so many other people who are of that mind, Mr. Knowlton!'—

'Not yourself?'

'I want the best berries,' said Diana, stopping before a cluster of bushes heavily laden.

'How about other things?'

Diana felt a pang at her heart, an odd desire to make some wild answer. But nothing could be cooler than what she said.

'I take them as I find them, Mr. Knowlton.'

He was helping her now again.

'What did you suppose I was thinking of, when I told you I wanted the best I could have?'

'I had no right to suppose anything. No doubt it is true of all sorts of things.'

'But I was thinking of one—did you guess what?'

Diana hesitated. 'I don't know, Mr. Knowlton,—I might guess wrong.'

'Then what made you say, "no doubt" I could have it?'

'I don't know, Mr. Knowlton,' said Diana, feeling irritated and worried almost past her power to bear. 'Don't you always have what you want?'

'Do you think I can?' he said eagerly.

'I fancy you do.'

'What did you think I meant by the "best" thing, then? Tell me—do tell me.'

'I thought you meant Miss Gertrude Masters,' Diana said, fairly brought to bay.

'You did! And what did you think I thought of Miss Diana Starling?'

He had stopped picking blackberries now, and was putting

his questions short and keenly. Diana's power of answering had come to an end.

'Hey!' said he, drawing her hand from the bush and stopping her work; 'what did you think I thought of *her?*—I have walked with her, and driven with her, and talked with her, in the house and out of the house, now all summer long; I have seen what she is like at home and abroad; what do you think I think of *her?*'

Baskets and berries had, figuratively, fallen to the ground; literally too, in Mr. Knowlton's case, for certainly both his hands were free, and had been employed while these words were spoken in gently and slowly gathering Diana into close bondage. There she stood now, hardly daring to look up; yet the tone of his questions had found its way to her inmost heart. She could not refuse one look, which they asked for. It gave her what she never forgot to her latest day.

'Does she know now?' he went on in a tone of mixed tenderness and triumph, like the expression of his face. 'My lily!—my camellia flower!—my sweet magnolia!—whatever there is most rare, and good, and perfect. My best of all things. Can I have the best, Di?'

Miss Gertrude Masters would have been equal to the situation, and doubtless would have met it with great equanimity; Diana was unused to most of the world's ways, and very new to this. She stood in quiet dignity, indeed; but the stains of crimson on cheek and brow flushed and paled like the lights of a sunset. All at the bottom of her deep sun-bonnet; was Mr. Knowlton to blame if he gently pushed it back and insinuated it off, till he had a full view?

'You know what is my "best" now,' he said. 'Can I have it, Diana?'

She tried to break away from him, and on her lip there broke that beautiful smile of hers; withal a little tremulous just then. It is rare on a grown woman's lip, a smile so very guileless and free; mostly it belongs to children. Yet not this smile, either.

'I should think you must know by this time,' she whispered.

I suppose he did ; for he put no more questions for a minute
or two.

'There's one more thing,' he said. 'Now you know what I
think of you ; what do you think of me, Diana ?'

'I think you are very imprudent,' she said, freeing herself
resolutely, and picking up her sun-bonnet. 'Anybody might
come, Mr. Knowlton.'

'Anybody might! But if you ever call me "Mr. Knowlton"
again—I'll do something extraordinary.'

Diana thought he would have a great many things to teach
her, beside that. She went at her fruit-picking with bewildered haste. She did not know what she was doing, but
mechanically her fingers flew and the berries fell. Mr.
Knowlton picked rather more intelligently ; but between them,
I must say, they worked very well. Ah, the blackberry field
had become a wonderful place ; and while the mellow purple
fruit fell fast from the branches, it seemed also as if years had
reached their fruition and the perfected harvest of life had
come. Could riper or richer be, than had fallen into Diana's
hands now ? than filled them now ? So it was, she thought.
And yet this was not life's harvest, only the bloom of the
flower ; the fruit comes not to its maturity with one sunny
day, and it needs more than sunshine. But let the fruit grow ;
it will come in time, even if it ripens in secret ; and meanwhile
smell the flower. It was the fragrance of the grape blossom
that filled the blackberry field ; most sweet, most evanishing,
most significant. Oddly, many people do not know it. But
it must be that their life has never brought them within reach
of its charm.

Two people in the field never knew how the shadows grew
long that day. No, not even though their colloquy was soon
interrupted, and by Gertrude Masters herself. She thenceforth claimed, and received, Mr. Knowlton's whole services ;
while Diana in her turn was assisted by Will Flandin, a young
farmer of Pleasant Valley, who gave his hands and his arms to
her help. It did not make much difference to Diana ; it might
have been an ogre, and she would not have cared ; so she
hardly noticed that Will, who had a glib enough tongue in

ordinary, was now very silent. Diana herself said nothing. She was listening to hidden music.

'There's a wonderful lot o' blackberries on Bear Hill,' Will remarked at last.

'Yes,' said Diana.

'Well, I guess we've cleaned 'em out pretty well for this time,' pursued he.

'Have we?' said Diana.

'Why, all these folks ha' been pickin' all day ; I should *think* they'd ha' made a hole in 'em.'

Silence fell again.

'How's the roads down your way?' began Mr. Flandin again.

'The roads? pretty well, I believe.'

'They're awful, up this way, to Bear Hill. I say, Miss Starling, how do you s'pose those people lives, in that village?'

'How do they? I don't know.'

'Beats me! they don't raise nothin', and they don't kill nothin',—'thout it's other folks's ; and what they live on I would jest like to know. Mother, she thinks a minister had ought to go and settle down among 'em ; but I tell her I'd like to see what a sheriff'd do fust. They don't live in no reg'lar good way, that's a fact.'

'Poor people!' said Diana. 'They don't even know enough to pick blackberries.'

'They hadn't no need to be so poor ef they would work,' said the young man. 'But I s'pose you've got a kind word for every one, ha'n't you, Miss Starling?'

'Diany,' said the voice of Joe Bartlett, who was pushing his way towards her through the bushes,—'Diany! Here you be! Here's your mother lookin' for ye. Got all you want? It's gettin' time to make tracks for hum. The sun's consid'able low.'

'I'm ready, Joe.'

'Give me one o' them pails, then, and we'll try ef we kin git through these pesky bushes. I vow! I wouldn't like to take Bear Hill for a farm, not on a long lease.'

They pushed and fought their way in the thicket for a long distance, till, as Joe remarked, they had surveyed the hill pretty well; Diana conscious all the time that Mr. Knowlton and Gertrude were following in their wake. That was near enough. She liked it so. She liked it even that in the crowd and the bustle of packing and hitching horses, and getting seated, there was no chance for more than a far-off nod and wave of the hand from the Elmfield party. They drove off first this time. And Diana followed at a little distance, driving Prince; Mrs. Starling declaring herself 'tuckered out.'

There was no sense of weariness on Diana. Never less in her life. She was glad the drive was so long; not because she was weary and wanted to rest, but because every nerve and sense seemed strung to a fine tension, so that everything that touched them sent waves of melody over her being. Truly the light was sweet that evening, for any eyes; to Diana's vision the sunbeams were solid gold, though refined out of all sordidness, and earth was heaped up and brimming over with riches. The leaves of the trees on the hill-sides sparkled in the new wealth of nature; the air scintillated with it; the water was full of it. Prince's hoofs trod in measure, and the wheels of the waggon moved rhythmically, and the evening breeze might have been the very spirit of harmony. The way was long, and before home was reached the light had faded and the sparkling was gone; but even that was welcome to Diana. She was glad to have a veil fall, for a while, over the brightness, and hide even from herself the new world into which she had entered. She knew it was there, under the veil; the knowledge was enough for the present.

CHAPTER IX.

MRS. STARLING'S OPINIONS.

It was well dusk when Prince stopped under the elm tree. The sun had gone down behind the low distant hills, leaving a white glory in all that region of the heavens; and shadows were settling upon the valleys. All household. wants and proprieties were disarranged; the thing to do was to bring up arrears as speedily as possible. To this Mrs. Starling and her daughter addressed themselves. The blackberries were put carefully away; the table set, supper cooked, for the men must have a warm supper; and after supper and clearing up there came a lull.

'If it warn't so late,' said Mrs. Starling,—' but it *is* too late, —I'd go at those berries.'

'Mother! Not to-night.'

'Well, no; it's 'most too late, as I said; and I *am* tired. I want to know if this is what folks call work or play? 'cause if it's play, I'd rather work, for my part. I believe I'd sooner stand at the wash-tub.'

'Than pick blackberries, mother?'

'Well, yes,' said Mrs. Starling; ' 'cause *then* I'd know when my work was done. If the sun hadn't gone down, we'd all be pickin' yet.'

'I am sure you could stop when you were tired, mother; couldn't you?'

'I never am tired, child, while I see my work before me; don't you know that? And it's a sin to let the ripe fruit go unpicked. I wonder what it grows in such a place for! Who were you with all day?'

'Different people.'

95

'Did Will Flandin find you?'

'Yes.'

'He was in a takin' to know where you were. So I just gave him a bit of a notion.'

'I don't see how *you* could know, mother; I had been going so roundabout among the bushes. I don't know where I was, myself.'

'Whenever you don't know that, Diana, stop and find out.'

Mrs. Starling was sitting before the stove in a resting attitude, with her feet stretched out towards it. Diana was busy with some odds and ends, but her mother's tone—or was it her own consciousness?—made her suddenly stop and look towards her. Mrs. Starling did not see this, Diana being behind her.

'Did it ever strike you that Will was sweet on you?' she went on.

'Will Flandin, mother?'

An inarticulate note of assent.

Diana did not answer, and instead went on with what she had been doing.

'Hey?' said Mrs. Starling.

'I hope he'll get cured of it, mother, if he is.'

'Why?'

'I don't know why,' said Diana, half laughing, 'except that he had better be sweet on some one else.'

'He's a nice fellow.'

'Yes, I think he is; as they go.'

'And he'll be very well off, Diana.'

'He's no match for me, then, mother; for I am well off now.'

'No, you ain't, child,' said Mrs. Starling. 'We have enough to live on, but that's all.'

'What more does anybody want?'

'You don't mean what you say, Diana!' cried her mother, turning upon her. 'Don't you want to have pretty things, and a nice house, and furniture to suit you, and maybe servants to do your work? I wonder who's particular, if you ain't! Wouldn't you like a nice carriage?'

'I like all these things well enough, mother; but they are not the first thing.'

'What is the first thing?' said Mrs. Starling shortly.

'I should say,—how I get them.'

'Oh!—I thought you were going to say the *man* was the first thing. That's the usual lingo.'

Diana was silent again.

'Now you can have Will,' her mother went on; 'and he would be my very choice for you, Diana.'

Diana made no response.

'He is smart; and he is good-lookin'; and he'll have a beautiful farm and a good deal of money ready laid up to begin with; and he's the sort to make it more and not make it less. And his mother is a first-rate woman. It's one of the best families in all Pleasant Valley.'

'I would rather not marry either of 'em,' said Diana, with a little half laugh again. 'You know, mother, there are a great many nice people in the world. I can't have all of 'em.'

'Who were you with all the forenoon?' Mrs. Starling asked suddenly.

'You went off and left me with the people from Elmfield. I was taking care of them.'

'I saw you come out of the field with them. What a popinjay that Masters girl is, to be sure! and Mrs.—what's her name?—the other, is not much better. Soft as oil, and as slippery. How on earth did *they* come to Bear Hill?'

'I suppose they thought it would be fun,' Diana said with constrained voice.

'Don't let anybody get sweet on you there, Diana Starling; not if you know what is good for you.'

'Where, mother?'

'*There.* At Elmfield. Among the Knowlton folks.'

'What's the matter with them?' Diana asked; but not without a touch of amusement in her voice, which perhaps turned the edge of her mother's suspicion. She went on, however, energetically.

'Poor and proud!' she said. 'Poor and proud. And that's about the meanest kind of a mixture there is. I don't mind if

G

folks *has* something to go on—why, airs come nat'ral to human
nature; I can forgive 'em anyhow, for I'm as proud as they
be. But when they *hain't* anything—and when they pile up
their pretensions so high they can't carry 'em steady—for my
part I'd rather keep out o' their way. They're no pleasure to
me ; and if they think they're an honour, it's an opinion I
don't share. Gertrude Masters ain't no better than a balloon ;
full of gas ; she hain't weight enough to keep her on her feet ;
and Mrs.—what's her name?—Genevy—she's as smooth as an
eel. And Evan is a monkey.'

' Mother ! what makes you say so ? '

' Why don't he shave himself, then, like other folks ? '

' Why, mother, it is just the fashion in the army to wear a
moustache.'

' What business has he to be in the army ? He ought to be
here helping his grandfather. I have no sort o' patience with
him.'

'Mother, you know they sent him to the Military Academy; of
course he could not help being in the army. It is no fault of his.'

' He could quit it, I suppose, if he wanted to. But he ain't
that sort. He just likes to wear gold on his shoulders, and a
stripe down his leg, and fancy buttons, and go with his coat
flying all open to show his white shirt. I think, when folks
have a pair of such broad shoulders, they're meant to do some
work ; but he'll never do none. He'll please himself, and hold
himself up high over them that *does* work. And he'll live to
die poor. I won't have you take after such a fellow, Diana ;
mind, I won't. I won't have *you* settin' yourself up above your
mother and despisin' the ways you was brought up to. And I
want you to be mistress o' Will Flandin's house and lands and
money ; and you can, if you're a mind to.'

Diana was a little uncertain between laughing and crying,
and thought best not to trust her voice. So they went up to
their rooms and separated for the night. But all inclination
to tears was shut out with the shutting of her door. Was not
the moonlight streaming full and broad over all the fields,
filling the whole world with quiet radiance? So came down
the clear, quiet illumination of her happiness upon all Diana's

soul. There was no disturbance; there was no shadow; there was no wavering of that full flood of still ecstasy. All things not in harmony with it were hidden by it. That's the way with moonlight.

And the daylight was sweeter. Early, Diana always saw it; in those prime hours of day when strength, and freshness, and promise, and bright hope are the speech and the eye-glance of nature. How much help the people lose who lose all that! When the sun's first look at the mountains breaks into a smile; when morning softly draws off the veil from the work there is to do; when the stir of the breeze speaks courage or breathes kisses of sympathy; and the clear blue sky seems waiting for the rounded and perfected day to finish its hours, now just beginning. Diana often saw it so; she did not often stop so long at her window to look and listen as she did this morning. It was a clear, calm, crisp morning, without a touch of frost, promising one of those mellow, golden, delicious days of September that are the very ripeness of the year; just yet six o'clock held only the promise of it. Like her life! But the daylight brought all the vigour of reality; and last night was moonshine. Diana sat at her window a few minutes drinking it all in, and then went to her dairy.

Alas! one's head may be in rare ether, and one's feet find bad walking spots at the same time. It was Diana's experience at breakfast.

'How are those pigs getting along, Josiah?' Mrs. Starling demanded.

'Wall, I don' know,' was the somewhat unsatisfactory response. 'Guess likely the little one's gettin' ahead lately.'

'He hadn't ought to!' said Mrs. Starling. 'What's the reason the others ain't gettin' ahead as fast as him?'

'He's a different critter—that's all,' said Josiah stolidly. 'He'll be the biggest.'

'They're all fed alike?'

'Fur's my part goes,' said Josiah; 'but when it comes to the eatin'—tell you! that little feller'll put away consid'able more'n his share. That's how he's growd so.'

'They are not any of 'em the size they ought to be, Josiah.'

'We ain't feedin' 'em corn yet.'

'But they are not as big as they were last year this time.'

'Don't see how you'll help it,' said Josiah. 'I ain't done nothin' to 'em.'

With which conclusion Mrs. Starling's ' help ' finished his breakfast and went off.

'There ain't the hay there had ought to be in the mows, neither,' Mrs. Starling went on to her daughter. 'I know there ain't; not by tons. And there's no sort o' a crop o' rye. I wish to mercy, Diana, you'd do somethin'.'

'Do what, mother?' Diana said gaily. 'You mean, you wish Josiah would do something.'

'I know what I mean,' said Mrs. Starling, 'and I commonly say it. That is, when I say anything. I *don't* wish anything about Josiah. I've given up wishin'. He's an unaccountable boy. There's no dependin' on him. And the thing is, he don't care. All he thinks on is his own victuals; and so long's he has 'em, he don't care whether the rest of the world turns round or no.'

'I suppose it's the way with most people, mother; to care most for their own.'

'But if I had hired myself to take care of other folks' things, I'd *do* it,' said Mrs. Starling. 'That ain't my way. Just see what I haven't done this morning already! and he's made out to eat his breakfast and fodder his cattle. I've been out to the barn and had a good look at the hay mow and calculated the grain in the bins; and seen to the pigs; and that was after I'd made my fire and ground my coffee and set the potatoes on to boil and got the table ready and the rooms swept out. Is that cream going to get churned to-day, Diana?'

'No, mother.'

'It's old enough.'

'It is not ready, though.'

'It ought to be. I tell you what, Diana, you must set your cream pot in here o' nights; the dairy's too cold.'

'Warm enough yet, mother. Makes better butter.'

'You don't get nigh so much, though. That last buttermilk

was all thick with floatin' bits of butter; and that's what I call wasteful.'

'I call it good, though.'

'There's where you make a mistake, Diana Starling; and if you ever want to be anything but a poor woman, you've got to mend. It's just those little holes in your pocket that let out the money; a penny at a time, to be sure; but by and by when you come to look for the dollars, you won't find 'em; and you'll not know where they're gone. And you'll want 'em.'

'Mother,' said Diana, laughing, 'I can't feel afraid. We have never wanted 'em yet.'

'You've been young, child. You will want 'em as you grow older. Marry Will Flandin, and you'll have 'em; and you may churn your cream how you like. I tell you what, Diana; when your arm ain't as strong as it used to be, and your back gets to aching, and you feel as if you'd like to sit down and be quiet instead of delvin' and delvin', *then* you'll feel as if 't would be handy to put your hand in your pocket and find cash somewhere. My! I wish I had all the money your father spent for books. Books just makes some folks crazy. Do you know it's the afternoon for Society meeting, Diana?'

'I had forgotten it. I shall not go.'

'One of us must,' said Mrs. Starling. 'I don't see how in the world I can, but I suppose I'll have to. You'll have to make the bread then, Diana. Yesterday's put me all out. And what are you going to do with all those blackberries? They're too ripe to keep.'

'I'll do them up this afternoon, mother. I'll take care of them.'

The morning went in this way, with little intermission. Mrs. Starling was perhaps uneasy from an undefined fear that something was going not right with Diana's affairs. She could lay hold on no clue, but perhaps the secret fear or doubt was the reason why she brought up, as if by sheer force of affinity, every small and great source of annoyance that she knew of. All the morning Diana had to hear and answer a string of suggestions and complainings like the foregoing. She was not unaccustomed to this sort of thing, perhaps; and doubtless she had her own hidden antidote to annoyance; yet it belonged still more to the large sweet nature of the girl, that though annoyed she was never irritated. Wrinkles never lined themselves on the fair smooth brow; proper token of the depth and calm of the character within.

CHAPTER X.

DINNER was over, and talk ceased, for Mrs. Starling went to dress herself for the sewing society, and presently drove off with Prince. Diana's motions then became as swift as they were noiseless. Her kitchen was in a state of perfected order and propriety. She went to dress herself then ; a modest dressing, for business, and kitchen business, too, must claim her all the afternoon ; but it is possible to combine two effects in one's toilet ; and if you had seen Diana that day, you would have comprehended the proposition. A common print gown, clean and summery-looking, showed her soft outlines at least as well as a more modish affair would ; and the sleeves rolled up to the elbows revealed Diana's beautiful arms. I am bound to confess she had chosen a white apron in defiance of possible fruit stains ; and the dark hair tucked away behind her ears gave the whole fair cheek and temple to view ; fair and delicate in contour, and coloured with the very hues of a perfect physical condition. I think no man but would like to see his future wife present such a picture of womanly beauty and housewifely efficiency as Diana was that day. And the best was, she did not know it.

She went about her work. Doubtless she had a sense that interruptions might come that afternoon ; however, that changed nothing. She had moulded her bread and put it in the pans and got it out of the way ; and now the berries were brought out of the pantry, and the preserving kettle went on the fire, and Diana's fingers were soon red with the ripe wine of the fruit. All the time she had her ears open for the sound

103

of a horse's hoofs upon the road; it had not come, so that a quick step outside startled her, and then the figure of Mr. Knowlton in the doorway took her by surprise. Certainly she had been expecting him all the afternoon; but now, whether it were the surprise or somewhat else, Diana's face flushed to the most lovely rose. Yet she went to meet him with simple frankness.

'I've not a hand to give you!' she said.

'Not a hand!' he echoed. 'What a mercy it is that I am independent of hands. Yesterday I should have been in despair;—to-day'—

'You must not abuse your privileges,' said Diana, trying to free herself. 'And O, Mr. Knowlton, I have a great deal of work to do.'

'So have I,' said he, holding her fast; and indeed she was too pretty a possession to be easily let go. 'Whole loads of talking, and no end of arrangements.—Di, I never saw you with such a charming colour. My beauty! Do you know what a beauty you are?'

'I am glad you think so,' she said.

'Think so? Wait till you are my wife, and I can dress you to please myself. I think you will be a very princess of loveliness.'

'In the meantime, Mr. Knowlton, what do you think of letting me finish my berries?'

'Berries?' he said, laughing. 'Tell me first, Di, what do you think of me?'

'Inconvenient,' said Diana. 'And I think, presuming. I *must* finish my berries, Mr. Knowlton.'

Evan, he said.

'Well; but let me do my work.'

'Do your work?—My darling! How am I going to talk to you if you are going into your work? However, in consideration of yesterday—you may.'

'What made you come to this door?' Diana asked.

'I knew you were here.'

'You would have been much more likely to find mother, most days.'

'Ah, but I met Prince, as I came along, with Mrs. Starling behind him; and then I thought'—

'What?'

'I remembered,' said Knowlton, laughing, 'that the same person cannot be in two places at once!'

The comfort of this fact being upon them, the two took advantage of it. Mr. Knowlton drew his chair close to the table over which Diana's fingers were so busy; and a talk began, which in the range and variety and arbitrary introduction of its topics, it would be in vain to try to follow. Through it all Diana's work went on, except now and then when her fingers made an involuntary pause. The berries were picked over, and weighed, and put over the fire, and watched and tended there; while the tall form of the young officer stood beside Diana as she handled her skimmer, and went back and forth as she went, helping her to carry her jars of sweetmeat.

'Have you told your mother?' Mr. Knowlton asked.

'No.'

'Why not?' he asked quickly.

'I did not think it was a good time, last night or this morning.'

'Does she not like me?'

'I think she wants to put some one else in your place, Evan.'

'Who?' he asked instantly.

'Nobody you need fear,' said Diana, laughing. 'Nobody I like.'

'Is there anybody you do like?'

'Plenty of people—that I like a little.'

'How much do you like me, Diana?'

She lifted her eyes and looked at him; calm, large, grey eyes, into which there had come a new depth since yesterday and an added light. She looked at him a moment, and dropped them in silence.

'Well?' said he eagerly. 'Why don't you speak?'

'I cannot,' said Diana.

'Why? I can speak to you.'

'I suppose people are different,' said Diana. 'And I am a woman.'

'Well, what then?'

She turned away, with the shyest, sweetest grace of reserve; turned away to her fruit, quite naturally; there was no shadow of affectation, nor even of consciousness. But her eyes did not look up again; and Mr. Knowlton's eyes had no interruption.

'Di, where do you think we shall go when we are married?'

'I don't know,' she said simply; and the tone of her voice said that she did not care. It was as quiet as the harebells when no wind is blowing.

'And *I* don't know!' Knowlton echoed with a half-sigh. 'I don't know where I am going myself. But I shall know in a day or two. Can you be ready in a week, do you think, Diana?'

'Shall you have to go so soon as that?' she asked with a startled look up.

'Pretty near. What of that? You are going with me. It may be to some rough out-of-the-way place; we never can tell; you know we are a sort of football for Uncle Sam to toss about as he pleases; but you are not afraid of being a soldier's wife, Di?'

She looked at him without speaking; a look clear and quiet and glad, like her voice when she spoke. So full of the thought of the reality he suggested, evidently, that she never perceived the occasion for a blush. Her eyes went through him, to the rough country or the frontier post where she could share—and annul—all his harsh experiences.

'What sort of places are those where you might go, Evan?'

'Nearly all sorts on the face of the earth, my beauty. I *might* be sent to the neighbourhood of one of the great cities; we should have a good time then, Di! I would wait for nothing; I could come and fetch you just as soon as I could get a furlough of a day or two. But they are apt to send us, the young officers, to the hardest places; posts beyond civilisation, out west to the frontier, or south to Texas, or across to the Pacific coast.'

'California!' Diana cried.

'California; or Oregon; or Arizona. Yes; why?'

'California is very far off.'

'Rather,' said Knowlton, with a half-sigh again. 'It don't make any difference, if we were once there, Diana.'

Diana looked thoughtful. It had never occurred to her, before this time, to wish that the country were not so extended; and certainly not to fancy that California and she had any interest in common. Lo, now it might be. 'How soon *must* you go, Evan?' she asked, as thoughts of longitude and latitude began to deepen the cloud shadow which had just touched her.

'A few days—a week or two more.'

'Is that all?'

'Can you go with me?' he whispered, bending forward to pick up a few of her berries, for the taste of which he certainly did not care at that moment.

And she whispered, 'No.'

'Can't you?'

'You know it's impossible, Evan.'

'Then I must go by myself,' he said, in the same half breath, stooping his head still so near that a half breath could be heard; and his hair, quite emancipated from the regulation cut, touched Diana's cheek. 'I don't know how I can! But, Di—if I can get a furlough at Christmas and come for you—will you be ready then?'

She whispered, 'Yes.'

'That is, supposing I am in any place that I can take you to,' he went on, after a hearty endorsement of the contract just made. 'It is quite possible I may not be! But I won't borrow trouble. This is the first trouble I ever had in my life, Di, leaving you.'

'They say prosperity makes people proud,' she said, with an arch glance at him.

'Proud?' echoed Knowlton. 'Yes, I *am* proud. I have a right to be proud. I do not think, Diana, there is such a pearl in all the waters of Arabia as I shall wear on my hand. I do not believe there is a rose to equal you in all the gardens of the world. Look up, my beauty, and let me see you. I shan't have the chance pretty soon.'

And yielding to the light touch of his fingers under her chin, caressing and persuading, Diana's face was lifted to view. It was like a pearl, for the childlike purity of all its lines; it was like enough a rose, too; like an opening rose, for the matter of that. Her thoughts went back to the elegance of Mrs. Reverdy and Gertrude Masters, and she wondered in herself at Mr. Knowlton's judgment of her; but there was too much of Diana ever to depreciate herself unworthily. She said nothing.

'I wonder what will become you best?' said Evan in a very satisfied tone.

'Become me?' said Diana, lifting her eyes.

'Yes. What's your colour?'

'I am sure I don't know,' said Diana, laughing. 'No one in particular, I guess.'

'Wear everything, can you? I shouldn't wonder! But I think I should like you in white. That's cold for winter—in some regions. I think I should like you in—let me see—show me your eyes again, Diana. If you wear so much rose in your cheeks, my darling,' said he, kissing first one and then the other, 'I should be safe to get you green. You will be lovely in blue. But of all, *except* white, I think I should like you, Diana, in royal red.'

'I thought purple was the colour of kings and queens,' Diana remarked, trying to get back to her berries.

'Purple is poetical. I am certain a dark, rich red would be magnificent on you; for it is you who will beautify the colour, not the colour you. I shall get you the first stuff of that colour I see that is of the right hue.'

'Pray don't, Evan. Wait,' said Diana, flushing more and more.

'Wait? I'll not wait a minute longer than till I see it. My beauty! what a delight to get things for you—and with you! Officers' quarters are sorry places sometimes, Diana; but won't it be fun for you and me to work transformations, and make our own world; that is, our own home? What does Mrs. Starling think of me?'

'I have told her nothing, Evan, yet. She was so busy this morning, I had not a good chance.'

'I'll confront her when she comes home this evening.'

'O no, Evan; leave it to me; I want to take a *good* time. She will not like it much anyhow.'

'I don't see really how she should. I have sympathy—no, I haven't! I haven't a bit. I am so full of my own side of the question, it is sheer hypocrisy to pretend I have any feeling for anybody else. When will you come down to Elmfield?'

'To Elmfield?' said Diana.

'To begin to learn to know them all. I want them to know you.'

'You have not spoken to them about me?'

'No,' said he, laughing; 'but I mean to.'

'Evan, don't say anything to anybody till mother has been told. Promise me! That would not do.'

'All's safe yet, Di. But make haste with your revelations; for I shall be here to-morrow night and every night now, and astonish her; and it isn't healthy for some people to be astonished. Besides, Di, my orders will be here in a week or two; and then I must go.'

'Do you like being under orders?' said Diana innocently.

Knowlton's grave face changed again; and laughing, he asked if *she* did not like it? and how she would do when she would be a soldier's wife, and so under *double* orders? And he got into such a game of merriment, at her and with her, that Diana did not know what to do with herself or her berries either. How the berries got attended to is a mystery; but it shows that the action of the mind can grow mechanical where it has been very much exercised. It can scarce be said that Diana thought of the blackberries; and yet, the jam was made and the wine prepared for in a most regular and faultless manner; the jars were filled duly, and nothing was burned, and all was done and cleared away before Mrs. Starling came home. Literally; for Mr. Knowlton had been sent away, and Diana had gone up to the sanctuary of her own room. She did not wish to encounter her mother that night. While the dew was not yet off her flowers, she would smell their sweetness alone.

CHAPTER XL

DIANA was not put to the trial next day of venturing her precious things to harsh handling. A very uncommon thing happened. Mrs. Starling was not well, and kept her bed.

She had caught cold, she confessed, by some imprudence the day before; and symptoms of pleurisy made it impossible that she should fight sickness as she liked to fight it, on foot. The doctor was not to be thought of; Mrs. Starling gave her best and only confidence to her own skill; but even that bade her lie by and 'give up.'

Diana had the whole house on her hands, as well as the nursing. Truth to tell, this last was not much. Mrs. Starling would have very little of her daughter's presence; still less of her ministrations. To be 'let alone' was her principal demand, and that Diana should 'keep things straight below.' Diana did that. The house went on as well as ever; and even the farm affairs received the needful supervision. Josiah Davis was duly ordered, fed, and dismissed; and when evening came, Diana was dressed in order, bright and ready for company. Company it pleased her to receive in the lean-to kitchen; the sound of voices and laughter beneath her would have roused Mrs. Starling to a degree of excitement from which it would have been impossible to keep back anything; and probably to a degree of consequent indignation which would have been capable of very informal measures of ejectment regarding the intruder. No; Diana could not risk that. She must wait till her mother's nerves and temper were at least in their ordinary state of wholesome calm, before she would shock them by the disclosures she had to make. And almost by their preciousness

110

to herself, Diana gauged their unwelcomeness to her mother.
It was always so. The two natures were so unlike, that not
even the long habit of years could draw them into sympathy.
They thought alike about nothing except the housewifely
matters of practical life. So these evenings when Mrs. Starling
was ill, Diana had her lamp and her fire in the lean-to kitchen;
and there were held the long talks with Mr. Knowlton which
made all the days of September so golden,—days when Diana's
hands were too busy to let her see him, and he was told he
must not come except at night; but through all the business
streamed the radiant glow of the last night's talk, like the
September sunlight through the misty air.

So the days went by; and Mrs. Starling was kept a
prisoner; pain and weakness warning her she must not dare
try anything else. And in their engrossment the two young
people hardly noticed how the time flew. People in Pleasant
Valley were not in the habit of paying visits to one another in
the evenings, unless specially invited; so nobody discovered
that Evan came nightly to Mrs. Starling's house; and if his
own people wondered at his absence from home, they could
do no more. Suspicion had no ground to go upon in any
particular direction.

The month had been glorious with golden leaves and golden
sunshine, until the middle was more than past. Then came a
September storm; an equinoctial, the people said; as furious
as the preceding days had been gentle. Whirlwinds of
tempest, and floods of rain; legions of clouds, rank after rank,
bringing the winds in their folds; or did the winds bring
them? All one day and night and all the next day, the storm
continued; and night darkened early upon Pleasant Valley
with no prospect of a change. Diana had watched for it a
little eagerly; Evan's visit was lost the night before, of course;
it was much to lose, when September days were growing
few; and now another night he could not come. Diana stood
at the lean-to door after supper, looking and making her conclusions sorrowfully. It was darkening fast; very dark it
would be, for there was no moon. The rain came down in
streams, thick and grey. The branches of the elm tree swung

and swayed pitilessly in the wind, beating against each other; while the wind whistled and shouted its intention of keeping on so all night. 'He can't come,' sighed Diana for the fifth or sixth time to herself; and she shut the door. It could be borne, however, to lose two evenings, when they had enjoyed so many together, and had so many more to look forward to; and with that mixture in her heart of content and longing,. which everybody knows, Diana trimmed her lamp and sat down to sew. How the wind roared! She must trim her fire too, or the room would be full of smoke. She made the fire up; and then the snare of its leaping flames and glowing coal bed drew her from her work; she sat looking and thinking, in a fulness of happiness to which all the roar of the storm only served for a foil. She heard the drip, drip of the rain; the fast-running stream from the overcharged eaves trough; then the thunder of the wind sweeping over the house in a great gust; and the whistle of the elm branches as they swung through the air like tremendous lithe switches, beating and writhing and straining in the fury of the blast. Looking into the clear, glowing flames, Diana heard it all, with a certain sense of enjoyment; when in the midst of it she heard another sound, a little thing, but distinguishable from all the rest; the sound of a foot upon the little stone before the door. Only one foot it could be in the world; Diana started up, and was standing with lips apart, facing the door, when it opened, and a man came in enveloped in a huge cloak, dripping at every point.

'Evan!' Diana's exclamation was, with an utterance between joy and dread.

'Yes,' said he as he came forward into the room,—'I've got orders.'

Without another word she helped relieve him of his cloak and went with it to the outer kitchen, where she hung it carefully to dry. As she came back, Evan was standing in front of the fire, looking gravely into it. The light danced and gleamed upon the gold buttons on his breast, and touched the gold bands on his shoulders; it was a very stately and graceful figure to Diana's eyes. He turned a little, took her into his arms, and then they both stood silent and still.

' I've got my orders,' Knowlton repeated in a low tone.

' To go soon, Evan ? '

' Immediately.'

' I knew it, when I heard your foot at the door.'

They were both still again, while the storm swept over the house in a fresh burst, the wind rushing by as if it was glad he was going and meant he should. Perhaps the two did not hear it; but I think Diana did. The rain poured down in a kind of fury.

' How could you get here, Evan ? ' she asked, looking up at him.

' I must. I had only to-night.'

' You are not *wet ?* '

' No, darling! Rain is nothing to me. How are you? and how is your mother ? '

' She is better. She is getting well.'

' And you? You are most like a magnolia tree, full of its white magnificent blossoms ; sweet in a kind of wealth of sweetness and bountiful beauty. One blossom would do for a comparison for ordinary women ; but you are like the whole tree.'

' Suppose I were to find comparisons for you ? '

' Ay, suppose you did. What would you liken me to ? ' said he with a sparkle of the eyes, which quite indisposed Diana from giving any more fuel to the fire that supplied it.

' What, Di? You might as well give me all the comfort you can to take away with me. I shall need it. And it will be long before I can come back for more. What am I like ? '

' Would you feel any better for thinking yourself like a pine tree? or a green hemlock? one of those up in our ravine of the brook ? '

' Ah, our ravine of the brook! Those days are all gone. I wish I were a green hemlock anywhere, with you a magnolia beside me ; or better, a climbing rose hanging upon me! If I could take you, Di!'

The pang of the wish was very keen in her ; the leap of the will towards impossibilities ; but she said nothing and stood quite motionless.

' I cannot come back for you at Christmas, Di.'

H

'Where are you going, Evan?'

'Where I would not take you, anyhow. I am under orders to report myself at a post away off on the Indian frontier, a long journey from here; and a rough, wild place never fit for such as you. Of course we young officers are the ones to be sent to such places; unless we happen to have influence at headquarters, which I haven't. But I shall not stay there for ever.'

'Must you go just where they send you?'

'Yes,' he said with a laugh. 'A soldier cannot choose.'

'Must you stay as long as they keep you there?'

'Yes, of course. But there is no use in looking at it gloomily, Di. The months will pass, give them time; and years are made of months. The good time will come at last. I'm not the first who has had to bear this sort of thing.'

'Will you have to stay *years* there?'

'Can't tell. I may. It depends on what is doing, and how much I am wanted. Probably I may have to stay two years at least; perhaps three.'

'But you can get a furlough and come for a little while, Evan?' said Diana; her voice sounded frightened.

'That's the worst of it!' said Knowlton. 'I don't know whether I can or not.'

'Why, Evan? don't they always?'

'Generally it can be done if the distance is not too great, and you are not too useful. You see there are seldom too *many* officers on hand, at those out-of-the-way posts.'

'Is there so much to do?' said Diana, half mechanically. Her thoughts were going farther; for grant the facts, what did the reason matter?

'There's a good deal to do sometimes,' Evan answered in the same way, thinking of more than he chose to speak. They stood silent again awhile. Diana was clasped in Knowlton's arms; her cheek rested on his shoulder; they both looked to the fire for consolation. Snapping, sparkling, glowing, as it has done in the face of so many of our sorrows, small and great, is there no consolation or suggestion to be got out of it? Perhaps from it came the suggestion at last that they should sit down. Evan brought a chair for Diana and placed one for himself close beside it, and they sat down, holding fast each other's hands.

Was it also the counsel of the fire that they should sit there all night? For it was what they did. The fire burned gloriously; the lamp went out; the red lights leaped and flickered all over floor and ceiling; and in front of the blaze sat the two, and talked; enough to last two years, you and I might say; but alas! to them it was but a whetting of the appetite that was to undergo such famine.

'If I could only take you with me, my darling!' Evan said for the twentieth time. And Diana was silent at first; then she said,

'It would be pleasant to go through hardships together.'

'No, it wouldn't!' said Evan. 'Not hardships for you, my beauty! They are all very well for me; in a soldier's line; but not for you!'

'A soldier's wife ought not to be altogether unworthy of him,' Diana answered.

'Nor he of her. So I wouldn't take you if I could where I am going. A soldier's wife will have hardships enough, first and last, no fear; but some places are not fit for women anyhow. I wish I could have seen Mrs. Starling, though, and had it out with her.'

'Had it out!' repeated Diana.

'Yes. I should have a little bit of a fight, shouldn't I? She *don't* like me much. I wonder why?'

'Evan,' said Diana after a minute's thought, 'if you are to be so long away, there is no need to speak to anybody about our affair just now. It *is* our affair; let it stay so. It is our secret. I should like it much better to keep it a secret. I don't want to hear people's talk. Will you?'

'But our letters, my dear; they will tell your mother.'

'Mother will not see mine. And she is not likely to see yours; I shall go to the post office myself. If she did, and found it out, I could keep *her* quiet easily enough. She would not want to speak, any more than I.'

Evan combated this resolution for some time. He wished to

have Diana friends with his sisters and at home at Elmfield.
But Diana had her own views, and desired so strongly to
keep her secret to herself, during the first part at least of
what threatened to be a long engagement, that at last he
yielded. It did not matter much to him, he said, away off
in the wilds.

So that subject was dismissed; and before the fantasia of
the flames they sat and composed a fantasia of life for themselves; as bright, as various, as bewitching, as evanishing;
the visions of which were mingled with the leaping and
changing purple and flame tints, the sparkle and the flash
of the fire. Diana could never stand before a fire of hickory
logs, and fail to see her life-story reappear as she had seen it
that night.

The hours went by.

'It's too bad to keep you up so, my darling!' Evan remarked. 'I am selfish.'

'No indeed! But you must want something, Evan! I had
forgotten all about it.'

He said he wanted nothing, but her; however, Diana's energies
were roused. She ran into the back kitchen, and came from
thence with the tea-kettle in her hands, filled. She was not
allowed to set it down, to be sure, but under her directions
it was bestowed in front of the glowing coals. Then, with
noiseless, rapid movements, she brought a little table to the
hearth and fetched cups and plates. And then she spread the
board. There was a cold ham on the big table, and round
white slices of bread, such as cities never see; and cake, light
and fruity; and yellow butter; and a cream pie, another
dainty that confectioners are innocent of; and presently the
fragrance of coffee filled the old lean-to to the very roof.
Evan laughed at her, but confessed himself hungry, and Diana
had it all her own way. For once, this rare once, she would
have the pleasure, she and Evan alone; many a day would
come and go before she might have it again. So she thought
as she poured coffee upon the cream in his cup. And whether
the pleasure or the pain were the keenest even then, I cannot
tell; but it was one of those minutes when one chooses the

pleasure, and will have it and will taste it, whatever lies at the bottom of the draught. The small hours of night, the fire-lit kitchen, the daintily-spread table, she and Evan at opposite sides of it; the pleasure of ministering, such as every woman knows; the beauty of her bread, the magnificence of her coffee, the perfection of her cookery, the exultation of seeing him enjoy it; while her heart was storing up its treasure of sorrow for the unfolding by and by, and knew it, and covered it up, and went on enjoying the minute. The criticism is sometimes made upon a writer here and there, that he talks too much about *eating;* and in a high-finished and artificial state of society it is indeed true that eating is eating, and nothing more. Servants prepare the viands, and servants bring them; and the result is more or less agreeable and satisfactory, but can hardly be said to have much of poetry or sentiment about it. The case is not so with the humbler livers on the earth's surface. Sympathy and affection and tender ministry are wrought into the very pie-crust, and glow in the brown loaves as they come out of the oven; and are specially seen in the shortcake for tea, and the favourite dish at dinner, and the unexpected dumpling. Among the working classes, too,—is it true only of them?— the meals are the breathing spaces of humanity, the resting spots, where the members of the household come together to see each other's faces for a moment at leisure, and to confer over matters of common interest that have no chance in the rush and the whirl of the hours of toil. At any rate, I know there was much more than the mere taste of the coffee in the cups that Diana filled and Knowlton emptied; much more than the supply of the bodily want in the bread they ate.

The repast was prolonged and varied with very much talk; but it was done at last. The kettle was set on one side, the table pushed back, and Evan looked at his watch. Still talk went on quietly for a good while longer.

'At what hour does your chief of staff open his barn doors?' said Evan, looking at his watch again.

'Early,' said Diana, not showing the heart-thrust the question had given her. 'Not till it is light, though.

' It will be desirable that I should get off before light, then. It is not best to astonish him on this occasion.'

' It is not near light yet, Evan?'

He laughed, and looked at her. ' Do you know, I don't know when that moment comes? I have not seen it once since I have been at Elmfield. It shows how little truth there is in the theories of education.'

Diana did not ask what he meant. She went to the door and looked out. It was profoundly dark yet. It was also still. The rain was not falling; the wind had ceased; hush and darkness were abroad. She came back to the fire and asked what o'clock it was. Evan looked. They had an hour yet; but it was an hour they could make little use of. The night was gone. They stood side by side on the hearth, Evan's arm around her; now and then repeating something which had been already spoken of; really endeavouring to make the most of the mere fact of being together. But the minutes went too fast. Again and again Diana went to the window; the second time saw, with that nameless pang at her heart, that the eastern horizon was taking the grey, grave light of coming dawn. Mr. Knowlton went out then presently, saddled his horse, and brought him out to the fence, all ready. For a few minutes they waited yet, and watched the grey light creeping up; then, before anything was clearly discernible through the dusky gloom, the last farewell was taken; Evan mounted and walked his horse softly away from the door.

CHAPTER XII.

DIANA sat down with her face in her hands, and was still. She felt like a person stunned. It was very still all around her. The fire gently breathed and snapped; the living presence that had been there was gone. A great feeling of loneliness smote her. But there was leisure for few tears just then; and too high-wrought a state of the nerves to seek much indulgence in them. A little while, and Josiah would be there with his pails of milk; there was something to be done first.

And quick, as another look from the window assured her. Things were becoming visible out of doors. Diana roused herself, though every movement had to be with pain, and went about her work. It was hard to move the chair in which Evan had been sitting; it was hard to move the table around which they had been so happy; even that little trace of last night could not be kept. Evan's cup, Evan's plate, the bit of bread he had left on it, Diana's fingers were dilatory and unwilling in dealing with them. But then she roused herself and dallied no longer. Table and cups and eatables were safely removed; the kitchen brushed up, and the table set for breakfast; the fire made in the outer stove, and the kettle put on; though the touch of the kettle hurt her fingers, remembering when she had touched it last. Every tell-tale circumstance was put out of the way, and the night of watching locked up among the most precious stores of Diana's memory. She opened the lean-to door then.

The morning was rising fair. Clouds and wind had wearied themselves out, as it might be; and nature was in a great hush. Racks of vapour were scattered overhead, slowly

119

moving away in some current of air that carried them; but
below there was not a breath stirring. A little drip, drip
from the leaves only told how heavily they had been sur-
charged; the long pendant branches of the elm hung moveless,
as if they were resting after last night's thrashing about. And
as Diana looked, the touches of gold began to come upon the
hills and then on the tree-tops. It was lovely and fair as
ever; but to Diana it was a changed world. She was not the
same, and nothing would ever be just the same as yesterday
it had been. She felt that, as she looked. She had lost and
she had gained. Just now the loss came keenest. The world
seemed singularly empty. The noise of entering feet behind
her brought her back to common life. It was Josiah and the
milk pails.

'Hain't set up all night, hev' ye?' was Josiah's startling
remark. 'I vow! you get the start of the old lady herself.
I b'ain't ready for breakfast yet, if you be.'

'It will be ready soon, Josiah.'

'Mornin's is gettin' short,' Josiah went on. 'One o' them
pesky barn doors got loose in the night, and it's beat itself
'most off the hinges, I guess. I must see and get it fixed afore
Mis' Starlin's round, or she'll be hoppin'. The wind was enough
to take the ruff off, but how it could lift that 'ere heavy latch,
I don't see.'

Diana went to the dairy without any discussion of the subject. Coming back to the kitchen, she was equally startled
and dismayed to see her mother entering by the inner door.
If there was one thing Diana longed for this morning, it was
to be alone. Josiah and the farm boys were hardly a hindrance.
She had thought her mother could not be.

'Are you fit to be down-stairs, mother?' she exclaimed.

'Might as well be down as up,' said Mrs. Starling. 'Can't
get well lying in bed. I'm tired to death with it all these
days; and last night I couldn't sleep half the night; seemed to
me I heard all sorts of noises. If I'd had a light I'd ha' got up
then. I thought the house was coming down about my ears;
and if it was, I'd rather be up to see.'

'The wind blew so.'

'You heard it too, did you? When did you come down, Diana? I hain't heard the first sound of your door. 'Twarn't light, was it?'

'I have been up a good while. But you are not fit to do the least thing, mother. I was going to bring you your breakfast.'

'If there's a thing I hate, it's, to have my meals in bed. I don't want anything, to begin with; and I can take it better here. What have you got, Diana? You may make me a cup of tea. I don't feel as though I could touch coffee. What's the use o' *your* getting up so early?'

'I've all to do, you know, mother.'

'No use in burning wood and lights half the night, though. The day's long enough. When did you bake?'

Diana answered this and several other similar household questions, and got her mother a cup of tea. But though it was accompanied with a nice bit of toast, Mrs. Starling looked with a dissatisfied air at the more substantial breakfast her daughter was setting on the table.

'I never could eat slops. Diana, you may give me some o' that pork. And a potato.'

'Mother, I do not believe it is good for you.'

'Good for me? And I have eat it all my life.'

'But when you were well.'

'I'm well enough. Put some of the gravy on, Diana. I'll never get my strength back on toasted chips.'

The men came in, and Mrs. Starling held an animated dialogue with her factotum about farm affairs; while Diana sat behind her big coffee-pot—not the one she had used last night, and wondered if that was all a dream; more sadly, if she should ever dream again. And why her mother could not have stayed in her room one day more. One day more!—

'He hain't begun to get his ploughing ahead,' said Mrs. Starling, as the door closed on the delinquent.

'What, mother?' Diana asked, starting.

'Ploughing. You haven't kept things a-going, as I see,' returned her mother. 'Josiah's all behind, as usual. If I could be a man half the time, I could get on. He ought to have had the whole west field ploughed while I've been sick.'

'I don't know so much about it as you do, mother.'

'I know you don't. You have too much readin' to do. There's a pane of glass broken in that window, Diana.'

'Yes, mother, I know it.'

'How did it come?'

'I don't know.'.

'You'll never get along, Diana, till you know everything that happens in your house. You aren't fit anyhow to be a poor woman. If you're rich, why, you can get a new pane of glass, and there's the end of it. I'm not so rich as all that comes to.'

'Getting a pane of glass, mother?'

'Without knowing what for.'

'But how does it help the matter to know what for? The glass must be got anyway.'

'If you know what for, it won't be to do another time. You'll find a way to stop it. I'll warrant, now, Diana, you haven't had the ashes cleared out of that stove for a week.'

'Why, mother?'

'It smokes. It always does smoke when it gets full of ashes; and it never smokes when it ain't.'

'There is no smoke *here*, surely '

'I smell it. I can smell anything there is about. I don't know whatever there was in the house last night that smelled like coffee; but I a'most thought there was somebody makin' it down-stairs. I smelled it as plain as could be. If I could ha' got into my shoes, I believe I would ha' come down to see, just to get rid of the notion, it worried me so. It beats me, now, what it could ha' been.'

Diana turned away with the cups she had been wiping, that she might not show her face.

'Don't you never have your ashes took up, Diana?' cried Mrs. Starling, who, when much exercised on household matters, sometimes forgot her grammar.

'Yes, mother.'

'When did you have 'em took up in this chimney?'

'I do not remember—yesterday, I guess,' said Diana vaguely.

'You never burnt all the ashes there is there since yesterday morning. You'd have had to sit up all night to do it; and burn a good lot o' wood on your fire, too.'

'Mother,' exclaimed Diana in desperation, 'I don't suppose everything is just as it would be if you'd been round all these days.'

'I guess it ain't,' said Mrs. Starling. 'There's where you are wanting, Diana. Your hands are good enough, but I wouldn't give much for your eyes. There's where you'd grow poor, if you weren't poor a'ready. Now you didn't know when that pane o' glass was broke. You'd go round and round, and a pane o' glass'd knock out here, and a quart of oil 'ud leak out there, and you'd lose a pound of flour between the sieve and the barrel, and you'd never know how or where.'

'Mother,' said Diana, 'you know I *never* spill flour or anything else; no more than you do.'

'No, but it would go, I mean, and you never the wiser. It ain't the way to get along, unless you mean to marry a rich man. Now look at that heap o' ashes! I declare, it beats me to know what you *have* been doing to burn so much wood here; and mild weather, too. Who has been here to see you, since I've been laid up?'

'Several people came to ask about you.'

'Who did? and who didn't? that came at all.'

'Joe Bartlett—and Mr. Masters—and Mrs. Delamater,—I can't tell you all, mother; there's been a good many.'

'Tell me the men that have been here.'

'Well, those I said; and Will Flandin, and Nick, and Mr. Knowlton.'

'Was *he* here more than once?'

'Yea.'

'How much more?'

'Mother, how do I know? I didn't keep count.'

'Didn't keep count, eh?' Mrs. Starling repeated. 'Must have been frequent company, I judge. Diana, you mind what I told you?'

Diana made no answer.

'You shall have nothing to do with him,' Mrs. Starling went on. 'You never shall. You sha'n't take up with any one that holds himself above me. I'll be glad when his time's up; and I hope it'll be long before he'll have another. Once he gets away, he'll think no more of *you*, that's one comfort.'

Diana knew that was not true; but it hurt her to have it said. She could stand no more of her mother's talk; she left her and went off to the dairy, till Mrs. Starling crept up-stairs again. Then Diana came and opened the lean-to door and looked out for a breath of refreshment. The morning was going on its way in beauty. Little clouds drifted over the deep blue sky; the mellow September light lay on fields and hills; the long branches of the elm swayed gently to and fro in the gentle air that drove the clouds. But oh for the wind and the storm of last night, and the figure that stood beside her before the chimney fire! The gladsome light seemed to mock her, and the soft breeze gave her touches of pain. She shut the door and went back to her work.

CHAPTER XIII.

FROM THE POST OFFICE.

MRS. STARLING'S room was like her; for use, and not for show, with some points of pride, and a general air of humble thrift. A patchwork quilt on the bed; curtains and valance of chintz; a rag carpet covering only part of the floor, the rest scrubbed clean; rush-bottomed chairs; and with those a secretary bureau of old mahogany, a dressing-glass in a dark carved frame, and a large oaken press. There were corner cupboards; a table holding work and work-basket; a spinning-wheel in a corner; a little iron stove, but no fire. Mrs. Starling lay down on her bed, simply because she was not able to sit up any longer; but she was scarcely less busy, in truth, than she had been down-stairs. Her eyes roamed restlessly from the door to the window, though with never a thought of the sweet September sunlight on the brilliant blue sky.

'Diana's queer this morning,' she mused. 'Yes, she was queer. What made her so mum? She was not like herself. Sailing round with her head in the clouds. And a little bit *blue*, too; what Diana never is; but she was to-day. What's up? I've been lying here long enough for plenty of things to happen; and she's had the house to herself. Knowlton has been here—she owned that; well, either he has been here too often, or not often enough. I'll find out which. She's thinkin' about him. Then that coffee—*was* it coffee, last night? I could have sworn to it; just the smell of fresh, steaming coffee. I didn't dream it. She wasn't surprised, either; she had nothing to say about it. She would have laughed at it once. And the ashes in the chimney! There's been a sight o' wood burned there, and just burned, too; they lay light, and hadn't been
126

swep' up. There's mischief! but Diana never shall go off with
that young feller; never! never! Maybe she won't have Will
Flandin; but she sha'n't have him.'

Mrs. Starling lay thinking and staring out of her window,
till she felt she could go down-stairs again. And then she
watched. But Diana had put every possible tell-tale circumstance out of the way. The very ashes were no longer where
her mother could speculate upon them; pies and cakes showed
no more suspiciously-cut halves or quarters; she had even been
out to the barn, and found that Josiah, for reasons of his own,
was making the door-latch and hinges firm and fast. It was
no time now to tell her mother her secret. Her heart was too
sore to brave the rasping speech she would be certain to provoke. And with a widely different feeling, it was too rich in
its prize to drag the treasure forth before scornful eyes. For
this was part of Diana's experience, she found; and the feeling
grew, the feeling of being rich in her secret possession; rich as
she never had been before; perhaps the richer for the secrecy.
It was all hers, this beautiful, wonderful love that had
come to her; this share in another person's heart and life;
her own wholly; no one might intermeddle with her joy;
she treasured it and gloated over it in the depths of her glad
consciousness.

And so, as the days went by, there was no change that her
mother could see in the sweet lines of her daughter's face.
Nothing less sweet than usual; nothing less bright and free;
if the eyes had a deeper depth at times, it was not for Mrs.
Starling to penetrate; and if the childlike play of the mouth
had a curve of beauty that had never until then belonged to it,
the archetype of such a sign did not lie in Mrs. Starling's nature.
Yet once or twice a jealous movement of suspicion did rise in
her, only because Diana seemed so happy. She reasoned with
herself immediately that Evan's absence could never have such
an effect, if her fears were true; and that the happiness must
therefore be referred to some purely innocent cause. Nevertheless, Mrs. Starling watched. For she was pretty sure that
the young soldier had pushed his advances while he had been
in Pleasant Valley; and he might push them still, though there

no longer. She would guard what could be guarded. She watched both Diana and other people, and kept an especial eye upon all that came from the post office.

Evan had gone to a distant frontier post; the journey would take some time; and it would be several days more still, in the natural course of things, before Diana could have a letter. Diana reasoned out all that, and was not anxious. For the present, the pleasure of expecting was enough. A letter from *him*; it was a fairylandish, weird, wonderful pleasure, to come to her. She took to studying the newspaper, and, covertly, the map. From the map she gained a little knowledge; but the columns of the paper were barren of all allusion to the matter which was her world, and Evan's. Newspapers are very partial sometimes. She was afraid to let her mother see how eagerly she scanned them. The map and Diana had secret and more satisfactory consultations. Measuring the probable route of Evan's journey by the scale of miles; calculating the rate of progress by different modes of travel; counting the nights, and places where he might spend them; she reckoned up over and over again the days that were probably necessary to enable him to reach his post. Then she allowed margins for what she did not know, and accounted for the blanks she could not fill up; and reasoned with herself about the engrossments which might on his first arrival hinder Evan from writing—for a few hours, or a night. So at last she had constructed a scheme by which she proved to herself the earliest day at which it would do to look for a letter, and the latest to which a letter might reasonably be delayed. Women do such things. How many men are worthy of it?

That farthest limit was reached, and no letter yet.

About that time, one morning the family at Elmfield were gathered at breakfast. It was not exactly like any other breakfast table in Pleasant Valley, for a certain drift from the great waves of the world had reached it; whereas the others were clean from any such contact. The first and the third generations were represented at the table; the second was wanting; the old gentleman, the head of the family, was surrounded by only his grand-daughters. Now old Mr. Bowdoin was as simple

and plain-hearted a man as all his country neighbours, if somewhat richer than most of them; he had wrought at the same
labour, and grown up with the same associations. He was not
more respectable than respected; generous, honest, and kindly.
But the young ladies, his grandchildren, Evan's sisters, were
different. They came to spend the summer with him, and they
brought fancies and notions from their far-away city life, which
made a somewhat incongruous mixture with the elemental
simplicity of their grandfather's house. All this appeared now.
The old farmer's plain strong features, his homespun dress and
his bowl of milk, were at one end of the table, where he presided heartily over the fried ham and eggs. Look where you
would beside, and you saw ruffled chintzes and little fly-away
breakfast-caps, and fingers with jewels on them. Miss
Euphemia had her tresses of long hair unbound and unbraided,
hanging down her back in a style that to her grandfather
savoured of barbarism; he could not be made to understand
that it was a token of the highest elegance. For these ladies
there was some attempt at elaborate and dainty cookery,
signified by sweetbreads and a puffed omelette; and Mrs.
Reverdy presided over a coffee-pot that was the wonder of
the Elmfield household, and even a little matter of pride to
the old squire himself; though he covered it with laughing
at her mimic fires and doubtful steam engines. Gertrude
Masters was still at Elmfield, the only one left of a tribe of
visitors who had made the old place gay through the summer.

'I have had an invitation,' said Mrs. Reverdy as she sent
her grandfather his cup of coffee. And she laughed. I wish I
could give the impression of this little laugh of hers, which, in
company, was the attendant of most of her speeches. A little
gracious laugh, with a funny air as if she were condescending,
either to her subject or herself, and amused at it.

'What is it, Vevay? what invitation?' inquired her sister;
while Gertrude tossed her mass of tresses from her neck, and
looked as if nothing at Pleasant Valley concerned *her*.

'An invitation to the sewing society!' said Mrs. Reverdy.
'We are all asked.' And the laugh grew very amused indeed.

'What do they do?' inquired Gertrude absently.

'O, they bring their knitting at two or three o'clock,—and have a good time to tell all the news till five or six; and then they have supper, and then they put up their knitting and go home.'

'What news can they have to tell at Pleasant Valley?'

'Whose hay is in first, and whose orchard will yield the most cider,' said Euphemia.

'Yes; and how all their children are, and how many eggs go in a pudding.'

'I don't believe they make puddings with eggs very often,' said the other sister again. 'Their puddings are more like hasty puddings, I fancy.'

'Some of 'em make pretty good things,' said old Mr. Bowdoin. 'Things you can't beat, Phemie. There's Mrs. Mansfield—she's a capital housekeeper; and Mrs. Starling. *She* can cook.'

'What do they expect you to do at the sewing meeting, Vevay?'

'Show myself, I suppose,' said Mrs. Reverdy.

'Well, I guess I'd go,' said her grandfather, looking at her. 'It would be as good a thing as you could do.'

'Go, grandpa? O, how ridiculous!' exclaimed Mrs. Reverdy, with her pretty face all wrinkled up with amusement.

'Go? yes. Why not?'

'I don't know how to knit; and I shouldn't know how to talk orchards and puddings.'

'I think you had better go. It is not a knitting society, as I understand it; and I am sure you can be useful.'

'Useful!' echoed Mrs. Reverdy. 'It's the last thing I know how to be. And I don't belong to the society, grandpa.'

'I shouldn't like them to think that,' said the old gentleman. 'You belong to me; and I belong to them, my dear.'

'Isn't it dreadful?' said Mrs. Reverdy in a low voice aside. 'Now he's got this in his head—whatever am I going to do?— Suppose I invite them all to Elmfield; how would you like that, sir?' she added aloud.

'Yes, my dear, yes,' said the old gentleman, pushing back his chair; for the cup of coffee was the last part of his break-

I

fast; 'it would be well done, and I should be glad of it. Ask 'em all.'

'You are in for it now, Vevay,' said Gertrude, when the ladies were left. 'How will you manage?'

'O, I'll give them a grand entertainment and send them away delighted,' said Mrs. Reverdy. 'You see, grandpa wishes it; and I think it'll be fun.'

'Do you suppose Evan really paid attentions to that pretty girl we saw at the blackberrying?'

'I don't know,' Mrs. Reverdy answered. 'He told me nothing about it. I should think Evan was crazy to do it; but men do crazy things. However, I don't believe it of him, Gerty. What nonsense!'

'I can find out, if she comes,' said Miss Masters. 'You'll ask her, Genevieve?'

So it fell out that an invitation to hold the next meeting of the sewing society at Elmfield was sent to the ladies accustomed to be at such meetings; and a great stir of expectation in consequence went through all Pleasant Valley. For Elmfield, whether they acknowledged it or not, was at the top of their social tree. The invitation came in due course to Mrs. Starling's house.

It came not alone. Josiah brought it one evening on his return from the Corners, where the store and the post office were, and Mrs. Reverdy's messenger had fallen in with him and entrusted to him the note for Mrs. Starling. He handed it out now, and with it a letter of more bulk and pretensions, having a double stamp and an unknown postmark. Mrs. Starling received both and Josiah's explanations in silence, for her mind was very busy. Curious as she was to know upon what subject Mrs. Reverdy could possibly have written to her, she lingered yet with her eyes upon this other letter. It was directed to 'Miss D. Starling.'

'That's a man's hand,' said Mrs. Starling to herself. 'He's had the assurance to go and write to her, I do believe!'

She stood looking at it, doubtful, suspicious, uneasy; then turned into the dairy for fear Diana might surprise her, while she opened Mrs. Reverdy's note. She had a vague idea that both epistles might relate to the same subject. But this one was innocent enough, at least. Hiding the large letter in her bosom, she came back and gave the invitation to Diana, whose foot she had heard.

'At Elmfield! What an odd thing! Will you go, mother?'

'I always go, don't I? What's the reason I shouldn't go now?'

'I didn't know whether you would like to go there.'

'What if I don't? No, I don't care particularly about goin' to Elmfield; they're a kind o' stuck up folks; but I'll go to let them see that I ain't.'

There was silence for a little; then Mrs. Starling broke it by inquiring if Diana had finished her chintz gown. Diana had.

'I'd wear it, if I was you.'

'Why, mother?'

'Let 'em see that other folks can dress as well as them.'

'O, mother, my dresses are nothing alongside of theirs.'

'What's the reason they ain't?' inquired Mrs. Starling, looking incredulous.

'Their things are beautiful, mother; more costly a great deal; and fashionable. We can't make things so in Pleasant Valley. We don't know how.'

'I don't see any sense in that,' rejoined Mrs. Starling. 'One fashion's as good as another. Anyhow, there's better-lookin' folks in Pleasant Valley than ever called themselves Bowdoin, or Knowlton either. So be as smart as you can, Diana. I guess you needn't be ashamed of yourself.'

Diana thought of nothing less. Indeed, she thought little about her appearance. While she was putting on her bright chintz dress, there was perhaps a movement of desire that she might seem pleasant in the eyes of Evan's people—something that *he* need not be ashamed of; but her heart was too full of richer thoughts to have much room for such as these. For Evan had chosen her; Evan loved her; the secret bond between them nothing on earth could undo; and any day now that first letter of his might arrive, which her eyes were bright only to think of looking upon. Poor Diana! that letter was jammed up within the bones of Mrs. Starling's stays.

CHAPTER XIV.

A MEETING AT ELMFIELD.

It was one of the royal days of a New England autumn; the air clear and bracing and spicy; the light golden and glowing, and yet softened to the dreamiest, richest, most bounteous aureole of hope, by a slight impalpable haze; too slight to veil anything, but giving its tender flattery to the landscape nevertheless. And through that to the mind. Who can help but receive it? Suggestions of waveless peace, of endless delight, of a world-full glory that must fill one's life with riches, come through such a light and under such a sky. Diana's life was full already; but she took the promise for all the years that stretched out in the future. The soft autumn sky where the clouds were at rest, having done their work, bore no symbol of the storms that might come beneath the firmament; the purple and gold and crimson of nature's gala dress seemed to fling their soft luxury around the beholder, enfolding him, as it were, from all the dust and the dimness and the dulness of this world's working days for evermore. So it was to Diana; and all the miles of that long drive, joggingly pulled along by Prince, she rode in a chariot of the imagination, traversing fields of thought and of space, now to Evan and now with him; and in her engrossment spoke never a word from the time she mounted into the waggon till they came in sight of Elmfield. And Mrs. Starling had her own subjects for thought, and was as silent on her part. She was thinking all the way what she should do with that letter. Suppose things had gone too far to be stopped? But Diana had told her nothing; she was not bound to know by guess-work. And if this were the *beginning*

132

of scrious proposals, then it were better known to but herself only. She resolved finally to watch Diana and the Elmfield people this afternoon; she could find out, she thought, whether there were any matter of common interest between them. With all this, Mrs. Starling's temper was not sweetened.

Elmfield was a rare place. Not by the work of art or the craft of the gardener at all; for a cunning workman had never touched its turf or its plantations. Indeed it had no plantations, other than such as were intended for pure use and profit; great fields of Indian corn, and acres of wheat and rye, and a plot of garden cabbages. Mrs. Reverdy's power of reform had reached only the household affairs. But the corn and the rye and the cabbages were out of sight from the immediate home field; and there the grace of nature had been so great that one almost forgot to wish that anything had been added to it. A little river swept, curving in sweet leisure, through a large level tract of greenest meadows. In front of one of these large curves the house stood, but well back, so that the meadow served instead of a lawn. It had no foreign beauties of tree growth to adorn it, nor needed them; for along the bank of the river, from space to space, irregularly, rose a huge New England elm, giving the shelter of its canopy of branches to a wide spot of turf. The house added nothing to the scene, beyond the human interest; it was just a large old farmhouse, nothing more; draped, however, and half covered up by other elms and a few fir trees. But in front of it lay this wide, sunny, level meadow, with the wilful little stream meandering through, with the stately old trees spotting it and breaking its monotony; and in the distance a soft outline of hills, not too far away, and varied enough to be picturesque, rounded in the whole picture. A picture one would stand long to look at; thoroughly New England and characteristic; gentle, home-like, lovely, with just a touch of wildness, intimating that you were beyond the rules of conventionality. Being New England folk themselves, Mrs. Starling and Diana of course would not read some of these features. They only thought it was a 'fine place.'

Long before they got there this afternoon, before anybody

got there, the ladies of the family gathered upon the wide old piazza.

'It's as good as a play,' said Gertrude Masters. 'I never saw such society in my life, and I am curious to know what they will be like.'

'You have seen them in church,' said Euphemia.

'Yes, but they all feel poky there. I can't tell anything by that. Besides, I don't hear them talk. There's somebody now!'

'Too fast for any of our good sewing friends,' said Mrs. Reverdy; 'and there is no waggon. It's Mr. Masters, Gerty! How he does ride; and yet he sits as if he was upon a rocking-horse.'

'I don't think he'd sit very quiet upon a rocking-horse,' said Gerty. And then she lifted up her voice and shouted musically a salutation to the approaching rider.

He alighted presently at the foot of the steps, and throwing the bridle over his horse's head, joined the party.

'So delighted!' said Mrs. Reverdy graciously. 'You are come just in time to help us take care of the people.'

'Are you going to entertain the nation?' asked Mr. Masters.

'Only Pleasant Valley,' Mrs. Reverdy answered with her little laugh; which might mean amusement at herself or condescension to Pleasant Valley. 'Do you think they will be hard to entertain?'

'I can answer for one,' said the minister. 'And looking at what there is to see from here, I could almost answer for them all.' He was considering the wide sunlit meadow, where the green and the gold, yea, and the very elm shadows, as well as the distant hills, were spiritualized by the slight soft haze.

'Why, what is there to see, Basil?' inquired his cousin Gertrude.

'The sky.'

'You don't think that is entertaining, I hope? If you were a polite man, you would have said something else.'

She was something to see herself, in one sense, and the

something was pretty, too; but very self-conscious. From her flow of curly tresses down to the rosettes on her slippers, every inch of her showed it. Now the best dressing surely avoids this effect; while there is some, and not bad dressing either, which proclaims it in every detail. The crinkles of Gertrude's hair were crisp with it; her French print dress, beautiful in itself, was made with French daintiness and worn with at least equal coquettishness; her wrists bore two or three bracelets both valuable and delicate; and Gertrude's eyes, pretty eyes too, were audacious with the knowledge of all this. Audacious ·in a sweet, secret way, understand; they were not bold eyes, openly. Her cousin looked her over, with a glance quite recognisant of all I have described, yet destitute of a shade of compliment or even of admiration; very clear and very cool.

'Basil, you don't say all you think!' exclaimed the young lady.

'Not always,' said her cousin. 'We have it on Solomon's authority, that a "fool uttereth all his mind. A wise man keepeth it till afterwards."'

'What are you keeping?'

But the answer was interrupted by Mrs. Reverdy.

'Where shall we put them, do you think, Mr. Masters? I'm quite anxious. Here, on the verandah, do you think?—or on the green, where we mean to have supper? or would it be better to go into the house?'

'As a general principle, Mrs. Reverdy, I object to houses. When you can, keep out of them. So I say. And there comes one of your guests. I will take my horse out of the road.'

Mrs. Reverdy objected and protested and ran to summon a servant, but the minister had his way and led his horse off to the stable. While he was gone, the little old green waggon which brought Miss Barry came at a soft jog up the drive and stopped before the door. Mrs. Reverdy came flying out and then down the steps to help her alight.

'It's a long ways to your place, Mrs. Reverdy; I declare, I'm kind o' stiff,' said the old lady as she mounted to the piazza. There she stood still and surveyed the prospect. And her conclusion burst forth in an unequivocal, 'Ain't it elegant!'

'I am delighted you like it,' said Mrs. Reverdy with her running laugh. 'Won't you sit down?'

'I hain't got straightened out yet, after drivin' the horse so long. It does put me in a kind o' cramp, somehow, to drive, —'most allays.'

'Is the horse so hard-mouthed?'

'La! bless you, I never felt of his mouth. He don't do nothin'; I don't expect he would do nothin'; but I allays think he's a horse, and there's no tellin'.'

'That's very true,' said Mrs. Reverdy, the laugh of condescending acquiescence mingled with a little sense of fun now. 'But do sit down; you'll be tired standing.'

'There's Mrs. Flandin's waggin, I guess, comin'; she was 'most ready when I come by. Is this your sister?'—looking at Gertrude.

'No, the other is my sister. This is Miss Masters; a cousin of your minister.'

'I thought she was, maybe,—your sister, I mean,—because she had her hair the same way. Ain't it very uncomfortable?' This to Gertrude.

'It is very comfortable,' said the young lady; 'except in hot weather.'

'Don't say it is!' quoth Miss Barry, looking at the astonishing hair while she got out her needles. 'Seems to me I should feel as if my hair never was combed.'

'Not if it *was* combed, would you?' said Gertrude gravely.

'Well, yes; seems to me I should. I allays liked to have my hair sleeked up as tight as I could get it; and then I knowed there warn't none of it flyin'. But la! it's a long time since I was young, and there's new fashions. Is the minister your cousin?'

'Yes. How do you like him?'

'I hain't got accustomed to him yet,' said the little old lady, clicking her needles with a considerate air. 'He ain't like Mr. Hardenburgh, you see; and Mr. Hardenburgh was the minister afore him.'

'What was the difference?'

'Well—Mr. Hardenburgh, you could tell he was a minister as fur as you could see him; he had that look. Now Mr. Masters haint; he's just like other folks; only he's more pleasant than most.'

'Oh, he is more pleasant, is he?'

'Well, seems to me he is,' said the little old lady. 'It allays makes me feel kind o' good when he comes alongside. He's cheerful. Mr. Hardenburgh *was* a good man, but he made me afeard of him; he was sort of fierce, in the pulpit and out of the pulpit. Mr. Masters ain't nary one.'

'Do you think he's a good preacher, then?' said Gertrude demurely, bending over to look at Miss Barry's knitting.

'Well, I do!' said the old lady. 'There! I ain't no judge; but I love to sit and hear him. 'Tain't a bit like a minister, nother, though it's in church; he just speaks like as I am speakin' to you; but he makes the Bible kind o' interestin'.'

It was very well for Gertrude that Mrs. Carpenter now came to take her seat on the piazza, and the conversation changed. She had got about as much as she could bear. And after Mrs. Carpenter came a crowd; Mrs. Flandin, and Mrs. Mansfield, and Miss Gunn, and all the rest, with short interval, driving up and unloading and joining the circle on the piazza; which grew a very wide circle indeed, and at last broke up into divisions. Gertrude was obliged to suspend operations for a while, and use her eyes instead of her tongue. Most of the rest were inclined to do the same; and curious glances went about in every direction, not missing Miss Masters herself. Some people were absolutely tongue-tied; others used their opportunity.

'Don't the wind come drefful cold over them flats in winter?' asked one good lady who had never been at Elmfield before. Mrs. Reverdy's running little laugh was ready with her answer.

'I believe it does; but we are never here in winter. It's too cold.'

'Your gran'ther's here, ain't he?' queried Mrs. Salter.

'Yes, O yes; grandpa is here, of course. I don't suppose anything would draw him away from the old place.'

'How big is the farm?' went on the first speaker.

Mrs. Reverdy did not know; three or four hundred acres, she believed. Or it might be five. She did not know the difference!

'I guess your father misses you when you all go away,' remarked Mrs. Flandin, who had hardly spoken, at least aloud.

The reply was prevented, for Mrs. Starling's waggon drew up at the foot of the steps, and Mrs. Reverdy hastened down to give her assistance to the ladies in alighting. Gertrude also suspended what she was saying, and gave her undivided attention to the view of Diana.

She was only a country girl, Miss Masters said to herself. Yet what a lovely figure, as she stood there before the waggon; perfectly proportioned, light and firm in action or attitude, with the grace of absolute health and strength and faultless make. More; there always is more to it; and Gertrude felt that without in the least having power to reason about it; felt in the quiet pose and soft motion those spirit indications of calm and strength and gracious dignity, which belonged to the fair proportions and wholesome soundness of the inward character. The face said the same thing when it was turned, and Diana came up the steps; though it was seen under a white sun-bonnet only; the straight brows, the large quiet eyes, the soft creamy colour of the skin, all testified to the fine physical and mental conditions of this creature. And Gertrude felt as she looked that it would not have been very surprising if Evan Knowlton or any other young officer had lost his heart to her. But she isn't dressed, thought Gertrude; and the next moment a shadow crossed her heart as Diana's sun-bonnet came off, and a wealth of dark hair was revealed, knotted into a crown of nature's devising, which art could never outdo. 'I'll find out about Evan,' said Miss Masters to herself.

She had to wait. The company was large now, and the buzz of tongues considerable; though nothing like what had been in Mrs. Starling's parlour. So soon as the two newcomers were fairly seated and at work, Mrs. Flandin took up the broken thread of her discourse.

'Ain't your father kind o' lonesome here in the winters, all by himself?'

'My grandfather, you mean,' said Mrs. Reverdy.

'I mean your grandfather. I forgot you ain't his own; but it makes no difference. Don't he want you to hum all the year round?'

'I daresay he would like it.'

'He's gettin' on in years now. How old is Squire Bowdoin?'

'I don't know,' said Mrs. Reverdy. 'He's between seventy and eighty, somewhere.'

'You won't have him long with you.'

'O, I hope so!' said Mrs. Reverdy lightly, and with the unfailing laugh which went with everything; 'I think grandpa is stronger than I am. I shouldn't wonder if he'd outlive *me*.'

'Still, don't you think it is your duty to stay with him?'

Mrs. Reverdy laughed again. 'I suppose we don't always do our duty,' she said. 'It's too cold here in the winter—after October or September—for me.'

'Then it is not your duty to be here,' said her sister Euphemia, somewhat distinctly. But Mrs. Flandin was bound to 'free her mind' of what was upon it.

'I should think the Squire'd want Evan to hum,' she went on.

'It would be very nice if Evan could be in two places at once,' Mrs. Reverdy owned conciliatingly.

'Where *is* Captain Knowlton now?' asked Mrs. Boddington.

'O, he is not a captain yet,' said Mrs. Reverdy. 'He is only a lieutenant. I don't know when he'll get any higher than that. He's a great way off—on the frontier—watching the Indians.'

'I should think it was pleasanter work to watch sheep,' said Mrs. Flandin. 'Don't it make you feel bad to have him away so far?'

'O, we're accustomed to having him away, you know; Evan has never been at home; we really don't know him as well as strangers do. We have just got a letter from him at his new post.'

They had got a letter from him! Two bounds Diana's heart made: the first with a pang of pain that they should have the earliest word; the next with a pang of joy, at the certainty that hers must be lying in the post office for her. The blood flowed and ebbed in her veins with the violent action of extreme excitement. Yet nature did for this girl what only the practice and training of society do for others; she gave no outward sign. Her head was not lifted from her work; the colour of her cheek did not change; and when a moment after she found Miss Masters at her side, and heard her speaking, Diana looked and answered with the utmost seeming composure.

'I've been trying ever since you came to get round to you,' Gertrude whispered. 'I'm so glad to see you again.'

But here Mrs. Flandin broke in. She was seated near.

'Ain't your hair a great trouble to you?'

Gertrude gave it a little toss and looked up.

'How do you get it all flying like that?'

'Everybody's hair is a trouble,' said Gertrude. 'This is as little as any.'

'Do you sleep with it all round your shoulders? I should think you'd be in a net by morning.'

'I suppose you would,' said Gertrude.

'Is that the fashion now?'

'It is one fashion,' Miss Masters responded.

'If it warn't, I reckon you'd do it up pretty quick. Dear me! what a thing it is to be in the fashion, I do suppose!'

'Don't you like it yourself, ma'am?' queried Gertrude.

'Never try. *I've* something else to do in life.'

'Well, but there's no *harm* in being in the fashion, Mis' Flandin,' said Miss Gunn. 'The minister said he thought there warn't.'

'The minister had better take care of himself,' Mrs. Flandin retorted.

Whereupon they all opened upon her. And it could be seen that for the few months during which he had been among them, the minister had made swift progress in the regards of the people. Scarce a tongue now but spoke in his praise or his justification, or called Mrs. Flandin to account for her hasty remark.

'When you're all done, I'll speak,' said that lady coolly. 'I'm not a man-worshipper—never was; and nobody's fit to be worshipped. *I* should like to see the dominie put down that grey horse of his.'

'Are grey horses fashionable?' inquired Mrs. Reverdy, with her little laugh.

'What would he do without his horse?' said Mrs. Boddington. 'How could he fly round Pleasant Valley as he does?'

'He ain't bound to fly,' said Mrs. Flandin.

'How's he to get round to folks, then?' said Mrs. Salter. 'The houses are pretty scattering in these parts; he'd be a spry man if he could walk it.'

'Seems to me that 'ere grey hoss is real handy,' said quiet Miss Barry, who never contradicted anybody. 'When Meliny was sick, Mr. Masters 'd be there, to our house, early in the mornin' and late at night; and he allays had comfort with him. There! I got to set as much by the sight o' that grey hoss, you wouldn't think; just to hear him come gallopin' down the road did me good.'

'Yes; and so it was to our house, when Liz was overturned,' said Mary Delamater. 'He'd be there every day, just as punctual as could be; and he could never have walked over. It's a cruel piece of road between our house and his'n.'

'I don't want him to walk,' said Mrs. Flandin; 'there's more ways than one o' doin' most things; but I *do* say, all the ministers ever I see druv a team; and it looks more religious. To see the minister flyin' over the hills like a racer is altogether too gay for my likin's.'

'But he ain't gay,' said Miss Gunn, looking appalled.

'He's mighty spry, for anybody that gets up into a pulpit on the Sabbath and tells his fellow-creatures what they ought to be doin'.'

'But he does do that, Mrs. Flandin,' said Diana. 'He speaks plain enough, too.'

'I *do* love to hear him!' said Miss Barry. 'There, his words seem to go all through me, and clear up my want of understandin'; for I never was smart, you know; but seems to me I see things as well agin when he's been talkin' to me. I say, it was a good day when he come to Pleasant Valley.'

'He ain't what you call an eloquent man,' said Miss Babbage, the schoolmaster's sister.

'What is an "eloquent man," Lottie Babbage?' Mrs. Boddington asked. 'It's a word, I know; but what is the thing the word means? Come, you ought to be good at definitions.'

'Mr. Masters don't pretend to be an eloquent man!' cried Mrs. Carpenter.

'Well, tell; come! what do you mean by it? I'd like to know,' said Mrs. Boddington. 'I admire to get my idees straight. What is it he don't pretend to be?'

'I don't think he pretends to be anything,' said Diana.

'Only to have his own way wherever he goes,' added Diana's mother.

'I'd be content to let him have his own way,' said Mrs. Carpenter. 'It's pretty sure to be a good way; that's what *I* think. I wisht he had it, for my part.'

'And yet he isn't eloquent?' said Mrs. Boddington.

'Well,' said Miss Babbage with some difficulty, 'he just says what he has got to say, and takes the handiest words he can find; but I've heard men that eloquent that they'd keep you wonderin' at 'em from the beginning of their sermon to the end; and you'd got to be smart to know what they were sayin'. A child can tell what Mr. Masters means.'

'So kin I,' said Miss Barry. 'I'm thankful I kin. And I don't want a man more eloquent than he is, for my preachin'.'

'It ain't movin' preachin',' said Mrs. Flandin.

'It moves the folks,' said Mrs. Carpenter. 'I don't know what you'd hev, Mis' Flandin; there's Liz Delamater, and Florry Mason, jined the church lately; and old Lupton; and

my Jim,' she added with softened voice; 'and there's several
more serious.'

No more could be said, for the minister himself came upon
the scene at this instant.   There was not an eye that did not
brighten at the sight of him, with the exception of Mrs. Starling
and Diana; there was not a lady there who was not manifestly
glad to have him come near and speak to her; even Mrs.
Flandin herself, beside whom the minister presently sat down
and entered into conversation respecting some new movement
in parish matters, for which he wished to enlist her help.
General conversation returned to its usual channels.

'I can't stand this,' whispered Gertrude to Diana; 'I am
tired to death.   Do come down and walk over to the river
with me.   Do! you can work another day.'

Diana hesitated; glanced around her.   It was manifest that
this was an exceptional meeting of the society, and not for the
purposes of work chiefly.   Here and there needles were suspended in lingering fingers, while their owners made subdued
comments to each other or used their eyes for purposes of
information getting.   One or two had even left work, and
were going to the back of the house, through the hall, to see
the garden.   Diana not very unwillingly dropped her sewing,
and followed her conductor down the steps and over the
meadow.

CHAPTER XV.

CATECHIZING.

'THE sun isn't hot, through all this cloud,' said Gertrude, 'so I don't mind it. We'll get into the shade under the elm yonder.'

'There is no cloud,' said Diana.

'No cloud! What is it, then? *Something* has come over the sun.'

'No, it's haze.'

'What is haze?'

'I don't know. We have it in Indian summer, and sometimes in October, like this.'

'Isn't it hot?' said Gertrude; 'and last week we were having big fires. It's such queer weather. Now this shade is nice.'

Under one or two of the elm canopies along the verge of the little river some rustic seats had been fixed. Gertrude sat down. Diana stood, looking about her. The dreamy beauty through which she had ridden that afternoon was all round her still; and the meadow and the scattered elms, with the distant softly-rounded hills, were one of New England's combinations, in which the gentlest beauty and the most characteristic strength meet and mingle. But what was more yet to Diana, she was among Evan's haunts. Here *he* was at home. There seemed to her fancy to be a consciousness of him in the silent trees and river; as if they would say if they could,—as if they were saying mutely,—'We know him—we know him; and we are old friends of his. We could tell you a great deal about him.'

'Elmfield is a pretty place,' said Gertrude. She had been

144

eyeing her companion while Diana was receiving the confidences of the trees.

'Lovely!'

'If it didn't grow so cold in winter,' said the young lady, shrugging her airy shoulders.

'I like the cold.'

'I should like to have it always hot enough to wear muslin dresses. Come, sit down. Evan put these seats here.'

But Diana continued standing.

'Did you hear that woman scolding because he don't stay here and give up his army life?'

'She takes her own view of it,' said Diana.

'Do *you* think he ought to give up everything to take care of his grandfather?'

'I daresay his grandfather likes to have him do as he is doing.'

'But it must be awfully hard, mustn't it, for them to have him so far away, and fighting the Indians?'

'Is he fighting the Indians?' Diana asked quietly; though she made the words quiet, she knew, by sheer force of necessity. But quiet they were; slow, and showing no eagerness; while her pulse had made one mad jump, and then seemed to stand still.

'O, the Indians are always making trouble, you know, on the frontier; that's what our men are there for, to watch them. I didn't mean that Evan was fighting just at this minute; but he might be, any minute. Shouldn't you feel bad if he was your brother?'

'Mrs. Reverdy doesn't seem to be uneasy.'

'She? no,' said Gertrude with a laugh; 'nothing makes *her* uneasy. Except thinking that Evan has fallen in love with somebody.'

'She must expect that sooner or later,' said Diana, with a calmness which told her companion nothing.

'Ah, but she would rather have it later. She don't want to lose Evan. She is very proud of him.'

'Would she lose him in such a case?' Diana asked, smiling, though she wished the talk ended.

K

'Why, you know brothers are good for nothing to sisters after they are married—worse! they are tantalizing. You are obliged to see what you used to have in somebody else's possession—and much more than ever you used to have; and it's tiresome. I'm glad I've no brothers. Basil is a good deal like a brother, and I am jealous of *him*.'

'It must be very uncomfortable to be jealous,' said Diana.

'Horrid! You saw a good deal of Evan, didn't you?'

A question that might have embarrassed Diana if she had not had an instant perception of the intent of it. She answered thereupon with absolute self-possession.

'I don't know what you would call a "good deal." I saw what *I* call a good deal of him that day in the blackberry field.'

'Don't you think he is charming?'

Diana laughed, and was vexed to feel her cheeks grow warm.

'That's a word that belongs to women.'

'Not to many of 'em!' said Gertrude, with a slight turning up of her pretty nose. Then, struck with the fine, pure face and very lovely figure before her, she suddenly added, 'Didn't he think you charming?'

'Are you laughing at me?' said Diana.

'No, indeed I am not. Didn't he?' said Gertrude caressingly.

Amusement almost carried off the temptation to be provoked. Diana laughed merrily as she answered, 'Do you think a person of so good taste would?'

'Yes, I do,' said Gertrude, half sulkily, for she was baffled, and besides, her words spoke the truth. 'I am sure he did. Isn't life very stupid up here in the mountains, when visitors are all gone away?'

'I don't think so. We never depend upon visitors.'

'It has been awfully slow at Elmfield since Mr. Knowlton went away. We sha'n't stay much longer. I can't live where I can't dance.'

'What is that?' said a voice close at hand—a peculiarly clear, silvery voice.

'Cousin Basil!' cried Gertrude, starting. 'What did you come here for? I brought Miss Starling here to have a good talk with her.'

'Have you had it?'

'I haven't had time. I was just beginning.'

'What! about dancing?'

'I was not speaking for you to hear. I was relieving myself by the confession that I can't live—happily, I mean—without it.'

'Choice of partners immaterial?'

'I couldn't bear a dull life!'

'Nor I.'

He looked as if he certainly did not know what dulness was, Diana thought. She listened, much amused.

'But you think it is wrong to dance, don't you?' Gertrude went on.

'"Better not" is wrong to a Christian,' he replied.

'It must be dreadful to be a Christian!'

'Because—?' he said, with a quiet and good-humoured glance and tone of inquiry.

'O, because it is slavery. So many things you cannot do, and dresses you cannot wear.'

'By what rule?' Mr. Masters asked.

'O, people think you are dreadful if you do those things; the Church, and all that. So I think it is a great deal better to keep out of it, and make no pretensions.'

'Better to keep out of what? let me understand,' said the minister. 'You are getting my ideas in a very involved state.'

'No, I am not! I say, it is better to make no profession.'

'Better than what? What is the alternative?'

'O, you know. Now you are catechizing me. It is better to make no profession, than to make it and not live up to it.'

'I understand. That is to say, it is wicked to pay your debts with counterfeit notes, so it is better not to pay them at all.'

'Nonsense, Basil! I am not talking of paying debts.'

'But I am.'

'What have debts got to do with it?'

'I beg your pardon. I understood you to declare your dis-
approbation of false money, and your preference for another
sort of dishonesty.'

'Dishonest, Basil! there is no dishonesty.'

'By what name do you call it?'

He was speaking gravely, though with a surface pleasantry;
both gravity and pleasantry were of a very winning kind.
Diana looked on and listened, much interested, as well as
amused; Gertrude puzzled and impatient, though unable to
resist the attraction. She hesitated, and surveyed him.

'There can't be dishonesty unless where one owes something.'

'Precisely'— he said, glancing at her. His hands were
busy at the time with a supple twig he had cut from one of
the trees, which he was trimming of its leaves and buds.

'What do I owe?' said the beauty, throwing her tresses of
hair off from her shoulders.

He waited a bit, the one lady looking defiant, the other
curious; and then he said, with a sort of gentle simplicity that
was at the same time uncompromising,

'"The Lord hath made all things for himself."'

Gertrude's foot patted the turf; after a minute she
answered,

'Of course you say that because you are a clergyman.'

'No, I don't. I am stating a fact, which I thought it likely
you had forgotten.'

Gertrude stood up, as if she had got enough of the conversation. Diana wished for another word.

'It is a fact,' she said; 'but what have we to do with it?'

'Only to let the Lord have his own,' said the minister with
a full look at her.

'How do you mean, Mr. Masters? I don't understand.'

Gertrude was marching over the grass leading to the house.
The other two followed.

'When you have contrived and made a thing, you reckon it
is your own, don't you? and when you have bought something,
you think it is at your disposal?'

Certainly ; but'—

" *You* were bought with a price." '

' Of course, God has a right to dispose of us,' Diana assented in an ' of course' way.

' *Does* he?' said the minister. Then, seeing her puzzled expression, he went on—' He cannot dispose of you as he wishes, without your consent.'

Diana stopped short, midway in the meadow. ' I do not in the least understand, Mr. Masters,' she said. ' How does he wish to dispose of me?'

'When you are his own, he will let you know,' said the minister, beginning to stroll onward again ; and no more words passed till they were nearing the house, when he said suddenly, ' Whom do you think you belong to now?'

Diana's thought made an instant leap at the words, a leap over hundreds of miles of intervening space, and alighted beside a fine officer-like figure in a dark blue military coat with straps on the shoulders. That was where she ' belonged,' she thought ; and a soft rose colour mantled on her cheek, and deepened, half with happiness, half with pride. The question that had provoked it was forgotten ; and the neighbourhood of the house was now too near to allow of the inquiry being pressed or repeated. The minister, indeed, was aware that for some time he and his companion had been facing a battery ; but Diana was in happy unconsciousness ; it was the thought of nothing present or near which made her eyes droop and her cheeks take on such a bloom of loveliness.

Among the eyes that beheld, Mrs. Starling's had not been the least keen, though she watched without seeming to watch. She saw how the minister and her daughter came slowly over the meadow, engaged with each other's conversation, while Miss Masters tripped on before them. She noticed the pause in their walk, Diana's slow, thoughtful step ; and then, as they came near, her flush and her downcast eye.

' The minister's talk's very interestin',' whispered Mrs. Carpenter in her ear.

' Not to me,' said Mrs. Starling, wilfully misunderstanding.

'Some folks think so, I know. I can't somehow never get along with him.'

'And Diana sha'n't,' was her inward resolve; 'but she can't be thinkin' of the other feller.'

As if to try the question at the moment, Mrs. Reverdy appeared at the top of the steps, just as the minister and Diana got to the foot of them. She was in high glee, for her party was going off nicely, and the tables were just preparing for supper.

'We want nothing now but Evan,' she said with her unfailing laugh. 'Miss Starling, don't you think he might have come for this afternoon, just to see so many friends?'

Diana never knew where she got the coolness to answer, 'How long a journey is it, Mrs. Reverdy?'

'O, I don't know! How far is it, Mr. Masters?—a thousand miles?—or two thousand? I declare I have no idea. But love laughs at distances, they say.'

'Is Cupid a contractor on this road?' inquired the minister gravely.

'A contractor!' exclaimed Mrs. Reverdy, laughing,—'oh, dear, what a funny idea! I never thought of putting it so. But I didn't know but Miss Starling could tell us.'

'Do you know anything about it, Miss Diana?' asked the minister.

'About what?'

'Why Lieutenant Knowlton is not here this afternoon?'

Diana knew that several pairs of eyes were upon her. It was a dangerous minute. But she had failed to discern in Mrs. Reverdy or in Gertrude any symptom of more than curiosity; and curiosity she felt she could meet and baffle. It was impertinent, and it was unkind. So, though her mind was at a point which made it close steering, she managed to sheer off from embarrassment and look amused. She laughed in the eyes that were watching her, and answered carelessly enough to Mr. Masters' question that she 'dared say Mr. Knowlton would have come if he could.' Mrs. Starling put up her work with a sigh of relief; and the rest of the persons concerned felt free to dismiss the subject from their minds and pay attention to the supper.

It was a great success, Mrs. Reverdy's sewing party. The excellent entertainment provided was heartily enjoyed, all the more for the little stimulus of curiosity which hung about every article and each detail of the tea-table. Old Mr. Bowdoin delighted himself in hospitable attentions to his old neighbours, and was full of genial and gratified talk with them. The stiffness of the afternoon departed before the tea and coffee; and when at last the assembly broke up, and a little file of country waggons drove away, one after another, from the door, it was with highly gratified loads of people.

Diana may be quoted as a single exception. In the tremor of her spirits which followed the bit of social navigation noticed above, she had hardly known how anything tasted at the supper; and the talk she had heard without hearing. There was nothing but relief in getting away.

The drive home was as silent between her and her mother as the drive out had been. Mrs. Starling was full of her own cogitations. Diana's thoughts were not like that,—hard-twisted and hard-knotted lines of argument, growing harder and more twisted towards their end; but wide flowing and soft changing visions, flowing sweet and free as the clouds borne on the air-currents of heaven; catching such colours, and drifting as insensibly from one form into another. The evening kept up the dreamy character of the afternoon, the haze growing duskier as the light waned; till the tender gleam of a full moon began to supply here and there the glory of the lost sunlight. It was a colder gleam, though; and so far, more practical than that flush of living promise which a little while ago had filled the sky and the world. Diana's thoughts centred on Evan's letter. Where was it? When should she get it? Josiah, she knew, had been to the post office that morning, and brought home nothing! She wished she could go to the post office herself; she sometimes had done so; but she would not like to take Evan's letter, either, from the knowing hands of the postmaster. She might not be able to command her looks perfectly.

'They don't know how to make soda biscuit down yonder.'
Mrs. Starling broke out abruptly, just as their drive was near
ended.

'Don't they?' said Diana absently.

'All yellow!' said Mrs. Starling disdainfully. 'Nobody
would ever know there was any salaratus in *my* biscuit—or in
yours either.'

'Except from the lightness, mother.'

'The lightness wouldn't tell what made 'em light,' said
Mrs. Starling logically. 'They had salaratus in their pickles too.'

'How could you tell?'

'Tell? As if I couldn't tell! Tell by the colour.'

'Ours are green too.'

'Not green like that. I would despise to make my pickles
green that way. I'd as soon paint 'em.'

'It was very handsome, mother, the supper altogether.'

'Hm! It was a little too handsome,' said Mrs. Starling,
'and that was what they liked about it. I'd like to know
what is the use o' having great clumsy forks of make-believe
silver '—

'O, they were real, mother.'

'Well, the more fools if they were. I'd like to know what
is the use of having great clumsy forks of silver, real or make-
believe, when you can have nice, sharp, handy steel ones, and
for half or a quarter the price?'

Diana liked the silver forks, and was silent.

'I could hardly eat my pickles with 'em. I couldn't, if they
had been *mine;* but Genevieve's cucumbers were spongy.'

To Diana's relief, their own door was gained at this moment.
She did not know what her mother's discourse might end in,
and was glad to have it stopped. Yet the drive had been
pretty!

The men had had their supper, which had been left ready
for them; and Josiah's care had kept up a blazing fire in the
lean-to kitchen. Diana went up-stairs to change her dress,
for she had the dishes now to wash up; and Mrs. Starling
stood in front of the fire-place, pondering. She had been
pondering all the time of the drive home, as well as much of

" Mrs Starling hesitated, with her hand on the letter, till the sound of
Diana's step in the house decided her action."

the time spent at Elmfield; she believed she had come to a conclusion, and yet she delayed her purpose. It was clear, she said to herself, that Diana did not care for Lieut. Knowlton; at least not much; her fancy might have been stirred. But what is a girl's fancy? Nothing worth considering. Letters, if allowed, might nourish the fancy up into something else. She would destroy this first one. She had determined on that. Yet she lingered. Conscience spoke uneasily. What if she were misled by appearances, and Diana had more than a fancy for this young fellow? Then she would crush it! Nobody would be the wiser, and nobody would die of grief; those things were done in stories only. Mrs. Starling hesitated nevertheless, with her hand on the letter, till the sound of Diana's step in the house decided her action. She was afraid to wait; some accident might overthrow all her arrangements; and with a hasty movement she drew the packet from her bosom and tucked it under the forestick, where a bed of glowing nutwood coals lay ready. Quick the fire caught the light tindery edges, made a little jet of excitement about the large wax seal, fought its way through the thick folds of paper, and in a moment had left only a mock sheet of cinder, with mock marks of writing still traceable vividly upon it. A letter still, manifestly, sharp-edged and square; it glowed at Mrs. Starling from its bed of coals, with the curious impassiveness of material things; as if the happiness of two lives had not shrivelled within it. Mrs. Starling stood looking. What had been written upon that fiery scroll? It was vain to ask now; and hearing Diana coming down-stairs, she took the tongs and punched the square cinder that kept its form too well. Little bits of paper, grey cinder with red edges, fluttered in the draught, and flew up in the smoke.

'What are you burning there, mother?' said Diana.

And Mrs. Starling answered a guilty 'Nothing,' and walked away. Diana looked at the little fluttering cinders, and an uneasy sensation came over her, that yet took no form of suspicion; and passed, for the thing was impossible. So near she came to it.

Why had Mrs. Starling not at least read the letter before destroying it? The answer lies in some of the strange, hidden involutions of feeling and consciousness, which are hard to trace out even by the person who knows them best. After the thing was done, she wished she had read it. It may be she feared to find what would stay her hand, or make her action difficult. It may be that certain stirrings of conscience warned her that delay might defeat her whole purpose. She was an obstinate woman by nature; obstinate to the point of wilful blindness when necessary; and to do her justice, she was perfectly incapable of estimating the gain or the loss of such an affection as Diana's, or of sympathizing with the suffering such a nature may know. It was not in her; she had no key to it; grant the utmost mischief that she supposed it even possible she might be doing, and it was as a summer gale to the cyclone of the Indian seas.

So her conscience troubled her little, and that little was soon silenced. Perhaps not quite forgotten; for it had the effect, not to make her more than usual tender of her daughter and indulgent towards her, as one would expect, but stern, carping, and exacting beyond all her wont. She drove household matters with a tighter rein than ever, and gave Diana as little time for private thought or musing as the constant and engrossing occupation of her hands could leave free. But, however, thoughts are not chained to fingers. Alas! what troubled calculations Diana worked into her butter, those weeks; and how many heavy possibilities she shook down from her fingers along with the drops of water she scattered upon the clothes for the ironing. Her very nights at last became filled with the anxious cogitations that never ceased all the day; and Diana awoke morning after morning unrefreshed and weary from her burdened sleep, and from dreams that reproduced in fantastic combinations the perplexities of her waking life. Her face began to grow shadowed and anxious, and her tongue was still. Mrs. Starling had generally done most of the talking; she did it all now.

Days passed on, and weeks. Mrs. Starling did not find out that anything was the matter with Diana; partly because she was determined that nothing should be the matter, and partly because young Flandin came about the house a good deal, and Mrs. Starling thought Diana to be vexed, or perhaps in a state of vexed indecision about him. And in addition, she was a little anxious herself, lest another letter should come and somehow reach the hands it was meant for. Having gone so far already, Mrs. Starling did not mean to spoil or lose her work for want of a few finishing touches. She watched the post office as never in her life, for any cause, she had watched it before.

CHAPTER XVI.

DIANA would have written to Mr. Knowlton to get her mystery solved; she was far too simple and true to stand upon needless punctilio; but she did not know how to address to him a letter. Evan himself had not known when he parted from her; the information came in that epistle that never reached her hands, that first letter. Names and directions had all perished in the flames, and for want of them Diana could do nothing. Meanwhile, what would Evan think? He would expect an answer, and a quick answer, to his letter; he was looking for it now, no doubt; wondering why it did not come, and disappointed, and fearing something wrong. That trouble, of fearing something wrong, Diana was spared; for she knew that the family at Elmfield had heard, and all was well; but sometimes her other troublesome thoughts made her powerless hands come together with a clasp of wild pain. How long must she wait now? how long would Evan wait, before in desperation he wrote again? And where was her letter? for it had been written and sent; that she knew;—was it lost? was it stolen? Had somebody's curiosity prevailed so far, and was her precious secret town property by this time? Every day became harder to bear; every week made the suspense more intolerable. Mrs. Starling was far out in one of her suppositions. Will Flandin came a good deal about the house, it is true; but Diana hardly knew he was there. If she thought about it at all, she was half glad, because his presence might serve to mask her silence and abstraction. She was conscious of both, and the effort to cover the one and hide the other was very painful sometimes.

October glories were passed away, and November days grew

shorter and shorter, colder and more dreary. It seemed now and then to Diana that summer had gone to a distance from which it could never revisit her. And after those days of constant communication with Evan, the blank cessation of it, the ignorance of all that had befallen or was befalling him, the want of a word of remembrance or affection, grew almost to a blank of despair.

It was late in the month.

'What waggon's that stopping?' exclaimed Mrs. Starling one afternoon. Mother and daughter were in the lean-to. Diana looked out, and saw with a pang of various feelings what waggon it was.

'Ain't that the Elmfield folks?'

'I think so.'

'I know so. I thought Mrs. Reverdy and the rest had run away from the cold.'

'Didn't you know Miss Masters had been sick?'

'How should I know it?'

'I heard so. I didn't know but you had heard it.'

'I can't hear things without somebody tells me. Go along up-stairs, Diana, and put on something.'

Diana obeyed, but she was very quick about it; she was nervously afraid lest while she was absent some word should be said that she would not have lost for the whole world. What had they come for, these people? Was the secret out, perhaps, and had they come to bring her a letter? Or to say why Evan had not written? Could he have been sick? A feverish whirlwind of thoughts rushed through Diana's head while she was fastening her dress; and she went down and came into the parlour with two beautiful spots of rose colour upon her cheeks. They were fever-spots. Diana had been pale of late; but she looked gloriously handsome as she entered the room. Bad for her. A common-looking woman might have heard news from Evan; the instant resolve in the hearts of the two ladies who had come to visit her was, that this girl should hear none.

They were, however, exceedingly gracious and agreeable. Mrs. Reverdy entered with flattering interest into all the

matters of household and farm detail respecting which Mrs.
Starling chose to be communicative; responded with details
of her own. How it was impossible to get good butter made,
unless you made it yourself. How servants were unsatisfactory,
even in Pleasant Valley; and how delightful it was to be able
to do without them, as Mrs. Starling did and Diana.

'I should like it of all things,' said Mrs. Reverdy with her
unfailing laugh; a little, well-bred, low murmur of a laugh.
'It must be so delightful to have your biscuits always light
and never tasting of soda; and your butter always as if it
was made of cowslips; and your eggs always fresh. We never
have fresh eggs,' continued Mrs. Reverdy, shaking her head
solemnly;—'never. I never dare to have them boiled.'

'What becomes of them?' said a new voice; and Mr.
Masters entered the field—in other words, the room. Diana's
heart contracted with a pang; was this another hindrance in
the way of her hearing what she wanted? But the rest of the
ladies welcomed him.

'Charming!' said Mrs. Reverdy; 'now you will go home
with us.'

'I don't see just on what you found your conclusion.'

'O, you will have made your visit to Mrs. Starling, you
know; and then you will have nothing else to do.'

'There spoke a woman of business!' said the minister.

'Yes, why not?' said the lady. 'I was just telling Mrs.
Starling how I should delight to do as she does, without
servants, and how pleasant I should find it; only, you know,
I shouldn't know how to do anything if I tried.' Mrs. Reverdy
seemed to find the idea very entertaining.

'You wouldn't like to get up in the morning to make your
biscuits,' said Gertrude.

'O yes, I would! I needn't have breakfast very early, you know.'

'The good butter wouldn't be on the table if you didn't,'
said Mrs. Starling.

'Wouldn't it? Why? Does it matter when butter is made,
if it is only made right?'

'No; but the trouble is, it cannot be made right after the
sun is an hour or two high.'

'An hour or two!' Mrs. Reverdy uttered a little scream.

'Not at this time of year, mother,' interposed Diana.

'Do you get up at these fearful times?' inquired Miss Masters languidly, turning her eyes full upon the latter speaker.

Diana scarce answered. Would all the minutes of their visit pass in these platitudes? could nothing else be talked of? The next instant she blessed Mr. Masters.

'Have you heard from the soldier lately?' he asked.

'O yes! we hear frequently,' Mrs. Reverdy said.

'He likes his post?'

'I really don't know,' said her sister, laughing; 'a soldier can't choose, you know. I fancy they have some rough times out there; but they manage to get a good deal of fun too. Evan's last letter told of buffalo hunting, and said they had some very good society too. You wouldn't expect it, on the outskirts of everything; but the officers' families are very pleasant. There are young ladies, sometimes; and every one is made a great deal of.'

'Where is Mr. Knowlton?' Diana asked. She had been working up her courage to dare the question; it was hazardous; she was afraid to trust her voice; but the daring of desperation was on her, and the words came out with sufficiently cool utterance. A keen observer might note a change in Mrs. Reverdy's look and tone.

'O, he's in one of those dreadful posts out on the frontier; too near the Indians; but I suppose if there weren't Indians there wouldn't be forts, and they wouldn't want officers or soldiers to be in them,' she added, looking at Mr. Masters, as if she had found a happy final cause for the existence of the aborigines of the country.

'What is the name of the place?' Diana asked.

'I declare I have forgotten. Fort ——, I can't think of any name but Vancouver, and it isn't that. Gertrude, what is the name of that place? Do you know, I can't tell whether it is in Arizona or Wisconsin!' And Mrs. Reverdy laughed at her geographical innocence.

Gertrude 'didn't remember.'

'He's not so far off as Vancouver, I think,' said Mr. Masters.

'No,—O no, not so far as that; but he might just as well. When you get to a certain distance, it don't signify whether it is more or less; you can't get at people, and they can't get at you. *You* have seemed to be at that distance lately, Basil. What a dreadful name! How came you to be called such a name?'

'Be thankful it is no worse,' said the minister gravely. 'I might have been called Lactantius.'

'Lactantius! Impossible. Was there ever a man named Lactantius?'

'Certainly.'

''Tain't any worse than Ichabod,' remarked Mrs. Starling.

'Nothing can be worse than Ichabod,' said Mr. Masters in the same dry way. 'It means, "The glory is departed."'

'The Ichabods I knew, never had any glory to begin with,' said Mrs. Starling.

But the minister laughed at this, and so gaily that it was infectious. Mrs. Starling joined in, without well knowing why; the lady visitors seemed to be very much amused. Diana tried to laugh, with lips that felt rigid as steel. The minister's eye came to hers too, she knew, to see how the fun went with her. And then the ladies rose, took a very flattering leave, and departed, carrying Mr. Masters off with them.

'I am coming to look at those books of yours soon,' he said, as he shook hands with Diana. 'May I?'

Diana made her answer as civil as she could, with those stiff lips; how she bade good-bye to the others she never knew. As her mother attended them to the garden gate, she went up the stairs to her room, feeling now it was the first time that the pain *could not be borne.* Seeing these people had brought Evan so near, and hearing them talk had put him at such an impossible distance. Diana pressed both hands on her heart, and stood looking out of her window at the departing carriage. What could she do? Nothing that she could think of, and to do nothing was the intolerable part of it. Any, the most tedious and lingering action, yes, even the least hopeful, anything that would have been action, would have made the pain supportable; she could have drawn breath then, enough for life's purposes; now she was stifling. There was some mystery; there was something wrong; some mistake, or misapprehension, or malpractice; *something*, which if she could put her hand on, all would be right. And it was hidden from her; dark; it might be near or far, she could not touch it, for she could not find it. There was even no place for suspicion to take hold, unless the curiosity of the post office, or of some prying neighbour; she did not suspect Evan; and yet there was a great throb at her heart with the thought that in Evan's place *she* would never have let things rest. Nothing should have kept the silence so long unbroken; if the first letter got no answer, she would have written another. So would Diana have done now, without being in Evan's place, if only she had had his address. And that cruel woman to-day! did she know, or did she guess, anything? or was it another of the untoward circumstances attending the whole matter?

It came to her now, a thought of regret that she had not ventured the disagreeableness and told her mother long ago of her interest in Evan. Mrs. Starling could take measures that her daughter could not take. If she pleased, that is; and the doubt also recurred, whether she would please. It was by no means certain; and at any rate now, in her mortification and pain, Diana could not invite her mother into her counsels. She felt that as from her window she watched the receding waggon, and saw Mrs. Starling turn from the gate and walk in. Uncompromising, unsympathizing, even her gait and the set of her head and shoulders proclaimed her to be. Diana was alone with her trouble.

An hour afterwards she came down as usual, strained the milk, skimmed her cream, went through the whole little routine of the household evening; her hands were steady, her eye was true, her memory lost nothing. But she did not speak one word, unless, which was seldom, a word was spoken to her. So went on the next day, and the next. November's days were trailing along, December's would follow; there was no change from one to another; no variety. Less than ever before; for, with morbid sensitiveness, Diana shrank from visitors and visiting. Every contact gave her pain.

L

Meanwhile, where was Evan's second letter? On its way, and in the post office.

It was late in November; Diana was sitting at the door of the lean-to, where she had been sitting on that June day when our story began. She was alone this time, and her look and attitude were sadly at variance with that former time. The November day was not without a charm of its own which might even challenge comparison with the June glory; for it was Indian summer time, and the wonder of soft spiritual beauty which had settled down upon the landscape, brown and bare though that was, left no room to regret the full verdure and radiant sunlight of high summer. The indescribable loveliness of the haze and hush, the winning tender colouring that was through the air and wrapped round everything, softening, mellowing, harmonizing somehow even the most unsightly; hiding where it could not beautify, and beautifying where it could not hide, like Christian charity; gave a most exquisite lesson to the world, of how much more mighty is spirit than matter. Diana did not see it, as she had seen the June day; her arms were folded, lying one upon another in idle fashion; her face was grave and fixed, the eyes aimless and visionless, looking at nothing and seeing nothing; cheeks pale, and the mouth parted with pain and questioning, its delicious childlike curves just now all gone. So sitting, and so abstracted in her own thoughts, she never knew that anybody was near till the little gate opened, and then with a start she saw Mr. Masters coming up the walk. Diana rose and stood in the doorway; all traces of country-girl manners, if she had ever had any, had disappeared before the dignity of a great and engrossing trouble.

'Good evening!' she said quietly, as they shook hands. 'Mother's gone out.'

'Gone out, is she?' said Mr. Masters, but not with a tone of particular disappointment.

'Yes. I believe she has gone to the Corner—to the post office.'

'The Corner is a good way off. And how do you do?'

Diana thought he looked at her a little meaningly. She answered in the customary form, that she was well.

'That says a great deal—or nothing at all,' the minister remarked.

'What?' said Diana, not comprehending him.

'That form of words,—"I am well."'

'It is very apt to mean nothing at all,' said Diana, 'for people say it without thinking.'

'As you did just now.'

'Perhaps—but I *am* well.'

'Altogether?' said the minister. 'Soul and mind and body?'

The word read dry enough; his manner, his tone, half gentle, half bold, with a curious inoffensive kind of boldness, took from them their dryness and gave them a certain sweet acceptableness that most persons knew who knew Mr. Masters. Diana never dreamed that he was intrusive, even though she recognised the fact that he was about his work. Nevertheless she waived the question.

'Can anybody say that he is well *so?*' she asked.

'I hope he can. Do you know the old lady who is called Mother Bartlett?'

'O yes.'

'Do you think she would hesitate about answering that question? or be mistaken in the answer?'

'But what do you mean by it exactly?' said Diana.

'Don't you know?'

'I suppose I do. I know what it means to be well in body. I have been well all my life.'

'How would you characterize that happy condition?'

'Why,' said Diana, unused to definitions of abstractions, but following Mr. Masters' lead as people always did, gentle or simple,—'I mean, or it means, sound and comfortable, and fit for what one has to do.'

'Excellent,' said the minister. 'I see you understand the subject. Cannot those things be true of soul and mind as well as of body?'

'What is the difference between soul and mind?' said Diana.

'A clear departure,' said the minister, laughing; then gravely, 'Do you read philosophy?'

'I don't know'— said Diana. 'I read, or I used to read, a good many sorts of books. I haven't read much lately.'

The minister gave her another keen look while she was attending to something else, and when he spoke again it was with a change of tone.

'I had a promise once that I should see those books.'

'Any time,' said Diana eagerly; 'any time!' For it would be an easy way of entertaining him, or of getting rid of him. Either would do.

'I think I proposed a plan of exchange, which might be to the advantage of us both.'

'To mine, I am sure,' said Diana. 'I don't know whether there can be anything you would care for among the books up-stairs; but if there should be— Would you like to go up and look at them?'

'I should,—if it would not give you too much trouble.'

It would be no trouble just to run up-stairs and show him where they were; and this Diana did, leaving him to overhaul the stock at his leisure. She came down and went on with her work.

Diana's heart was too sound and her head too clear to allow her to be more than to a certain degree distressed at not hearing from Evan. She did not doubt him more than she doubted herself; and not doubting him, things must come out all right by and by. She was restive under the present pain; at times wild with the desire to find and remove the something, whatever it was, which had come between Evan and her; for this girl's was no calm, easy-going nature, but one with depths of passionate reserve and terrible possibilities of suffering or enjoying. She had been calm all her life until now, because these powers and susceptibilities had been in an absolute poise; an equilibrium that nothing had shaken. Now the depths were stirred, and at times she was in a storm of impatient pain; but there came revulsions of hope and quiet lulls, when the sun almost shone again under the clearance made by faith and

hope. One of these revulsions came now, after she had set the
minister to work upon her books.   Perhaps it was simple
reaction ; perhaps it was something caught from the quiet
sunshiny manner and spirit of her visitor ; but at her work in
the kitchen Diana grew quite calm-hearted. She fancied she
had discerned somewhat of more than usual earnestness in
the minister's observation of her, and she began to question
whether her looks or behaviour had furnished occasion. Perhaps she had not been ready enough to talk ; poor Diana knew
it was often the case now ; she resolved she would try to mend
that when he came down. And there was, besides, a certain
lurking impatience of the bearing of his words ; they had
probed a little too deep, and after the manner of some morbid
conditions, the probing irritated her. So by and by, when Mr.
Masters came down with a brown volume in his hand, and
offered to borrow it if she would let him lend her another of
different colour, Diana met him and answered quite like herself,
and went on—

' Mr. Masters, how *can* people be always well in body, mind,
and spirit, as you say ? I am sure people's bodies get sick
without any fault of their own ; and there are accidents ; and
just so there are troubles. People can't help troubles, and
they can't be " well " in mind, I suppose, when they are in
pain ? '

' Are you sure of that ? ' the minister answered quietly,
while he turned to the window to look at something in the
volume he had brought down with him.

' Why, yes ; and so are you, Mr. Masters, are you not ? '

' You need to know a great deal to be sure of anything,' he
answered in the same tone.

' But you are certain of this, Mr. Masters ? '

' I shouldn't like to expose myself to your criticism. Let us
look at facts. It seems to me that David was " well " when
he could say, " Thou hast delivered my soul from death, mine
eyes from tears, and my feet from falling." Also the man
described in another place—" He that dwelleth in the secret
place of the Most High shall abide under the shadow of the
Almighty." '

There came a slight quiver across Diana's face, but her words
were moved by another feeling.

'Those were people of the old times; I don't know anything
about them. I mean people of to-day.'

'I think Paul was "well" when he could say, "I have
learned, in whatsoever state I am, therewith to be content."'

'O, but that is nonsense, Mr. Masters!'

'It was Paul's experience.'

'Yes, but it cannot be the experience of other people. Paul
was inspired.'

'To write what was true, — not what was false,' said the
minister, looking at her. 'You don't think peace and content
come by inspiration, do you?'

'I did not think about it,' said Diana. 'But I am sure it is
impossible to be as he said.'

'I never heard Paul's truth questioned before,' said the
minister, with a dry sort of comicality.

'No, but, Mr. Masters,' said Diana, half by way of apology,
'I spoke from my own experience.'

'And he spoke from his.'

'But, sir,—Mr. Masters,—seriously, do you think it is
possible to be contented when one is in trouble?'

'Miss Diana, One greater than David or Paul said
this, "If a man love me, he will keep my words; and
my Father will love him; and we will come unto him,
and make our abode with him." Where there is that in-
dwelling, believe me, there is no trouble that can overthrow
content.'

'Content and pain together?' said Diana.

'Sometimes pain and very great joy.'

'You are speaking of what I do not understand in the
least,' said Diana. And her face looked half incredulous, half
sad.

'I wish you did know it,' he said. No more; only those few
words had a simplicity, a truth, an accent of sympathy and
affection, that reached the very depth of the heart he was
speaking to; as the same things from his lips had often reached
other hearts. He promised to take care of the book in his

hand, and presently went away, with one of the warm, frank, lingering grasps of the hand, that were also a characteristic of Basil Masters. Diana stood at the door watching him ride away. It cannot be said she was soothed by his words, and perhaps he did not mean she should be. She stood with a weary feeling of want in her heart; but she thought only of the want of Evan.

CHAPTER XVII.

THE USE OF LIVING.

IT was quite according to Diana's nature, that as the winter went on, though still without news of Evan, her tumult and agony of mind quieted down into a calm and steadfast waiting. Her spirit was too healthy for suspicion, too true for doubt; and put away doubt and suspicion, what was left but the assurance that there had been some accident or mistake; from the consequences of which she was suffering, no doubt, but which would all be made right, and come out clear so soon as there could be an opportunity for explanation. For that there was nothing to do, but to wait a little; with the returning mild weather, Evan would be able to procure a furlough, he would be at her side, and then—nothing then but union and joy. She could wait; and even in the waiting, her healthy spirit as it were sloughed off care, and came back again to its usual placid, strong, bright condition.

So the winter went; a winter which was ever after a blank in Diana's remembrance; and the cold weather broke up into the frosts and thaws that sugar-makers love; and in such a March day it was the word came to Mrs. Starling's house that old Squire Bowdoin was dead. The like weather never failed in after years to bring back to Diana that one day and its tidings, and the strange shock they gave her.

' 'Twas kind o' sudden,' said the news-bringer, who was Joe Bartlett; 'he was took all to once and jes' dropped—like a ripe chestnut.'

' Why like a ripe chestnut?' said Mrs. Starling sharply.

' Wall, I had to say suthin', and that come first. The Scripter does speak of a shock o' corn in his season, don't it, Mis' Starling?'

'What's the likeness between a shock o' corn and a chestnut, Joe? I can't abide to hear folks talk nonsense. Who's at Elmfield?'

'Ain't nary one there that had ought to be there; nary one but the help.'

'But they're comin'?' said Mrs. Starling, lifting up her head for the answer.

'Wall, I can't say. Evan, he's too fur; and I guess men in his place hain't their ch'ice. And his folks is flourishy kind o' bodies; I don't set no count on 'em, for my part.'

'Well, everybody else 'll be there, and shame 'em if they ain't,' said Mrs. Starling. 'How's your mother, Joe?'

'Wall, I guess *she's* ripe,' said Joe with a slow intonation, loving and reverent; 'but she's goin' to hold on to this state o' things yet awhile. Good day t' ye!'

Diana went to the old man's funeral with her mother; in a sort of tremble of spirits, looking forward to what she might possibly see or hear. But no one was there; no one in whom she had any interest; none of Mr. Bowdoin's grandchildren could make it convenient to come to his funeral. The large gathering of friends and neighbours and distant relations were but an unmeaning crowd to Diana's perceptions.

What difference would this change at Elmfield make in her own prospects? Would Mrs. Reverdy and her set come to Elmfield as usual, and so draw Evan as a matter of course? They might not, perhaps. But what difference could it be to Diana? Evan would come, at all events, and under any circumstances; even if his coming let the secret out, he would come, and nothing would keep him from it; the necessity of seeing her would be above all other except military necessities. Diana thought she wished the old gentleman had not died. But it could make no difference. As soon as he could, Evan would be there.

She returned to her quiet waiting. But now nature began to be noisy about her. It seemed that everything had a voice. Spring winds said, 'He is coming;' the perfume of opening buds was sweet with his far-off presence; the very gales that chased the clouds, to her fancy chased the minutes as well; the waking up of the household and farm activities, said that now Diana's inner life would come back to its wonted course and arrangements.

The spring winds blew themselves out; spring buds opened into full leafage; spring activities gradually merged into the steady routine of summer; and still Diana saw nothing, and still she heard nothing of Evan.

She was patient now by force of will; doggedly trusting. She *would* not doubt. None of the family came to Elmfield; so there was no news by the way that could reach her. Mrs. Starling watched the success of her experiment, and was satisfied. Will began to come about the house more and more.

It was near the end of summer, more than a year since her first introduction to Evan, that Diana found herself again one day at Mother Bartlett's cottage. She always made visits there from time to time; to-day she had come for no special reason, but a restlessness which possessed her at home. The old lady was in her usual chimney corner, knitting, as a year ago; and Diana, having prepared the mid-day repast and cleared away after it, was sitting on the doorstep at the open door; whence her eye went out to the hillside pasture and followed the two cows which were slowly moving about there. It was as quiet a bit of nature as could be found anywhere; and Diana was very quiet looking at it. But Mrs. Bartlett's eye was upon her much more than upon her work; which, indeed, could go on quite well without such supervision. She broke silence at last, speaking with an imperceptible little sigh.

'And so, dear, the minister preached his sermon about the fashions last Sabbath?'

'About fashion,' said Diana. 'He had promised it long ago.'

'And what did he say, dear?'

'He said, "The fashion of this world passeth away."'

'But he said something more, I suppose? *I* could have said that.'

'He said a great deal more,' replied Diana. 'It was a very curious sermon.'

'As I hain't heard it, and you hev, perhaps you'll oblige me with some more of it.'

'It was a very curious sermon,' Diana repeated. 'Not in the least like what you would have expected. There wasn't much about fashion in it; and yet, somehow it seemed to be *all* that.'

'What was his text?'

'I can't tell; something about "the grace of the fashion of it." I don't remember how the words went.'

'I know, I guess,' said the old lady. ''Twas in James, warn't it? Something like this—"The sun is no sooner risen with a burning heat"'—

'Yes, yes, that was it.'

'"— but it withereth the grass, and the flower thereof falleth, and the grace of the fashion of it perisheth."'

'That was it,' assented Diana.

'So he preached about the shortness of life?'

'No, not at all. He began with those words, and just a sentence or two—and it was beautiful, too, mother—explaining them; and then he said the Bible hadn't much in it directly speaking of our fashions; he would give us what there was, and let us make what we could of it; so he did.'

'You can make a good deal of it if you try,' said Mrs. Bartlett. 'And then, dear?'

'Then he went off, you'd never think where—to the last chapter of Proverbs; and he described the woman described there; and he made her out so beautiful and good and clever and wise, that somehow, without saying a word about fashion, he made us feel how *she* would never have had any concern about it; how she was above it, and five times more beautiful without, than she would have been with, the foolish ways of people now-a-days. But he didn't say that; you only felt it. I don't much believe there are any such women, mother.'

'I hope and believe you'll make just such a one, Diana.'

'I?' said the girl, with a curious intonation; then subsiding again immediately, she sat as she had sat at her own door a year ago, with arms folded, gazing out upon the summery hill pasture where the cows were leisurely feeding. But now her eyes had a steady, hard look, not busy with the sunshiny turf or the deep blue sky against which the line of the hill cut so soft and clear. *Then* the vision had been all outward.

'And that was his sermon?' said the old lady with a dash of disappointment.

'No! O no,' said Diana, rousing herself. 'He went on then —how shall I tell you? Do you remember a verse in the Revelation about the Church coming down as a bride adorned for her husband?'

'Ay!' said the old lady with a gratified change of voice. 'Well?'

'He went on to describe that adornment. I can't tell you how he did it; I can't repeat what he said; but it was inner adornment, you know; "all glorious within," I remember he said; and without a word more about what he started with, he made one feel that there is no real adornment but that kind, nor any other worth a thought. I heard Kate Boddington telling mother, as we came out of church, that she felt as cheap as dirt, with all her silk dress and new bonnet; and Mrs. Carpenter, who was close by, said *she* felt there wasn't a bit of her that would bear looking at.'

'What did your mother say?'

'Nothing. She didn't understand it, she said.'

'And, Di, how did you feel?'

'I don't think I felt anything, mother.'

'How come that about?'

'I don't know. I believe it seems to me as if the fashion of this world never passed away; it's the same thing, year in and year out.'

'What ails you, Diana?' her old friend asked after a pause.

'Nothing. I'm sort o' tired. I don't see how folks stand it, to live a long life.'

'But life has not been very hard to you, honey.'

'It needn't be *hard* for that,' Diana answered, with a kind of choke in her voice. 'Perhaps the hardest of all would be to go on an unvarying jog-trot, and to know it would always be so all one's life.'

'What makes life all of a sudden so tiresome to you, Di?'

'Something I haven't got, I suppose,' said the girl drearily.
' I have enough to eat and drink.'

' You ain't as bright as you used to be a year ago.'

' I have grown older, and have got more experience.'

' If life is good for nothin' else, Di, it's good to make ready for what comes after.'

' I don't believe that doctrine, mother,' said Diana energetically. ' Life is meant to be life, and not getting ready to live. '*Tisn't* meant to be all brown and sawdusty here, that people may have it more fresh and pleasant by and by.'

'No; but to drive them out o' this pasture, maybe. If the cows found always the grass long in the meadow, when do you think they'd go up the hill?'

A quick, restless change of position was the only answer to this; an answer most unlike the natural calm grace of Diana's movements. The old lady looked at her wistfully, doubtfully, two or three times up and down from her knitting, before speaking again. And then speaking was prevented, for the other door opened and the minister came in.

Basil was always welcome, whatever house or company he entered; he could fall in with any mood, take up any subject, sympathize in anybody's concerns. That was part of his secret of power, but that was not all. There was about him an *aura* of happiness, so to speak; a steadfastness of the inner nature, which gave a sense of calm to others almost by the force of sympathy; and the strength of a quiet will, which was, however, inflexible. All that was restless, uncertain, and unsatisfied in men's hearts and lives, found something in him to which they clung as if it had been an anchor of hope; and so his popularity had a very wide, and at first sight very perplexing range.

The two women in Mrs. Bartlett's cottage were glad to see him; and they had reason. Perhaps, for he was very quick, he discerned that the social atmosphere had been somewhat hazy when he came in; for through all his stay his talk was so bright and strong that it met the needs of both hearers. Even Diana laughed with him and listened to him; and when he rose to take leave, she asked if he came on horseback to-day?

'No; I am ease-loving. I borrowed Mr. Chalmers' buggy.'

'Which way are you going now, sir, if you please?'

He hesitated an instant, looked at her, and answered quite demurely, 'I think your way.'

'Would you be so kind as to take me so far as home with you, then?'

'I don't see any objection to that,' said Basil in the same cool manner. And Diana hastily took her bonnet and kissed her old friend, and in another minute or two she was in the buggy, and they were driving off.

If the minister suspected somewhat, he would spoil nothing by being in a hurry. He drove leisurely, saying that it was too hot weather to ask much exertion even from a horse; and making little slight remarks, in a manner so gentle and quiet as to be very reassuring. But if that was what Diana wanted, she wanted a great deal of it; for she sat looking straight between the edges of her sun-bonnet, absolutely silent, hardly even making the replies her companion's words called for. At last he was silent too. The good grey horse went very soberly on, not urged at all; but yet even a slow rate of motion will take you to the end of anything, given the time; and every minute saw the rods of Diana's road getting behind her. I suppose she felt that, and spoke at last in the desperate sense of it. When a person is under that urgency, he does not always choose his words.

'Mr. Masters, is there any way of making life anything but a miserable failure?'

The lowered cadences of Diana's voice, a thread of bitterness in her utterance, quite turned the minister's thought from anything like a light or a gay answer. He said very gravely,

'Nobody's life need be that.'

'How are you to get rid of it?'

'Of that result, you mean?'

'Yes.'

'Will you state the difficulty, as it appears to you?'

'Why, look at it,' said Diana, more hesitatingly; 'what do most people's lives amount to?—what does mine? To dress oneself, and eat and drink, and go through a round of things, which only mean that you will dress yourself and eat and drink again and do the same things to-morrow, and the next day;— what does it all amount to in the end?'

'Is life no more than that to you?'

Diana hesitated, but then, with a tone still lowered, said, 'No.'

The minister was silent now, and presently Diana went on again.

'The whole world seems to me just so. People live, and die; and they might just as well not have lived, for all that their being in the world has done. And yet they have lived— and suffered.'

More than she knew was told in the utterance of that last word. The minister was still not in a hurry to speak. When he did, his question came as a surprise.

'You believe the first chapter of Genesis, Miss Diana?'

'Certainly,' she said, feeling with downcast heart, 'O, now a sermon!'

'You believe that God made the earth, and made man to occupy it?'

'Yes—certainly.'

'What do you think he made him for?'

'I know what the catechism says,' Diana began slowly.

'No, no; my question has nothing to do with the catechism. Do you believe that the Creator's intention was that men should live purposeless lives, like what you describe?'

'I can't believe it.'

'Then what purpose are we here for? Why am I, and why are you, on the earth?'

'I don't know,' said Diana faintly. The talk was not turning out well for her wish, she thought.

'To find that out,—and to get in harmony with the answer, —is the great secret of life.'

'Will you help me, Mr. Masters?' said Diana humbly. 'It is all dark and wild to me,—I see no comfort in anything. If there were nothing better than this, one would rather *not* be on the earth.'

Mr. Masters might have pondered with a little surprise on
the strength of the currents that flow sometimes where the
water looks calm; but he had no time, and in truth was in
no mood for moralizing just then. His answer was somewhat
abrupt, though gentle as possible.

'What do you want, Miss Diana?'

But the answer to that was a choked sob, and then, breaking
all bounds of her habit and intention, a passionate storm of
tears. Diana was frightened at herself; but, nevertheless, the
sudden probe of the question, with the sympathetic gentleness
of it, and the too great contrast between the speaker's happy,
calm, strong content and her own disordered, distracted life,
suddenly broke her down. Neither, if you open the sluice-
gates to such a current, can you immediately get them shut
again. This she found, though greatly afraid of the conclusions her companion might draw. For a few minutes her
passion was utterly uncontrolled.

If Basil drew conclusions, he was not in a hurry to make
them known. He did not at that time follow the conversation
any further; only remarking cheerfully, and sympathetically
too, 'We must have some more talk about this, Miss Diana;
but we'll take another opportunity,' and so presently left her
at her own door, with the warm, strong grasp of the hand
that many a one in trouble had learned to know. There is
strange intelligence, somehow, in our fingers. They can say
what lips fail to say. Diana went into the house feeling that
her minister was a tower of strength and a treasury of
kindness.

She found company. Mrs. Flandin and her mother were
sitting together.

'Hev you come home to stay, Diana?' was her mother's
sarcastic salutation.

'How come you and the Dominie to be a ridin' together?'
was the other lady's blunter question.

'I had the chance,' said Diana, 'and I asked him to bring
me. It's too hot for walking.'

'And how come he to be in a buggy, so convenient? He
always goes tearin' round on the back of that 'ere grey horse,

I thought. I never see a minister ride so afore; and I don't *think*, Mis' Starling, it's suitable. What if he was to break his neck, on the way to visit some sick man ? '

' Jim Treadwell broke *his* neck out of a waggon,' responded Mrs. Starling.

' Ah, well! there ain't no security, no place; but don't it strike you, now, Mis' Starling, that a minister had ought to set an example of steady goin', and not turn the heads of the young men, and young women, with his capers? '

' He is a young man himself, Mrs. Flandin,' Diana was bold to say.

' Wall—I know he is,' said the lady in a disapproving way. ' I know he is; and he can't help it; but if I had my way, I'd allays have a minister as much as fifty year old. It looks better,' said Mrs. Flandin complacently; ' and it *is* better.'

' What is he to do all the first fifty years of his life, then ? '

' Wall, my dear, I hain't got the arrangement of things; I don't know. I know Will would hitch up and carry you anywheres you want to go—if it's a waggon you want any time.'

After that, Will made good his mother's promise, so far as intentions went. He was generally on hand when anything was to be done in which himself and his smart buggy could be useful. Indeed, he was very often on hand at other times; dropping in after supper, and appearing with baskets, which were found to contain some of the Flandin pears or the fine red apples that grew in a corner of the lot, and were famous. Some of his own bees' honey Will brought another time, and a bushel of uncommonly fine nuts. Of course this was in the fall, to which the weary weeks of Diana's summer had at length dragged themselves out. But if Will hoped that honey would sweeten Diana's reception of him and his attentions, as yet it did not seem to have the desired effect. In truth, though Will could never suspect it, her brain was so heavy with other thoughts that she was only in a vague and general way conscious of his presence; and of his officious gallantries scarcely aware. So little aware, indeed, of their bearing, that on two or three occasions she suffered herself to be conveyed

M

in Will's buggy to or from some gathering of the neighbours;
Mrs. Starling or Mrs. Flandin had arranged it, and Diana had
quite blindly fallen into the trap. And then the young man,
not unreasonably elated and inspirited, began to make his
visits to Mrs. Starling's house more frequent than ever. It
was little he did to recommend himself when he was there; he
generally sat watching Diana, carrying on a spasmodic and
interrupted conversation with Mrs. Starling about farm affairs,
and seizing the opportunity of a dropped spool or an unwound
skein of yarn to draw near Diana and venture some word to
her. Poor Diana felt in those days so much like a person
whose earthly ties are all broken, that it did not come into
her head in what a different light she stood to other eyes.

CHAPTER XVIII.

A SNOWSTORM.

As the weeks of September rolled away, they brought by the necessary force of associations a sharp waking up to Diana's torpor. These, last year, had been the weeks of her happiness; happiness had come to her dressed in these robes of autumn. light and colour; and now every breath of the soft atmosphere, every gleam from the changing foliage, the light's peculiar. tone, and the soft indolence of the hazy days, stole into the recesses of Diana's heart, and smote on the nerves that answered every touch with vibrations of pain. The Æolian harp that had sounded such soft harmonies a year ago, when the notes rose and fell in breathings of joy, clanged now with sharp and keen discords that Diana could scarcely bear. The time of blackberries passed without her joining the yearly party. which went as usual; she escaped that; but there was no escaping September. And when in due course the time for the equinoctial storms came, and the storms did not fail, though coming this year somewhat later than the last, Diana felt like a person wakened up to life to die the second time. Her mood all changed. From a dull, miserable apathy, which yet had somewhat of the numbness of death in it, she woke up to the intense life of pain, and to a corresponding, but in her most unwonted, irritability of feeling. All of a sudden, as it were, she grew sensitive to whatever in her life and surroundings was untoward or trying. She read through Will Flandin's devotion; she saw what her mother was 'driving at,' as she would have expressed it. And the whole reality of her relations to Evan and his relations to her stood in colours as distinct as those of the red and green maple leaves, and

179

unsoftened by the least haze of self-delusion. In the dash of the rain and the roar of the wind, in the familiar swirl of the elm branches, she read as it were her sentence of death. Before this she had not been dead, only stunned; now she was wakened up to die. Nature herself, which had been so kind a year ago, brought her now the irrevocable message. A whole year had gone by, a year of silence; it was merely impossible that Evan could be true to her. If he had been true, he would have overleaped all barriers, rather than let this silence last: but indeed he had no barriers to overleap; he had only to write; and he had plenty of time for it. *She* might have overleaped barriers, earlier in the year, if she could have known the case was so desperate; and yet, Diana reflected, she could not and would not, even so. It was well she had not tried. For if Evan needed to be held, she would not put out a finger to hold him.

Of this change in Diana's mood it is safe to say that nothing was visible. Feeling as if every nerve and sense were become an avenue of living pain, dying mentally a slow death, she showed nothing of it to others. Mind and body were so sound and strong, and the poise of her nature was matched with such a sweet dignity, that she was able to go through her usual round of duties in quite her usual way; 'die and make no sign.' Nothing was neglected in any wise, nothing was slurred or hurried over; thoroughly, diligently, punctually, she did the work from which all heart was gone out, and even Mrs. Starling, keen enough to see anything if only she had a clue to it, watched and saw nothing. For Diana's cheek had been pale for a good while now, and she had never been a talkative person, lately less than ever; so the fact that in these days she never talked at all did not strike her mother. But such power of self-containing is a dangerous gift for a woman.

No doubt the extreme bustle and variety of the autumn and early winter work helped Mrs. Starling to shut her eyes to what she did not want to see; helped Diana too. Fall ploughing and sowing were to be attended to; laying down the winter's butter, storing the vegetables, disposing of the grain, fatting cattle, wood cutting and hauling, and repairing of fences, which Mrs. Starling always had done punctually in the fall as soon as the ploughs were put up. For nothing under Mrs. Starling's care was ever left at loose ends; there was not a better farmer in Pleasant Valley than she. Then the winter closed in, early in those rather high latitudes; and pork-killing time came, when for some time nothing was even thought of in the house but pork in its varied forms,—lard, sausage, bacon, and hams, with extras of souse and head-cheese. Snow had fallen already; and winter was setting in betimes, the knowing ones said.

So came one Sunday a little before Christmas. It brought a lull in the midst of the pork business. Hands were washed finally for the whole day, and the kitchen 'redd up.' The weariness of Diana's nerves welcomed the respite; for business, which ofttimes is a help to bearing pain, in some moods aggravates it at every touch; and Diana was glad to think that she might go into her own room and lock the door and be alone with her misery. The day was cloudy and threatening, and Mrs. Starling had avowed her purpose not to go to church. She was 'tuckered out,' she said. 'And I am sure the Sabbath was given us for rest.' Diana made no answer; she was washing up the breakfast things.

'I guess we ain't early, neither,' Mrs. Starling went on. 'Well—one day in seven, folks must sleep; and I didn't get that headcheese out of my hands till 'most eleven o'clock. I guess it's first-rate, Diana; we'll try a bit this noon. Who's that stoppin'?—Will Flandin, if I see straight; that's thoughtful of him; now he'll take you to church, Di.'

Will he? thought Diana. Flandin came in. Dressed in his Sunday best he always seemed to Diana specially lumbering and awkward; and to-day his hair was massed into smoothness by means of I know not what bountiful lubrication, which looked very greasy and smelt very strong of cloves. His necktie was blue with yellow spots; about the right thing, Will thought; it was strange what a disgust it gave Diana. What's in a necktie?

'Goin' to snow, Will?' asked Mrs. Starling.

'Wall—guess likely. Not jes' yet, though.'

'Your mother got through with her pork?'

'Wall—I guess not. Seems to me, ef she was through, there wouldn't be so many pickle tubs round.'

'Good weight?'

'Wall—fair.'

'Ourn's better than that. Tell yeu what, Will, your pigs don't get the sunshine enough.'

'Don't reckon they know the difference,' said Will, smiling and glancing over towards Diana; but Diana was gone. 'Were you calculatin' to go to meetin' to-day, Mis' Starling?'

'Guess not to-day, Will. I'm gettin' too old to work seven days in a week—in pork-killin' time, anyhow. I'm calculatin' to stay at home. Diana's always for goin', though; she's gone to get ready, I guess. She ain't tired.'

Silence. Diana's room was too far off for them to hear her moving about, and Mrs. Starling sat down and stretched out her feet towards the fire. Both parties meditating.

'You and she hain't come to any understanding yet?' the lady began. Will shifted his position uneasily, and spoke not.

'I wouldn't wait *too* long, if I was you. She might take a notion to somebody else, you know, and then you and me'd be nowhere.'

'Has she, Mis' Starling?' Will asked, terrified.

'She hain't told *me* nothing of it, if she has; and I hain't seen her look sweet on anybody; but she might, you know, Will, if anybody came along that she fancied. I always like to get the halter over my horse's head, and then I know I've got him.'

The image suggested nothing but difficulty to Will's imagination. A halter over Diana's stately neck!

'I allays catch a horse by cornerin' him,' he said sheepishly, and again moving restlessly in his chair.

'That won't answer in this chase,' said Mrs. Starling. 'Diana 'll walk up to you of your own accord, if she comes at all; but you must hold out your hand, Will.'

'Ain't I a-doin' that all the while, Mis' Starling?' said Will, whom every one of his friend's utterances seemed to put farther and farther away from his goal.

'I reckon she'll come, all right,' said Mrs. Starling reassuringly; 'but, you know, girls ain't obliged to see anybody's hand till they have to. You all like 'em better for bein' skittish. I don't. She ain't skittish with me, neither; and she won't be with you, when you've caught her once. Take your time, only I wouldn't be *too* long about it, as I said.'

Poor Will! The sweat stood upon his brow with the prospect of what was before him, perhaps that very day; for what time could be better for 'holding out his hand' to Diana than a solitary sleigh ride? Then, if he held out his hand and she wouldn't see it!

Meanwhile.—Diana had, as stated, left the kitchen, and mounted the stairs with a peculiarly quick, light tread which meant business; for the fact was that she did discern the holding out of Will's hand, and was taking a sudden sheer. Nothing but the sheer was quite distinct to her mind as she set her foot upon the stair; but before she reached the top landing-place, she knew what she would do. Her mother was not going to church; Will Flandin was; and the plan, she saw, was fixed, that he should drive herself. Her mother would oblige her to go; or else, if she made a determined stand, Will on the other hand would not go; and she would have to endure him, platitudes, blue necktie, cloves, and all, for the remainder of the morning. Only one escape was left her. With the swiftness and accuracy of movement which is possible in a moment of excitement to senses and faculties habitually deft and true, Diana changed her dress, put on the grey, thick, coarse wrappings which were very necessary for any one going sleigh-riding in Pleasant Valley, took her hood in her hand, and slipped down the stairs as noiselessly as she had gone up. It was not needful that she should go through the kitchen, where her mother and her visitor were; there was a side door, happily; and without being seen or heard, Diana reached the barn.

The rest was easy. Prince was fast by his halter, instead of wandering at will over the sunny meadow; and without any delay or difficulty, Diana got his harness on and hitched him to the small cutter which was wont to convey herself and her mother to church and wherever else they wanted to go in winter time. Only Diana carefully took the precaution to remove the sleigh bells from the rest of Prince's harness; then she led him out of the barn where she had harnessed him, closed the barn doors securely, remembering how they had been left on another occasion, mounted, and drove slowly away. It had been a dreamy piece of work to her; for it had so fallen out that she had never once harnessed Prince again since that June day, when she, indeed, did not harness him, but had been about it, when somebody else had taken the work out of her hand. It was very bitter to Diana to handle the bridle and the traces that *he* had handled that day; she did it with fingers that seemed to sting with pain at every touch; her brain got into a whirl; and when she finally drove off, it was rather instinctively that she went slowly and made no sound, for Will and his hopes and his wooing and his presence had faded out of her imagination. She went slowly, until she, also instinctively, knew that she was safe, and then still she went slowly. Prince chose his own gait. Diana, with the reins slack in her hand, sat still and thought. There was no need for hurry; it was not near church time, not yet even church-going time; Will would be quiet for a while yet, before it would be necessary to make any hue-and-cry after the runaway; and she and Prince would be far beyond ken by that time. And meanwhile there was something soothing in the mere being alone under the wide grey sky. Nobody to watch her, nothing to exert herself about; for a few moments in her life, Diana could be still and drift.

Whither? She was beginning to feel that the chafing of home, her mother's driving and Will's courting, were becoming intolerable. Heart and brain were strained and sore; if she could be still till she died, Diana felt it to be the utmost limit of desirableness. She knew she was not likely to die soon; brain and nerve might be strained, but they were sound and whole; the whole capacity for suffering, the unimpaired energy for doing, were hers yet. And stillness was not likely to be granted her. It was inexpressibly suitable to Diana's mood

to sit quiet in the sleigh and let Prince walk, and feel alone, and
know that no one could disturb her. A few small flakes of snow
were beginning to flit aimlessly about; their soft, wavering
motion suggested nothing ruder than that same purposeless drift
towards which Diana's whole soul was going out in yearning.
If she had been in a German fairy tale, the snow-flakes would
have seemed to her spirits of peace. She welcomed them. She
put out her hand and caught two or three, and then brought
them close to look at them. The little fair crystals lay still
on her glove; it was too cold for them to melt. O to be like
that!—thought Diana,—cold and alone! But she was in no
wise like that, but a living human creature, warm at heart
and quick in brain; in the midst of humanity, obliged to fight
out or watch through the life-battle, and take blows and wounds
as they came. Ah, she would not have minded the blows or
the wounds; she would have girded herself joyfully for the
struggle, were it twice as long or hard; but now,—there was
nothing left to fight for. The fight looked dreary. She longed
to creep into a corner, under some cover, and get rid of it all.
No cover was in sight. Diana knew, with the subtle instinct
of power, that she was one of those who must stand in the
front ranks and take the responsibility of her own and probably
of others' destinies. She could not creep into a corner and be
still; there was work to do. And Diana never shirked work.
Vaguely, even now, as Prince walked along and she was
revelling, so to speak, in the loveliness and the peace of
momentary immunity, she began to look at the question, how
and where her stand must be and her work be done. Not as
Will Flandin's wife, she thought! No, she could never be
that. But her mother would urge and press it; how much
worry of that sort could she stand, when she was longing for
rest? Would her mother's persistence conquer in the end,
just because her own spirit was gone for contending? No;
never! Not Will Flandin, if she died for it. Anything else.

The truth was, the girl's life-hope was so dead within her,
that for the time she looked upon all things in the universe
through a veil of unreality. What did it matter, one thing or
the other? what did it signify any longer which way she took

through the wilderness of this world? Diana's senses were
benumbed; she no longer recognised the forms of things, nor
their possible hard edges, nor the perspectives of time. Life
seemed unending, long, it is true, to look forward to; but she
saw it, not in perspective, but as if in a nightmare it were all
in mass pressing upon her and taking away her breath. So
what did points here and there amount to? What did it
matter? any more than this snow which was beginning to
come down so fast.

Fast and thick; the aimless scattering crystals, which
had come fluttering about as if uncertain about reaching
earth at all, had given place to a dense, swift, driving
storm. Without much wind perceptible yet, the snowfall
came with a steady straight drift which spoke of an impel-
ling force somewhere, might it be only the weight of the
cloud reservoirs from which it came. It came in a way that
could no longer be ignored. The crystals struck Diana's face
and hands with the force of small missiles. But just now she
had been going through a grey and brown lonely landscape; it
was covered up, and nothing to see but this white downfall.
Even the nearest outlines were hidden; she could barely dis-
tinguish the fences on either hand of her road; nothing further;
trees and hills were all swallowed up, and the road itself was
not discernible at a very few paces' distance. Indeed, it was
not too easy to keep her eyes open to see anything, so beat the
crystals, sharp and fast, into her face. Diana smiled to herself,
to think that she was safe now from even distant pursuit; no
fear that Flandin would by and by come up with her, or even
make his appearance at the church at all that day; the storm
was violent enough to keep any one from venturing out of
doors, or to make any one turn back to his house who had
already left it. Diana had no thought of turning back; the
more impossible the storm made other people's travelling, the
better it was for hers. Prince knew the way well enough, and
could go to church like a Christian; she left the way to him,
and enjoyed the strange joy of being alone, beyond vision or
pursuit, set aside as it were from her life and life surroundings
for a time. What did she care how hard the storm beat? To

the rough treatment of life this was as the touch of a soft feather. Diana welcomed it; loved the storm; bent her head to shield her from the blast of it, and went on. The wind began to make itself known as one of the forces abroad, but she did not mind that either. Gusts came by turns, sweeping the snow in what seemed a solid mass upon her shoulder and side face; and then, in a little time more, there was no question of gusts, but a steady wild fury which knew no intermission. The storm grew tremendous, and everybody in Pleasant Valley was well aware that such storms in those regions did not go as soon as they came. Diana herself began to feel glad that she must be near her stopping-place. No landmarks whatever were visible, but she thought she had been travelling long enough, even at Prince's slow rate, to put most of the three miles behind her; and she grew a little afraid lest in the white darkness she might miss the little church; once past it, though never so little, and looking back would be in vain. It was a question if she would not pass it even with her best endeavour. In her preoccupation it had never once occurred to Diana to speculate on what she would find at the church, if she reached it; and now she had but one thought, not to miss reaching it. She had some anxious minutes of watching, for her rate of travelling had been slower than she knew, and there was a good piece of a mile still between her and the place when she began to look for it. Now she eyed with greatest care the road and the fences, when she could see the latter; and indeed it is poetical to speak of her seeing the road, for the tracks were all covered up. But at last Diana recognised a break in the fence at her left; checked Prince, turned his head carefully in that direction, found he seemed to think it all right, and presently saw just before her the long low shed in which the country people were wont to tie their horses for the time of divine service. Prince went straight to his accustomed place.

Diana got out. There was no need to tie Prince to-day. The usual equine sense of expediency would be quite sufficient to keep any horse under cover. She left the sleigh, and groped her way—truly it was not easy to keep on her feet, the wind blew so—till she saw the little white church just before her.

There was not a foot-track on the snow which covered the steps leading to the door. But the wind and the snow would cover up or blow away any such tracks in very short time, she reflected ;—yet,—what if the door were locked and nobody there! One moment her heart stood still. No; things were better than that; the door yielded to her hand. Diana went in, welcomed by the warm atmosphere, which contrasted so pleasantly with the wind and the snow-flakes, shut the door, shook herself, and opened one of the inner doors which led into the audience room of the building.

CHAPTER XIX.

OUT OF HUMDRUM.

WARM, how good and warm! but empty. Perfectly empty. Perfectly still. Empty pews, and empty pulpit; nobody, not a head visible anywhere. Not a breath to be heard. The place was awful; it was like the ghost of a church; all the life out of it. But how, then, came it to be warm? Somebody must have made the fires; where was somebody gone? And had none of all the congregation come to church that day? was it too bad for everybody? Diana began to wake up to facts, as she heard the blast drive against the windows, and listened to the swirl of it round the house. And how was she going to get home, if it was so bad as that? At any rate, here was still solitude and quiet and freedom; she could get warm and enjoy it for awhile, and let Prince rest; she would not be in a hurry. She turned to go to one of the corners of the room, where the stoves were screened off by high screens in the interest of the neighbouring pews; and then, just at the corner of the screen, from where he had been watching her, she saw Mr. Masters. Diana did not know whether to be sorry or glad. On the whole, she rather thought she was glad; the church was eerie all alone.

'Mr. Masters!—I thought nobody was here.'

'I thought nobody was going to be here. Good morning! Who else is coming?'

'Who else? Nobody, I guess.'

'How am I to understand that?'

'Just so,'—said Diana, coming up to the stove and putting her fingers out towards the warmth.

'Where is the other half of your family?'

189

'I left mother at home.'

'You came alone?'

'Yes, I came alone.' Diana began to wonder a little at the situation in which she found herself, and to revolve in her mind how she could make use of it.

'Miss Diana, you have dared what no one else has dared.'

'It was not daring,' said the girl. 'I did not think much of the storm, till I was so far on the way that it was as easy to come on as to go back.'

A light rejoinder, which would have been given to anybody else, was checked on Mr. Masters' lips by the abstracted, apart air with which these words were spoken. He gave one or two inquisitive glances at the speaker, and was silent. Diana roused herself.

'Has nobody at all come to church?'

'Nobody but Mr. St. Clair'—(he was the old sexton.) 'And he has such a bad cold that I took pity on him and sent him home. I promised him I would shut up the church for him— when it was necessary to leave it. *He* was in no condition to be preached to.'

He half expected Diana would propose the shutting up of the church at once, and the ensuing return home of the two people there; but instead of that, she drew up a stool and sat down.

'You will not be able to preach to-day,' she remarked.

'Not to much of a congregation,' said the minister. 'I will do my best with what I have.'

'Are you going to preach to me?' said Diana, with a ghost of a smile.

'If you demand it! You have an undoubted right.'

Diana sat silent. The warmth of the room was very pleasant. Also the security. Not from the storm, which howled and dashed upon the windows and raged round the building and the world generally; but from that other storm and whirl of life. Diana did not want just yet to be at home. Furthermore, she had a dim notion of using her opportunity. She thought how she could do it; and the minister, standing by, watched her, with some secret anxiety but an extremely calm exterior.

'You must give me the text, Miss Diana,' he ventured presently.

Diana sat still, musing. 'Mr. Masters,' she said at last, very slowly, in order that the composure of it might be perfect,— 'will you tell me what is the good of life?'

'To yourself, you mean?'

'Yes. For me—or for anybody.'

'I should say briefly, that God makes all His creatures to be happy.'

'Happy!' echoed Diana, with more sharpness of accent than she knew.

'Yes.'

'But, Mr. Masters, suppose—suppose that is impossible?'

'It never is impossible.'

'That sounds—like—mockery,' said Diana. 'Only you never do say mocking things.'

'I do not about this.'

'But, Mr. Masters!—surely there are a great many people in the world that are not happy?'

'A sorrowful truth. How comes Diana Starling to be one of them?'

And saying this, the minister himself drew up a chair and sat down. The question was daring, but the whole way and manner of the man were so quiet and gentle, so sympathizing and firm at once, that it would have lured a bird off its nest; much more the brooding reserve from a heart it is not nursing but killing. Diana looked at him, met the wise, kind, grave eye she had learned long ago to trust,—and broke down. All of a sudden; she had not dreamed she was in any danger; she was as much surprised as he was; but that helped nothing. Diana buried her face in her hands and burst into tears.

He looked very much concerned. Wisely, however, he kept perfectly quiet and let the storm pass; the little inner storm which caused the outer violence of winds and clouds to be for the time forgotten. Diana sobbed bitterly. When after a few minutes she checked herself, the minister went off and brought her a glass of water. Diana lifted her flushed face and drank it, making no word of excuse or apology. As he took the glass back, Mr. Masters spoke in the tone of mixed sympathy and authority—it was a winning kind of authority—which was peculiar to him.

'Now, Miss Diana, what is it?'

But there was a long pause. Diana was regaining self-command and searching for words. The minister was patient, and waited.

'There seems to be nothing left in life,' she said at last.

'Except duty, you mean?'

'There is enough of that; common sort of duties. But duty is very cold and bare if it is all alone, Mr. Masters.'

'Undoubtedly true. But who has told you that your life must be filled with only common sorts of duties?'

'It has nothing else,' said Diana despondently. 'And I look forward and see nothing else. And when I think of living on and on so—my brain almost turns, and I wonder why I was made.'

'Not to live so. Our Maker meant none of us to live a humdrum life; don't you know, we were intended for "glory, honour, and immortality"?'

'How can one get out of humdrum?' Diana asked disconsolately.

'By living to God.'

'I don't understand you.'

'You understand how a woman can live to a beloved human creature, doing everything in the thought and the joy of her affection.'

Was he probing her secret? Diana's breath came short; she sat with eyes cast down and a feeling of oppression; growing pale with her pain. But she said, 'Well?'

'Let it be God, instead of a fellow-creature. Your life will have no humdrum then.'

'But—one can only love what one knows,' said Diana, speaking carefully.

'Precisely. And the Bible cry to men is, that they would "know the Lord." For want of that knowledge, all goes wild.'

'Do you mean that that will take the place of everything

else?' said Diana, lifting her weary eyes to him. They were strong, beautiful eyes too, but the light of hope was gone, and all sparkle of pleasure, out of them. The look struck to the minister's heart. He answered, however, with no change of tone.

'I mean, that it more than takes the place of everything else.'

'Not replace what is lost,' said Diana sadly.

'More than replace it, even when one has lost all.'

'That can't be!—that must be impossible, sometimes,' said Diana. 'I don't believe you know.'

'Yes, I do,' said the minister gravely.

'People would not be human.'

'Very human—tenderly human. Do you really think, Miss Diana, that he who made our hearts, made them larger than he himself can fill?'

Diana sat silent a while, and the minister stood considering her; his heart strained with sympathy and longing to give her help, and at the same time doubting how far he might or dared venture. Diana on her part fearing to show too much, but remembering also that this chance might never repeat itself. The fear of losing it began to overtop all other fears. So she began again.

'But, Mr. Masters—this, that you speak of—I haven't got it; and I don't understand it. What shall I do?'

'Get it.'

'How?'

'Seek it in the appointed way.'

'What is that?'

'Jesus said, " He that hath my commandments and keepeth them, he it is that loveth me; and he that loveth me shall be loved of my Father; and I will love him, and *will manifest myself to him.*"'

'But I do not love him.'

'Then pray as Moses prayed,—"I beseech thee, show me thy glory."'

Diana's head sank a little. 'I have no heart to *give* to anything!' she confessed.

N

'What has become of it?' asked the minister daringly.

'Don't people sometimes lose heart without any particular reason?'

'No; never.'

'I have reason, though,' said Diana.

'I see that.'

'You do not know—?' said Diana, facing him with a startled movement.

'No. I know nothing, Miss Diana. I guess.'

She sat with her face turned from him for a while; then, perhaps reminded by the blast of wind and snow which at the moment came round the house furiously and beat on the windows, she went on hastily:

'You wonder to see me here; but I ran away from home, and I can't bear to go back.'

'Why?'

'Mr. Masters, mother wants me to'—Diana hesitated— 'marry a rich man.'

The minister was silent.

'He is there all the while—I mean, very often; he has not spoken out yet, but mother has; and she favours him all she can.'

'You do not?'

'I wish I could never see him again!' sighed Diana.

'You can send him away, I should think.'

'I can't, till he asks my leave to stay. And I am so tired. He came to take me to church this morning; and I ran away before it was time to go.'

'You cannot be disposed of against your will, Miss Diana.'

'I seem to have so little will now. Sometimes I am almost ready to be afraid mother and he together will tire me out. Nothing seems to matter any more.'

'That would be a great mistake.'

'Yes!'—said Diana, getting up from her chair and looking out towards the storm with a despairing face;—'people make mistakes sometimes. Mr. Masters, you must think me very strange—but I trust you—and I wanted help so much'—

'And I have not given you any.'

'You would if you could.'

'And I will if I can. I have thought of more than I have spoken. When can I see you again, to consult further? It must be alone.'

'I don't know. This is my chance. Tell me now. What have you thought of?'

'I never speak about business on Sunday,' said the minister, meeting Diana's frank eyes with a slight smile which was very far from merriment.

'Is this business?'

'Partly of that character.'.

'I don't know, then,' said Diana. 'We must take our chance. Thank you, Mr. Masters.'

'May I ask what for?'

'For your kindness.'

'I should like to be kind to you,' said he. 'Now the present practical question, which cannot be put off, Miss Diana, is—how are you going to get home?'

'And you?'

'That is a secondary matter, and easily disposed of. I live comparatively near by. It is out of the question that you should drive three miles in this storm.'

Both stood and listened to the blast for a few minutes. There was no denying the truth of his words. In fact, it would be a doubtful thing for a strong man to venture himself and his beast out in the fury of the whirling wind and snow; for a woman, it was not to be thought of. Mr. Masters considered. For him to take Diana, supposing the storm would let him, to the house of some near neighbour, would be awkward enough, and give rise to endless and boundless town talk. To carry her home, three miles, was, as he had said, out of the question. To wait, both of them, in the church, for the storm's abating, was again not a desirable measure, and would furnish even richer food for the tongues of the parish than the other alternatives would. To leave her, or for her to leave him, were alike impossible. Mr. Masters was not a man who usually hesitated long about any course of action, but he was puzzled to-day. He walked up and down in one of the aisles,

thinking; while Diana resumed her seat by the stove. Her
simplicity and independence of character did not allow her to
greatly care about the matter; though she, too, knew very well
what disagreeable things would be said, at home and elsewhere, and what a handle would be made of the affair, both
against her and against the minister. For his sake, she was
sorry; for herself, what did anything much matter? This
storm was an exceptional one; such as comes once in a year
perhaps, or perhaps not in several years. The wind had risen
to a tempest; the snow drove thick before it, whirling in the
eddies of the gust, so as to come in every possible direction,
and seemingly caught up again before it could reach a resting-
place. The fury of its assault upon the church windows made
one thing at least certain; it would be a mad proceeding now
to venture out into it, for a woman or a man either. And it
was very cold; though happily the stoves had been so
effectually fired up, that the little meeting-house was still
quite comfortable. Yet the minister walked and walked.
Diana almost forgot him; she sat lost in her own thoughts.
The lull was soothing. The solitude was comforting. The
storm, which put a barrier between her and all the rest of the
world, was a temporary friend. Diana could find it in her
heart to wish it were more than temporary. To be out
of the old grooves of pain is something, until the new
ones are worn. To forsake scenes and surroundings which
know all our secrets is sometimes to escape beneficially their
persistent reminders of everything one would like to forget.
Diana felt like a child that has run away from school, and so
for the present got rid of its lessons; and sat in a quiet sort
of dull content, listening now and then to the roar of the blast,
and hugging herself that she had run away in time. Half an
hour more, and it would have been too late, and Will and her
mother would have been her companions for all day. How
about to-morrow? Diana shuddered. And how about all the
to-morrows that stretched along in dreary perspective before
her? Would they also, all of them, hold nothing but those
same two persons? Nothing but an endless vista of butter-
making and pork-killing on one hand, and hair-oil scented with

"'Well! said the voice of the minister suddenly beside her, 'what do you think of the prospect?'"

Page 197.

cloves on the other? It would be better far to die, if she could die; but Diana knew she could not.

'Well!' said the voice of the minister suddenly beside her, 'what do you think of the prospect?'

Diana's eyes, as they were lifted to his face, were full of so blank a life-prospect, that his own face changed, and a cloud came over its brightness.

'We can't get away,' he said. 'Not at present, unless we were gulls; and gulls never fly in these regions. Do you mind waiting?'

'I do not mind it at all,' said Diana; 'except for you. I am sorry for you to have to stay here with me.'

'There isn't anybody I would rather stay with,' said the minister, half humorously. 'Now, can you return the compliment?'

'Yes indeed!' said Diana earnestly. 'There isn't anybody else I would half as lieve stay with.'

'Apparently you have some confidence in me?' he said in the same tone.

'I have confidence in nobody else,' said Diana sadly. 'I know you would help me if you could.'

They were silent a few minutes after that, and when Mr. Masters began to speak again, it was in a different tone; a gentle, grave tone of business.

'I have been doing some hard thinking,' he said, 'while I have been walking yonder; and I have come to the conclusion that the present is an exceptional case and an exceptional time. Ordinarily I do not let business—private business—come into Sunday. But we are brought here together, and detained here, and I have come to the conclusion that this is the business I ought to do. I have only one parishioner on my hands to-day,' he went on with a slight smile, 'and I may as well attend to her. I am going to tell you my plan. I shall not startle you? Just now you allowed that you had confidence in me?'

'Yes. I will try to do whatever you say I ought to do.'

'That I cannot tell,' said he gravely, 'but I will unfold to you my plan. You have trust in me. So have I in you, Diana; but I have more. So much more, that it would make me

happy to go through my life with you.   I know,'—he said as
he met her startled look up to him,—' I know you do not love
me, I know that; but you trust me; and I have love enough
for two.   That has been true a great while.   Suppose you
come to me and let me take care of you.   Can you trust me to
that extent?'

Diana's lips had grown white with fear and astonishment.
' You do not know!'—she gasped.   But his answer was steady
and sweet.

' I think I do.'

' All?'

' All I need to know.'

'It would be very, very wrong to you, Mr. Masters!' said
Diana, hiding her face.

'No,' he answered in the same gentle way.   'To give me
what I long for?'

' But—but—I have *nothing* to give in return,' she said,
answering not the form of his words, but the reality under
them.

' I will take my risk of that.   I told you, I have enough for
both.   And I might add, to last out our lives.   I only want to
have the privilege of taking care of you.'

'My heart is dead!'—cried Diana piteously.

'Mine isn't.   And yours is not.   It is only sick, but not
unto death; and I want to shelter and nurse it to health again.
May I?'

'You cannot,' said Diana.   'I am not worth anybody's
looking at any more.   There is no life left in me.   I am not
good enough for you, Mr. Masters.   You ought to have a whole
heart, and a large one, in return for your own.'

' I do not want any return,' said he.   'Not at present,
beyond that trust which you so kindly have given me.   And
if I never have any more, I will be content, Diana, to be
allowed to do all the giving myself.   You must spend your
life somewhere.   Can you spend it anywhere better than at
my side?'

' No,'—Diana breathed rather than spoke.

'Then it's a bargain?' said he, taking her hand.   Diana did not withdraw it, and stooping down he touched his lips gently to hers. This was so unlike one of Evan's kisses, that it did not even remind Diana of them. She sat dazed and stunned, hardly knowing how she felt, only bewildered; yet dimly conscious that she was offered a shelter, and a lot which, if she had never known Evan, she would have esteemed the highest possible. An empty lot now, as any one must be; an unequal exchange for Mr. Masters; an unfair transaction; at the same time, for her, a hiding-place from the world's buffetings. She would escape so from her mother's exactions and rule; from young Flandin's following and pretensions; from the pointed finger of gossip. True, that finger had never been levelled at her, not yet; but every one who has a secret sore spot knows the dread of its being discovered and touched. And Diana had never been wont to mind her mother's exactions, or to rebel against her rule; but lately, for a year past, without knowing or guessing the wrong of which her mother had been guilty, Diana had been conscious of an underlying want of harmony somewhere. She did not know where it was; it was in the air; for nature's subtle sympathies find their way and know their ground far beyond the sphere of sense or reason. Something adverse and something sinister she had vaguely felt in her mother's manner, without having the least clue to any possible cause or motive. Suspicion was the last thing to occur to Diana's nature; so she suspected nothing; nevertheless felt the grating and now and then the jar of their two spirits one against the other. It was dimly connected with Evan, too, in her mind, without knowing why; she thought, blaming herself for the thought, that Mrs. Starling would not have been so determinately eager to get her married to Will Flandin if Evan Knowlton had never been thought to fancy her. This was a perfectly unreasoning conclusion in Diana's mind; she could give no account of it; but as little could she get rid of it; and it made her mother's ways lately hard to bear. The minister, she knew instinctively, would not let a rough wind blow on her face; at his side neither criticism nor any sort of human annoyance could reach her; she would have only her own deep heart-sorrow to bear on to the end. But what sort of justice was this towards him? Diana lifted her head, which had been sunk in musing, and looked round. She had heard nothing for a while; now the swirl and rush of the storm were the first thing that struck her senses; and the first thought, that no getting away was possible yet; then she glanced at Mr. Masters. He was there near her, just as usual, looking at her quietly.

'Mr. Masters,' she burst forth, 'you are very good!'

'That is right,' he said, with a sort of dry comicality which belonged to him. 'I hope you will never change your opinion.'

'But,' said Diana, withdrawing her eyes in some confusion, 'I think I am not. I think I am doing wrong.'

'In what?'

'In letting you say what you said a little while ago. You have a heart, and a big one. I have not any heart at all. I can't give you what you would give me; I haven't got it to give. I never shall have anything to give.'

'The case being so as you put it,' said the minister quite quietly, 'what then? You cannot change the facts. I cannot take back what I have given; it was given long ago, Diana, and remains yours. The least you can do, is to let me have what is left of you and take care of it. While I live I will do that, and ask no reward.'

'You will get tired of it,' said Diana, with her lip trembling.

'Will I?' said he, taking her hand. And he added no more, but through the gentle, almost careless intonation, Diana felt and knew the very truth, that he never would. She left her hand in his clasp; that too was gentle and firm, like the man; he seemed a tower of strength to Diana. If only she could have loved him! Yet she thought she was glad that he loved her. He was something to lean upon; some one who would be able to give help. They sat so, hand in hand, for a while, the storm roaring against the windows and howling round the building.

'Don't you think,' the minister began again with a tender, light accent, 'it will be part of my permanent duty to preach to you?'

'I dare say; I am sure I want it enough,' said Diana.

'Is not this a good opportunity?'

'I suppose it is. We cannot get away.'

'Never mind; the wind will go down by and by. It has been blowing on purpose to keep us here. Diana, do you think a good God made any of his creatures to be unhappy?'

'I don't know, Mr. Masters. He lets them be unhappy.'

'It is not his will.'

'But he takes away what would make them happy?'

'What do you think would do that?'

'I suppose it is one thing with one person, and another with another.'

'True; but take an instance.'

'It is mother's happiness to have her farm and her dairy and her house go just right.'

'Is she happy if it does?'

'She is very uncomfortable if it don't.'

'That is not my question,' said the minister, smiling. 'Happiness is not a thing that comes and goes with the weather, or the crops, or the state of the market;—nor even with the life and death and affection of those we love.'

'I thought it did'— said Diana rather faintly.

'In that case it would be a changeable, insecure thing; and being that, it would cease to be happiness.'

'Yes. I thought human happiness was changeable and uncertain.'

'Do you not feel that such conditions would spoil it? No; God loves us better than that.'

'But, Mr. Masters,' said Diana in some surprise, 'nobody in this world can be sure of keeping what he likes?'

'Except one thing.'

'What can that be?'

'Did you never see anybody who was happy independent of circumstances?'

Diana reflected. 'I think Mother Bartlett is.'

'I think so too.'

'But she is the only person of whom that is true in all Pleasant Valley.'

'How comes she to be an exception?'

Diana reflected again, but this time without finding an answer.

'Isn't it, that she has set her heart on what cannot fail her nor be insufficient for her?'

'Religion, you mean?'

'I do not mean religion.'

'What then?' Diana asked in new surprise.

'I mean—Christ.'

'But—isn't that the same thing?'

'Not exactly.   Christ is a person.'

'Yes—but'—

'And *he* it is that can make happy those who know him. Do you remember he said, "He that cometh to me shall never hunger, and he that believeth on me shall never thirst"?'

Looking up at the speaker and following his words, they somehow struck Diana rather hard. Her lips suddenly trembled, and she looked down.

'You do not understand it,' said the minister, 'but you must believe it.   Poor hungry lamb, seeking pasture where there is none,—where it is withered,—come to Christ!'

'Do you mean,' said Diana, struggling for voice and self-command, but unable to look up, for the minister's hand was on her shoulder and his words had been very tenderly spoken,—'do you mean, that when everything *is* withered, he can make it green again?'

The minister answered in the words of David, which were the words of the Lord: ' "He shall be as the light of the morning, when the sun riseth, even a morning without clouds ; as the tender grass springeth out of the earth by clear shining after rain." '

Diana bent her head lower.   Could such refreshment and renewal of her own wasted nature ever come to pass?   She did not believe it; yet perhaps there was life yet at the roots of the grass which scented the rain.   The words swept over her as the breath of the south wind.

' "The light of a morning without clouds" '—she repeated when she could speak.

'Christ is all that, to those who know him,' the minister said.

'Then I do not know him,' said Diana.

'Did you think you did?'

'But how *can* one know him, Mr. Masters?'

'There is only one way. It is said, "God, who created the light out of darkness, hath *shined in our hearts*, to give the light of the glory of the knowledge of Christ."'

'How?'

'I cannot tell. As the sun rises over the hills, and suddenly the gold of it is upon everything, and the warmth of it.'

'When?'

'I don't know that either,' said Mr. Masters, gently touching Diana's brow, as one touches a child's, with caressing fingers. '*He* says: "Ye shall find me when ye shall search for me with all your heart."—"If thou criest after knowledge, and liftest up thy voice for understanding; if thou seekest her as silver, and searchest for her as for hid treasures; then shalt thou understand the fear of the Lord, and *find the knowledge of God*."'

Diana sat still awhile and neither of them spoke; then she said, speaking more lightly:

'I think you have preached a beautiful sermon, Mr. Masters.'

'It's a beautiful sermon,' assented the minister; 'but how much effect will it have?'

'I don't know,' said Diana. 'I don't seem to have energy enough to take hold of anything.' Then after a little she added—'But if anybody can help me, I am sure it is you.'

'We will stand by one another, then,' said he, 'and do the best we can.'

Diana did not make any denial of this conclusion; and they sat still without more words, for some time, each busied with his own separate train of musings. Then Diana felt a little shiver of cold beginning to creep over her; and Mr. Masters roused himself.

'This is getting serious!' said he, looking at his watch. 'What o'clock do you think it is? One, and after. Am I to make up the fires again? We cannot stir at present.'

Neither, it was found, could he make up the fires. For the
coal bin was in the cellar or underground vault, to which the
entrance was from the outside; and looking from the window,
Mr. Masters saw that the snow had drifted on that side to the
height of a man, covering the low door entirely.   Hours of
labour would be required to clear away the snow enough to
give access to the coal; and the minister had not even a
shovel. At the same time, the fires were going down, and the
room was beginning to get chilly under the power of the
searching wind, which found its way in by many entrances.
The only resource was to walk. Mr. Masters gave Diana his
arm, and she accepted it, and together they paced up and down
the aisle. It was a strange walk to Diana; her companion was
rather silent, speaking only a few words now and then; and it
occurred to her to wonder whether this, her first walk with
him, was to be a likeness of the whole; a progress through
chilly and empty space. Diana was not what may be called an
imaginative person, but a thought of this kind came over her.
It did not make her change her mind at all respecting the
agreement she had entered into; if it were to be so, better she
should find herself at his side, she thought, than anywhere else.
She was even glad, in a dull sort of way, that Mr. Masters
should be pleased; pleasure for her was gone out of the world.
Honour him she could, and did, from the bottom of her heart;
but that was all. It was well, perhaps, for her composure that
whatever pleasure her companion might feel in their new relations, he did not make the feeling obtrusively prominent. He
was just his usual self, with a slight confidence in his manner
to her which had not appeared before.

So they walked.

'Diana,' said Mr. Masters suddenly, 'have you brought no
lunch with you?'

'I forgot it. At least,—I was in such a hurry to get out of
the house without being seen, I didn't care about anything
else. If I had gone to the pantry, they would have found out
what I was doing.'

'And I brought nothing to-day, of all days. I am sorry, for
your sake.'

'I don't mind it,' said Diana. 'I don't feel it.'

'Nor I,—but that proves nothing. This won't do. It is two o'clock. We *must* get away. It will be growing dark in a little while more. The days are just at the shortest.'

'I think the storm isn't quite so bad as it was,' said Diana.

They stood still and listened. It beat and blew, and the snow came thick; still the exceeding fury of the blast seemed to be lessened.

'We'll give it a quarter of an hour more,' said the minister. 'Diana—we have had preaching, but we have had no praying.'

She assented submissively, to his look as well as his words, and they knelt down together in the chancel. Mr. Masters prayed, not very long, but a prayer full of the sweetness and the confidence and the strength of a child of God who is at home in his Father's presence; full of tenderness and sympathy for her. Diana's mind went through a series of experiences in the course of that short prayer. The sweetness and the confidence of it touched her first with the sense of contrast, and wrung tears from her that were bitter; then the speaker got beyond her depth, into regions of feeling where she could not follow him nor quite understand, but that, she knew, was only because he was at home where she was so much a stranger; and her thoughts made a leap to the admiration of *him*, and then to the useless consideration, how happy she might have been with this man had not Evan come between. Why had he come, just to win her and prove himself unworthy of her? But it was done, and not to be undone. Evan had her heart, worthy or unworthy; she could not take it back; there was nothing left for her but to be a cold shadow walking beside this good man, who was so full of all gentle and noble affections. Well, she was glad, since he wanted her, that she might lead her colourless existence by his side. That was the last feeling with which she rose from her knees.

CHAPTER XX.

SETTLED.

It was a very wild storm yet through which Mr. Masters drove Diana home. Still the wind blew hard, and the snow came driving and beating down upon their shoulders and faces in thick white masses; and the drifts had piled up in some places very high. More than once the sleigh, Prince and all, was near being lodged in a snow-bank, from which the getting free would have been a work of time; Mr. Masters had to get out and do some rather complicated engineering; and withal, through the thick and heavy snowfall it was difficult to see what they were coming to. Patience and coolness and good driving got the better of dangers, however, and slowly the way was put behind them. They met nobody.

'Mr. Masters,' said Diana suddenly, 'you will have to stay at our house to-night. You can never get back.'

'I don't believe Mrs. Starling will let me go,' said the minister.

Diana did not know exactly how to understand this. It struck a sort of chill to her, that he was intending at once to proclaim their new relations to each other; yet she could find nothing to object, and indeed she did not wish to object.

'Mother will not be pleased,' she ventured after a pause.

'No, I do not expect it. We have got to face that. But she is a wise woman, and will know how to accommodate herself to things when she knows she can't help it. I will put Prince up and give him some supper, and then we will see.'

Diana accordingly went in alone. But, as it happened, Mrs. Starling was busied with some affairs in the outer kitchen; and Diana passed through and got up to her own room without
206

any encounter. She was glad. Encounters were not in her line. She was somewhat leisurely, therefore, in taking off her wrappings and changing her dress. And as the minister was on the other hand as soon done with his ministrations to Prince as circumstances and the snow permitted, it fell out that they re-entered the kitchen almost at the same moment, though by different doors. It was the lean-to kitchen, the only place where fire was kept on Sunday; and indeed that was the usual winter dwelling-room, a little outer kitchen serving for all the dirty work. It was in what I should call dreary Sunday order; which means, order without life. The very chairs and tables seemed to say forlornly that they had nothing to do. Not so much as an open book proclaimed that the mistress of the place was any better off. However, she had other resources; for even as the minister came in from the snow, and Diana from up-stairs, Mrs. Starling herself made her appearance from the outer kitchen with a pan of potatoes in her hand.

Mrs. Starling liked neither to be surprised, nor to seem so. Moreover, from the outer kitchen door she had seen Prince and the sleigh going to the barn, and seen, too, who was driving him. With the cunning of an Indian, she had made a sudden tremendous leap to conclusions; how arrived at, I cannot say; there is a faculty in some natures that is very like a power of intuition. So she came in now with a manner that was undeclarative of anything but grimness; gave no sign of either surprise or curiosity; vouchsafed the minister only a scant little nod of welcome, and to Diana scarce a look; and set her pan of potatoes on the table, while she went into the pantry for a knife.

'Do you want those peeled, mother?' Diana asked.

'Must have something for supper, I suppose.'

'Shall I do it?'

'No. I guess you've done enough for one day.'

'*I* have,' said Mr. Masters. 'And if you had driven these three miles in the snow, you would know it. May I have some supper, Mrs. Starling?'

'There'll be enough, I guess,' said the mistress of the house,

with her knife flying round the potato in hand in a way that
showed both practice and energy. Then presently, with a
scarce perceptible glance up at her daughter, she added,

'Where have you been?'

'To church, mother.'

'To church!'—scornfully. 'What did you do there?'

'She heard preaching,' said the minister, in that very quiet
and composed way of his, which it was difficult to fight
against. Few people ever tried; if any one could, it was Mrs.
Starling.

'I guess there warn't many that had the privilege?' she said
inquiringly.

'Not many,' said the minister. 'I never had a smaller
audience—in church—to preach to.'

'Folks had better be at home such a day, and preach to
themselves.'

'I quite agree with you. So I brought Diana back as soon
as I could. But we have been two hours on the way.'

Mrs. Starling's knife flew round the potatoes; her tongue
was silent. Diana began to set the table. Sitting by the
corner of the fire to dry the wet spots on his clothes, the
minister watched her. And Mrs. Starling, without looking,
watched them both; and at last, having finished her potatoes,
seized the dish and went off with it; no doubt to cook the
supper, for savoury fumes soon came stealing in. Diana made
coffee, not without a strange back look to a certain stormy
September night when she had made it for some one else.
It was December now—a December which no spring would
follow; so what mattered anything, coffee or the rest? If
there were any blessing left for her in the world, she believed
it would be under Mr. Masters' protection and in his goodness. She felt dull and in a dream, but she believed that.

The three had supper alone. Conversation, as far as Mrs.
Starling was concerned, went on the pattern that has been
given. Mr. Masters was at the whole expense of the entertainment, mentally; and he talked with the ease and pleasant-
ness that seemed natural to him, of things that could not help
interesting the others; even Diana in her deadness of heart,

even Mrs. Starling in her perversity, pricked up their ears and listened. I don't believe, either, he even found it a difficult effort; nothing ever seemed difficult to Mr. Masters that he had to do; it was always done so graciously, and as if he were enjoying it himself. So no doubt he was. Certainly this evening; though Mrs. Starling did not speak many words, and Diana spoke none. So supper was finished, and the mistress and her guest moved their chairs to the fire, while Diana busied herself in putting up the things, going in and out from the pantry.

'You'll have to keep me to-night, Mrs. Starling,' said the minister.

'I knew that when I saw you come in,' responded the lady, not over graciously.

'I am not going to receive hospitality under false pretences, though,' said the minister. 'If I rob, I won't steal. Mrs. Starling, Diana and I have come to an agreement.'

'I knew that too,' returned the lady defiantly.

'According to which agreement,' pursued the other, without change of a hair, 'I am coming again, some other time, to take her away, out of your care into mine.'

'There go two words to that bargain,' said Mrs. Starling, after a half-minute's pause.

'Two words have been spoken; mine and hers. Now we want yours.'

'Diana's got to take care of me.'

'Does that mean that she is never to marry?'

'It don't mean anything ridiculous,' said Mrs. Starling; 'so it don't mean that.'

'I should not like to say anything ridiculous. Then, if she may marry, it only remains that she and you should be suited. Do you object to me as a son-in-law?'

It is impossible to convey the impression of the manner, winning, half humorous, half dry, supremely careless and confident, in which all this was said on the minister's part. It was something almost impossible at the moment to withstand, and it fidgeted Mrs. Starling to be under the power of it. Her grudge against the minister was even increased by it, and yet she could not give vent to the feeling.

O

'I'm not called upon to make objections against you in any way,' she answered rather vaguely.

'That means, of course, that you have no objections to make?'

'I don't make any,' said Mrs. Starling shortly.

'I must be content with that,' said Mr. Masters, smiling. 'Diana, your mother makes no objection.' And rising, he went and gravely kissed her.

I do not know what tied Mrs. Starling's tongue. She sat before the fire with her hands in her lap, in an inward fury of dull displeasure; she had untold objections to this arrangement; and yet, though she knew she must speak now or never, she could not speak. Whether it were the spell of the minister's manner, which, as I said, worked its charm upon her as it did upon others; whether it were the prick of conscience, warning her that she had interfered once too often already in her daughter's life affairs; or whether, finally, she had an instinctive sense that things were gone too far for her hindering hand, she fumed in secret, and did nothing. She was a woman of sense; she knew that if a man like Mr. Masters loved her daughter, and had got her daughter's good-will, it would be an ill waste of strength on her part to try to break the arrangement. It might be done; but it would not be worth the scandal and the confusion. And she was not sure that it could be done.

So she sat chewing the cud of her mortification and ire, giving little heed to what words passed between the others. It had come to this! She had schemed, she had put a violent hand upon Diana's fate, to turn it her own way, and now *this* was the way it had gone! All her wrong deeds for nothing! She had purposed, as she said, that Diana should take care of her; therefore Diana should not marry any poor and proud young officer, nor any officer at all, to carry her away beyond reach and into a sphere beyond and above the sphere of her mother. No, Diana must marry a rich young farmer; Will Flandin would just do; a man who would not dislike or be anywise averse to receive such a mother-in-law into his house, but reckon it an added advantage. Then her home would be

secure, and her continued rule; and ruling was as necessary to
Mrs. Starling as eating. She would have a larger house and
business to manage, and withal need not do herself more than
she chose; having Diana, she would be sure of everything else
she wanted. Now she had lost Diana. And only to a poor
parson when all was done! Would it have been better to let
her marry the officer? For Mrs. Starling had a shrewd guess
that such would have been the issue of things if she had let
them alone. Diana could not so have been more out of her
power or out of her sphere; for Mrs. Starling had a certain
assured consciousness that she would not 'fit' in the minister's
family, and that, gentle as he was, he would rule his house and
his wife himself. She sat brooding, hardly hearing what was
said by either of the others; and indeed, the discourse was not
very lively; till Mr. Masters rose and bade them good night.
And then Mrs. Starling still went on musing. Why had she
not interfered at the right moment, to put a stop to this affair?
She had let the moment go, and the thought vexed her; and
her mood was not at all sweetened by the lurking doubt
whether she could have stopped it if she had tried. Mrs.
Starling could not abide to meet with her match, and sorely
hated her match when she found it. What if she were to tell
Diana of those letters of Evan? But then Diana would be
off to the ends of the earth with *him*. Better keep her in
the village, perhaps. Mrs. Starling grew more and more
impatient.

'Diana, you are a big fool!' she burst out.

Diana at that moment thought *not*. She did not answer.
Both were sitting before the wide fireplace, and Diana had not
moved since Mr. Masters left them.

'What sort of a life do you expect you are going to have?'

'I don't know, mother.'

'You, who might marry the richest man in town!—And
live in plenty, and have just your own way, and everything
you want! You *are* a fool! Do you know what it means to
be a poor minister's wife?'

'I shall know, I suppose. That is, if Mr. Masters is poor.
I don't know whether he is or not.'

'He is, of course !   They all are.'

' Well, mother.   You have taught me how to keep house on a little.'

' Yes, you and me ; that's one thing.   It's another thing when you have a shiftless man hanging round, and a dozen children or so, and expected to be civil to all the world. They always have a house full of children, and they are all shiftless.'

' Who, mother ? '

' Poor ministers.'

' Father hadn't—and wasn't.'

' He was as shiftless a man as ever wore shoe-leather ; he wasn't a bit of help to a woman.   All he cared for was to lose his time in his books ; and that's the way this man 'll do, and leave you to take the brunt of everything.   *Your* time 'll go in cookin' and mendin' and washin' up ; and you'll have to be at everybody's beck and call at the end o' that.   If there's anything *I* hate, it's to be in the kitchen and parlour both at the same time.'

Diana was silent.

' You might have lived like a queen.'

' I don't want to live like a queen.'

' You might have had your own way, Diana.'

' I don't care about having my own way.'

' I wish you would care, then, or had a speck of spirit. What's life good for ? '

' I wish I knew '—said Diana wearily, as she rose and set back her chair.

' You never will know, in that man's house.   I do think, ministers are the meanest lot o' folks there is ; and that you should go and take one of them ! '—

' It is the other way, mother ; he has taken me,' said Diana, half laughing at what seemed to her the disproportion between her mother's passion and the occasion for it.

' You were a fool to let him.'

' I don't think so.'

' You'll be sorry yet.'

' Why ? '

'They're a shiftless lot,' said Mrs. Starling rather evasively, 'the whole of 'em. And this one has a way of holding his own in other folk's houses that is intolerable to me! I never liked him, not from the very first.'

'I always liked him,' said Diana simply; and she went off to her room. She had not expected that her mother would favour the arrangement; on the contrary; and it had all been settled much more easily than she had looked for.

CHAPTER XXI.

UNSETTLED.

So things were settled, and Mrs. Starling made no attempt to unsettle them; on the other hand, she fell into a condition of permanent unrest, which I do not know how to characterize. It was not ill-humour exactly; it was not displeasure, or if, it was displeasure at herself; but it was contrary to all Mrs. Starling's principles to admit that, and she never admitted it. Her farm servant, Josiah, described her as being always now in an 'aggravated' state; and Diana found her society very uncomfortable. There was never a word spoken pleasantly, by any chance, about anything; good was not commended, and ill was not deplored; but both, good and ill, were taken up in the same sharp, acrid, cynical tone, or treated with the like restless mockery. Mrs. Starling found no fault with Diana, other than by this bitter manner of handling every subject that came up; at the same time she made the little house where they lived together a place of thunderous atmosphere, where it was impossible to draw breath freely and peacefully. They were very much shut up to one another, too. That Sunday storm in December had been followed by successive falls of snow, so deep that the ways were encumbered, and travelling more difficult than usual in Pleasant Valley even in winter. There was very little getting about between the neighbours' houses; and the people let their social qualities wait for spring and summer to develop themselves. Diana and her mother scarcely saw anybody. Dick Boddington at rare intervals looked in. Joe Bartlett once or twice came with a message from his mother; once Diana had gone down to see her. Even Mr. Masters made his appearance at the little brown farm-house

214

less frequently than might have been supposed; for, in truth, Mrs. Starling's presence made his visits rather unsatisfactory; and besides the two kitchen fires, there was none other in the house to which Diana and he could withdraw and see each other alone. So he came only now and then, and generally did not stay very long.

To Diana, all this while, the coming or the going, the solitude or the company, even the good or ill humours of her mother, seemed to be of little importance. She lived her own shut-up, deadened, secret life through it all, and had no nerves of sensation near enough to the surface to be affected much by what went on outside of her. What though her mother was all the while in a rasped sort of state? it could not rasp Diana; she seemed to wear a coat of mail. Neighbours? no neighbours were anything to her one way or another; if she could be said to like anything, it was to be quite alone and see and hear nobody. Her marriage she looked at in the same dull way; with a thought, so far as she gave it a thought, that in the minister's house her life would be more quiet, and peace and good-will would replace the eager disquiet around her which, without minding it, Diana yet perceived. More quiet and better, she hoped her life would be; her life and herself; she thought the minister was getting a bad bargain of it, but since it was his pleasure, she thought it was a good thing for her; every time she met the gentle kind eyes and felt the warm clasp of his hand, Diana repeated the assurance to herself. The girl had sunk again into mental torpor; she did not see nor hear nor feel; she lived along a mechanical sort of life, having relapsed into her former stunned condition. Not crushed—there was too much of Diana's nature for one blow or perhaps many blows to effect that; not beaten down, like some other characters; she went on her way upright, alert, and strong, doing and expecting to do the work of life to its utmost measure; all the same, walking as a ghost might walk through the scenes of his former existence; with no longer any natural conditions to put her at one with them, and only conscious of her dead heart. This state of things had given way in the fall to a few months of incessant and very live pain; with her betrothal to

the minister Diana had sunk again into the dulness of apathy.
But with a constitution mental and physical like hers, so full
of sound life-blood, so true and strong, in the nature of things
this state of apathetic sleep could not last for ever. And the
time of final waking came.

The winter had dragged its length away. Spring had come,
with its renewal of all the farm and household activities. Diana
stood up to her work and did it, day by day, with faultless
accuracy, with blameless diligence. She was too useful a helper
not to be missed unwillingly from any household that had once
known her; and Mrs. Starling's temper did not improve. It
had been arranged that Diana's marriage should take place
about the first of June. Spring work over, and summer going
on its orderly way, she could be easiest spared then, she
thought; and Mrs. Starling, seeing it must be, made no particular objection. Beyond the time, nothing had been talked of
yet concerning the occasion. So it was a hitherto untouched
question, when Mrs. Starling asked her daughter one day,—
'What sort of a wedding are you calculatin' to have?'

'What sort of a wedding? I don't know,' said Diana.
'What do you mean by a wedding?'

'The thing is, what *you* mean by it. Don't be a baby,
Diana Starling! Do you mean to ask your friends to see you
married?'

'I don't want anybody, I am sure,' said Diana. 'And I am
sure Mr. Masters does not care.'

'Are you going to be married in a black gown?'

'Black! No; but I do not care what kind of a gown it is,
further than that.'

'I don't think you care much about the whole thing,' said
Mrs. Starling, looking at her. 'If I was you, I wouldn't be
married just to please somebody else, without it pleased myself too. That's what *I* think.'

Poor Diana thought of Mr. Masters' face as she had seen it
the last time; and it seemed to her good to give somebody else
pleasure, even if pleasure were gone and out of the question for
her. This view of the question, naturally, she did not make
public.

'What *are* you going to marry this man for?' said Mrs. Starling, standing straight up (she had been bending over some work) and looking hard at her daughter.

'I hope he'll make a good woman of me,' Diana said soberly.

'If you had a little more spunk, you might make a good man of him; but you aren't the woman to do it. He wants his pride taken down a bit.'

'But what about the day, mother?' said Diana, who preferred not to discuss this subject.

'Well, if you haven't thought of it, I have; and I'm going to ask all the folks there are; and we've got to make a spread for 'em, Diana Starling, so we may as well be about it.'

'Already!' said Diana. 'It's weeks yet.'

'They'll run away, you'll find; and the cake'll be better for keepin'. You may go about stonin' the fruit as soon as you're a mind to.'

Diana said no more, but stoned her raisins and picked over her currants and sliced her citron, with the same apathetic want of realization which lately she had brought to everything. It might have been cake for anybody else's wedding that she was getting ready, so little did her fingers recognise the relation of the things with herself. The cake was made and baked and iced and ornamented. And then Mrs. Starling's activities went on to other items of preparation. Seeing Diana would be married, she meant it should be done in a way the country-side would not forget; neither should Mrs. Flandin make mental comparisons, pityingly, of the wedding that was, with the wedding that would have been with her son for the bridegroom. Baking and boiling and roasting and jellying went on in quantity, for Mrs. Starling was a great cook, and could do things in style when she chose. The house was put in order; fresh curtains hung up, and the handsomest linen laid out, and greens and flowers employed to cover and deck the severely plain walls and furniture. One thing more Mrs. Starling wished for which she was not likely to have, the presence of one of the Elmfield family on the occasion. She would have liked some one of them to be there, in order that sure news of the whole might go to Evan and beyond possibility

of doubt; for a lurking fear of his sudden appearing some time
had long hidden in Mrs. Starling's mind. I do not know what
she feared in such a case. Of the two, Evan was hardly
more distasteful to her as a son-in-law than the minister was;
though it is true that her action in the matter of burning the
letters had made her hate the man she had injured. This
feeling was counterbalanced, I confess, by another feeling of
the delight it would be to see Mr. Masters nonplussed; but on
the whole, she preferred that Evan should keep at a distance.

All the work and confusion of these last few weeks claimed
Diana's full time and strength, as well as her mother's; she
had scarcely a minute to think; and that was one reason, no
doubt, why she went through them with such unchanged composure. They were all behind her at last. Everything was in
order and readiness, down to the smallest particular; and it
was with a dull sense of this that Diana went up to her room
the last night before her wedding day. It was all done, and
the time was all gone.

She went in slowly, went to the window, opened it and sat
down before it. June had come again; one day of June was
passed, and to-morrow would be the second. Through the
bustle of May, Diana had hardly given a look to the weather
or a thought to the time of year; it greeted her now at her
window like a dear old friend that she had been forgetting.
The moon, about an hour high, gave a gentle illumination
through the dewy air, revealing plainly enough the level
meadows, and the hills which made their distant bordering.
The scent of roses and honeysuckles was abroad; just under
Diana's window there was a honeysuckle vine in full blossom,
and the rich, peculiar fragrance came in heavily-laden puffs of
air; the softest of breezes brought them, stirring the little
leaves lazily, and just touched Diana's face, sweet and tender,
reminding, caressing. Reminding of what? For it began to
stir vaguely and uneasily in Diana's heart. Things not thought
of before put in a claim to be looked at. This her home and
sanctuary for so many years, it was to be hers no longer. This
was the last night at her window, by her honeysuckle vine.
She would not have another evening the enjoyment of her

wonted favourite view over the fields and hills; she had done with all that. Other scenes, another home, would claim her; and then slowly rose the thought that her freedom was gone; this was the last time she would belong to herself. Oddly enough, nothing of all this had come under consideration before. Diana had been stunned; she had believed for a long time that she was dead, mentally; she had been, as it were, in a slumber, partly of hopelessness, partly of pre-occupation; now the time of waking had come; and the hidden life in her stirred and rose and shivered with the consciousness that it *was* alive and in its full strength, and what it meant for it to be alive now. As I said, Diana's nature was too sound and well-balanced and strong for any-thing to crush it, or even any part of it; and now she knew that the nerves of feeling she thought Evan had killed for ever, were all astir and quivering, and would never be fooled into slumbering again. I cannot tell how all this dawned and broke to her consciousness. She had sat down at her window a calm, weary-hearted girl, placid, and with even a dull sort of content upon her; so she had sat and dreamed awhile; and then June and moonlight, and her honeysuckle, and the roses, and the memory of her free childish days, and the image of her lost lover, and the thought of where she was standing, by degrees—how gently they did it, too—roused her and pricked her up to the consciousness of what she was going to do. What was she going to do? Marry a man who had no real place in her heart. She had thought it did not matter; she had thought she was dead; now all at once she knew that she was alive in every fibre, and that it mattered fearfully. The idea of Mr. Masters stung her, not as novel-writers say, 'almost to mad-ness,'—for there was no such irregularity in Diana's round, sound, healthy nature,—but to pain that seemed unbearable. No confusion in her brain, and no dulness now; on the con-trary, an intense consciousness of all that her position involved. She had made a mistake like many another; unlike many, she had found it out early. She was going to marry a man to whom she had no love to give; and she knew now that the life she must thenceforth lead would be daily torture. Almost the worse because she had for Mr. Masters so deep a respect and so true an appreciation. And he loved her; of that there was no question; the whole affection of the best man she had ever known was bestowed upon her, and in his hopes he saw doubtless a future when she would have learnt to return his love. 'And I never shall,' thought Diana. 'Never, as long as I live. I wonder if I shall get to hate him because I am obliged to live with him? All the heart I have is Evan's, and will be Evan's; it don't make any difference that he was not worthy of me, as I suppose he wasn't; I have given, and I cannot take back. And now I must live with this other man!'—Diana shuddered already.

She shed no tears. Happy are they whose grief can flow; part of the oppression, at least, flows off with tears, if not part of the pain. Eyes wide open, staring out into the moonlight; a rigid face, from which the colour gradually ebbed and ebbed away, more and more; so Diana kept the watch of her bridal eve. As the moon got higher, and the world lay clearer revealed under its light, shadows grew more defined, and objects more recognisable, it seemed as if in due proportion the life before Diana's mental vision opened and displayed itself, plainer and clearer; as she saw one, she saw the other. If Diana had been a woman of the world, her strength of character would have availed to do what many a woman of the world has not the force for; she would have drawn back at the last minute and declined to fulfil her engagement. But in the sphere of Diana's experience such a thing was unheard of. All the proprieties, all the conditions of the social life that was known to her, forbade even the thought; and the thought never came to her. She felt just as much bound, that is, as irrecoverably, as she would be twenty-four hours later. But she was like a caged wild animal. The view of the sweet moonlit country became unbearable at last, and she walked up and down her floor; she had a vague idea of tiring herself so that she could sleep. She did get tired of walking, but no sleep came; and at last she sat down again before her window to watch another change that was coming over the landscape. The moon was down, and a cool grey light, very unlike her soft glamour, was

stealing into the sky and upon the world. Yes, the day was
coming; the clear light of a matter-of-fact, work-a-day
creation. It was coming, and she must meet it, and march
on in the procession of life, which would leave no one out. If
she could go alone! But she must walk by another's side now.
And to that other, the light of this grey dawn, if he saw it,
brought only thoughts of joy. Could she help his being disappointed? Would she be able to help his finding out what a
dreadful mistake he had made, and she? 'I *must*,' thought
Diana, and set her teeth mentally; 'he must *not* know how I
feel; he does not deserve that. He deserves nothing but good,
of me or of anybody. I will give him all I can, and he shall
not know how I do it.'

With a recoil in every fibre of her nature, Diana turned to
take up her life burden. She felt as if she had had none till
now.

CHAPTER XXII.

NEW LIFE.

THE first week of Diana's marriage was always a blank in her memory. The one continual, intense strain of effort to hide from her husband what she was thinking and feeling swallowed up everything else. Mr. Masters had procured a comfortable little light rockaway, and avoiding all public thoroughfares and conveyances, had driven off with Diana among the leafy wildernesses of the White Mountains; going where they liked and stopping where they liked. It was more endurable to Diana than any other way of spending those days could have been; the constant change and activity, and the variety of new things always claiming attention and admiration, gave her all the help circumstances could give. They offered abundance of subjects for Mr. Masters to talk about; and Diana could listen, and with a word or two now and then get along quite passably. But of all the beauty they went through, of all the glory of those June days, of all the hours of conversation that went on, Diana kept in her memory but the one fact of continual striving to hinder Mr. Masters from seeing her heart. She supposed she succeeded; she never could tell. For one other thing forced itself upon her consciousness as the days went on—a growing appreciation of this man whom she did not love. His gentleness of manner, his tender care and consideration for her, the even sweetness of temper which nothing disturbed and which would let nothing disturb her, playing with inconveniences which he could not remove; and then, beneath all that, a strength of character and steady force of will which commanded her utmost respect and drew forth her fullest confidence. It hurt Diana's conscience terribly that
222

she had given this man a wife who, as she said to herself, was utterly unworthy of him; to make this loss good, so far as any possible service or life-work could, she would have done anything or submitted to anything. It was the one wish left her.

'What do you think of going home?' Mr. Masters asked suddenly one evening. They had come back from a glorious ramble over the nearest mountain, and were sitting after supper in front of the small farm-house where they had found lodging, looking out upon the view. Twilight was settling down upon the green hills. Diana started and repeated his word.

'Home?'

'Yes. I mean Pleasant Valley,' said the minister, smiling. 'Not the house where I first saw you. There are one or two sick people, from whom I do not feel that I can be long away.'

'You always think of other people first!' said Diana, almost with a sigh.

'So do you.'

'No, I do not. I do not think I do. It seems to me I have always thought most of myself.'

'You can begin now, then, to do better.'

'In thinking of you first, you mean? O yes, I do. I will. But you think of people you do not care for.'

'No, I don't. Never. You cannot think of people you do not care for, in the way you mean. They will not come into your head.'

'How can one do, then, Basil? How do you do?'

'Obviously, the only way is to care for them.'

'Who is sick in Pleasant Valley?'

'Nobody you know. One is an old man who lives back on the mountain; the other is a woman near Blackberry Hill.'

'Blackberry Hill? do you go there?'

'Now and then.'

'But those are dreadful people there.'

'Well,' said the minister, 'they want help so much the more.'

'Help to live, do you mean? They do stealing enough for that.'

'Nobody *lives* by stealing,' said the minister. 'It is one of the ways of death; and help to live is just what they want. But "how shall they believe on him of whom they have not heard? and how shall they hear without a preacher?"'

'And do you *preach* to them in that place?'

'I try.'

'But there is no church there?'

'When you have got anything to do,' said the minister, with a dry sort of humorousness which belonged to him, 'it is best not to be stopped by trifles.'

'Where do you preach, then, Basil?'

'Wherever I can find a man or a woman to listen to me.'

'In the houses?' exclaimed Diana.

'Why not?'

'Well, we never had a minister in Pleasant Valley like you before.'

'Didn't you?'

'I don't believe anybody ever went to those people to preach to them, until you went.'

'They had a good deal of that appearance,' Mr. Masters assented.

'But,' Diana began again after a short pause,—'to go back; Basil, you do not *care* for those people?'

'I think I do,' said the minister very quietly.

'I suppose you do!' said Diana, in a sort of admiration. 'But how can you?'

'Easy to tell,' was the answer. 'God made them, and God loves them; I love all that my Father loves. And Christ died for them; and I seek the lost whom my Master came to save. And there is not one of them but has in him the possibility of glory; and I see that possibility, and when I see it, Diana, it seems to me a small thing to give my life, if need be, that it may be realized.'

'I am not good enough to be your wife!' said Diana, sinking her head. And her secret self-abasement was very deep.

'Does that mean that you object to the cutting short of our holiday?' the minister asked, in his former tone of dry humorous suggestion.

'I?' said Diana, looking up and meeting his eyes. 'No, certainly. I am ready for whatever you wish, and whenever you wish.'

'I don't wish it at all,' said the minister, giving a somewhat longing look at the green wilderness before them, of which the lovely hilly outlines were all that the gathering twilight left distinct. 'But the thing is, Di, I cannot play when I ought to be working.'

It made little difference to Diana. Indeed, she had a hope that in her new home she would find, as she always had found in her old home, engrossing duties that would make her part easier to get through, and in some measure put a check to the rush of thought and feeling. So with her full consent the very next day they set out upon their journey home. It was not a great journey, indeed; a long day's drive would do it; their horse was fresh, and they had time for a comfortable rest and dinner at mid-day. The afternoon was very fair, and as they began to get among the hills overlooking Pleasant Valley, something in air or light reminded Diana of the time, two years ago, when she had gone up the brook with Evan. She began to talk to get rid of her thoughts.

'What a nice, comfortable little carriage this is, Basil! Where did it come from?'

'From Boston.'

'From Boston! I thought there was nothing like it in Pleasant Valley, that ever I saw. But how did you get it from Boston?'

'Where's the difficulty?' said the minister, sitting at ease sideways on the front seat and looking in at her. He had put Diana on the back seat, that she might take a more resting position than there was room for beside him.

'Why, it's so far.'

'Railway comes to Manchester. I received it there, and that is only ten miles. I rode Saladin over a few days ago, and drove him back. I had ordered the set of harness sent with the rockaway. Ecco!'

'Echo?' said Diana. 'Where?'

P

'A very sweet echo,' said the minister, smiling. 'Didn't you hear it?'

'No. But, Basil, do you mean that this carriage is yours?'

'No; it is yours.'

'Mine! then you have bought it! Didn't it cost a great deal?'

'I thought not. If you like it, certainly not.'

'O, Basil, you are very good!' said Diana humbly. 'But indeed I do not want you to go to any expense, ever, for me.'

'I am not a poor man, Diana.'

'Aren't you? I thought you were.'

'What right had you to think anything about it?'

'I thought ministers were always poor.'

'I am an exception, then.'

'And—Basil—you never acted like a rich man.'

'I am not going to, Di. Do you want to act like a rich woman?'

Spite of her desperate downheartedness, Diana could not help laughing a little at his manner.

'I do not wish anything different from you,' she answered.

'It is best for every reason, if you would use money to advantage in a place like this, not to make a show of it. And in other places, if you would use it to advantage, you *cannot* make a show of it. So it comes to the same thing. But short of that, Di, we can do what we like.'

'I know what you like,'—she said.

'I shall find out what you like. In the first place, where do you think you are going?'

'Where? I never thought about it. I suppose to Mrs. Persimmon's.'

'I don't think you would like that. The place was not exactly pleasant; and the house accommodations did very well for me, but would not have been comfortable for you. So I have set up housekeeping in another locality. Do you know where a woman named Cophetua lives?'

'I never heard of her.'

'Out of your beat. She lives a little off the road to the Blackberry Hill. I have taken her house, and put a woman in it to do whatever you want done.'

'I? But we never kept help, since I can remember, Basil; not house help.'

'Well? That proves nothing.'

'But I don't need anybody—I can do all that we want.'

'You will find enough to do.'

Mr. Masters quickened the pace of his horse, and Diana sat back in the carriage, half dismayed. She longed to lose herself in work, and she wished for nothing less than eyes to watch her.

It was almost evening when they got home. The place was, as Mr. Masters had said, out of what had been Diana's way hitherto; in a part of Pleasant Valley which was a one side of the high road. The situation was very pretty, overlooking a wide sweep of the valley bottom, with its rich cultivation and its encircling border of green wooded hills. As to the house, it was not distinguished in any way beyond its compeers. It was rather low; it was as brown as Mrs. Starling's house; it had no giant elms to hang over it and veil its uncomelinesses. But just behind it rose a green hill; the house, indeed, stood on the lower slope of the hill, which fell off more gently towards the bottom; behind the house it lifted up a very steep, rocky wall, yet not so steep but that it was grown with beautiful forest trees. Set off against its background of wood and hill, the house looked rather cosy. It had been put in nice order, and even the little plot of ground in front had been cleared of thistles and hollyhocks, which had held a divided reign, and trimmed into neatness, though there had not been time yet for grass or flowers to grow.

Within the house about this time, at one of the two lower front windows, a little woman stood looking out and speculating on the extreme solitariness of the situation. She had nobody to communicate her sentiments to, or she could have been eloquent on the subject. The golden glow and shimmer of the setting sun all over the wide landscape, it may be said with truth, she did not see; to her it was nothing but 'sunshine,' a natural and necessary accessory of the sun's presence, when clouds did not happen to come over the sky. I think she really saw nothing but the extreme emptiness of the picture

before her; just that one fact, that there was nothing to see.
Therefore it was on various accounts an event when the
rockaway hove in sight, and the grey horse stopped before the
gate. It did not occur to Miss Collins then to go out to the
carriage to receive bundles or baskets or render help generally;
she had got something to look at, and she looked. Only when
the minister, having tied Saladin's head, came leading the way
through the little courtyard to the front door, did it occur to
his 'help' to open the same. There she stood, smiling the
blankest of smiles, which made Diana want to get rid of her
on the instant.

'Well, of all things!' was her salutation uttered in a high
key. 'If it ain't you! I never was so beat. Why, I didn't
look for ye this long spell yet.'

'Won't you let us come in, Miss Collins, seeing we are
here?'

'La! I'm glad to see ye, fust-rate,' was the answer as she
stepped back; and stepping farther back as Mr. Masters advanced, at last she pushed open the door of her kitchen, which
was the front room on that side, and backed in, followed by
the minister and, at a little interval, by his wife. Miss Collins
went on talking. 'How do, Mis' Masters? I speck I can't be
under no mistake as to the personality, though I hain't had
the pleasure o' a introduction. But I thought honeymoon
folks allays make it last as long as they could?' she went on,
turning her eyes from Diana to the minister again; 'and you
hain't been no time at all.'

'What have you got in the house, Miss Collins? anything
for supper? I am hungry,' said the latter.

'Wall—happiness makes some folks hungry,—and some, they
say, it feeds 'em,' Miss Collins returned. 'Folks is so unlike!
But if you're hungry, Mr. Masters, you'll have to have sun'thin.'

Leaving her to prepare it, with a laughing twinkle in his
eye the minister led Diana out of that room and along a short
passage to another door. The passage was very narrow, the
ceiling was low, the walls whitewashed, the wainscoting blue;
and yet the room which they entered, though sharing in all
the items of this description, was homely and comfortable. It

was furnished in a way that made it seem elegant to Diana. A warm-coloured dark carpet on the floor, two or three easy-chairs, a wide lounge covered with chintz, and chintz curtains at the windows. On the walls here and there single shelves of dark wood put up for books, and filled with them; a pretty lamp on the little leaf table, and a wide fireplace with bright brass andirons. The windows looked out upon the wooded mountain-side. Diana uttered an exclamation of surprise and admiration.

'This is your room, Di,' said the minister. 'The kitchen has the view: I did think of changing about and making the kitchen here; but the other room has so long been used in that way, I was afraid it would be a bad exchange. However, we will do it yet, if you like.'

'Change? why, this room is beautiful!' cried Diana.

'Looks out into the hill.'

'O, I like that.'

'Don't make it a principle to like everything I do,' said he, smiling.

'But I *do* like it, Basil; I like it better than the other side,' said Diana. 'I just love the trees and the rocks. And you can hear the birds sing. And the room is most beautiful.'

Mr. Masters had opened the windows, and there came in a spicy breath from the woods, together with the wild warble of a wood-thrush. It was so wild and sweet, they both were still to listen. The notes almost broke Diana's heart, but she would not show that.

'What do you think that bird is saying?' she asked.

'I don't know what it may be to *his* mind; I know what it is to mine. Pray, what does it say to yours?'

'It is too plaintive for the bird to know what it means,' said Diana.

'Probably. I have no doubt the ancients were right when they felt certain animals to be types of good and others of evil. I think it is true, in detail and variety. I have the same feeling. And in like manner, carrying out the principle, I hear one bird say one thing and another another, in their countless varieties of song.'

' Did the ancients think that?'

' Don't you remember the distinction between clean beasts and unclean?'

' I thought that was ordered.'

' It was ordered to be observed. The distinction was felt before.'

They were again silent a moment, while the thrush's song filled the air with liquid rejoicing.

' That bird,' said Diana slowly, ' sings as if he had got somewhere above all the sins and troubles and fights of life; I mean, as if he were a human being who had got there.'

' That will do,' said the minister.

' But that's impossible; so why should he sing it?'

' Take it the other way,' said the minister, smiling.

' You mean '—said Diana, looking up, for she had sat down before the open window, and he stood by her side;—' you mean, he would not sing a false note?'

' Nor God make a promise he would not fulfil. Come up-stairs.'

' But, Basil!—how could the bird's song be a promise from God?'

' Think;—he gave the song, Diana. As has been said of visible things in nature, so it may be said of audible things,— every one of them is *the expression of a thought of God.*'

He did not wait for an answer, and Diana's mind was too full to give one. Up-stairs they went. The room over Diana's was arranged to be Mr. Masters' study; the other, above the kitchen, looked out upon a glorious view of the rich valley and its encompassing hills; both were exceedingly neat and pretty in their furniture and arrangements, in all of which Diana's comfort had been sedulously cared for. Her husband showed her the closet for her boxes, and opened the huge press prepared for her clothes; and taking off her bonnet, welcomed her tenderly home. But it seemed to Diana as if everything stifled her, and she would have liked to flee to the hills, like the wild creatures that had their home there. Her outward demeanour, for all that, was dignified and sweet. Whatever she felt, she would not give pain.

'You are too good to me,' she murmured. 'I will be as good as I can, Basil, to you.'

'I know it,' said he.

'And I think I had better begin,' she presently added more lightly, 'by going down and seeing how Miss Collins and supper are getting on.'

'I daresay they will get on to some sort of consummation.'

'It will be a better consummation if you let me go.'

Perhaps he divined something of her feeling, for he made no objection, and Diana escaped ; with a sense that her only refuge was in action. To do something, no matter what, and stop thinking. Yet, when she went down-stairs, she went first to the back room and to the open window, to see if she could catch the note of the thrush once more. It came to her like a voice from the other world. He was still singing; somewhere up amid the cool shades of the hemlocks and oaks on the hill, from out the dusky twilight of their tops ; sending his tremulous trills of triumph down the hillside, he was undoubtedly having a good time. Diana listened a minute, and then went to the kitchen. Miss Collins was standing in front of the fire contemplating it, or the kettle she had hung over it.

'Where is Mr. Masters' supper?' Diana began.

'Don't you take none?' was the rejoinder.

'I mean, what can we have?'

'You can have all there is. And there ain't nothin' in the house but what's no 'count. If I'd ha' knowed—honeymoon folks wants sun'thin' tip-top, been livin' on the fat o' the land, I expect; and now ye're come home to pork ; and that's the hull on't.'

'Pork will do,' said Diana, 'if it is good. Have you no ham?'

'Lots. That's pork, ain't it?'

'Eggs?'

'Yes, there's eggs.'

'Potatoes?'

'La, I didn't expect ye'd want potatoes at this time o' day.'

Diana informed herself of the places of things, and set herself and Miss Collins vigorously to work. The handmaid looked on somewhat ungraciously at the quiet, competent energy of her superior, the smile on her broad mouth gradually fading.

'Reckon you don't know me,' she remarked presently.

'Yes, I do,' said Diana; 'you are Jemima Collins, that used to live at the post office. How came you here?'

'Wall, there's nothin' but changes in the world, I expect; that's *my* life. Mis' Reems, to the post office, had her mother come home to live with her; owin' to her father gettin' his arm took off in some 'chinery, which was the death o' him; so the mother come home to her daughter, and then they made it out as they two was equal to all there was to do; and I don't say they warn't; but that was reason enough why they didn't want me no longer. And then I stayed with Miss Gunn a spell, helpin' her get her house cleaned; and then the minister made out as he wanted a real 'sponsible person for to take care o' *his* house, and Miss Gunn she told him what she knowed about me; and so I moved in. La, it's a change from the post office! It was sort o' lively there; allays comin' and goin', and lots o' news.'

Diana made no answer. The very mention of the post office gave her a sort of pang; about that spot her hopes had hovered for so long, and with such bitter disillusionizing. She sent Miss Collins to set the table in the other room, and presently, having finished her cookery, followed with it herself.

CHAPTER XXIII.

SUPPER AT HOME.

THE windows were open still, and the dusky air without was full of cool freshness. In the wide fireplace the minister had kindled a fire; and in a little blue teapot he was just making the tea; the kettle stood on the hearth. It was as pretty and cheerful a home view as any bride need wish to see for the first evening in her new house. Diana knew it, and took the effect, which possibly was only heightened by the consciousness that she wished herself five hundred miles away. What the picture was to her husband she had no idea, nor that the crowning feature of it was her own beautiful, sweet presence. Miss Collins brought in the prepared dishes, and left the two alone.

'I see I have fallen into new hands,' the minister remarked presently. 'Mrs. Persimmon never cooked these eggs.'

'You must have been tired of living in that way, I should think.'

'No,—I never get tired of anything.'

'Not of bad things?'

'No. I get rid of them.'

'But how can you?'

'Different ways.'

'Can you do everything you want to, Basil?' his wife asked, with an incredulous sort of admiration.

'I'll do everything you want me to do.'

'You have already,—and more,' she said with a sigh.

'How will your helpmeet in the other room answer the purpose?'.

'I have never been used to have anybody, you know, Basil; and I do not need any one. I can do all easily myself.'

'I know you can. I do not wish you should.'

'Then what will you give me to do?'

'Plenty.'

'I don't care what—if I can only be busy. I cannot bear to be idle. What shall I do, Basil?'

'Is there nothing you would like to study, that you have never had a chance to learn?'

'Learn?' said Diana, a whole vista of possible new activities opening all at once before her mind's eye;—'O yes! I would like to learn—to study. What, Basil?'

'What would you like to take hold of?'

'I would like—Latin.'

'Latin!' cried the minister. 'That's an excellent choice. Greek too?'

'I would like to learn Greek, very much. But I suppose I must begin with one at once.'

'How about modern languages?'

'You know,' said Diana shyly,—'I can have no teacher but you.'

'And you stand in doubt as to my qualifications? Prudent!'

'I will learn anything you like to teach me,' said Diana; and her look was both very sweet and very humble; withal had something of an anxious strain in it.

'Then there's another thing; don't you want to help me?'

'How?'

'In my work.'

'How can I?'

'I don't believe you know what my work is,' said the minister dryly. 'Do you, now?'

'I thought I did,' said Diana.

'Preaching sermons, to wit!' said the minister. 'But that is only one item. My business is to work in my Master's vineyard.'

'Yes; and I thought that was how you did it.'

'But a man may preach many sermons, and do never a bit of work,—of the sort I mentioned.'

'What is the sort, then, Basil?'

'I'll show you when we get away from the table. It is time you knew.'

So, when the supper tray and Miss Collins were gone, the minister took his Bible and made Diana sit down beside him where they could both look over it.

'Your notion of a minister is, that he is a sort of machine to make sermons?'

'I never thought you were a *machine*, of any sort,' said Diana gently.

'No, of course not; but you thought that was my special business, didn't you? Now look here.—"Son of man, I have made thee a watchman unto the house of Israel; therefore hear the word at my mouth, and give them warning from me."'

'A watchman'—Diana repeated.

'It is a responsible post, too, for see over here,—"If the watchman see the sword come, and blow not the trumpet, and the people be not warned; if the sword come, and take any person from among them, he is taken away in his iniquity; *but his blood will I require at the watchman's hand.*"'

'Do you mean, Basil'—

'Yes, I mean all that. You can understand now what was in Paul's mind, and what a great word it was, when he said to the Ephesian elders, "I take you to record this day, that I am pure from the blood of all men." He had done his whole duty in that place!'

'I never felt that old Mr. Hardenburgh warned us against anything,' Diana remarked.

'Did I?'

'You began to make me uncomfortable almost as soon as you came.'

'That's good,' said the minister quietly. 'Now see these words, Diana,—"Go ye into all the world, and tell the good news to everybody."'

'"Preach the gospel"'—said Diana.

'That is simply, telling the good news.'

'Is it?'

'Certainly.'

'But, Basil, it never seemed so.'

'There was a reason for that. "As cold waters to a thirsty soul, so is good news from a far country." You were not thirsty, that is all.'

'Basil,' said Diana, almost tremulously, 'I think I am now.'

'Well,' said her husband tenderly, 'you know who could say, and did say, "If any man thirst, let him come unto ME and drink." "I am the bread of life; he that cometh to me shall never hunger, and he that believeth on me shall never thirst."'

That bringing together of need and supply, while yet Need does not see how it is to stretch out its hand to take the supply—how sharp and how pitiful it makes the sense of longing! Diana drooped her head till it touched Basil's arm; it seemed to her that her heart would fairly break.

'But that doesn't mean'—she said, bringing out her words with hesitation and difficulty,—'that does not mean hunger of every sort?'

'Yes.'

'Of earthly sorts, Basil? how can it? people's desires for so many things?'

'Is there any limit or qualification to the promise?'

'N—o; not there.'

'Is there anywhere else?'

Diana was silent.

'There is none anywhere, except the limit put by the faith of the applicant. I have known a person starving to death, relieved for the time even from the pangs of bodily hunger by the food which Christ gave her. There is no condition of human extremity for which he is not sufficient.'

'But,' said Diana, still speaking with difficulty, 'that is for some people.'

'For some people—and for everybody else.'

'But—he would not like to have anybody go to him just for such a reason.'

'He will never ask *why* you came, if you come. He was in this world to relieve misery, and to save from it. "Him that cometh to me I will in no wise cast out," is his own word. He will help you if you will let him, Diana.'

Diana's head pressed more heavily against Basil's arm; the temptation was to break out into wild weeping at this contact of sympathy, but she would not. Did her husband guess how much she was in want of help? That thought half frightened her. Presently she raised her head and sat up.

'Here is another verse,' said her husband, 'which tells of a part of my work. "Go ye into the highways, and as many as ye shall find, *bid to the marriage.*"'

'I don't understand '—

'"The kingdom of heaven is like unto a certain king which made a marriage for his son,"—it means rather a wedding entertainment.'

'How, Basil?'

'The Bridegroom is Christ. The bride is the whole company of his redeemed. The time is by and by, when they shall be all gathered together, all washed from defilement, all dressed in the white robes of the king's court which are given them, and delivered from the last shadow of mortal sorrow and infirmity. Then in glory begins their perfected, everlasting union with Christ; then the wedding is celebrated; and the supper signifies the fulness and communion of his joy in them, and their joy in him.'

Basil's voice was a little subdued as he spoke the last words, and he paused a few minutes.

'It is my business to bid people to that supper,' he said then; 'and I bid you, Di.'

'I will go, Basil.'

But the words were low and the tears burst forth, and Diana hurried away.

CHAPTER XXIV.

THE MINISTER'S WIFE.

Diana plunged herself now into business. She was quite in earnest in the promise she had made at the end of the conversation last recorded; but to set about a work is one thing and to carry it through is another; and Diana did not immediately see light. In the meanwhile, the pressure of the bonds of her new existence was only to be borne by forgetting it in intense occupation. Her husband wanted her to study many things; for her own sake and for his own sake he wished it, knowing that her education had been exceedingly one-sided and imperfect; he wanted all sources of growth and pleasure to be open to her, and he wanted full communion with his wife in his own life and life-work. So he took her hands from the frying-pan and the preserving kettle, and put dictionaries and philosophies into them. On her part, besides the negative incitement of losing herself and her troubles in books, Diana's mental nature was too sound and rich not to take kindly the new seeds dropped into the soil. She had gone just far enough in her own private reading and thinking to be all ready to spring forward in the wider sphere to which she was invited, and in which a hand took hers to help her along. The consciousness of awakening power, too, and of enlarging the bounds of her world, drew her on. Sometimes in Basil's study, where he had arranged a place for her, sometimes down-stairs in her own little parlour, Diana pored over books and turned the leaves of dictionaries; and felt her way along the mazes of Latin stateliness, or wondered and thrilled at the beauty of the Greek words of the New Testament as her husband explained them to her. Or she wrought out problems; or she wrote abstracts; or she

238

dived into depths of philosophical speculation. Then Diana began to learn French, and very soon was delighting herself in one or other of a fine collection of French classics which filled certain shelves in the library. There was, besides all the motives above mentioned which quickened and stimulated her zeal for learning, another very subtle underlying cause which had not a little to do with her unflagging energy in pursuit of her objects. Nay, there were two. Diana did earnestly wish to please her husband, and for his sake to become, so far as cultivation would do it, a fit companion for him. That she knew. But she scarcely knew, how beneath all that, and mightier than all that, was the impulse to make herself worthy of the other man whose companion now she would never be. Subtle, as so many of our springs of action are, unrecognised, it drove her with an incessant impulse. To be such a woman as Evan would have been proud of; such a one as he would have liked to stand by his side anywhere; one that he need not have feared to present in any society. Diana strove for it, and that although Evan would never know it, and it did not in the least concern him. And as she felt from time to time that she was attaining her end and coming nearer and nearer to what she wished to be, Diana was glad with a secret joy, which was not the love of knowledge, nor the pride of personal ambition, nor the duty of an affectionate wife. As I said, she did not recognise it; if she had, I think she would have tried to banish it.

One afternoon she was sitting by her table at the study window, where she had been very busy, but was not busy now. The window was open; the warm summer air came in, and over the hills and the lowland the brilliance and glow of the evening sunlight was just at its brightest. Diana sat gazing out, while her thoughts went wandering. Suddenly she pulled them up; and her question was rather a departure, though standing in a certain negative connection with them.

'Basil, I can't make out just what *faith* is.'

'Cannot you?'

'No. Can you help me? The Bible says, "*believe*," "*believe*." I believe. I believe everything it tells me, and you tell me; but I have not *faith*.'

'How do you know that?'

'If I had, I should be a Christian.'

'And you think you are not?'

'I am sure I am not.'

'Are you willing?'

'I think I—am willing,' Diana answered slowly, looking out into the sunlight.

'If you are right, then faith must be something more than mere belief.'

'What more is it?' she said eagerly, turning her face towards him now.

'I think the heart has its part in it as well as the head, and it is with the heart that the difficulty lies. In true Bible faith, the heart gives its confidence where the intellect has given its assent. "*With the heart* man believeth unto righteousness." That is what the Lord wants;—our personal trust in him; unreserved and limitless trust.'

'Trust?' said Diana. 'Then why cannot I give it? why don't I?'

'That is the question to be answered. But, Di, the heart *cannot* yield that confident trust, so long as there is any point in dispute between it and God; so long as there is any consciousness of holding back something from him or refusing something to him. Disobedience and trust cannot go together. It is not the child who is standing out in rebellion who can stretch out his hand for his father's gifts, and know that they will be given.'

'Do you think I am rebelling, Basil?'

'I cannot see into your heart, Di.'

'What could I be "holding back" from God?'

'Unconditional surrender.'

'Surrender of what?'

'Yourself—your will. When you have made that surrender, there will be no difficulty about trusting. There never is.'

Diana turned to the window again, and leaning her head on her hand, sat motionless for a long time. Sunlight left the bottom lands and crept up the hills and faded out of the sky. Dusk and dews of twilight fell all around, and the dusk

" It was after a very long time of this silence that she rose, came to the
table where he was sitting, and knelt down beside it."

Page 241.

deepened till the stars began to shine out here and there.
Sweet summer scents came in on the dew-freshened air; sweet
chirrup of insects made their gentle running commentary on
the silence; Miss Collins had long ago caused the little bell
with which she was wont to notify her employers that their
meals were ready, to sound its tinkling call to supper; but
Diana had not heard it, and the minister would not disturb
her. It was after a very long time of this silence that she
rose, came to the table where he was sitting, and knelt down
beside it.

'I believe,' she said. 'And I *trust*, Basil.'

He took her hand, but said nothing otherwise. He could
not see her face, for she had laid it down upon some books,
and besides the room was very dusky now. But when he
expected some further words which should tell of relief or joy,
to his surprise he felt that Diana was weeping, and then that
her tears had grown into a storm. Most strange for her, who
very rarely let him or any one see the outbursts of such feeling;
indeed, even by herself she was very slow to come to the indulgence of tears. It was not her way. Now, before she was
aware, they were flowing; and as it is with some natures, if
you open the sluice-gates at all, a flood pours forth which
makes it impossible to shut them again for a while. And this
time I think she forgot that anybody was by. He was puzzled.
Was it joy or sorrow? Hard for herself to tell, there was so
much of both in it. For, with the very first finding of a sufficient refuge and help for her trouble, Diana had brought her
burden to his feet, and there was weeping convulsively; partly
from the sense of the burden, partly with the sense of laying
it down, and with the might of that infinite sympathy the
apprehension of which was beginning to dawn upon her now
for the first time. What is it like? O, what is it like? It is
the 'Dayspring from on high.' Basil could not read all she
was feeling and spell it out. But I think he had a sort of
instinct of it, and felt that his wife was very far from him, in this
her agony of joy and sorrow; for he kept motionless, and his
broad brow, which never was wrinkled, was very grave. One
hand he laid lightly upon Diana's shoulder, as if so to remind

Q

her of his presence and close participation in all that concerned her; otherwise he did not interrupt her nor make any claim upon her attention.

Gradually Diana's sobs ceased; and then she grew utterly still; and the two sat so together, for neither of them knew how long. At last Diana raised her head.

' You have had no supper all this while!' she said.

' I have had something much better,' said he, gently kissing her cheek.

' To see me cry?' said Diana. ' I don't know why I cried.'

' I think I do. Don't you feel better for it?' ·

' Yes. Or else, for that which made me do so. Come down, Basil.'

At tea she was perfectly herself and quite as usual, except for the different expression in her face. It was hardly less grave than before, but something dark had gone out and something light had come in.

' I can face the Sewing Society now,' she remarked towards the end of the meal.

' The Sewing Society!' her husband echoed. ' Is that much to face?'

' I have not been once since I was married. And they make so much fuss about it, I must go now. They meet to-morrow at mother's.'

' What do they sew?'

' They pretend to be making up a box for some missionary out west.'

' I guess there is no pretence about it.'

' Yes, there is. They have been eight months at work upon a box to go to Iowa somewhere, to a family very much in want of everything; and the children and mother are almost, or quite, I guess, in rags, and the ladies here are comfortably doing a little once a week, and don't even expect to have the box made up till Christmas time. Think of the people in Iowa waiting and waiting, with hardly anything to put on, while we meet once a week and sew a little, and talk, and have supper.'

' How would you manage it?'

' I would send off the box next week, Basil.'

'So would I. Suppose now we do?'

'Send off a box?'

'Yes. I will give you the money;—you can go—I will drive you—down to Gunn's, and you can get there whatever you think would be suitable, and we will have the fun to ourselves.'

The colour flushed into Diana's face; it was the first flush of pleasure that had come there in a long while.

'You are very good, Basil!' she said. 'Don't you think I could drive Saladin?'

'Where?'

'Anywhere. I mean, that I could go to places then without troubling you to drive me.'

'I can stand so much trouble. It is not good for a man to live too easy.'

'But it might be convenient for you sometimes.'

'So it might, and pleasant for you. No, I should not like to trust you to Saladin. I wonder if your mother would let me have Prince, if I offer her a better horse in exchange. Perhaps I can do better than that. We will see.'

'O, Basil, you must not get another horse for me!'

'I will get anything I like for you.'

'But do you mean, and keep Saladin too?'

'I mean that. Saladin is necessary to me.'

'Then don't, Basil. I can tell you, people will say you are extravagant if you have two horses.'

'I cannot help people talking scandal.'

'No; but it will hurt your influence.'

'Well, we will feel the pulse of the public to-morrow. But I think they would stand it.'

They drove down to Mrs. Starling's the next day. Mr. Masters had other business, and must go farther. Diana went in alone. She was early, for she had come to help her mother make the preparations; and at first these engrossed them both.

'Well,' said Mrs. Starling, when some time had passed,— 'how do you get along with your husband?'

Diana's eyes opened slightly. 'It would be a very strange person that could not get on with Mr. Masters,' she answered.

'Easy, is he? I hate easy men! The best of 'em are helpless enough; but when you get one of the easy sort, they are contented if every door hangs on one hinge.'

Diana made no answer.

' How does your girl get along? '

' Very well. Pretty well.'

' What you want with a girl, I don't see.'

' I didn't either. But Mr. Masters wants me to do other things.'

' Set you up to be a lady. Well, the world's full o' fools.'

' I am as busy, mother, as ever I was in my life.'

' Depends on what you call business. Making yourself unfit for business, I should say. Call it what you like. I suppose he is your humble servant, and just gives you your own way.'

' He is not that sort of man at all, mother. He is as kind as can be; but he is nobody's humble servant.'

' Then I suppose you are his. There is somebody now, Diana; it's Kate Boddington. Do go in and take care of her, —you can do so much,—and keep her from coming out here where I am.'

' Well, Di!' exclaimed her relative as Diana met her. 'Ain't it a sight to see *you* at the sewin' meetin'! Why haven't you been before? Seems to me, you make an uncommon long honeymoon of it.'

Diana's natural sweetness and dignity, and furthermore, the great ballast of old pain and new gladness which lay deep down in her heart, kept her quite steady and unruffled under all such breezes. She had many of the like to meet that day; and the sweet calm and poise of her manner through them all would have done honour to the most practised woman of the world. Most of her friends and neighbours here collected had scarce seen her since her marriage, unless in church; and they were curious to know how she would carry herself, and curious in general about many things. It was a sort of battery that Diana had to face, and sometimes a masked battery; but it was impossible to tell whether a shot hit.

' What I want to know,' said Mrs. Boddington, ' is, where the minister and you made it up, Di. You were awful sly about it!'

' Ain't that so?' chimed in Mrs. Carpenter. ' I never had no notion o' what was goin' on—not the smallest idee; and I was jest a sayin' one day to Miss Gunn, or somebody—I declare I don't know now who 'twas, I was so dumbfounded when the news come, it took all my memory away;—but I was jes' a sayin' to somebody, and I remember it because I'd jes' been after dandelion greens and couldn't find none; they was jest about past by then, and bitter; and we was a settin' with our empty baskets; and I was jes' tellin' somebody, I don't know who 'twas, who I thought would make a good wife for the minister, when up comes Mrs. Starling's Josiah and reaches me the invitation. "There!" says I; " if he ain't a goin' to have Diana Starling!" I was beat.'

' I daresay you could have fitted him just as well,' remarked Mrs. Starling.

' Wall, I don't know. I was thinkin',—but I guess it's as well not to say now what I was thinkin'.'

' That's so!' assented Miss Barry. ' I don't believe he thinks nobody could ha' chosen for him no better than he has chosen for himself.'

' Men never do know what is good for them,' Mrs. Salter remarked, but not ill-naturedly; on the contrary, there was a gleam of fun in her face.

' I'm thankful, any way, he hain't done worse,' said another lady. ' I used to be afraid he would go and get himself hitched to a fly-away.'

' Euphemie Knowlton?' said Mrs. Salter. ' Yes, I used to wonder if we shouldn't get our minister's wife from Elmfield. It looked likely at one time.'

' Those two wouldn't ha' pulled well together, ne—ver,' said another.

' I should like to know how he and Di's goin' to pull together?' said Mrs. Flandin acidly. ' He's goin' one way, and she another.'

' Do you think so, Mrs. Flandin?' asked the lady thus in a very uncomplimentary manner referred to.

' Wall—ain't it true?' said Mrs. Flandin judicially.

' I do not think it is true.'

'Wall, I'm glad to hear it, I'm sure,' said the other; 'but there's a word in the Scriptur' about two walking together when they ain't agreed.'

'Mr. Masters and I are agreed,' said Diana, while her lips parted in a very slight smile, and a lovely tinge of rose-colour came over her cheeks.

'But not in everything, I reckon?'

'In everything I know,' said Diana steadily, while a considerable breeze of laughter went round the room. Mrs. Flandin was getting the worst of it.

'Then it'll be the worse for him!' she remarked with a jerk at her sewing. Diana was silent now, but Mrs. Boddington took it up.

'Do you mean to say, Mis' Flandin, you approve of quarrels between man and wife? and quarrels in high places, too?'

'High places!' echoed Mrs. Flandin. 'When it says that a minister is to be the servant of all!'

'And ain't he?' said Mrs. Carpenter. 'Is there a place or a thing our minister don't go to if he's wanted? and does he mind whether it's night or day, or rough or smooth? and does he care how fur it is, or how long he goes without his victuals? I will say, I never did see a no more self-forgetful man than is Mr. Masters; and I've a good right to know, and I say it with feelin's of gratitude.'

'That's jes' so,' said Miss Barry, her eyes glistening over her knitting, which they did not need to watch. And there was a hum of assent through the room.

'I'm not sayin' nothin' agin *him*,' said Mrs. Flandin in an injured manner; 'but what I was hintin', I warn't *sayin'* nothin', is that he's married a '—

'A beauty '—said Mrs. Boddington.

'I don't set no count on beauty,' said the other. 'I allays think, ef a minister is a servant of the Lord, and I hope Mr. Masters is, it's a pity his wife shouldn't be too. That's all.'

'But I am, Mrs. Flandin,' said Diana quietly.

'What?'

' A servant of the Lord.'

' Since when ? ' demanded the other incredulously.

' Does it matter since when?' said Diana, with a calm
gentleness which spoke for her. ' I was not always so, but I
am now.'

' Hev *you* met with a change?' the other asked, again
judicially, and critically.

' Yes.'

' Ain't that good news, now!' said Miss Barry, dropping
her knitting and fairly wiping her eyes.

' I hope your evidence is clear,' said the other lady.

' Do you want to hear what they are?' said Diana. ' I have
come to know the Lord Jesus—I have come to believe in him
—I have given myself to be his servant. As truly his servant,
though not so good a one, as my husband is. But what he
bids me, I'll do.'

The little assembly was silent, silent all round. Both the
news and the manner of the teller of it were imposing.
Decided, clear, calm, sweet, Diana's grey eyes as well as her
lips gave her testimony ; they did not shrink from other eyes,
nor droop in hesitation or difficulty ; as little was there a line
of daring or self-assertion about them. The dignity of the
woman struck and hushed her companions.

' Our minister 'll be a happy man, I'm thinkin',' said good
Mrs. Carpenter, speaking out what was the secret thought of
many present.

' You haven't joined the church, Diana,' said Mrs. Starling
harshly.

' I will do that the first opportunity, mother.'

' That's your husband's doing. I allays knew he'd wile a
bird off a bush!'

' I am very thankful to him,' said Diana calmly.

That calm of hers was unapproachable. It would neither
take offence nor give it ; although, it is true, it did irritate
some of her neighbours and companions by the very distance
it put between them and her. Diana was different from them,
and growing more different; yet it was hard to find fault.
She was so handsome, too ; that helped the effect of superiority.

And her dress; what was there about her dress? It was a pale
lilac muslin, no ways remarkable in itself; but it fell around
lines so soft and noble, and about so queenly a carriage, it
waved with so quiet and graceful motions, there was a temptation to think Diana must have called in dressmaking aid that
was not lawful—for the minister's wife.   As the like often
happens, Diana was set apart by a life-long sorrow from all
their world of experience,—and they thought she was proud.

'What did you pay for that muslin, Diana?' Mrs. Flandin
asked.

'Fifteenpence.'

'Du tell! well, I should ha' thought it was more,' remarked
Miss Gunn.   'It's made so elegant.'

'I made it myself,' said Diana, smiling.

'Du tell!' said Miss Gunn again, reviewing the gown.   For,
as I hinted, its draperies were graceful, their lovely lines being
unbroken by furbelows and flummery; and the sleeves were
open and half long, with a full ruffle which fell away from
Diana's beautiful arms.

'How Phemie Knowlton used to dress!' Miss Gunn went
on, moved by some hidden association of ideas.

'I wonder is nobody ever comin' back to Elmfield?' said
Mrs. Boddington.   'They don't do nothin' with the place, and
it's just waste.'

The talk wandered on; but Diana's thoughts remained fixed.
They had flown back over the two years since Evan and she
had their explanation in the blackberry field, and for a little
while she sat in a dream, feeling the stings of pain, that
seemed, she thought, to grow more lively now instead of less.
The coming in of Mr. Masters roused her, and with a sort of
start she put away the thought of Evan, and of days and joys
past for ever, and forcibly swung herself back to present
things.   People were very well-behaved after her husband
came, and she did her part, she knew, satisfactorily; for she
saw his eye now and then resting on her or meeting hers with
the hidden smile in it she had learned to know.   And besides,
nothing was ever dull or commonplace where he was; so even
in Mrs. Starling's house and Mrs. Flandin's presence, the rest

of the evening went brightly off. And then, driving home, through the light of a young moon and over the quiet country, Diana watched the wonderful calm line where the hill-tops met the sky; and thought, surely, with the talisman she had just found of heavenly love and sympathy and strength, she could walk the rest of her way through life and bear it till the end. Then, by and by, beyond that dividing line of eternity, there would be bright heaven, instead of the dusky earth. If only she could prevent Basil from knowing how she felt, and so losing all peace in life himself. But his peace was so fixed in heaven, she wondered if anything on earth could destroy it? She would not try that question.

CHAPTER XXV.

MISS COLLINS' WORK.

IT was well for Diana that she had got a talisman of better power than the world can manufacture. It was well for her, too, that she followed up earnestly the clue to life which had been given her. If you have a treasure-house of supplies, and are going to have to get to it in the dark by and by, it is good to learn the way very well while the light is there. For weeks Diana gave herself before all other things to the study of her Bible, and to better understanding of faith's duties and privileges. In all this, Basil was a great help; and daily his wife learned more and more to admire and revere the mind and temper of the man she had married. Reverence would have led surely to love, in such a nature as Diana's; but Diana's heart was preoccupied. What love could not do, however, conscience and gratitude did as far as possible. Nothing that concerned Basil's comfort or honour was uncared for by his wife. So, among other things, she never entrusted the care of his meals entirely to Miss Collins; and quite to that lady's discomfiture, would often come into the kitchen and prepare some nice dish herself, or superintend the preparation of it. Miss Collins resented this. She shared the opinion of some of the ladies of the Sewing Society, that Mrs. Masters was quite proud and needed to be 'taken down' a bit; and if she got a good chance, she had it in her mind to do a little of the 'taking down' herself.

It was one evening late in September. Frosts had hardly set in yet, and every change in the light and colour carried Diana's mind back to Evan and two years ago, and mornings and evenings of that time which were so filled with nameless
250

joys and hopes. Diana did not give herself to these thoughts, nor encourage them; they came with the suddenness and the start of lightning. Merely the colour of a hill at sunset was enough to flash back her thoughts to an hour when she was looking for Evan; or a certain sort of starlight night would recall a particular walk along the meadow fence; or a gust and whiff of the wind would bring with it the thrill that belonged to one certain stormy September night that never faded in her remembrance. Or the smell of coffee sometimes, when it was just at a certain stage of preparation, would turn her heart-sick. These associations and remembrances were countless and incessant always under the reminders of the September light and atmosphere; and Diana could not escape from them, though as soon as they came she put them resolutely away.

This evening Mr. Masters was out. Diana knew he had gone a long ride and would be tired,—that is, if he ever could be tired,—and would be certainly ready for his supper when he came in. So she went out to make ready a certain dish of eggs which she knew he liked. Such service as this she could do, and she did. There was no thoughtful care, no smallest observance, which could have been rendered by the most devoted affection, which Diana did not give to her husband. Except, —she never offered a kiss, or laid her hand in his or upon his shoulder. Happily for her, Basil was not a particularly demonstrative man; for every caress from him was 'as vinegar upon nitre;' she did not show repulsion, that was all.

'I guess I kin do that, Mis' Masters,' said her handmaid, who always preferred to keep the kitchen for her own domain. Diana made no answer. She was slowly and delicately peeling her eggs, and probably did not notice the remark. Miss Collins, however, resented the neglect.

'Mr. Masters is gone a great deal. It's sort o' lonesome up here on the hill. Dreadfully quiet, don't you think it is?'

'I like quiet,' Diana answered absently.

'Du, hey? Wall, I allays liked life. I never could get too much o' that. I should like a soldier's life uncommon,—if I was a man.'

Diana had finished peeling her eggs, and now began to wash a bunch of green parsley which she had fetched from the garden, daintily dipping it up and down in a bowl of spring-water.

'It was kind o' lively down to the post office,' Miss Collins remarked again, eyeing the beautiful half-bared arm and the whole figure, which in its calm elegance was both imposing and irritating to her. Miss Collins, indeed, had a very undefined sense of the beautiful; yet she vaguely knew that nobody else in Pleasant Valley looked so or carried herself so; no other woman's dress adorned her so, or was so set off by the wearer; although Diana's present attire was a very simply-made print gown, not even the stylish ladies of Elmfield produced an equal effect with their French dresses. And was not Diana 'Mis' Starling's daughter'? And Diana seemed not to hear or care what she had to say!

'Everybody comes to the post office,' she went on grimly; 'you hev only to watch, and you see all the folks, and you know all that is goin' on. An' that suits me 'xactly.'

'But you had nothing to do with the post office,' said Diana. 'How could you see everybody?'

'You keep your eyes open, and you'll see things, most places,' said Miss Collins. 'La! I used to be in and out; why shouldn't I? And now and then I'd say to Miss Gunn— "You're jest fagged out with standin' upon your feet; you jes' go in there and sit down by the fire, and don't let the pot bile over and put it out; and I'll see to the letters and the folks." And so she did, and so I did. It was as good as a play.'

'How?' said Diana, feeling a vague pain at the thought of the post office; that place where her hopes had died. Somehow there was a vague dread in her heart also, without any reason.

'Wall—you git at folk's secrets—if they have any,' Miss Collins answered, suddenly checking her flow of words. Diana did not ask again; the subject was disagreeable. She began to cut up her parsley deftly with a sharp knife; and her hand-maid stood and looked at her.

'Some folks thought, you know, at one time, that Mr. Masters was courtin' Phemie Knowlton. I didn't let on, but la! I knowed it warn't so. Why, there warn't never a letter come from her to him, nor went from him to her.'

'She was here herself,' said Diana; 'why should they write? You could tell nothing by that.'

'She warn't here after she had gone away,' said Miss Collins; 'and that was jes' the time when I knowed all about it. I knowed about other people too.'

That was also the time after Evan had quitted Pleasant Valley. Yet Diana did not know why she could not keep herself from trembling. If Evan *had* written, then, this Jemima Collins and her employer, Miss Gunn, would have known it and drawn their conclusions. Well, they had no data to go upon now.

'Bring me a little saucepan, Jemima, will you?'

Jemima brought it. Now her mistress (but she never called her so) would be away and off in a minute or two more, and leave her to watch the saucepan, she knew, and her opportunity would be over. Still she waited to choose her words.

'You ain't so fond o' life as I be,' she observed.

'Perhaps not,' said Diana. 'I do not think I should like a situation in the post office.'

'But I should ha' thought you'd ha' liked to go all over the world and see everything. Now Pleasant Valley seems to me something like a corner. Why didn't you?'

'Why didn't I what?' said Diana, standing up. She had been stooping down over her saucepan, which now sat upon a little bed of coals.

'La! you needn't look at me like that,' said Miss Collins, chuckling. 'It's no harm. You had your ch'ice, and you chose it; only *I* would have took the other.'

'The other what? *What* would you have taken?'

'Wall, I don't know,' said Miss Collins; 'to be sure, one never does know till one is tried, they say; but if I had, I think I should ha' took 'tother one.'

'I do not understand you,' said Diana, walking off to the

table, where she began to gather up the wrecks of the parsley stems. She felt an odd sensation of cold about the region of her heart, physically very disagreeable.

'You are hard to make understand, then,' said Miss Collins. 'I suppose you know you had two sweethearts, don't you? And sure enough you had the pick of the lot. 'Taint likely you've forgotten.'

'How dare you speak so?' asked Diana, not passionately, but with a sort of cold despair, eyeing her handmaiden.

'Dare?' said the latter. 'Dare what? I ain't saying nothin'. 'Tain't no harm to have two beaus; you chose your ch'ice, and *he* hain't no cause to be uncontented, anyhow. About the 'tother one I don't say nothin'. I should think he *was*, but that's nat'ral. I s'pose he's got over it by now. You needn't stand and look. He's fur enough off, too. Your husband won't be jealous. You knowed you had two men after you.'

'I cannot imagine why you say that,' Diana repeated, standing as it were at bay.

'How I come to know? That's easy. Didn't I tell you I was in the post office? La, I know. I see the letters.'

'Letters!' cried Diana, in a tone which forthwith made Miss Collins open all the eyes she had. It was not a scream; it was not even very loud; yet Miss Collins went into a swift calculation to find out what *was* in it. Beyond her ken, happily; it was a heart's death-cry.

'Yes,' she said stolidly; 'I said letters. Ain't much else goin' at the post office, 'cept letters and papers; and I ain't one o' them as sets no count by the papers. La, what do I care for the news at Washington? I don't know the folks; they may all die or get married for what I care; but in Pleasant Valley I know where I be, and I know who the folks be. And that's what made me allays like to get a chance to sort the letters, or hand 'em out.'

'You never saw many letters of mine,' said Diana, turning away to hide her lips, which she felt were growing strange. But she must speak; she must know more.

'N—o,' said Miss Collins; 'not letters o' your writin',—ef you mean that.'

'Letters of mine of any sort. I don't get many letters.'

'Some of 'em's big ones, when they come. My! didn't I use to wonder what was in 'em! Two stamps, and *three* stamps. I s'pose feelin's makes heavy weight.' Miss Collins laughed a little.

'Two stamps and three stamps?' said Diana fiercely;— 'how many were there?'

'I guess I knowed of three. Two I handed out o' the box. myself; and Miss Gunn, she said there was another. There was no mistakin' them big letters. They was on soft paper, and lots o' stamps, as I said.'

'You gave them out? Who to?'

'To Mis' Starlin' herself. I mind partic'lerly. She come for 'em herself, and she got 'em. You don't mean she lost 'em on her way hum? They was postmarked some queer name, but they come from Californy; I know that. You hain't never forgotten 'em? I've heerd it's good to be off with the old love before you are on with the new; but I never heerd o' folks forgettin' their love-letters. La, 'tain't no harm to have love-letters. Nobody can cast that up to ye. You have chosen your ch'ice, and it's all right. I reckon most folks would be proud to have somebody else thrown over for them.'

Diana heard nothing of this. She was standing, deaf and blind, seeming to look out of the window; then slowly, moved by some instinct, not reason, she went out of the kitchen and crept up-stairs to her own room and laid herself upon her bed. Deaf and blind; she could neither think nor feel; she only thought she knew that she was dead. The consciousness of the truth pressed upon her to benumbing; but she was utterly unable to separate points or look at the connection of them. She had lived and suffered before; now she was crushed and dead; that was all she knew. She could not even measure the full weight of her misery; she lay too prostrate beneath it.

So things were, when very shortly after the minister came in. He had put up his horse, and came in with his day's work behind him. Diana's little parlour was bright, for a smart fire was blazing; the evenings and mornings were cool now in Pleasant Valley; and the small table stood ready for supper, as

Diana had left it. She was up-stairs, probably; and up-stairs he went, to wash his hands and get ready for the evening; for the minister was the neatest man living. There he found Diana laid upon her bed, where nobody ever saw her in the day-time; and furthermore, lying with that nameless something in all the lines of her figure which is the expression not of pain but of despair; and those who have never seen it before, read it at first sight. How it should be despair, of course, the minister had no clue to guess; so, although it struck him with a sort of strange chill, he supposed she must be suffering from some bodily ailment, in spite of the fact that nobody had ever known Diana to have so much as a headache in her life until now. Her face was hid. Basil went up softly and laid his hand on her shoulder, and felt so the slight convulsive shiver that ran over her. But his inquiries could get nothing but monosyllables in return; hardly that; rather inarticulate utterances of assent or dissent to his questions or proposals. Was she suffering? Yes. What was the cause? No intelligible answer. Would she not come down to tea? No. Would she have anything? No. Could he do anything for her? No.

'Diana,' said her husband tenderly, 'is it bad news?'

There was a pause, and he waited.

'Just go down,' she managed with great difficulty to say. 'There is nothing the matter with me. I'll come by and by. I'll just lie still a little.'

She had not shown her face, and the minister quietly withdrew, feeling that there was more than appeared on the surface. There was enough appearing on the surface to make him uneasy; and he paid no attention to Miss Collins, who brought in the supper and bustled about rather more than was necessary.

'Don't ring the bell, Jemima,' Mr. Masters said. 'Mrs. Masters is not coming down.'

Miss Collins went on to make the tea. That was always Diana's business.

'What ails her?' she asked abruptly.

'You ought to know,' said the minister. 'What did she complain of?'

'Complain!' echoed the handmaiden. 'She was as well as you be, not five minutes afore you come in.'

'How do you know?'

'Guess I had ought to! Why, she was in the kitchen talkin' and fiddle-faddlin' with them eggs; she thinks I ain't up to 'em. There warn't nothin' on earth the matter with her then. She had sot the table in here and fixed up the fire, and then she come into the kitchen and went to work at the supper. There ain't never nothin' the matter with her.'

The minister made no sort of remark, nor put any further inquiry, nor looked even curious. Miss Collins, however, *did*. Her brain got into a sudden confusion of possibilities. Pouring out the tea, she stood by the table reflecting what she should say next.

'I guess she's mad at me,' she began slowly. 'Or maybe she's afeard you'll be mad with her. La! 'tain't nothin'. I told her you'd never be jealous. 'Tain't no harm for a girl to have two beaus, is it?'

The minister gave her a quick look from under his brows, and replied calmly that he 'supposed not.'

'Wall, I told her so; and now she's put out 'cause I knowed o' them letters. La, folks that has the post office can't help but know more o' what concerns their fellow-creatures than other folks does. I handled them myself, you see, and handed them out; leastways two o' them; that warn't no fault o' mine nor of anybody's. La, she needn't to mind!'

'How much tea did you put in, Jemima?'

'I don't know, Mr. Masters. I put in a pinch. Mrs. Masters had ought to ha' been here to make it herself. She knows how you like it.'

'I like more than such a pinch as this was. If you will empty the teapot, I will make a cup for myself. That will do, thank you.'

Left alone, Mr. Masters sat for a little while with his head on his hand, neglecting the supper. Then he roused himself and went on to make some fresh tea. And very carefully and nicely he made it, poured out a cup and prepared it, put it on a little tray then, and carried it steaming and fragrant up to

R

his wife's room. Diana was lying just as he had left her. Mr. Masters shut the door, and came to the bedside.

'Di,' said he gently, 'I have brought you a cup of tea.'

There was neither answer nor movement. He repeated his words. She murmured an unintelligible rejection of the proposal, keeping her face carefully covered.

'No,' said he, 'I think you had better take it. Lift up your head, Di, and try. It is good.'

The tone was tender and quiet, nevertheless Diana had known Mr. Masters long enough to be assured that when he had made up his mind to a thing, there was no bringing him off it. She would have to take the tea; and as he put his hand under her head to lift her up, she suffered him to do it. Then he saw her face. Only by the light of a candle, it is true; but that revealed more than enough. So wan, so deathly pale, so dark in the lines round the eyes, and those indescribable shadows which mental pain brings into a face, that her husband's heart sank down. No small matter, easy to blow away, had brought his strong beautiful Diana to look like that. But his face showed nothing, though indeed she never looked at it; and his voice was clear and gentle just as usual in the few words he said. He held the cup to her lips, and after she had drank the tea and lay down again, he passed his hand once or twice with a tender touch over her brow and the disordered hair. Then, with no more questions or remarks, he took away the candle and the empty cup, and Diana saw him no more that night.

CHAPTER XXVI.

THINGS UNDONE.

THE mischief-maker slept peacefully till morning. Nobody else. Diana did not keep awake, it is true; she was at that dull stage of misery when something like stupor comes over the brain; she slumbered heavily from time to time. Nature does claim such a privilege sometimes. It was Basil who watched the night through; watched and prayed. There was no stupor in his thoughts; he had a very full, though vague, realization of great evil that had come upon them both. He was very near the truth, too, after an hour or two of pondering. Putting Miss Collins' hints, Diana's own former confessions, and her present condition together, he saw, clearer than it was good to see, the probable state of affairs. And yet he was glad to see it; if any help or bettering was ever to come, it was desirable that his vision should be true, and his wisdom have at least firm data to act upon. But what action could touch the case?—the most difficult that a man can have to deal with. Through the night Basil alternately walked the floor and knelt down, sometimes at his study table, sometimes before the open window, where it seemed almost as if he could read signs of that invisible sympathy he was seeking. The air was a little frosty, but very still; he kept up a fire in his chimney, and Basil was not one of those ministers who live in perpetual terror about draughts; it was a comfort to him to-night to look off and away from earth, even though he could not see into heaven. The stars were witnesses to him and for him, in their eternal calmness. 'He calleth them all by their names; for that he is strong in power, not one faileth. Why sayest thou, O Jacob, and speakest, O Israel, My way is hid from

the Lord, and my judgment is passed over from my God?'—
And in answer to the unspoken cry of appeal that burst forth
as he knelt there by the window—'O Lord, my strength, my
fortress, and my refuge in the day of affliction!'—came the
unspoken promise : ' The mountains shall depart, and the hills
be removed ; but my kindness shall not depart from thee,
neither shall the covenant of my peace be removed, saith the
Lord that hath mercy on thee.' The minister had something
such a night of it as Jacob had before his meeting with Esau ;
with the difference that there was no lameness left the next
morning. Before the dawn came up, when the stars were
fading, Basil threw himself on the lounge in his study, and
went into a sleep as deep and peaceful as his sleeps were wont
to be. And when he rose up, after some hours, he was entirely
himself again ; refreshed and restored and ready for duty.
Neither could anybody, that day or afterwards, see the slightest
change in him from what he had been before.

He went out and attended to his horse ; the minister always
did that himself. Then came in and changed his dress, and
went through his morning toilet with the usual dainty care.
Then he went in to see Diana.

She had awaked at last out of her slumberous stupor, sorry to
see the light and know that it was day again. Another day!
Why should there be another day for her? what use? why
could she not die and be out of her trouble? Another day!
and now would come, had come, the duties of it; how was she
to meet them? how could she do them? life energy was gone.
She was dead ; how was she to play the part of the living, and
among the living? What mockery! And Basil, what would
become of him? As for Evan, Diana dared not so much in
her thoughts as even to glance his way. She had risen half
up in bed—she had not undressed at all—and was sitting with
her arms slung round her knees, gazing at the daylight and
wondering vaguely about all these things, when the door
between the rooms swung lightly open. If she had dared,
Diana would have crouched down and hid her face again ; she
was afraid to do that ; she sat stolidly still, gazing out at the
window. Look at Basil she could not. His approach filled

her with so great a feeling of repulsion that she would have liked to spring from the bed and flee,—anywhere, away and away; where she would see him no more. No such flight was possible. She sat motionless and stared at the window, keeping down the internal shiver which ran over her.

Basil came with his light quick step and stood beside her; took her hand and felt her pulse.

'You are not feeling very well, Di,' he said gravely.

'Well enough,'—said Diana. 'I will get up and be down presently.'

'Will you?' said he. 'Now I think you had better not. The best thing you can do will be to lie still here and keep quiet all day. May I prescribe for you?'

'Yes. I will do what you please,' said Diana. She never looked at him, and he knew it.

'Then this is what I think you had better do. Get up and take a bath; then put on your dressing-gown and lie down again. You shall have your breakfast up here—and I will let nobody come up to disturb you.'

'I'm not hungry. I don't want anything.'

'You are a little feverish—but you will be better for taking something. Now you get your bath—and I'll attend to the breakfast.'

He kissed her brow gravely, guessing that she would rather he did not, but knowing nevertheless that he might and must; for he was her husband, and however gladly she, and unselfishly he, would have broken the relation between them, it subsisted and could not be broken. And then he went downstairs.

'Where's Mis' Masters?' demanded Jemima when she brought in the breakfast-tray, standing attention.

'Not coming down.'

'Ain't anything ails her, is there?'

'Yes. But I don't know how serious. Give me the kettle, Jemima; I told her to lie still, and that I would bring her a cup of tea.'

'I'll take it up, Mr. Masters; and you can eat your breakfast.'

'Thank you. I always like to keep my promises. Fetch in
the kettle, Jemima.'

Jemima dared not but obey. So when Diana, between dead
and alive, had done as she was bid, taken her bath, and wrapped
in her dressing-gown was laid upon her bed again, her husband
made his appearance with a little tray and the tea. There had
been a certain bodily refreshment about the bath and the
change of dress, but with that little touch of the everyday
work of life there had come such a rebellion against life in
general and all that it held, that Diana was nearly desperate.
In place of dull despair, had come a wild repulsion against
everything that was left her in the world; and yet the girl
knew that she would neither die nor go mad, but must just live
and bear. She looked at Basil and his tray with a sort of
impatient horror.

'I don't want anything!' she said. 'I don't want anything!'

'Try the tea. It is out of the green chest.'

Diana had learned, as I said, to know her husband pretty
well; and she knew that though the tone in which he spoke
was very quiet, and for all a certain sweet insistence in it could
scarcely be said to be urging, nevertheless there was under it
something to which she must yield. His will had never had clashed
with hers once; nevertheless Diana had seen and known that
whatever Basil wanted to do with anybody, he did. Everybody
granted it to him, somehow. So did she now. She raised
herself up and tasted the tea.

'Eat a biscuit—.'

'I don't want it. I don't want anything, Basil.'

'You must eat something, though,' said he. 'It is bad
enough for me to have to carry along with me all day the
thought of you lying here; I cannot bear in addition the
thought of you starving.'

'O no, I am not starving,' Diana answered; and unable to
endure to look at him or talk to him, she covered her face with
her hands, leaning it down upon her knees. Basil did not say
anything, nor did he go away; he stood beside her, with an
outflow of compassion in his heart, but waiting patiently. At
last he touched her smooth hair with his hand.

'Di,' said he gently, 'look up and take something.'

She hastily removed her hands, raised her head, swallowed the tea, and managed to swallow the biscuit with it. He leaned forward and kissed her brow as he had done last night.

'Now lie down and rest,' said he. 'I must ride over to Blackberry Hill again—and I do not know how long I may be kept there. I will tell Jemima to let no visitors come up to bother you. Lie still and rest. I will give you a pillow for your thoughts, Di.—"Under the shadow of thy wings will I make my refuge, until these calamities be overpast."'

He went away; and Diana covered her face again. She could not bear the light. Her whole nature was in uproar. The bath and dressing, the tea, her husband's presence and words, his last words especially, had roused her from her stupor, and given her as it were a scale with which to measure the full burden of her misery. There was no item wanting, Diana thought, to make it utterly immeasurable and unbearable. If she had married a less good man, it would have been less hard to spoil all his hopes of happiness ; if he had been a weaker man, she would not have cared about him at all. If any hand but her own mother's had dashed her cup of happiness out of her hand, she would have had there a refuge to go to. Most girls have their mothers. If Evan had not been sent to so distant a post—but when her thoughts dared turn to Evan, Diana writhed upon her bed in tearless agony. Evan, writing in all the freshness and strength of his love and his trust in her, those letters ;—waiting and looking for her answer ;—writing again and again ; disappointed all the while ; and at last obliged to conclude that there was no faith in her, and that her love had been a sham or a fancy. What had he not suffered on her account! even as she had suffered for him. But that he should think *so* of her was not to be borne ; she would write. Might she write? From hiding her head on her pillow, Diana sat bolt upright now and stared at the light as if it could tell her. Might she write to Evan, just once, this once, to tell him how it had been ? Would that be any wrong against her husband ? Would Basil have any right to forbid her? The uneasy sense of doubt here was met by a furious rebellion against any authority that would interfere with her doing herself—as she said—so much justice, and giving herself and Evan so much miserable comfort. Could there be a right to hinder her? Suppose she were to ask Basil?—But what disclosures that would involve! Would he bear them, or could she? Better write without his knowledge. Then, on the other hand, Basil was so upright himself, so true and faithful, and trusted her so completely. No, she never could deceive his trust, not if she died. O that she could die! But Diana knew that she was not going to die. Suppose she charged her mother with what she had done, and get *her* to write and confess it? A likely thing, that Mrs. Starling would be wrought upon to make such a humiliation of herself! She was forced to give up that thought. And indeed she was not clear about the essential distinction between communicating directly herself with Evan, and getting another to do it for her. And what had been Mrs. Starling's motive in keeping back the letters? But Diana knew her mother, and that problem did not detain her long.

For hours and hours Diana's mind was like a stormy sea, where the thunder and the lightning were not wanting any more than the wind. Once in a while, like the faint blink of a sun-ray through the clouds, came an echo of the words Basil had quoted—' In the shadow of thy wings will I make my refuge '—but they hurt her so that she fled from them. The contrast of their peace with her turmoil, of their intense sweetness with the bitter passion which was wasting her heart; the hint of that harbour for the storm-tossed vessel, which could only be entered, she knew, by striking sail; all that was unbearable. I suppose there was a whisper of conscience, too, which said, ' Strike sail, and go in ! '—while passion would not take down an inch of canvas. *Could* not, she said to herself. Could she submit to have things be as they were? submit, and be quiet, and accept them, and go her way accepting them, and put the thought of Evan away, and live the rest of her life as though he had no existence? That was the counsel Basil would give, she had an unrecognised consciousness; and for the present, pain was easier to bear than that. And now memory flew back over the years, and took up again the thread of her relations with Evan, and traced them to their beginning; and went over all the ground, going back and forward, recalling every meeting, and reviewing every one of those too scanty hours. For a long while she had not been able to do this, because Evan, she thought, had been faithless, and in that case she really never had had what she thought she had in him. Now she knew he was not faithless, and she had got the time and him back again, and she in a sort revelled in the consciousness. And with that came then the thought, 'Too late!'—She had got him again only to see an impassable barrier set between which must keep them apart for ever. And that barrier was her husband. What the thought of Basil, or rather what his image was to Diana that day, it is difficult to tell; she shunned it whenever it appeared, with an intolerable mingling of contradictory feelings. Her fate,—and yet more like a good angel to her than anybody that had ever crossed the line of her path; the destroyer of her hope and joy for ever,—and yet one to whom she was bound, and to whom she owed all possible duty and affection; she wished it were possible never to see him again in the world, and at the same time there was not another in the world of whom she believed all the good she believed of him. His image was dreadful to her. Basil was the very centre-point of her agonized struggles that day. To be parted from Evan she could have borne, if she might have devoted herself to the memory of him and lived in quiet sorrow; but to put this man in his place!—to belong to him, to be his wife—

In proportion to the strength and health of Diana's nature was the power of her realization and the force of her will. But also the possibility of endurance. The internal fight would have broken down a less pure and sound bodily organization. It was characteristic of this natural soundness and sweetness, which was mental as well as physical, that her mother's part in the events which had destroyed her happiness had very little of her attention that day. She thought of it with a kind of sore wonder and astonishment, in which resentment had almost no

share. 'O, mother, mother!'—she said in her heart; but she
said no more.

Miss Collins came up once or twice to see her, but Diana lay
quiet, and was able to baffle curiosity.

'Are ye goin' to git up and come down to supper?' the
handmaid asked in the second visit, which occurred late in the
afternoon.

'I don't know. I shall do what Mr. Masters says.'

'You don't look as ef there was much ailin' you;—and yet
you look kind o' queer, too. I shouldn't wonder a bit ef you
was a gettin' a fever. There's a red spot on one of your cheeks
that's like fire. T'other one's pale enough. You must be in a
fever, I guess, or you couldn't lie here with the window open.'

'Leave it open—and just let me be quiet.'

Miss Collins went down, marvelling to herself. But when
Basil came home he found the flush spread to both cheeks, and
a look in Diana's eyes that he did not like.

'How has the day been?' he asked, passing his hand over
the flushed cheek and the disordered hair. Diana shrank and
shivered and did not answer. He felt her pulse.

'Diana,' said he, 'what is the matter with you?'

She stared at him, in the utter difficulty of answering.
'Basil'—she began, and stopped, not finding another word
to add. For prevarication was an accomplishment Diana knew
nothing of. She closed her eyes, that they might not see the
figure standing there.

'Would you like me to fetch your mother to you?'

'No,' she said, starting. 'O no! Don't bring her, Basil.'

'I will not,' said he kindly. 'Why should she not come?'

'Mother? never. Never, never! Not mother. I can't bear
her'— said Diana strangely.

Mr. Masters went down-stairs looking very grave. He took
his supper, for he needed it; and then he carried up a cup of
tea, fresh made, to Diana. She drank it this time eagerly;
but there was no lightening of his grave brow when he carried
the cup down again. Something was very much the matter,
he knew now, as he had feared it last night. He debated with
himself whether he had better try to find out just what it

was. Miss Collins, by a judicious system of suggestion and inquiry, might be led perhaps to reveal something without knowing that she revealed anything; but the minister disliked that way of getting information when it could be dispensed with. He had enough knowledge to act upon; for the rest he was patient, and could wait.

That night he knew Diana did not sleep. He himself passed the night again in his study, though not in the struggles of the night before. He was very calm, stedfast, diligent; that is, his usual self entirely. And, watching her without her knowing he watched, he knew by her breathing and her changes of position that it was a night of no rest on her part. Once he saw she was sitting up in the bed; once he saw that she had left it and was sitting by the window.

The next day the minister did not leave home. He had no more urgent business anywhere, he thought, than there. And he found Diana did not make up by day what she had lost by night; she was always staring wide awake whenever he went into the room; and he went whenever there was a cup of tea or a cup of broth to be taken to her, for he prepared it and carried it to her himself.

It happened in the course of the afternoon that Prince and the old little green waggon came jogging along and landed Mrs. Starling at the minister's door. This was a very rare event; Mrs. Starling came at long intervals to see her daughter, and made then a call which nobody enjoyed. To-day Miss Collins hailed the sight of her. Indeed, if the distance had not been too much, Miss Collins would have walked down to carry the tidings of Diana's indisposition; for, like a true gossip, she scented mischief where she could see none. The minister would let her have nothing to do with his wife; and if he were out of the house and she got a chance, she could make nothing of Diana. Nothing certain; but nothing either that lulled her suspicions. Now, with Mrs. Starling, there was no telling what she might get at. The lady dismounted and came into the kitchen, looking about her, as always, with sharp eyes.

'How d'ye do?' said she. 'Where is Diana?'

'I'm glad to see ye, Mis' Starling, and that's a fact,' said the handmaid. 'I was 'most a mind to walk down to 'your place to-day.'

'What's the matter? Where's Diana?'

'Wall, she's up-stairs. She hain't been down now for two days.'

'What's the reason?'

'Wall—sun'thin' ain't right; and I don't think the minister's clear what it is; and *I* ain't. She was took as sudden—you never see nothin' suddener—she come in here to fix a dish o' eggs for supper that she's mighty particler about, and don't think no one can cook eggs but herself; and I was talkin' and tellin' her about my old experiences in the post office—and she went up-stairs and took to her bed; and she hain't left it sen. Now ain't that queer? 'Cause she didn't say nothin' ailed her; not a word; only she went up and took to her bed; and she does look queer at you, that I will say. Mebbe it's fever a comin' on.'

There was a minute or two's silence. Mrs. Starling did not immediately find her tongue.

'What have the post office and your stories got to do with it?' she asked harshly. 'I should like to know.'

'Yes—,' said Miss Collins, drawing out the word with affable intonation,—'that's what beats me. What should they? But la! the post office is queer; that's what I always said. Everybody gits into it; and ef you're there, o' course you can't help knowin' things.'

'You weren't in the post office!' said Mrs. Starling. 'It was none of *your* business.'

'Warn't I?' said Miss Collins. 'Don't you mind better'n that, Mis' Starling? I mind you comin', and I mind givin' you your letters too; I mind some 'ticlar big ones, that had stamps enough on to set up a shop. La, 'tain't no harm. Miss Gunn, she used to feel a sort o' sameness about allays takin' in and givin' out, and then she'd come into the kitchen and make cake mebbe, and send me to 'tend the letters and the folks. And then it was as good as a play to me. Don't you never git tired o' trottin' a mile in a bushel, Mis' Starlin'? So I was jest a tellin' Diany '—

'Where's the minister?'

'Most likely he's where she is—up-stairs. He won't let nobody else do a hand's turn for her. He takes up every cup of tea, and he spreads every bit of bread and butter; and he tastes the broths; you'd think he was anythin' in the world but a minister; he tastes the broth, and he calls for the salt and pepper, and he stirs and he tastes; and then—you never see a man make such a fuss, leastways *I* never did—he'll have a white napkin and spread over a tray, and the cup on it, and saucer too, for he won't have the cup 'thout the saucer, and then carry it off.—Was your husband like that, Mis' Starling? He was a minister, I've heerd tell.'

Mrs. Starling turned short about without answering, and went up-stairs.

She found the minister there, as Miss Collins had opined she would; but she paid little attention to him. He was just drawing the curtains over a window where the sunlight came in too glaringly. As he had done this, and turned, he was a spectator of the meeting between mother and child. It was peculiar. Mrs. Starling advanced to the foot of the bed, came no nearer, but stood there looking down at her daughter. And Diana's eyes fastened on hers with a look of calm, cold intelligence. It was intense enough, yet there was no passion in it; I suppose there was too much despair; however, it was, as I said, keen and intent, and it held Mrs. Starling's eyes like a vice. Those Mr. Masters could not see; the lady's back was towards him; but he saw how Diana's eyes pinioned her, and how strangely still Mrs. Starling stood.

'What's the matter with you?' she said harshly at last.

'You ought to know,'—said Diana, not moving her eyes.

'I ain't a conjuror,' Mrs. Starling returned with a sort of snort. 'What makes you look at me like that?'

Diana gave a short, sharp laugh. 'How can you look at me?' she said. 'I know all about it, mother.'

Mrs. Starling with a sudden determination went round to the head of the bed and put out her hand to feel Diana's pulse. Diana shrank away from her.

'Keep off!' she cried. 'Basil, Basil, don't let her touch me.'

'She is out of her head,' said Mrs. Starling, turning to her son-in-law, and speaking half loud. 'I had better stay and sit up with her.'

'No,' cried Diana. 'I don't want you. Basil, don't let her stay. Basil, Basil!'—

The cry was urgent and pitiful. Her husband came near, arranged the pillows, for she had started half up; and putting her gently back upon them, said in his calm tones,—'Be quiet, Di; you command here. Mrs. Starling, shall we go down-stairs?'

Mrs. Starling this time complied without making any objection; but as she reached the bottom she gave vent to her opinion.

'You are spoiling her!'

'Really—I should like to have the chance.'

'What do you mean by that?'

'Just the words. I should like to spoil Di. She has never had much of that sort of bad influence.'

'That sounds very weak, to me,' said Mrs. Starling.

'To whom should a man show himself weak, if not toward his wife?' said Basil carelessly.

'Your wife will not thank you for it.'

'I will endeavour to retain her respect,' said Basil in the same way; which aggravated Mrs. Starling beyond bounds. Something about him always did try her temper, she said to herself.

'Diana is going to have a fever,' she spoke abruptly.

'I am afraid of it.'

'What's brought it on?'

'I came home two evenings ago and found her on the bed.'

'You don't want me, you say? Who do you expect is going to sit up with her and take care of her?'

'I will try what I can do, for the present.'

'You can't manage that and your out-door work too.'

'I will manage *that*'—said Basil significantly.

'And let your parish work go? Well, I always thought a minister was bound to attend to his people.'

'Yes. Isn't my wife more one of my people than anybody else? Will you stay and take a cup of tea, Mrs. Starling?'

' No; if you don't want me, I am going. What will you do if Diana gets delirious? I think she's out of her head now.'

' I'll attend to her,' said Basil composedly.

Half suspecting a double meaning in his words, Mrs. Starling took short leave, and drove off. Not quite easy in her mind, if the truth be told, and glad to be out of all patience with the minister. Yes, if she had known how things would turn—if she had known—perhaps she would not have thrown that first letter into the fire; which had drawn her on to throw the second in, and the third. Could any son-in-law, could Evan Knowlton, at least, have been more untoward for her wishes than the one she had got? More unmanageable he could not have been; nor more likely to be spooney about Diana. And now what if Diana really should have a fever? People talk out in delirium. Well—the minister would keep his own counsel; she did not care, she said. But all the same, she did care; and she would fain have been the only one to receive Diana's revelations, if she could have managed it. And by what devil's conjuration had the truth come to be revealed, when only the fire and she knew anything about it? Mrs. Starling chewed the cud of no sweet fancy on her road home.

CHAPTER XXVII.

BONDS.

DIANA did become ill. A few days of such brain work as she had endured that first twenty-four hours were too much even for her perfect organization. She fell into a low fever, which at times threatened to become violent, yet never did. She was delirious often; and Basil heard quite enough of her unconscious revelations to put him in full possession of the situation. In different portions, Diana went over the whole ground. He knew sometimes that she was walking with Evan, taking leave of him; perhaps taking counsel with him, and forming plans for life; then wondering at his silence, speculating about ways and distances, tracing his letters out of the post office into the wrong hand. And when she was upon that strain, Diana would break out into a cry of ' O mother, mother, mother !'— repeating the word with an accent of such plaintive despair that it tore the heart of the one who heard it.

There was only one. As long as this state of things lasted, Basil gave himself up to the single task of watching and nursing his wife. And amid the many varieties of heart-suffering which people know in this world, that which he tasted these weeks was one of refined bitterness. He came to know just how things were, and just how they had been all along. He knew what Diana's patient or reticent calm covered. He heard sometimes her fond moanings over another name; sometimes her passionate outcries to the owner of that name to come and deliver her; sometimes—she revealed that too—even the repulsion with which she regarded himself. ' O, not this man !' she said one night, when he had been sitting by her and hoping that she was more quiet. ' O, not this man! It was a mistake. It was all a mistake. People ought to take better care at the post office. Tell Evan I didn't know; but I'll come to him now just as soon as I can.'

Another time she burst out more violently. 'Don't kiss me!' she exclaimed. 'Don't touch me. I won't bear it. Never again. I belong to somebody else, don't you know? You have no business to be here.' Basil was not near her, indeed she would not have recognised him if he had been; he was sitting by the fire at a distance; but he knew whom she was addressing in her mournful ravings, and his heart and courage almost gave way. It was very bitter; and many an hour of those nights the minister spent on his knees at the bed's foot, seeking for strength and wisdom, seeking to keep his heart from being quite broken, striving to know what to do. Should he do as she said, and never kiss her again? Should he behave to her in the future as a mere stranger? What was best for him and for her? Basil would have done that unflinchingly, though it had led him to the stake, if he could know what the best was. But he did not quite give up all hope, desperate as the case looked; his own strong cheerful nature and his faith in God kept him up. And he resolutely concluded that it would not be the best way nor the hope-fullest, for him and Diana, bound to each other as they were, to try to live as strangers. The bond could not be broken; it had better be acknowledged by them both. But if Basil could have broken it and set her free, he would have done it at any cost to himself. So, week after week, he kept his post as nurse at Diana's side. He was a capital nurse. Untireable as a man, and tender as a woman; quick as a woman, too, to read signs and answer unspoken wishes; thoughtful as many women are not; patient with an unending patience. Diana was herself at times, and recognised all this. And by degrees, as the slow days wore away, her disorder wore away too, or wore itself out, and she came back to her normal condition in all except strength. That was very failing, even after the fever was gone. And still Basil kept his post. He began now, it is true, to attend to some pressing outside duties, for which in the weeks just past he had provided a substitute; but morn-

S

ing, noon, and night he was at Diana's side. No hand but his own might ever carry to her the meals which his own hand had no inconsiderable share in preparing. He knew how to serve an invalid's breakfast with a refinement of care which Diana herself before that would not have known how to give another, though she appreciated it and took her lesson. Then nobody could so nicely and deftly prop up pillows and cushions so as to make her rest comfortably for the taking of the meal; no one had such skilful strength to enable a weak person to change his position. For all other things, Diana saw no difference in him; nothing told her that she had betrayed herself, and she betrayed herself no more. Dull and listless she might be; that was natural enough in her weak state of convalescence; and Diana had never been demonstrative towards her husband; it was no new thing that she was not demonstrative now. Neither did he betray that he knew all she was trying, poor child, to hide from him. He was just as usual. Only, in Diana's present helpless condition, he had opportunity to show tenderness and care in a thousand services which in her well days she would have dispensed with. And he did it, as I said, with the strength of a man and the delicacy of a woman. He let nobody else do anything for her.

Did he guess how gladly she would have escaped from all his ministrations? did he know what they were to Diana? Probably not; for with all his fineness of perception he was yet a man; and I suppose, reverse the conditions, there never was a man yet who would object to have one woman wait upon him because he loved another. Yet Basil did know partly and partly guess; and he went patiently on in the way he had marked out for himself, upheld by principle and by a great tenacity of purpose which was part of his character. Nevertheless, those were days of pain, great and terrible even for him; what they were to Diana he could but partially divine. As health slowly came back, and she looked at herself and her life again with eyes unveiled by disease, with the pitiless clearness of sound reason, Diana wished she could die. She knew she could not; she could come no nearer to it than a passing thought; her pulses were retaking their sweet regularity; her nerves were strung again, fine and true; only muscular strength seemed to tarry. Lying there on her bed and looking out over the snow-covered fields, for it was mid-winter by this time, Diana sometimes felt a terrible impulse to fly to Evan; as if she could wait only till she had the power to move. The feeling was wild, impetuous; it came like a hurricane wind, sweeping everything before it. And then Diana would feel her chains, and writhe, knowing that she could not and would not break them. But how ever was life to be endured? life with this other man? And how dreadful it was that he was so good, and so good to her! Yes, it would be easier if he did not care for her so well, far easier; easier even if he were not himself so good. The power of his goodness fettered Diana; it was a spell upon her. Yes, and she wanted to be good too; she would not forfeit heaven because she had lost earth; no, and not to gain earth back again. But how was she to live? And what if she should be unable always to hide her feeling, and Basil should come to know it? how would *he* live? What if she had said strange things in her days and nights of illness? They were all like a confused misty landscape to her; nothing taking shape; she could not tell how it might have been. Restless and weary, she was going over all these and a thousand other things one day, as she did every day, when Basil came in. He brought a tray in his hand. He set it down, and came to the bedside.

'Is it supper-time already?' she asked.

'Are you hungry?'

'I ought not to be hungry. I don't think I am.'

'Why ought you not to be hungry?'

'I am doing nothing, lying here.'

'I find that is what the people say who are doing too much. Extremes meet,—as usual.'

He lifted Diana up, and piled pillows and cushions at her back till she was well supported. Nobody could do this so well as Basil. Then he brought the tray and arranged it before her. There was a bit of cold partridge, and toast; and Basil filled Diana's cup from a little teapot he had set by the fire. The last degree of nicety was observable in all these preparations. Diana ate her supper. She must live, and she must eat, and she could not help being hungry; though she wondered at herself that she could be so unnatural.

'Where could you get this bird?' she asked at length, to break the silence which grew painful.

'I caught it.'

'Caught it?   *You!*   Shot it, do you mean?'

'No. I had not time to go after it with a gun. But I set snares.'

'I never knew partridges were so good,' said Diana, though something in her tone said, unconsciously to her, that she cared not what was good or bad.

'You did not use your advantages. That often happens.'

'I had not the advantage of being able to get partridges,' said Diana languidly.

'The woods are full of them.'

'Don't you think it is a pity to catch them?'

'For you?' said Basil. He was removing her empty plate, and putting before her another with an orange upon it, so accurately prepared that it stirred her admiration.

'Oranges!' cried Diana. 'How did you learn to do everything, Basil?'

'Don't be too curious,' said he. As he spoke, he softly put back off her ear a stray lock of the beautiful brown hair, which fell behind her like a cloud of wavy brightness. Even from that touch she inwardly shrank; outwardly she was impassive enough.

'Basil,' said Diana suddenly, 'didn't I talk foolishly sometimes?—when I was sick, I mean.'

'Don't you ever do it when you are well?'

'Do I?'

'What do you think?' said he, laughing, albeit his heart was not merry at the moment; but Diana's question was naive.

'I did not think I was in the habit of talking foolishly.'

'Your thoughts are true and just, as usual. It is so far from being in your habit, that it is hardly in your power,' he said tenderly.

Diana ate her orange, for she was very fond of the fruit,

and it gave occupation to hands and eyes while Basil was standing by. She did not like his evasion of her question, and pondered how she could bring it up again, between wish and fear. Before she was ready to speak the chance was gone. As Basil took away her plate, he remarked that he had to go down to see old Mrs. Barstow; and arranging her pillows anew, he stooped down and kissed her.

Left alone, Diána sat still propped up in bed and stared into the fire, which grew brighter as the light without waned. How she rebelled against that kiss! 'No, he has no right to me!' she cried in her passionate thoughts; 'he has no right to me! I am Evan's; every bit of me is Evan's, and nobody's else. O, how came I to marry this man? and what shall I do? I wonder if I shall go mad?—for I am not going to die. But how is it possible that I can live *so?*'

She was slow in regaining strength. Yet little by little it came back, like a monarch entering a country that has rebelled against him. By and by she was able to sit up. Her husband had a luxurious easy-chair sent from Boston for her and placed in her room; and one evening, it was in February now, Diana got up and put herself in it. She had never known such a luxurious piece of furniture in her life; she was dressed in a warm wrapper also provided by her husband, and which seemed to her of extravagant daintiness; and she sank into the depths of the one and the folds of the other with a helpless feeling of Basil's power over her, symbolized and emphasized by these things. Presently came Basil himself, again bringing her supper. He placed a small table by her side and set the tray there; put the teapot down by the fire; and taking a view of his wife, gave a slight smile at the picture. He might well, having so good a conscience as this man had. Diana was one of those magnificent women who look well always and anywhere; with a kitchen apron on and hands in flour, or in the dishabille of careless undress; but as her husband saw her then, she was lovely in an exquisite degree. She was wrapped in a quilted dressing-gown of soft grey stuff, with a warm shawl about her shoulders; her beautiful abundant hair, which she had been too weak of hand, and of heart too, to dress elaborately, lay piled

about her head in loose, bright, wavy masses, much more picturesque than Diana would have known how to make them by
design. I think there is apt, too, to be about such women a
natural grace of motion or of repose ; it was her case. To think
of herself or the appearance she might at any time be making,
was foreign to Diana; the noble grace of unconsciousness,
united to her perfectness of build, made her always faultless in
action or attitude. If she moved or if she sat, it might have
been a duchess, for the beautiful unconscious ease with which
she did it. Nature's high breeding; there is such a thing, and
there is such an effect of it when the constitution of mind and
body are alike noble.

Basil poured out her cup of tea, and divided her quail, and
then sat down. It was hard for her to bear.

'You are too good to me,' said Diana humbly.

'I should like to see you prove that.'

'I am not sure but you are too good to everybody.'

'Why? how can one be too good?'

'You won't get paid for it.'

'I think I shall,' said Basil, in a quiet confident way he
had, which was provoking if you were arguing with him. But
Diana was not arguing with him.

'Basil, *I* can never pay you,' she said, with a voice that
faltered a little.

'You are sure of that in your own mind?'

'Very sure!'

'I am a man of a hopeful turn of nature. Shall I divide
that joint for you?'

'My hands cannot manage a quail!' said Diana, yielding her
knife and fork to him. 'What can make me so weak?'

'You have had fever.'

'But I have no fever now, and I do not seem to get my
strength back.'

'After the unnatural tension, Nature takes her revenge.'

'It is very hard on you!'

'What?'

Diana did not answer. She had spoken that last word with
almost a break in her voice ; she gave her attention now dili-

gently to picking the quail bones. But when her supper was done, and the tray delivered over to Miss Collins, Basil did not, as sometimes he did, go away and leave her, but sat down again and trimmed the fire. Diana lay back in her chair, looking at him.

'Basil,' she said at last after a long silence,—'do you think mistakes, I mean life-mistakes, can ever be mended in this world?'

'You must define what you mean by mistakes,' he said without looking at her. 'There are no *mistakes*, love, but those which we make by our own fault.'

'O but yes there are, Basil!'

'Not what *I* mean by mistakes.'

'Then what do you call them? When people's lives are all spoiled by something they have had nothing to do with—by death, or sickness, or accident, or misfortune.'

'I call it,' said Basil slowly, and still without looking at her, —'I call it, when it touches me or you, or other of the Lord's children,—God's good hand.'

'O no, Basil! people's wickedness cannot be his hand.'

'People's wickedness is their own. And other evil I believe is wrought by the prince of this world. But God will use people's wickedness, and even Satan's mischief, to his children's best good; and so it becomes, in so far, his blessed hand. Don't you know he has promised, "There shall no evil happen to the just"? And that "all things shall work together for good to them that love God"? His promise does not fail, my child.'

'But, Basil,—loads of things do happen to them which *cannot* work for their good.'

'Then what becomes of the Lord's promise?'

'He cannot have made it, I think.'

'He has made it, and you and I believe it.'

'But, Basil, it is impossible. I do not see how some things *can* ever turn to people's good.'

'If any of the Lord's children were in doubt upon that point, I should recommend him to ask the Lord to enlighten him. For the heavens may fall, Diana, but "the word of our God shall stand for ever."'

Diana felt her lips quivering, and drew back into the shadow to hide them.

'But there can be no kindness in some of these things that I am thinking about,' she said as soon as she could control her voice; and it sounded harsh even then.

'There is nothing but kindness. When I would not give you strong coffee a while ago, in your fever, do you think I was influenced by cruel motives?'

'I could never believe anything but good of you, Basil.'

'Thank you. Do you mean, that of Christ you *could*?'

'No—' said Diana, hesitating; 'but I thought, perhaps, he might not care.'

'He had need to be long-suffering!' said Basil; 'for we do try his patience, the best of us. "He has borne our griefs and carried our sorrows," Diana; down into humiliation and death; that he might so earn the right to lift them off our shoulders and hearts; and one of his children doubts if he cares!'

'But he does not lift them off, Basil,' said Diana; and her voice trembled with unshed tears.

'He will'—said her husband.

'When?'

'As soon as we let him.'

'What must I do to let him?'

'Trust him wholly. And follow him like a child.'

The tears came, Diana could not hinder them; she laid her face against the side of her chair where Basil could not see it.

CHAPTER XXVIII.

EVAN'S SISTER.

SLOWLY from this time Diana regained strength, and by degrees took again her former place in the household. To Miss Collins' vision she was 'the same as ever.' Basil felt she was not.

Yet Diana did every duty of her station with all the care and diligence she had ever given to it. She neglected nothing. Basil's wardrobe was kept in perfect order; his linen was exquisitely got up; his meals were looked after, and served with all the nice attention that was possible. Diana did not in the least lose her head, or sit brooding when there was something to do. She did not sit brooding at any time, unless at rare intervals. Yet her husband's heart was very heavy with the weight which rested on hers, and truly with his own share as well. There was a line in the corners of Diana's sweet mouth which told him, nobody else, that she was turning to stone; and the light of her eye was, as it were, turned inward upon itself. Without stopping to brood over things, which she did not, her mind was constantly abiding in a different sphere away from him, dwelling afar off, or apart in a region by itself; he had her physical presence, but not her spiritual; and who cares for a body without a soul? All this time there was no confidence between them. Basil knew, indeed, the whole facts of the case, but Diana did not know he knew. He wished she would speak, but believed now she never would; and he could not ask her. Truly he had his own part to bear; and withal his sorrow and yearning tenderness for her. Sometimes his heart was nigh to break. But Diana's heart was broken.

Was it comfort, or was it not comfort, when near the end of spring a little daughter was born to them? Diana in any circumstances was too true a woman not to enter upon a mother's riches and responsibilities with a full heart, not to enter thoroughly into a mother's joy and dignity; it was a beautiful something that had come into her life, so far as itself was concerned; and no young mother's hands ever touched more tenderly the little pink bundle committed to them, nor ever any mother's eyes hung more intently over her wonderful new possession. But lift the burden from Diana's heart her baby did not. There was something awful about it, too, for it was another bond that bound her to a man she did not love. When Diana was strong enough, she sometimes shed floods of tears over the little unconscious face, the only human confidant she dared trust with her secret. Before this time her tears had been few; something in the baby took the hardness from her, or else gave one of those inexplicable touches to the spring of tears which we can neither resist nor account for. But the baby's father was as fond of her as her mother, and had a right to be, Diana knew; and that tried her. She grudged Basil the right. On the whole, I think, however, the baby did Diana good. As for Basil, it did him good. He thanked God, and took courage.

The summer had begun when Diana was able to come downstairs again. One afternoon she was there, in her little parlour, come down for a change. The windows were open, and she sat thinking of many things. Her easy-chair had been moved down to this room; and Diana, in white, as Basil liked to see her, was lying back in it, close beside the window. June was on the hills, and in the air, and in the garden; for a bunch of red roses stood in a glass on the table, and one was fastened at Diana's belt and another stuck in her beautiful hair. Not by her own hands, truly; Basil had brought in the roses a little while ago and held them to her nose, and then put one in her hair and one in her belt. Diana suffered it, all careless and unknowing of the exquisite effect, which her husband smiled at, and then went off; for his work called him. She had heard his horse's hoof-beats, going away at a gallop; and the sound carried her thoughts back, away, as a little thing will, to a time when Mr. Masters used to come to her old home to visit her mother and her, and then ride off so. Yes, and in those days another came too; and June days were sweet then as now; and roses bloomed; and the robins were whistling then also, she remembered; did *their* fates and life courses never change? was it all June to them, every year? How the robins whistled their answer!—'all June to them, every year!' And the smell of roses did not change, nor the colour of the light; and the fresh green of the young foliage was deep and bright and glittering to-day as ever it was. Just the same! and a human life could have all sweet scents and bright tints and glad sounds fall out of it, and not to come back! There is nothing but duty left, thought Diana; and duty with all the sap gone out of it. Duty was left a dry tree; and more, a tree so full of thorns that she could not touch it without being stung and pierced. Yet even so; to this stake of duty she was bound.

Diana sat cheerlessly gazing out into the June sunlight, which laughed at her with no power to gain a smile in return; when a step came along the narrow entry, and the doorway was filled with Mrs. Starling's presence. Mother and daughter looked at each other in a peculiar way they had now; Diana's face cold, Mrs. Starling's face hard.

'Well!' said the latter,—'how are you getting along?'

'You see, I am down-stairs.'

'I see you're doing nothing.'

'Mr. Masters won't let me.'

'Humph! When *I* had a baby four weeks old, I had my own way. And so would you, if you wanted to have it.'

'My husband will not let me have it.'

'That's fool's nonsense, Diana. If you are the girl I take you for, you can do whatever you like with your husband. No man that ever lived would make *me* sit with my hands before me. Who's got the baby?'

'Jemima.'

'How's Jemima to do her work and your work too? She can't do it.'

'No, but Mr. Masters is going to get another person to help take care of baby'

' A nurse!' cried Mrs. Starling aghast.

' No, not exactly; but somebody to help me.'

' Are you turned weak and sickly, Diana?'

' No, mother.'

' Then you don't want another girl, any more than a frog wants an umbrella. Put your baby in the crib and teach her to lie there, when you are busy. That's the way you were brought up.'

' You must talk to Mr. Masters, mother.'

' I don't want talk to Mr. Masters—I've got something else to do. But you can talk to him, Diana, and he'll do what you say.'

' It's the other way, mother. I must do what he says.' Diana's tone was peculiar.

' Then you're turned soft.'

' I think I am turned hard.'

' Your husband is easy to manage—for you.'

' Is he?' said Diana. ' I am glad it isn't true. I despise men that are easy to manage. I am glad I can respect him, at any rate.'

Mrs. Starling looked at her daughter with an odd expression. It was curious and uncertain; but she asked no question. She seemed to change the subject; though perhaps the connection was close.

' Did you hear the family are coming to Elmfield again this summer?'

Diana's lips formed the word ' no;' the breath of it hardly got out.

' Yes, they're coming, sure enough. Phemie will be here next week; and her sister, what's her name?—Mrs. Reverdy— is here now.'

Silence.

' I suppose they'll fill the house with company, as they did last time, and cut up their shines as usual. Well! they don't come in my way. But you'll have to see 'em, I guess.'

' Why?'

' You know they make a great to-do about your husband in that family. And Genevieve Reverdy seems uncommonly fond of you. She asked me no end of questions about you on Sabbath.'

There flushed a hot colour into Diana's cheeks, which faded away and left them very pale.

'She hasn't grown old a bit,' Mrs. Starling went on, talking rather uneasily; 'nor she hain't grown wise, neither. She can't ask you how you do without a giggle. And she had dressed herself to come to church as if the church was a fair and she was something for sale. Flowers, and feathers, and laces, and ribbons, a little there and a little here; bows on her gloves, and bows on her shoes, and bows on her gown. I believe she would have tucked some into the corners of her mouth, if they would have stayed.'

Diana made no reply. She was looking out into the sunlit hillside in view from her window, and had grown visibly whiter since her mother came in. Mrs. Starling reviewed her for that instant with a keen, anxious, searching gaze, which changed before Diana turned her head.

'I can't make out, for my part, what such folks are in the world for,' she went on. 'They don't do no good, to themselves nor to nobody else. And fools mostly contrive to do harm. Well—she's coming to see you; she'll be along one of these days.'

'To see me!' Diana echoed.

'So she says. Maybe it's all flummery. I daresay it is; but she talked a lot of it. You'd ha' thought there warn't any one else in the world she cared about seeing.'

Mrs. Starling went up-stairs at this point to see the baby, and Diana sat looking out of the window with her thoughts in wild confusion of pain. Pain and fright, I might say. And yet her senses took the most delicate notice of all there was in the world outside to attract them. Could it be June, once so fair and laughing, that smote her now with such blows of memory's hammer? or was it Memory using June? She saw the bright glisten of the leaves upon the hillside, the rich growth of the grass, the fair beams of the summer sun; she noticed minutely the stage of development which the chestnut blossoms had reached; one or two dandelion heads; a robin

redbreast that was making himself exceedingly at home on the
little spread of greensward behind the house. I don't know if
Diana's senses were trying to cheat her heart; but from one
item to another her eye went and her mind followed, in a
maze of pain that was not cheated at all, till she heard her
mother's steps forsake the house. Then Diana's head sank.
And then, even at the moment, as if the robin's whistle had
brought them, the words came to her—'Call upon me in the
day of trouble; I will deliver thee, and thou shalt glorify me.'
An absolute promise of the Lord to his people. Could it be
true, when trouble was beyond deliverance? And then came
Basil's faith to her help; she knew how he believed every word,
no matter how difficult or impossible; and Diana fell on her
knees and hid her face, and fled to the one only last refuge of
earth's despairing children. How even God could deliver her,
Diana did not see, for the ground seemed giving way beneath
her feet; but it is the man who cannot swim who clutches the
rope for life and death; and it is when we are hopeless of our
own strength that we throw ourselves utterly upon the one
hand that is strong. Diana was conscious of little else but of
doing that; to form a connected prayer was beyond her; she
rather held up the promise, as it were with both hands, and
pleaded it mutely and with the intensity of one hovering between life and death. The house was still, she feared no disturbance; and she remained motionless, without change of
posture either of mind or body, for some length of time.
Gradually the 'I will deliver thee '—'I will deliver thee '—
began to emphasize itself to her consciousness, like a whisper
in the storm, and Diana burst into a terrible flood of tears.
That touch of divine sympathy broke her heart. She sobbed
for minutes, only keeping her sobs too noiseless to reach and
alarm Miss Collins' ears; till her agony was softened and
changed at last into something more like a child's exhausted
and humble tears, while her breast rose and fell so, pitifully.
With that came also a vague floating thought or two. 'My
duty—I'll do my duty—I'll do my duty.'

It was over, and she had risen and was resting in her chair,
feeling weaker and yet much stronger than before; waiting

till she could dare show her face to Miss Collins; when a little low tap was heard at the front door. Company? But Diana had noticed no step and heard no wheels. However, there was no escape for her if it were company. She waited, and the tap was repeated. I don't know what about it this second time sent a thrill all down Diana's nerves. The doors were open, and seeing that Miss Collins did not stir, Diana uttered a soft 'Come!' She was hardly surprised at what followed; she seemed to know by instinct what it would be.

'Where shall I come?' asked a voice, and a pair of brisk high-heeled shoes tripped into the house, and a little trilling laugh, equally light and meaningless, followed the words. 'Where shall I come? It's an enchanted castle—I see nobody.'

But the next instant she could not say that, for Diana showed herself at the door of her room, and Mrs. Reverdy hastened forward. Diana was calm now, with a possession of herself which she marvelled at even then. Bringing her visitor into the little parlour, she placed herself again in her chair, with her face turned from the light.

'And here I find you! O you beautiful creature!' Mrs. Reverdy burst out. 'I declare, I don't wonder at—anything!' and she laughed. The laugh grated terribly on Diana. 'I wonder if you know what a beauty you are?' she went on;—'I declare!—I didn't know you were half so handsome. Have you changed, since three years ago?'

'I think I must,' Diana said quietly.

'But where have you been? Living here in Pleasant Valley?' was the next not very polite question.

'People do live in Pleasant Valley. Did you think not?' Diana answered.

'O yes. No. Not what we call life, you know. And you were always handsome; but three years ago you were just Diana Starling, and now—you might be anybody!'

'I am Mr. Masters' wife,' said Diana, setting her teeth as it were upon the words.

'Yes, I heard. How happened it? Do you know, I am afraid you have done a great deal of mischief? O, you hand-

some women!—you have a great deal to account for. Did you
never think you had another admirer?—in those days long ago,
you know?'

'What if I had?' Diana said almost fiercely.

'O, of course,' said Mrs. Reverdy with her laugh again,—
'of course it is nothing to you now; girls are hard-hearted
towards their old lovers, I know that. But weren't you a
little tender towards him once? He hasn't forgotten his part,
I can tell you. You mustn't be *too* hard-hearted, Diana.'

If the woman could have spoken without laughing! That
little meaningless trill at the end of everything made Diana
nearly wild. She could find no answer to the last speech, and
so remained silent.

'Now I have seen you again, I declare I don't wonder at
anything. I was inclined to quarrel with him, you know,
thinking it was just a boyish foolish fancy that he ought to get
over; I was a little out of patience with him; but now I see
you, I take it all back. I declare, you're a woman the men
might rave about. You mustn't mind if they do.'

'There is another question—whether my husband will mind.'
She said the words with a hard, relentless force upon herself.

'Is he jealous?' laughing.

'He has no reason.'

'Reason! O, people are jealous without reason; they don't
wait for that. Better without than with. How is Mr. Masters?
is he one of that kind? And how came he to marry you?'

'You ought not to wonder at it, with the opinion you have
expressed of me.'

'O no, I don't wonder at all! But somebody else wanted
to marry you too; and somebody else thought he had the best
right. I am afraid you flirted with him. Or was it with Mr.
Masters you flirted? I didn't think you were a girl to flirt;
but I see! You would keep just quietly still, and they would
flutter round you, like moths round a candle, and it would be
their own fault if they both got burned. Has Mr. Masters got
burned? My poor moth has singed his wings badly, I can
tell you. I am very sorry for him.'

'So am I,' Diana said gravely.

'Are you? Are you really? Are you sorry for him? May I tell him you are sorry?'

'You have not said whom you are talking about,' Diana answered, with a coldness which she wondered at when she said it.

'O, but you know! There is only one person I could be talking about. There is only one I could care enough about to be talking for him. You cannot help but know. May I tell him you say you are sorry for him? It would be a sort of comfort, and he wants it.'

'You must ask Mr. Masters.'

'What?'

'That.'

'Whether I may tell Evan you are sorry for him?'

'Whether you may tell that to anybody.'

'I don't want to tell it to but one,' said Mrs. Reverdy, laughing. 'What has Mr. Masters to do with it?'

'He is my husband.' And calmly as Diana said it, she felt as if she would like to shriek out the words to the birds on the hillside—to the angels, if there were angels in the air. Yet she said it calmly.

'But do you ask your husband about everything you do or say?'

'If I think he would not like it.'

'But that is giving him a great deal of power,—too much. Husbands are fallible, as well as wives,' said Mrs. Reverdy, laughing.

'Mr. Masters is not fallible. At least, I never saw him fail in anything. If he ever made a mistake, it was when he married me.'

'And you?' said Mrs. Reverdy. 'Didn't you make a mistake too?'

'In marrying somebody so much too good for me—yes,' Diana answered.

The little woman was a good deal baffled.

'Then have you really no kind word for Evan? must I tell him so?'

Diana felt as if her brain would have reeled in another minute.

T

Before she could answer, came the sound of a little wailing cry from the room up-stairs, and she started up. That movement was sudden, but the next were collected and slow. 'You will excuse me,' she said,—'I hear baby,'—and she passed from the room like a princess. If her manner had been less discouraging, I think Mrs. Reverdy would have still pursued her point, and asked leave to follow her and see the baby; but Diana's slow, languid dignity and gracious composure imposed upon the little woman, and she gave up the game; at least for the present. When Miss Collins, set free, hurried down, Mrs. Reverdy was gone.

CHAPTER XXIX.

HUSBAND AND WIFE.

HAD she no kind word for Evan? Diana felt as if her heart would snap some one of its cords, and give over its weary beating at once and for ever. No kind word for Evan? her beloved, her betrayed, her life-treasure once, towards whom still all the wealth of her heart longed to pour itself out; and she might not send him one kind word? And he did not know that she had been true to him; and yet he had remained true to her. Might he not know so much as that, and that her heart was breaking as well as his? Only it would not break. All the pain of death without its cessation of consciousness. Why not let him have one word to know that she loved him still, and would always love him? Truth—truth and duty—loyal faith to her husband, the man whom in her mistake she had married. O, why could not such mistakes be undone! But they never could, never. It was a living death that she was condemned to die.

I cannot say that Diana really wavered at all in her truth; but this was an hour of storm never to be remembered without shuddering. She had her baby in her arms, but the mother's instincts were for the time swallowed up in the stormier passions of the woman. She cared for it and ministered to it, tenderly as ever, yet in a mechanical, automatic sort of way, taking no comfort and finding no relief in her sweet duty. It was the roar of the storm and the howling of temptation which overwhelmed every other voice in her heart. Then there were practical questions to be met. Mrs. Reverdy and her family at Elmfield, who could guarantee that Evan would not get a furlough and come there too? Mrs. Reverdy's words seemed

to have some ultimate design, which they had not indeed
declared; they had the air of somewhat different from mere
aimless rattle or mischievous gossip. Suppose Evan were to
come? What then?

The baby went off to sleep, and was laid away in its crib,
and the mother stood alone at the window wrestling with her
pain. She felt helpless in the grasp of it as almost never
before. Danger was looming up and threatening dark in the
distance; there might be a whirlwind coming out of that
storm quarter, and how was she going to stand in the whirlwind? Beyond the wordless cry which meant 'Lord help
me!'—Diana could hardly pray at all at this moment; and
the feeling grew that she must have human help. 'Tell Basil'
—a whisper said in her heart. She had shunned that thought
always; she had judged it no use; now she was driven to it.
He must know the whole. Perhaps then he could tell her
what to do.

As soon as Diana's mind through all its tossings and turnings
had fixed upon this point, she went immediately from thought
to action. It was twilight now, or almost. Basil would not
come home in time for a talk before supper; supper must be
ready, so as to have no needless delay. She could wait, now
she knew what she would do; though there was a fire burning
at heart and brain. She went down-stairs and ordered something to be got ready for supper; finished the arrangement
of the tea-table, which her husband liked to have very dainty;
picked a rose for his plate, though it seemed dreadful mockery;
and as soon as she heard his step at the door she made the
tea. What an atmosphere of sweet, calm brightness he
brought in with him, and always brought. It struck Diana
now with the kind of shiver which a person in a fever feels at
the touch of fresh air. Yet she recognised the beauty of it,
and it fortified her in her resolve. She would be true to this
man, though she died for it! There was nothing but truth in
him.

She got through the meal-time as she could; swallowed
tea, and even ate bread, without knowing how it tasted,
and heard Basil talk without knowing what he said. As

soon as she could she went up-stairs to the baby, and waited till her husband should come too. But when he came, he came to her, and did not go to his study.

'Basil, I want to speak to you—will you come into the other room?' she said huskily.

'Won't this room do to talk in?'

'No. It is over the kitchen.'

'Jemima knows I never quarrel'— said Basil lightly; however, he led the way into the study. He set a chair for Diana and took another himself, but she remained standing.

'Basil—is God good?' she said.

'Yes. Inexpressibly good.'

'Then why does he let such things happen?'

'Sit down, Di. You are not strong enough to talk standing. Such things? What things?'

'Why does he let people be tempted above what they can bear?'

'He never does—his children—if that is what you mean. He always provides a way of escape.'

'Where?'

'At Christ's feet.'

'Basil, how can I get there?' she said with a sob.

'You *are* there, my darling,' he said, putting her gently into the easy-chair she had disregarded. 'Those who trust in him, his hand never lets go. They may seem to themselves to lose their standing—they may not feel the ground under their feet —but he knows; and he will not let them fall. If they hold fast to him, Diana.'

'Basil, you don't know the whole.'

'Do you want to tell me?'

Her voice was abrupt and hoarse; his was calm and cool as the fall of the dew.

'I want to tell you if I can. But I shall hurt you.'

'I am very willing, if it eases you. Go on.'

'It won't ease me. But you must know it. You ought to know. O, Basil, I made such a mistake when I married you!'—

She did not mean to say anything so bitter as that; she

was where she could not measure her words. Perhaps his face
paled a little ; in the faint light she could not see the change
of colour. His voice did not change.

'What new has brought that up?'

'Nothing new. Something old. O Basil—his sister has
been here to-day to see me.'

'Has she?' His voice did change a little then. 'What
did she come for?'

'I don't know. And *he* will be here, perhaps, by and by.
O Basil, do you know who it is? And what shall I do?'

Diana had sprung up from her chair and dropped down on
the floor by her husband's side, and hid her face in her hands
on his knee. His hand passed tenderly, sorrowfully, over the
beautiful hair, which lay in disordered, bright, soft masses over
head and neck. For a moment he did not speak.

'Basil—do you know who it is?'

'I know.'

'What shall I do?'

'What do you want to do, Diana?'

'Right—' she said, gasping, without looking up.

'I am sure of it!' he said tenderly. 'Well, then—the only
way is, to go on and do right, Diana.'

'But how can I? how shall I? Suppose he comes? O
Basil, it was all a mistake ; he wrote, and mother kept back
the letters, and I never got them ; he sent them, and I never
got them ; and I thought he was not true and it did not matter
what I did, and I honoured you above everything, Basil—and
so—and so—I did what I did '—

'What cannot be undone.'

'No—' she said, shivering.

He passed his hands again over her soft hair, and bent down
and kissed it.

'You honour yourself too, Diana, as well as me.'

'Yes—' she said, under breath.

'And you honour our God, who has let all this come upon
us both?'

'But, O Basil! how could he? how could he?'

'I don't know.'

'And yet you say he is good?'

'And so you say too. The only good; the utterly, perfectly good; who loves his people, and keeps his promises, and who has said that all things shall work together for the good of those that love him.'

'How can such a thing as this?' she said faintly.

'Suppose you and I cannot see how? Then faith comes in and believes it without seeing. We shall see by and by.'

'But Basil—suppose—Evan—comes?'

'Well?'

'Suppose—he came—here?'

'Well, Diana?'

She was silent then, but she shook and trembled and writhed. Her head was still where she had laid it; her face hidden.

'You are going through as great a trial, my poor wife, as almost ever falls to the lot of a mortal. But you will go through it, and come out from it; and then it will be found to have been "unto praise and honour and glory"—by and by.'

'O how can you tell?'

'I trust in God. And I trust you.'

'But I think he will come—here to Pleasant Valley, I mean. And if he comes—here, to this house, I mean'—

'What then?'

'What do you want me to do?'

'About seeing him?'

'Yes.'

'What you like best to do, Diana.'

'Basil—he does not know.'

'What does he not know?'

'About the letters or anything. He has never heard—never a word from me.'

'There was an understanding between you before he went away?'

'O yes!'

Both were silent again for a time; silent and still. Then Diana spoke timidly:

'Do you think it would be wrong for him to know?'

Her husband delayed his answer a little; truly, if Diana had something to suffer, so had he; and I suppose there was somewhat of a struggle in his own mind to be won through; however, the answer when it came was a quiet negative.

'May I write and tell him?'

He bent down and kissed her fingers as he replied— 'I will.'

'O Basil,' said the woman at his feet, 'I have wished I could die a thousand times!—and I am well and strong, and I cannot die.'

'No,' he said gravely; 'we must not run away from our work.'

'Work!' said Diana, sitting back now and looking up at him;—'what work?'

'The work our Master has given us to do to glorify him. To fight with evil and overcome it; to endure temptation, and baffle it; to carry our banner of salvation through the thick of the smoke and the fire, and never let it fall.'

'I am so weak, I cannot fight.'

'The fight of faith you can. The only sort of fighting that can prevail. Faith lays hold of Christ's strength, and so comes off more than conqueror. All you can do, is to hold fast to him.'

'O Basil! why does he let such things happen? why does he let such things happen? Here is my life broken—and yours; both broken and ruined.'

'No,' the minister answered quietly,—'not mine, nor yours. Broken, if you will, but not ruined. Neither yours nor mine, Diana. With the love of Christ in our hearts, that can never be. He will not let it be.'

'It is all ruined,' said Diana; 'it is all ruined. I am full of evil thoughts, and no good left. I have wished to die, and I have wanted to run away—I felt as if I must '—

'But instead of dying or running away, you have stood nobly and bravely to your post of suffering. Wait and trust. The Lord means good to us yet.'

'What possible good?'

'Perhaps, that being stripped of all else, we may come to know him.'

' Is it necessary that people should be stripped of all before they can do that?'

'Sometimes.'

Diana stood still, and again there was silence in the room. The soft June air, heavy with the breath of roses, floated in at the open window, bringing one of those sharp contrasts which make the heart sick with memory and longing; albeit the balsam of promise be there too. People miss that. 'Now men see not the bright light that is in the clouds;' and how should they? when the darkness of night seems to have fallen, how can they even remember that behind that screen of darkness there is a flood of glory? There came in sounds at the window too, from the garden and the wood on the hillside; chirruping sounds of insects, mingled with the slight rustle of leaves and the trickle of water from a little brook which made all the noise it could over the stones in its way down the hill. The voices were of tender peace; the roses and the small life of nature all really told of love and care which can as little fail for the Lord's children as for the furniture of their dwelling-place. Yet that very unchangeableness of nature hurts, which should comfort. Diana stood still, desolate, to her own sense seeming a ruin already; and her husband sat in his place, also still, but he was calm. They were quiet long enough to think of many things.

'You are very good, Basil!' Diana said at last.

It was one of those words which hurt unreasonably. Not because they are not true words and heartily meant, but because they are the poor substitute for those we would like to hear, and give us an ugly scale to measure distances and differences by. Basil made no sort of answer. Diana stood still. In her confusion of thoughts she did not miss the answer. Then she began again.

'Evan—I mean, Basil!'—and she started;—'I wish we could get away.'

' From Pleasant Valley?'

'Yes.'

'My work is here.'

Is mine here too? thought Diana, as she slowly went away into the other room.   What is mine?   To die by this fire that burns in me; or to freeze stiff in the cold that sometimes almost stops my heart's beating?   She came up to the side of her baby's crib and stood there looking, dimly conscious of an inner voice that said her work was not death.

CHAPTER XXX.

SUNSHINE.

A FEW days later, the minister came home one evening with a message for his wife.

'Good old Mother Bartlett is going home, Diana, and she wants to see you.'

'Home? Is she dying, do you mean?'

'*She* does not mean it. To her, it is entering into life.'

'But what's the matter?'

'You know she had that bad cold. I think the treatment was worse than the disease; and under the effects of both, her strength seems to have given way. She is sinking quietly.'

'I will go down there in the morning.'

So the next day, early, Basil drove his wife down and left her at the cottage. It was somehow to Diana's feeling just such another day as had been that other wonderful one when she had seen Evan first, and he harnessed Prince, and they came together over this very road. Perhaps soon Evan would be riding there again, without her, as she was going now without him. Never together again, never together again! and what was life to either of them apart? Diana went into the cottage walking as one in a dream.

The cottage was in nice order, as usual, though no woman's hand had been about. Joe, rough as he was, could be what his friends called 'real handy;' and he had put everything in trim and taken all care for his mother's comfort before he went out. The minister had told him Diana would be there; so after he had done this he went to his work. Mrs. Bartlett was lying on her bed in the inner room. Diana kissed her, with a heart too full at the moment to speak.

209

'Did the minister bring you?' the old lady askéd.

'Yes. Are you all alone?'

'The Lord never leaves his children alone, dear. They leave him sometimes. Won't you open the winders, Diana? Joe forgot that, and I want to see the sun.'

Diana rolled up the thick paper shades which hung over the windows, and put up the sashes. Summer air poured in, so full of warmth and brightness and sounds of nature's activity, that it seemed to roll up a tide of life to the very feet of the dying woman. She looked, and drew a deep breath or two.

'That's good!' she said. 'The Lord made the sunshine. Now sit down, dear; I want to see you. Sit down there, where I *can* see you.'

'Does Joe leave you here by yourself?'

'He knew you was comin'. Joe's a good boy. But I don't want him nor nobody hangin' round all the time, Diana. There ain't nothin' to do; only he forgot the winders, and I want to look out and see all my riches.'

'Your riches, Mother Bartlett?'—And she was not going to live but a few days more. Diana wondered if her senses were wandering. But the old lady smiled; the wise, sweet smile that Diana knew of old.

'Whose be they, then?' she asked.

'You mean, all this pretty summer day?'

'Ain't it pretty? And ain't the sunshine clear gold? And ain't the sky a kind of an elegant canopy? And it's all mine, and all it covers, and he that made it too; and seein' what he makes, puts me in mind of how rich he is and what more he kin do. How's the baby?'

For some little time the baby was talked of, in both present and future relations.

'And you're very happy, Diana?' the old woman asked. 'I hain't seen you now for quite a spell—'most all winter.'

'I ought to be'—Diana answered, hesitating.

'Some things folks does because they had ought to,' remarked the old lady, 'but bein' happy ain't one of 'em. The whole world had ought to be happy, if you put it so. The Lord wants 'em to be.'

'Not happy '—said Diana hastily.

'Yes. 'Tain't his fault if they ain't.'

'How can he want everybody to be happy, when he makes them so unhappy ?'

'He?—the Lord? He don't make nobody unhappy, child. How did that git in your head ?'

'Well, it comes to the same thing, Mother Bartlett. He lets things happen.'

'He hain't chained up Satan yet, if that's what you mean. But Satan can't do no harm to the Lord's children. He's tried, often enough, but the Lord won't let him.'

'But, Mother Bartlett, that's only a way of talking. I don't know if it is Satan does it, but every sort of terrible thing comes to them. How can you say it's not evil ?'

''Cause the good Lord turns it to blessing, dear. Or if he don't, it's 'cause they won't let him. O' course it is Satan does it—Satan and his ministers. "Every good gift and every perfect gift cometh down from the Father of lights, with whom is no variableness, neither shadow of turning." How should he be kind to-day and unkind to-morrow ?'

Diana could not trust her voice, and was silent. The old woman looked at her, and said in a changed tone presently,

'What's come to you, Diana Masters? You had ought to be the happiest woman there is livin'.'

Diana could not answer.

'*Ain't* you, dear ?' Mrs. Bartlett added tenderly.

'I didn't mean to speak of myself,' Diana said, making a tremendous effort to bring out her words unconcernedly ; 'but I get utterly puzzled sometimes, Mother Bartlett, when I see such things happen—such things as do happen, and to good people too.'

'You ain't the fust one that's been puzzled that way,' returned the old woman. 'Job was all out in his reckoning once ; and David was as stupid as a beast, he says. But when chillen gets into the dark, they're apt to run agin sun'thin' and hurt theirselves. Stay in the light, dear.'

'How can one, always ?'

'O, child, jes' believe the Lord's word. That'll keep you near him; and there is no darkness where he is.'

'What *is* his word, that I must believe?—about this, I mean.'

'That he loves us, dear; loves us tender and true; like you love your little baby, only a deal more; and truer, and tenderer. For a woman *may* forget her sucking child, but he never will forget. And all things he will make to "work together for good to them that love him."'

Diana shook and trembled with the effort to command herself, and not burst into a storm of weeping, which would have betrayed what she did not choose to betray. She sat by the bedpost, clasping it, and with the same clasp as it were holding herself. For a moment *she* had 'forgotten her sucking child,' —the words came home; and it was only by that convulsive hold of herself that she could keep from crying out. With her face turned away from the sick woman, she waited till the convulsion had passed; and then said in measured, deliberate accents,

'It is hard to see how some things can turn out for good— some things I have known.'

'Well, you ain't infinite, be you?' said Mrs. Bartlett. 'You can't see into the futur'; and what's more, you can't see into the present. You don't know what's goin' on in your own heart—not as *he* knows it. No more you ain't almighty to change things. If I was you, I would jest trust him that is all-wise, and knows everything, and almighty, and kin do what he likes.'

'Then why don't he make people good?'

'I said, he can do what he likes. He don't like to do people's own work for 'em. He *doos* make 'em good, as soon as they're willin' and ask him. But the man sick with the palsy had to rise and take up his bed and walk; and what's more, he had to believe fust he could do it. I know the Lord gave the power, but the man had his part, you see.'

'Mother Bartlett,' said Diana, rousing herself, 'you must not talk so much.'

'Don't do me no harm, Diana.'

'But you have talked enough. Now let me give you your broth.'

'Then you must talk. I hain't so many opportunities o' social converse that I kin afford to let one of 'em slip. You must talk while I'm eatin'.'

But Diana seemed to have nothing to say. She watched the spoonfuls of broth in attentive silence.

'What's new, Diana? there allays is sun'thin'.'

'Nothing new. Only '—said Diana, correcting herself, 'the Knowltons are coming back to Elmfield. Mrs. Reverdy *is* come.'

'Be the hull o' them comin'?'

'I believe so.'

'What for?'

'I don't know. To enjoy the summer, I suppose.'

'That's their sort,' said the old woman slowly. 'Jest to get pleasure. I used for to see 'em flyin' past here in all the colours o' the rainbow—last time they was in Pleasant Valley.'

'But God made the colours of the rainbow,' said Diana.

'So he did,' the old lady answered, laughing a little. 'So he did; and the colours of the flowers, which is the same colours, to be sure; but what then, Diana?'

'I was thinking, Mother Bartlett—it cannot displease him that we should like them too.'

'No, child, it don't; nor it don't displease him to have us wear 'em, nother,—if we could only wear 'em as innercently as the flowers doos. If you kin, Diana, you may be as scarlet as a tulip or as bright as a marigold, for all I care.'

'But people are not any better for putting on dark colours,' said Diana.

'They're some modester, though.'

'Why?'

'They ain't expectin' that folks 'll be lookin' at 'em.'

'Mr. Masters likes me to wear bright dresses.'

'Then do it, child. It's considerable of a pleasure to have his eyes pleased. Do you know what a husband you've got, Diana?'

'Yes.'

'He's 'most like one o' them flowers himself. He's so full o' the sweetness the Lord has put into him, and he's jest as unconscious that he's spreadin' it wherever he goes.'

Diana was silent. She would have liked again to burst into tears; she controlled herself as before.

'That ain't the way with those Knowlton girls; nor it ain't the way they wear their fine colours, neither. Can't you get a little sense into their heads, Diana?'

'I? They think nothing of me, Mother Bartlett.'

'Maybe not, two years ago, but they will now. You're the minister's wife, Diana. They allays sot a great deal by him.'

Diana was chewing the cud of this, when Mrs. Bartlett asked again,

'Who's sick in the place?'

'Quite a number. There's Mrs. Wilson at the tavern; she's sinking at last; my husband sees her every day. Then old Josh Lightfoot—he's down with I don't know what; very sick. Mrs. Saddler has a child that has been hurt; he was pitched off a load of hay and fell upon a fork; his mother is distracted about him, and it is all Mr. Masters can do to quiet her. And Lizzie Satterthwaite is going slowly, you know, in consumption, and *she* expects to see him every day. And that isn't all; for over in the village of Bromble there is sickness—I suppose there always is in that miserable place.'

'And the minister goes there too, I'll be bound?'

'O yes. He goes everywhere, if people want him. It takes twenty miles of riding a day, he told me, just to visit all these people that he must see.'

'Ay, ay,' said the old woman contentedly; 'enjoyment ain't the end of life, but to do the will of God; and he's doin' it. And enjoyment comes that way too; ay, ay! "an hundred-fold now, in this world, and in the world to come eternal life." I hain't ever been able to do much, Diana; but it has been sweet—his service—all along the way; and now I'm goin' where it'll be nothin' but sweetness for ever.'

A little tired, perhaps, with talking, for she had talked with a good deal of energy, the old lady dozed off into a nap; and Diana sat alone with the summer stillness, and thought over

and over some of the words that had been said. It was the
hush of the summer stillness, and also the full pulse of the
summer life that she felt as she sat there; not soothing to
inaction, but stirring up to loving doing. A warm breath of
vital energy, an odorous witness-bearing of life fruitfulness,
a hum and a murmur of harmonious forces in action, a depth
of colour in the light and in the shadow, which told of the
richness and fulness of the natural world. Nothing idle,
nothing unfruitful, nothing out of harmony, nothing in vain.
How about Diana Masters, and her work and her part in the
great plan? Again the gentle summer air which stole in,
laden with such scents and sweets, rich and bountiful out of
the infinite treasury, spoke of love at the heart of creation.
But there were cold winds, too, sometimes; icy storms; desola-
tions of tempests; they had been here not long ago. True,
but yet it was not those, but *this* which carried on the life of
the world; this was the 'Yes,' and those others the 'No,' of
creation; and an affirmative is stronger than a negative any
day, by universal acknowledgment. Moreover, that 'No'
was in order to this 'Yes;' gave way before it, yielded to it;
and life reigned in spite of death. Vaguely Diana's mind felt
and carried on the analogy, and the reasoning from analogy,
and drew a chill, far-off hope from it. For it was the time of
storm and desolation with her now, and the summer sun had
not come yet. She sat musing while the old lady slumbered.

'Hullo, Diany! here you be!' exclaimed the voice of Joe
Bartlett, suddenly breaking in. 'Here's your goodman out-
side, waitin' for you, I guess; his horse is a leetle skittish.
What ails your mother?'

'My mother?'

'Yes. Josh says—you see, I've bin down to mill to git
some rye ground, and he was there; and what's more, he had
the start of me, and I had to wait for him, or I wouldn't ha'
stood there chatterin' while the sun was shinin' like it is to-
day; that ain't my way. But Josh says she's goin' round
groanin' at sun'thin'—and that ain't *her* way, nother. Mind
you, it ain't when anybody's by; I warrant you, she don't give
no sign *then* that anythin's botherin' her; Josh says it's when

U

she's alone. I didn't ask him how he come to know so much, and so little; but I wisht I had,' Joe finished his speech laughing.

Diana took her hat, kissed the old woman, and went out to her husband, who was waiting for her. And some miles of the drive were made in silence. Then as the old brown house came in sight, with the weeping elms over the gate, Diana asked her husband to stop for a minute or two. He reined up under the elm trees and helped Diana out, letting her, however, go in alone.

Diana was not often here, naturally; between her and her mother, who never in the best of times had stood near together or shared each other's deeper sympathies, a gulf had opened. Besides, the place was painful to Diana on other accounts. It was full of memories and associations; she always seemed to herself when there as a dead person might on revisiting the place where once he had lived; she felt dead to all but pain, and the impression came back with sharp torture that once she used to be alive. So, as the shadow of the elm branches fell over her now, it hurt her inexpressibly. She was alive when she had dwelt under them; yes, she and Evan too. She hurried her steps and went in at the lean-to door.

It was now long past mid-day. The noon meal was over, apparently, and every sign of it cleared away. The kitchen was in spotless order; but beside the table sat Mrs. Starling, doing nothing; an unheard-of state of affairs. Diana came farther in.

'Mother '—

'Well, Diana,'—said Mrs. Starling, looking up. 'What's brought you now?'

'I've been down to see Mrs. Bartlett—she sent for me— and I thought I would step in as I went by. Mr. Masters is outside.'

'Well, I've no objection,' said Mrs. Starling ambiguously.

'How do you do?'

'Middling.'

'Is all getting on well with the farm and the dairy?'

'I don't let it be no other way.'

Diana saw that something was wrong, but knew also that if she were to find it out it would be by indirect ways.

'May I go into the pantry and get some milk? I've been a good while from home, and I'm hungry.'

'Go along,' said her mother ungraciously. 'I should think likely, if *you* are hungry, your baby is too. That's a new way of doing things. 'Twarn't ever my way. A woman that's got a baby ought to attend to it. An' if she don't, her husband ought to make her.'

'I've not been gone so long as all that comes to,' said Diana; and she went into the pantry, her old domain. The pans of milk looked friendly at her; the sweet clean smell of cream carried her back—it seemed ages—to a time when she was as sweet and clean. 'Yet it is not my fault,'—she said to herself,—' it is *hers*—all hers.' She snatched a piece of bread and a glass of milk, and swallowed it hastily. Then, as she came out, she saw that one of her mother's hands lay bandaged up in her lap under the table.

'Mother,—what's the matter with your hand?'

'O, not much.'

'But what? It's all tied up. Have you burned it?'

'No.'

'What then? Cut yourself?'

'I should like to know how I should go to work to cut my right hand! Don't make a fuss about nothing, Diana. It's only scalded.'

'Scalded! How?'

'I shall never be able to tell that, to the end of my days,' said Mrs. Starling. 'If pots and kettles and that could be possessed, I should know what to think. I was making strawberry preserve—and the kettle was a'most full, and it was first rate preserve, and boiling, and almost done, and I had just set it down on the hearth; and then, I don't know how to this day, I stumbled—I don't know over what—and my arm soused right in.'

'Boiling sweetmeat!' cried Diana. 'Mother, let me see. It must be dreadfully burned.'

'It's all done up,' said Mrs. Starling coldly. 'I was real put out about my preserves.'

'Have you had dinner?'

'I never found I could live 'thout eating.'

'Who got dinner for you, and cleared away?'

'Nobody. I did it myself.'

'For the men and all!'

'Well, *they* don't count to live without eatin', no mor'n I do,' said Mrs. Starling with a short laugh.

'And you did it with one hand?'

'Did you ever know me to stop in anything I had to do for want of a hand?' said Mrs. Starling scornfully.

No, thought Diana to herself; nor for want of anything else, even though it were right or conscience. Aloud she only said,

'I must go home to baby'—

'You had better, I should think,' her mother broke in.

'Can I do anything for you first?'

'You can see for yourself, there is nothing to do.'

'Shall I come back and stay with you to-night?'

'You had better ask the Dominie.'

'Mother, he *never* wants me to do anything but just what is right,' Diana said seriously. Mrs. Starling lifted up her head and gave a curious searching look into her daughter's face. What was she trying to find?

'That's one turtle dove,' she said. 'And are you another, and always bob your head when he bobs his'n?'

Diana wondered at this speech; it seemed to her, her mother was losing ground even in the matter of language. No thought of irritation crossed her; she was beyond trifles now. She made no answer; she merely bade her mother good-bye, and hurried out. And for a long while the drive was again in silence. Then, when the grey horse was walking up a hill, Diana spoke in a meditative sort of way.

'Basil—you said enjoyment was not the end of life'—

'Did I?' he answered gravely.

'If you didn't, it was Mother Bartlett. You *do* say so, I suppose?'

'Yes. It is not the end of life.'

'What is, then?'

'To do the will of God. And by and by, if not sooner, enjoyment comes that way too, Diana. And when it comes that way, it stays, and lasts.'

'How long?'

'For ever and ever!'

Diana waited a few minutes and then spoke again.

'Basil—I want to consult you.'

'Well, do it.'

'Ought I to leave my mother to live alone, as she is? She is not young now.'

'What would you do?'

'If I knew, Basil, I would like it to be what I *ought* to do.'

'Would you take her to live with you?'

'If you would?—and she would.'

Basil put his arm round his wife and bent down and kissed her. He would not have done it if he could have guessed how she shrank.

'If you will take life on those terms,' he said, 'then it will be true for you that "sorrow may endure for a night, but joy cometh in the morning."'

It will be the morning of the resurrection, then, thought Diana; but she only replied,

'What "terms," Basil, do you mean?'

'Doing the Lord's will. His will is always good, Diana, and brings sweet fruit; only you must wait till the fruit is ripe, my child.'

'Then what about mother?'

'I do not believe she would come to us.'

'Nor I. Suppose she would let us come to her?'

'Then I would go,—if you wished it.'

'I don't wish it, Basil. I was thinking, if I could bear it? But the thought will not out of my head, that she ought not to be alone.'

'Then do what is in thine heart,' the minister said cheerfully.

CHAPTER XXXI.

A JUNE DAY.

MRS. STARLING hesitated when Diana proposed her plan; she would think of it, she said. But when she began to think of it, the attractions were found irresistible. To have her grandchild in the house beside her, perhaps with a vague thought of making up to her daughter in some unexplained way for the wrong she had done; at any rate, to have voices and life in the house again, instead of the bare silence; voices of people that belonged to her own blood; Mrs. Starling found that she could not give up the idea, once it got into her head. Then she objected that the house was too small.

The minister said he would put up an addition of a couple of rooms for himself and Diana, and Diana's old room could serve as a nursery.

'Who wants a nursery?' Mrs. Starling demanded. Her idea of a nursery was the whole house and all out of doors. The minister laughed, and said that was not *his* idea; and Mrs. Starling was fain to let it pass. She was human, though she was not a good woman; and Diana's proposal to come back to her had, though she would never allow it even to herself, touched both her heart and her conscience. Somewhere very deep down and out of sight, nevertheless it was true; and it was true that she had been very lonely; and she let the minister have his own way, undisputed, about the building.

The carpenters were set to work at once, and at home Diana quietly made preparations for a removal in the course of a few months. She buried herself in business as much as ever she could, to still thought and keep her nerves quiet; for con-

310

stantly, daily and nightly now, the image of Evan was before
her, and the possibility that he might any day present himself
in very flesh and blood. No precautions were of any avail; if
he chose to seek her out, Diana could not escape him unless
by leaving Pleasant Valley; and that was not possible. Would
he come? She looked at that question from every possible
point of the compass, and from every one the view that presented itself was that he would come. Nay, he ought not; it
would be worse than of no use for them to see each other; and
yet, something in Diana's recollections of him, or, it might be,
something in the consciousness of her own nature, made her
say to herself that he would come. How should she bear it?
She almost wished that Basil would forbid it, and take measures
to make it impossible; but the minister went his way unmoved
and quiet as usual; there was neither fear nor doubt on his
broad fair brow. Diana respected him immensely; and at
times felt a great pang of grief that his face should wear such
a shade of gravity as was habitual to it now. Knowing him so
well as she did by this time, she could guess that though the
gravity never degenerated into gloom, the reason was to be
found solely and alone in the fact that Basil's inner life was
fed by springs which were beyond the reach of earthly im-
poverishing or disturbing. How much better she thought him
than herself!—as she looked at the calm, stedfast beauty of
his countenance, which matched his daily life and walk. No
private sorrow touched that. Never thinking of himself nor
seeking his own, he was busy from morning till night with the
needs of others; going from house to house, carrying help,
showing light, bringing comfort, guiding into the way, point-
ing out the wrong; and at home,—Diana knew with what glad
resort he went to his Bible and prayer for his own help and
wisdom, and wrought out the lessons that were to be given
openly in the little hillside church. Diana knew, too, what
flowers of blessing were springing up along his path; what
fruits of good. 'The angel of the church' in Pleasant Valley
he was, in a sense most true and lovely, although that be not
the original bearing of the phrase in the Revelation, where
Alford thinks, and I think, no human angels are intended.

Nevertheless, that was Basil here; and his wife, who did not love him, honoured him to the bottom of her heart.

And in her self-reproach and her humility, Diana wrote bitterer things against herself than there was any need. For she, too, was doing her daily work with a lovely truth of aim and simpleness of purpose. With all the joys of life crushed out, she was walking the way which had become so weary with a steady foot, and with hands ready and diligent to do all they found to do. In another sort from her husband, the fair, calm, grave woman was the angel of her household. I can never tell you how beautiful Diana was now. If the careless light glance of the girl was gone, there was now, instead, the deeper beauty of a nature that has loved and suffered; that ripening process of humanity, without which it never comes to its full bloom and fruitage; though that be a very material image for the matter in hand. And there was besides in Diana the dignity of bearing of one who is lifted above all small considerations of every kind; that is, not above small duties, but above petty interests. Therefore, in this woman, who had never seen and scarcely imagined courts, even in the minister's house in Pleasant Valley, there was the calm poise and grace which we associate in our speech and thoughts with the highest advantages of social relations. So extremes sometimes meet. In Diana it was due to her inborn nobility of nature and the sharp discipline of sorrow; in aid of which practically came also her perfection of physical health and form. It must be remembered, too, that she had been now for a good while in the close companionship of a man of great refinement and culture, and that both study and conversation had lifted her by this time far out of the intellectual sphere in which the beginning of our story found her.

The carpenters were going on vigorously with their work on the new rooms adding to Mrs. Starling's house; and Diana was making, as she could from time to time, her little preparations for the removal, which, however, could not take place yet for some time. It was in the beginning of July. Diana was up-stairs one day, looking over the contents of a trunk, and cutting up pieces for patchwork. Windows were open, of course, and the scent of new hay came in with the warm air. Haymaking was going on all over Pleasant Valley. By and by Miss Collins put her head in.

'Be you fixed to see folks?'

'Who wants me?'

'Well, there's somebody comin'; and I reckon it's one or other o' them fly-aways from Elmfield.'

'Here?' said Diana, starting up and trembling.

'Wall, there's one of 'em comin', I guess—I see the carriage —and I thought maybe you warn't ready to see no one. When one gets into a trunk it's hard to get out again. So I thought I'd jes' come and tell ye. There she is comin' up the walk. Hurry, now.'

Down went Miss Collins to let the visitor in, and Diana did hurry and changed her dress. What can she be come for? she questioned with herself meanwhile; for it was Mrs. Reverdy, she had seen. No good! no good! But nobody would have guessed that Diana had ever been in a hurry, that saw her entrance the next minute upon her visitor. That little lady felt a sort of imposing effect, and did not quite know how to do what she had come for.

'I always think there has come some witchery over my eyes,' she said with her invariable little laugh of ingratiation, 'when I see you. I always feel a kind of new surprise. Is it the minister that has changed you so? What's he done?'

'Changed me?' Diana repeated.

'Why, yes; you *are* changed. You are not like what you were two years ago—three years ago—how long is it?'

'It is three years ago,' said Diana, trying to smile. 'I am three years older.'

'O, it isn't that. *I'm* three years older. I suppose I didn't see enough of you then to find you out. It was my fault. But if you had married somebody belonging to me, I can tell you, I should have been very proud of my sister-in-law.'

She laughed at the compliment she was making, laughed lightly; while Diana inwardly shook, like a person who has received a sudden sharp blow, and staggers in danger of losing his footing. Did she waver visibly before her adversary's eyes, she wondered? She was sure her colour did not change. She found nothing to say in any case; and after a moment her vision cleared and she had possession of herself again.

'I am saucy,' said Mrs. Reverdy, smiling, 'but nobody thinks of minding anything I say. That's the good of being little and insignificant, as I am.'

Diana was inclined to wish her visitor would not presume upon her harmlessness.

'I should as soon think of being rude to a duchess,' Mrs. Reverdy went on; 'or to a princess. I don't see how Evan ever made up his mind to go away and leave you.'

'Is it worse to be rude to a duchess than to other people?' Diana asked, seizing the first part of this speech as a means to get over the last.

'I never tried,' said Mrs. Reverdy; 'I never had·the opportunity, you know. I might have danced with the Prince of Wales, perhaps, when he was here. I know a lady who did, and she said she wasn't afraid of *him*. If you had been there, I am sure she would not have got the chance.'

'You forget, I am not a dancer.'

'O, not now, of course—but then you wouldn't have been a minister's wife.'

'Why should not a minister's wife dance as well as other people?'

'O, I don't know!' said Mrs. Reverdy lightly; 'but they never do, you know. They are obliged to set an example.'

'Of what?'

'Of everything that is proper, I suppose. Don't you feel that everybody's eyes are upon you, always, watching everything you do?'

A good reminder! But Diana answered simply that she never thought about it.

'Don't you! Isn't the minister always reminding you of what people will think?'

'No. It isn't his way.'

'Doesn't he? Why, without being a minister, that is what my husband used always to be doing to me. I was a little giddy, you know,' said Mrs. Reverdy, laughing; 'I was very young; and I used to have plenty of admonitions.'

'I believe Mr. Masters thinks we should only care about God's eyes,' Diana said quietly.

Mrs. Reverdy startled a little at that, and for a moment looked grave. From Diana she had not expected this turn.

'I never think about anything!' she said then with a laugh, that looked as if it were meant to be one of childlike ingenuousness. 'Don't think me very bad. Everybody can't be good and discreet like you and Mr. Masters.'

'Very few people are like Mr. Masters,' Diana assented.

'We all know that. And in the daily beholding of his superiority, have you quite forgotten everything else?—your old lover and all?'

'Whom do you mean?' Diana asked, with a calm coldness at which she wondered herself.

'I mean Evan, to be sure. You know he was your old lover. He wants to see you. He has not forgotten you, at any rate. Have you entirely forgotten him? Poor fellow! he has had a hard time of it.'

'I have not forgotten Mr. Knowlton at all,' Diana said with difficulty, for it seemed to her that her throat was suddenly paralyzed.

'You have not forgotten him? I may tell him that? Do you know, he raves about you?—I wish you could hear him once. He is Captain Knowlton now, you must understand; he has got his advancement early; but one or two people died, and somebody else was removed out of his way; and so he stepped into his captaincy. Lucky fellow! he always has been lucky; except just in one thing; and he thinks that spoils all. May he come and see you, Diana? He has given me no peace until I would come and ask you, and he will never have any peace, that I can see, if you refuse him. Poor fellow! there he is out there all this time, champing the bit worse than the horses.'

And the woman said it all with her little civil smile and laugh, as if she were talking about sugar plums.

'Is he here?' cried Diana.

' With the horses—waiting to know the success of my mission; and I have been afraid to ask you, for fear you should say no; and I *cannot* carry back such an answer to him.   May I tell him to come in ? '

' Why should he not come to see me, as well as any other friend ? ' said Diana.   But the quiver in her voice gave the answer to her own question.

' Of course ! ' said Mrs. Reverdy, rising with a satisfied face. ' There is no reason in the world why he should not, if you have kindness enough left for him to let him come.   Then I'll go out and tell him to come in ; for the poor fellow is sitting on swords' points all this while.'   And laughing at her supposed happy professional allusion, the lady withdrew.

Diana flew up the stairs to her own room.   She did not debate much the question whether she ought to see Evan ; it came to her rather as a thing that she *must* do ; there was no question in the case.   However, perhaps the question only lay very deep down in her consciousness, for the justification presented itself, that to refuse to see him would be to confess both to his sister and himself that there was danger in it.   Diana never could confess that, whatever the fact.   So, answering dumbly the doubt that was as wordless, without stopping a moment she caught up her sleeping baby out of its cradle, and drawing the cradle after her went into her husband's study.   Basil was there, she knew, at work.   He looked up as she came in. Diana drew the cradle near to him, and carefully laid the still sleeping, fair and fat little bundle from her arms down in it again ; this was done gently and deliberately enough ; no hurry and no perturbation.   Then she stood upright.

' Basil, will you take care of her ?   He is come.'

The minister looked up into his wife's face ; he knew what she meant.   And he felt as he looked at her, how far she was from him.   There was no smile on Diana's lips, indeed ; on the contrary, an intensity of feelings that were not pleasurable ; and yet, and yet—he who has looked for the light of love in an eye and missed it long, knows it when he sees it, even though it be not for him.   The four eyes met each other steadily.

' Shall I see him ? ' Diana asked.

Basil stretched out his hand to her. ' I can trust you, Diana.'
She put her cold hand in his for a minute and hurried away.
Then, as she reached the other room, she heard in the hall
below a step, the step she had not heard for years; and her
heart made one spring back over the interval. In the urgency
of action, Diana's colour had hardly changed until now; now
she turned deadly white, and for one instant sank on her knees
by her bedside with her heart full of a mute, unformed prayer
for help. It was fearful to go on, but she must go on now;
she must see Evan; he was there; questions were done; and
as she went down-stairs, while her face was white, and pain
almost confused her senses, there was a stir of keen joy at her
heart—fierce, like that of a wild beast which has been robbed
of its prey but has got it again. She tried for self-command,
and as one mean towards it forced herself to go deliberately.
No hasty steps should be heard on the stairs or on the floor.
Even so, the way was short; a moment, and she had entered
the room, and she and Evan were face to face once more.

Face to face, and yet neither dared look at the other. He
was standing, waiting for her; she came a few paces into the
room and stood still opposite him; they did not touch each
other's hands; they made no show of greeting. How should
they? in each other's presence indeed they were, with but a
small space of transparent air between, to the sense; and yet,
a barrier mountains high, of impassable ice, to the mind's
apprehension. You could have heard a pin drop in the room;
the two stood there, a few yards apart, not even looking at
each other, yet intensely conscious each all the while of the
familiar outlines and traits so long unseen, so well known by
heart. Breathing the air of the same room again, and nevertheless miles and miles apart; that was what they were
feeling. The miles could not be bridged over; what use to
try to bridge over the yards? Diana was growing whiter, if
whiter could be; Evan's head sank lower. At last the man
succumbed; sat down; buried his head in his hands, and
groaned aloud. Diana stood like a statue, but looking at
him now.

What is it in little things which has such power over us? As Diana stood there looking, it was little things which stabbed her as if each were a sharp sword. The set of Evan's shoulders, the waves of his hair, the very gold shoulder-straps on the well-remembered blue uniform undress; his cap which lay on her table, with its service symbols. Is it that the sameness of these material trifles seems to assert that nothing is changed, and so makes the change more incredible and dreadful? I cannot describe the woful pain which the sight of these things gave Diana. With them came the fresh remembrance of all the manly beauty and grace of Evan in which she had once sunned herself, and the contrast of her husband. Not that Basil's personal appearance was ever to be despised, any more than himself; his figure was good, and his face had a beauty of its own, possibly a higher kind of beauty; but it was not the type of a hero of romance; and Evan's, to Diana's fancy, *was;* and it had been her romance. She stood still, motionless, breathless. If anybody spoke, it must be he. But at last she trembled too much to stand, and she sat down too.

'How has it happened, Diana?' Evan asked without looking up.

'I don't know,'—she said just above her breath.

'How could you do so?'

Well, it suited him well to reproach her! What matter? Things could not be more bitter than they were. She did not try to answer.

'You have ruined both our lives. *Mine* is ruined; I am ruined. I shall never be worth anything now. I don't care what becomes of me.'

As she still did not answer, he looked up, and their eyes met. Once meeting, they could not quit each other. Diana's gaze was sad enough, but eager with the eagerness of long hunger. His was sharp with pain at first, keen with unreasonable anger; one of the mind's resorts from unbearable torment. Then as he looked it changed and grew soft; and finally, springing up, he went over to where she sat, dropped on his knees before her, and seizing her hands kissed them one after the other till tears began to mingle with the kisses. She was passive; she could not drive him off; she felt that she and he must have this one moment to bury their past in; it was only when her hands were growing wet with his tears that she roused herself to an effort.

'Evan—Evan—listen to me! You mustn't—remember, I am a man's wife.'

'How could you?'

'I did not know what I was doing.'

'Have you given up loving me?'

'What is the use of talking of it, Evan? I am another man's wife.'

'But there are such things as divorces.'

'Hush! Do not speak of such a thing.'

'I must speak of it. Whom do you love? tell me that first.'

'No one has a right to ask me such a question.'

'*I* have a right,' cried the young man; 'for I have been deceived, cheated, robbed of my own; and I have a right to get back my own. Diana, speak! do you love me less than you used to do? Tell me that.'

'I do not change, Evan.'

'Then you have no business to be anybody's wife but mine. Nothing can hinder *that*, Diana.'

'Stop! You are not to speak so. I will not hear it.'

'You are mine, Diana.'

'I *was* yours, Evan!' she said tenderly, bending her head over him till her lips touched his hair. 'We have been parted, and it is over—over for this world. You must go your way, and I must go mine. And you must not say, I am ruined.'

'Do not you say it?'

'I must not.'

'It is the truth for me, if I do not have you with me.'

'It is not the truth,' she said with infinite tenderness in her manner. 'Not ruined, Evan. We can go our way and do our work, even if we are not happy. *That* is another thing.'

'Then you are not happy?' he said eagerly.

Diana did not reply.

'Why should we not be happy?' he went on passionately,

looking up now into her face. 'You are mine, Diana—you belonged to me first, you have been mine all along; only I have been robbed of you ;—pure robbery ; nothing else. And has not a man a right to his own, wherever and whenever he finds it ? You had given yourself first to me. That is irrevocable.'

'No'—she said with the same gentleness, in every tone of which lurked an unutterable sorrow ; it would have broken her husband's heart to hear her ; and yet she was quiet, so quiet that she awed the young officer a little. 'No—I had promised to give myself to you; that is all.'

'You gave me your heart, Di ? '

She was silent, for at the moment she could not speak.

'Di !'—he insisted.

'Yes.'

'That is enough. That is all.'

'It is not all. Since then I have '—

'How could you do it, Diana? how could you do it, after your heart was mine? *while* your heart was mine ! '

'I was dead,' she said in the same low, slow, impressive way. 'I thought I was dead,—and that it did not matter any more what I did, one way or another. I thought I was dead ; and when I found out that there was life in me yet, it was too late.' A slight shudder ran over her shoulders, which Evan, however, did not see.

'And you doubted me ! ' said he.

'I heard nothing '—

'Of course !—and that was enough to make you think I was nothing but a featherhead ! '—

'I thought I was not good enough for you,' she said softly.

'Not good enough ! ' cried Evan. 'When you are just a pearl of perfection—a diamond of loveliness—more than all I knew you would be—like a queen rather than like a common mortal. And I could have given you a place fit for you ; and here you are '—

'Hush ! ' she said softly, but it stopped him.

'*Why* did you never hear from me ? I wrote, and wrote, and O, Diana, how I looked for something from you ! I walked miles on the way to meet the waggon that brought our mails; I could hardly do my duty, or eat, or sleep, at last. I would ride then to meet the post-carrier, though it did not help me, for I could not open the bags till they were brought into the post; and then I used to go and gallop thirty miles to ride away from myself. *Why* did you never write one word?'

'I did not know your address,' she said faintly.

'I gave it you, over and over.'

'You forget,—I never got the letters.'

'What became of them?'

'I don't know.'

'What was her motive?'

'I suppose—I don't know.'

'What do you suppose?'

'What is the use of talking about it, Evan?'

'My poor darling!' said he, looking up in her face again; 'it has been hard on you too. Oh Di! my Di! I cannot lose you!'—

He was still kneeling before her, and she put her two hands on his head, smoothing or rather pushing back the short locks from his temples on either side, looking as one looks one's last on what one loves. Her eyes were dry, and large with pain which did not allow the eyelids their usual droop; her mouth was in the saddest lines a woman's lips can take, but they did not tremble.

'Hush,' she said again softly. 'I am lost to you. That is over. Now go and do a man's work in the world, and if I hear of you, let me hear good.'

'Haven't you got one kiss for me?'

She bent lower down, and kissed his brow. She kissed it twice; but the manner of the woman was of such high and pure dignity that the young officer, who would else have had no scruple, did not dare presume upon it. He took no more than she gave; bent his head again when she took her hands away, and covered his face, as at first. They were both still awhile.

'Evan—you must go,' she whispered.

'When may I come again?'

She did not answer.

X

'I am coming very soon again, Di. I must see you often—
I must see you *very* often, while I am here. I cannot live if I
do not see you. I do not see how I can live any way!'

'Don't speak so.'

'How do *you* expect to bear it?' he asked jealously.

'I don't know. We shall find as the days come.'

'Life looks so long!'—

'Yes. But we have got something to do in it.'

'I have not. Not now.'

'Every one has. And a brave man, or a brave woman, will
do what he has to do, Evan.'

'I am not brave, except in the way every man is brave.
When may I come, Diana? To-morrow?'

'O no!'

'Why not? Then when?'

'Not this week.'

'But this is Tuesday.'

'Yes. And Mrs. Reverdy is waiting for you all this while.'

'I have been waiting all these years. She don't know what
waiting means. Mayn't I come again before Monday?'

'Certainly not. You must wait till then, and longer.'

'I am not going to wait longer. Then Monday, Diana?'

He stretched out his hand to her, and she laid hers within it.
The first time that day; the first time since so many days.
Hands lingered, were slow to unclasp, loath to leave the touch
which was such exquisite pain and pleasure at once. Then,
without looking again, slowly, deliberately, as all her movements had been made, Diana withdrew from the room; not
bearing, perhaps, to stay and have him leave her, or doubting of
her power to make him go, or unable to endure anything more
for this time. She left him standing there, and slowly went
up the stairs. But the moment she got to her room she
stopped, and stood with her hands pressed upon her heart,
listening; every particle of colour vanishing from her face, and
her eyes taking a strained look of despair; listening to the
footsteps that, also slowly, now went through the hall. When
they went out and had quitted the house, she flew to the window. She watched to see the stately figure go along the little

walk and out at the gate; she had hardly dared to look at him down-stairs. Now her eye sought out every well-known line and trait with an eagerness like the madness of thirst. Yes, he had grown broader in the shoulders; his frame was developed; he had become more manly, and so even finer in appearance than ever. Without meaning it, Diana drew comparisons. How well he walked! what a firm, sure, graceful gait! How beloved of old time was the officer's undress coat, and the little cap which reminded Diana so inevitably of the time when it was at home on her table or lying on a chair near! Only for a minute or two she tasted the bitter-sweet pang of associations; and then cap and wearer were passed from her sight.

CHAPTER XXXII.

WIND AND TIDE.

How that night went by it would be useless to try to tell. Some things cannot be described. A loosing of all the bands of law and order in the material world we call chaos; and once in a while the mental nature of some poor mortal falls for a time into a like condition. No hold of anything, not even of herself; no clear sense of anything, except of the disorder and pain; no hope at the moment that could fasten on either world, the present or the future; no will to lay hold of the unruly forces within her and reduce them to obedience. An awful night for Diana, such as she never had spent, nor in its full measure would ever spend again. Nevertheless, through all the confusion, under all the tumult, there was one fixed point; indeed, it was the point round which all the confusion worked, and which Diana was dimly conscious of all the while; one point of action. At the time she could not steady herself to look at it; but when the dawn came up in the sky, with its ineffable promise of victory by and by,—and when the rays of the sun broke over the hills with their golden performance of conquest begun, strength seemed to come into her heart. Certainly light has no fellowship with darkness; and the spiritual and the material are more closely allied, perhaps, than we wot of. Diana washed herself and dressed, and felt that she had done with yesterday.

It was a worn and haggard face that was opposite Basil at the breakfast table; but she sat there, and poured out his tea with not less care than usual. Except for cups of tea, the meal was not much more than a pretence. After it was done, Diana followed her husband to his study.

'Basil,' she said, 'I must go away.'

Mr. Masters started, and asked what she meant.

'I mean just that,' said Diana. 'I must go away. Basil, help me!'

'Help you, my child?' said he; 'I will help you all I can. But sit down, Diana; you are not able to stand. Why do you want to go away?'

'I must.'

'Where do you wish to go?'

'I do not know. I do not care. Anywhere.'

'You have no plan?'

'No; only to get away.'

'Why, Diana?' he said very tenderly. 'Is it necessary?'

'Yes, Basil. I must go.'

'Do you know that it would be extremely difficult for me to leave home just at present? There are so many people wanting me.'

'I know that. I have thought of all that. You cannot go. Let me go, and baby.'

'Where, my dear?'

'I don't know,' she said with almost a sob. 'You must know. You must help me, Basil.'

Basil looked at her, and took several turns up and down the room, in sorrow and perplexity.

'What is your reason, Di?' he asked gently. 'If I understood your thought better, I should know better how to meet it.'

'I must be away,' said Diana vaguely. 'I must not be here. I mustn't be where I can see—anybody. Nobody must know where I am, Basil—do you understand? You must send me away, and you must not tell *anybody*.'

The minister walked up and down, thinking. He let go entirely the thought of arguing with Diana. She had the look at moments of a creature driven to bay; and when not so, the haggard, eager, appealing face filled his inmost heart with grief and pity. Nobody better than Basil could manage the unreasonable and bring the disorderly to obedience; he had a magical way with him; but now he only meditated how Diana's wish was to be met. It was not just easy, for he had few family connections in the world, and she had none.

'I can think of nobody to whom I should like to send you,' he said. 'Unless'—

He waited, and Diana waited; then he finished his sentence.

'I was going to say, unless a certain old grandaunt of mine. Perhaps she would do.'

'I do not care where or who it is,' said Diana.

'I care, though.'

'Where does she live?'

'On Staten Island.'

'Staten Island?' repeated Diana.

'Yes. It is near New York; about an hour from the city, down the bay.'

'The bay of New York?'

'Yes.'

'May I go there?' said Diana. 'That would do.'

'How soon do you wish to go?'

'To-day, if I could!' she said with a half-caught breath. 'Can I, Basil? To-day is best.'

Mr. Masters considered again.

'Will you be ready to go by the seven o'clock train this evening?'

'Yes. O yes!'

'Very well. We will take that.'

'*We?*' Diana repeated. 'Must I take you, Basil, away from your work? Cannot I go alone?'

He looked up at her with a very sweet grave smile as he answered, 'Not possibly.'

'I am a great deal of trouble'—she said with a woful expression.

'Go and make your preparations,' he said cheerfully; 'and I will tell you about Aunt Sutphen when we are off.'

There was no bustle in the house that day, there was no undue stir of making arrangements; but at the time appointed Diana was ready. She had managed to keep Miss Collins in the dark down to the very last minute, and answered her questions then with, 'I can't tell you. You must ask Mr.

Masters.' And Diana knew anybody might as well get the Great Pyramid to disclose its secrets.

That night's train took them to Boston. The next morning they went on their way towards New York; and so far Mr. Masters had found no good time for his proposed explanations. Diana was busied with the baby, and contrived to keep herself away from him or from communication with him. He saw that she was engrossed, preoccupied, suffering, and that she shunned him; and he fell back and waited. In New York, he established Diana in a hotel and left her, to go himself alone to the Island and have an interview with his aunt.

Diana, alone in a Broadway hotel, felt a little like a person shipwrecked in mid-ocean. What was all this bustling, restless, driving multitude around her like, but the waves of the sea, to which Scripture likens them? and the roar of their tumult almost bewildered her senses. Proverbially there is no situation more lonely to the feeling than the midst of a strange crowd; and Diana, sitting at her window and looking down into the busy street, felt alone and cast adrift as she never had felt in her life before. *Her* life seemed done, finished, as far as regarded hope or joy; nothing left but weary and dragging existence; and the eager hurrying hither and thither of the city crowd struck on her view as aimless and fruitless, and so very drear to look at. What was it all for?—seeing life was such a thing as she had found it. The wrench of coming away from Pleasant Valley had left her with a reaction of dull, stunned, and strained nerves; she was glad she had come away, glad she was no longer there; and that was the only thing she was glad of in the wide, wide world.

Some degree of rest came with the quiet of those hours alone in the hotel. Basil was gone until the evening, and Diana had time to recover a little from the fatigue of the journey, and in the perfect solitude also from the overstrain of the nerves. She began to remember Basil's part in all this, and to be sensible how true and faithful and kind he was; how very unselfish, how patient with her and with pain. Diana could have wept her heart out over it, if that would have done any good; and indeed supposing that she could have

shed tears at all, which she could not just then. She only felt
sore and sorry for her husband; and then she took some pains
with her toilet, and refreshed herself so as to look pleasant to
his eyes when he came home.

He came home only to a late supper. He looked somewhat
weary, but his eye brightened when he saw Diana, and he came
up and kissed her.

'Diana—God is good,' he said to her.

'Yes,' she answered, looking up drearily. 'I believe it.'

'But you do not feel it yet. Well, remember, it is true,
and you will feel it some day. It is all right with Aunt Sutphen.'

'She will let me come?'

'She is glad to have you come. The old lady is very much
alone. And she does me the honour to say that she expects
my wife will know how to behave herself.'

'What does she mean by that?' said Diana, a little startled.

'I don't know! Aunt Sutphen has her own notions respecting behaviour. I did not inquire, Diana; knowing that, whatever her meaning might be, it was the same thing so far as
you are concerned.'

'Basil—you are very good!' Diana said after a pause and
with a trembling lip.

'I can take compliments from Aunt Sutphen,' he said with
a bit of his old dry humorous manner, 'but from you I don't
know what to do with them. Come to supper, Di; we must
take the first boat for Clifton to-morrow morning, if we can,
to let me get back on my way to Pleasant Valley.'

The first boat was very early. The city, however, had long
begun its accustomed roar, so that the change was noticeable
and pleasant as soon as the breadth of a few furlongs was put
between the boat and the wharf. Stillness fell, only excepting
the noise made by the dash of the paddle-wheels and the
breathing and groaning of the engine; and that seemed quiet-
ness to Diana, in contrast with the restless hum and roar of the
living multitude. The bay and its shores sparkled in the early
sunlight; the sultry, heated atmosphere of the city was most
refreshingly replaced by the cool air from the salt sea. Diana
breathed it in, filling her lungs with it.

'How good this is!' she said. 'Basil, I should think it was dreadful to live in such a place as that.'

'Makes less difference than you would think, when you once get accustomed to it.'

'O, do you think so? It seems to me there is nothing pleasant there to see or to hear.'

'Ay, you are a true wood-thrush,' said her husband. 'But there is plenty to do in a city, Diana; and that is the main thing.'

'So there is in the country.'

'I sometimes think I might do more,—reach more people, I mean,—if I were somewhere else. But yes, Di, I grant you, apart from that one consideration, there is no comparison. Green hills are a great deal better company than hot brick walls.'

'And how wonderful, how beautiful, this water is!'

'The water is a new feature to you. Well, you will have plenty of it. Aunt Sutphen lives just on the edge of the shore. I am very sorry I cannot stay to see you domesticated. Do you mind it much, beginning here alone?'

'O no.'

Diana did not mind that or anything else, in her content at having reached a safe harbour, a place where she would be both secure and free. Lesser things were of no account; and alas! the presence of her husband just now with her was no pleasure. Diana felt at this time, that if she were to live and keep her reason she must have breathing space. Above all things, she desired to be quite alone; to have leisure to think and pray, and review her ground and set up her defences. Basil could not help her; he was better out of sight. So, when he had put her into the little carriage that was in waiting at the landing, and with a last gesture of greeting turned back to the boat, while Diana's eyes filled with tears, she was, nevertheless, nothing but glad at heart. She gathered her baby closer in her arms, and sat back in the carriage and waited.

It was only a short drive, and along the edge of the bay the whole distance. The smell of the salt water was strange and delicious. The morning was still cool. Now that she had left

the boat behind her, or rather the boat had left her, the stillness began to be like that of Pleasant Valley; for the light
wheels rolled softly over a smooth road. Then they stopped
before a low, plain-looking cottage.

It was low and plain, yet it was light and pleasant. Windows
opening like doors upon the piazza, and the piazza running
all round the house, and the pillars of the piazza wreathed
thick with honeysuckles, some of them, and some with climbing roses. The breath of the salt air was smothered in perfumes. Through one of the open window-doors Diana went
into a matted room, where everything gave her the instant
impression of neatness and coolness and quiet, and a certain
sweet summer freshness, which suited her exactly. There was
no attempt at richness of furnishing. Yet the old lady who
stood there waiting to receive her was a stately lady enough,
in a spotless morning dress of white, dainty and ruffled, and a
little close embroidered cap above her clustering grey curls.
The two looked at each other.

'So you're his wife?' said the elder lady. 'I declare, you're
handsomer than he is. Come in here, my dear; if you are as
good as he is, you are welcome.' She opened an inner door
and led the way into a bedchamber adjoining, opening like the
other room by window-doors upon the piazza, matted and cool
and furnished in white. All this Diana took in with the first
step into the room. But she answered Mrs. Sutphen's peculiar
welcome.

'Did you ever know anybody so good as he is, ma'am?'

'Breakfast will be on table as soon as you are ready,' Mrs.
Sutphen went on without heeding her words. 'It is half-past
seven, and I always have it at seven. I waited for you, and
now I want my cup of tea. How soon will you be ready?'

'Immediately.'

'What will you do with the baby?'

'I will lay her down. She is asleep.'

'You'll have to have somebody to look after her. Well,
come then, my dear.'

Diana followed the old lady, who was half imperative and
half impatient. She never forgot that hour in all her life,

everything was so new and strange. The windows open
towards the water, the fresh salt air coming in, the India
matting under her feet, made her feel as if she had got into
a new world. The dishes were also in part strange to her,
and her only companion fully strange. The good cup of tea
she received was almost the only familiar thing, for the very
bread was like no bread she had ever seen before. Diana
sipped her tea gratefully; all this novelty was the most welcome thing in the world to her overstrained nerves. She
sipped her tea as in a dream; the old lady studied her with
eyes wide awake and practical.

'Where did Basil pick you up, my dear?'

Diana started a little, looked up, and flushed.

'Where did you come from?'

'From the place where Mr. Masters has been settled these
three or four years.'

'In the mountains! What sort of people have you got
there? More of your sort?'

'They are all of my sort,' said Diana somewhat wonder-
ingly.

'Do you know what your sort is, my dear?'

'I do not understand'—

'I thought you did not. I'll change my question. What
sort of work is Basil doing there?'

'You know his profession?'—Diana said, not knowing much
better either how to take this question.

'Yes, yes. I know his profession; I ought to, for I wanted
him to be a lawyer. But don't you know, my dear, there are
all sorts of clergymen? There are some make sermons as
other men make bricks; and some more like the way children
blow soap-bubbles; all they care for is, how big they are, and
how high they will fly, and how long they will last. And I
have heard people preach,' the old lady went on, 'who seemed
most like as if they were laying out a Chinese puzzle, and you
had to look sharp to see where the pieces fitted. And some,
again, preach sermons as if they were a magistrate reading the
Riot Act, only they don't want the people to disperse by any
means. What is Basil's way?'

'He has more ways than all these,' said Diana, who could not help smiling.

'These among 'em?'

'I think not.'

'Go on, then, and tell me. What's he like in the pulpit?'

Diana considered how she should humour the old lady's wish.

'Sometimes he is like a shepherd leading his flock to pasture,' she began. 'Sometimes he is like a lifeboat going out to pick up drowning people. Sometimes it is rather a surgeon in an hospital, going round to find out what is the matter with people and make them well. Sometimes he is just the messenger of the Lord Jesus Christ, and all his business is to deliver his message and get people to hear it.'

Mrs. Sutphen looked at Diana over the table, and evidently pricked up her ears; but Diana spoke quite simply, rather slowly; she was thinking how Basil had often seemed to her in his ministry, in and out of the pulpit.

'My dear,' said the old lady, 'if your husband is like that, do you know you are married to quite a remarkable man?'

'I thought as much a great while ago.'

'And what sort of a pastor's wife do you make? You are a very handsome woman to be a minister's wife.'

'Am I? Why should not a handsome woman be the wife of a minister?'

'Why, she should, if she can make up her mind to it. Well, my dear, if you will have no more breakfast, perhaps you will like to go and rest. Do you enjoy bathing?'

Diana did not take the bearing of the question.

'I go into the water every morning,' the old lady explained. 'You had better do the same. It will strengthen you.'

'Into the water! You mean the salt water?'

'Of course I mean the salt water. There isn't any fresh water to go into, and no good if there was.'

'I never tried salt water. I never saw salt water before.'

'Do you good,' said the old lady. 'Well, go and sleep, my dear. Basil says you want rest.'

But that way of taking it was not Diana's need, or purpose.

She withdrew into her cool green-shaded room, and as the baby still slept, set open the blind doors which made that pleasant green shade, and sat down on the threshold to be quiet, and enjoy the view. The water was within a few rods of her window; nothing but a narrow strip of grass and a little picket fence intervening between the house and the sandy bit of beach. The waves were rolling in from the Narrows, which here were but a short distance to the eastward; and across the broad belt of waters she could see the low shore of Long Island on the other side. Diana put her head out of the door, and there, seven miles away to the west and north, she could see where a low, hovering, light smoke cloud told of the big city to which it owed its origin. Over the bay sails were flitting, not swiftly, for the air was only very gently stirring; but they were many, near and far, of different sizes and forms; and the mighty tide was rushing in with wonderful life and energy in its green waves. Diana's senses were like those of a person enchanted. She drew in the salt, lively air; she looked at the cool lights and shadows of the rushing water, over which here and there still hung bands of morning mist; she heard the lap of the waves upon the shore as they went by; and it was to her as if she had escaped from danger and perplexity into another world, where sorrow might be, indeed, but from which confusion and fear were banished.

The baby slept on, as if she had been broken off her rest by the novelties and inconveniences of travelling, and were making up for lost time; and Diana sat on the threshold of her door and thought. The lull was inexpressibly sweet, after the storm that had tossed her hither. It gave her repose just to remember that Evan could not find her out—and that Basil would leave her alone. Yes, both thoughts came in for a share in the deep-drawn breaths of relief which from time to time wrung themselves from Diana's breast. She knew it; she could not help it; and she soon forgot her husband in thinking of her lover. It seemed to her she might allow herself that indulgence now; now when she had put a gulf between them which he could not bridge over, and she would

not; now when she had brought a separation between them
which must for ever be final. For she would never see him
again. Surely now she might think of him, and let fancy
taste the sweet bitter drops that memory would distil for her.
Diana went back to the old time and lived in it for hours, till
the baby awoke and claimed her; and even then she went on
with her dream. She dreamed all day.

Next morning early, before she was awake, there came
a little imperative tap at her door. Diana sprang up and
opened it.

'I am going to take my bath,' said her hostess. 'Here's a
bathing dress—put it on and come along.'   ‸

'Now?' said Diana doubtfully.

'Why, of course now! Now's the time. Nobody 'll see
you, child; and if they do, it won't matter. Hundreds would
see you if you were at Long Branch or Newport. Come along;
you want bracing.'

I wonder if I do, thought Diana, as she clothed herself in
the loose gown of brown mohair; then slipped out after her
hostess. If she did, she immediately confessed to herself, this
was the thing to give it. The sun was not yet up; the morning air crisp and fresh and delicious; the water rolling gently
in from the Narrows again, in a mighty tide, but with no wind,
so sending up only little waves to the beach; however, they
looked somewhat formidable to Diana.

'How far do you go in?' she asked.

'As far as I can. I can't swim, child, so I keep to shore.
Come after me, here!'—

And she seized Diana's hand and marched in ahead of her,
and marched on, till Diana would have stopped, but the old
lady's hand pulled her along.

It was never to be forgotten, that first taste of salt water.
When they were in the flood up to their necks, her companion
made her duck her head under; it filled Diana's mouth and
eyes at the first gasp with salt water, but what a new freshness
of life seemed at the same time to come into her! How her
brain cleared, and her very heart seemed to grow strong, and
her eyesight true in that lavatory! She came out of the water

for the moment almost gay, and made her toilette with a vigour
and energy she had not brought to it in many a day. Breakfast was better to her, and the old lady was contented with
what she said about it.

Yet Diana sat and dreamed again all day after that, watching the rolling tide of waters, and letting her thoughts run on
in as uninterrupted a flow. She dreamed only about Evan;
she went over old times and new, old impressions and new;
she recalled words and looks and tones and gestures, of long
ago and lately; at Pleasant Valley she had not dared; here
she thought it was safe, and she might take the indulgence.
She recalled all Evan's looks. How he had improved! More
stately, more manly, more confident (could that be?), more
graceful; with the air of command replacing a comparative
repression of manner (only comparative), even as the full, thick,
curly moustache replaced a velvety dark line which Diana well
remembered. As he had been then, she had fancied him perfect; as he was now, he was to the eye far finer yet. Basil
could not compare with him. Ah, why did fancy torture her
by ever bringing forward the comparison! Basil never pre-
tended to wear a moustache, and the features of his face were
not so regular, and his eye was not so brilliant, and the
indescribable air of authority was not there, nor the regulated
grace of movement. True, Basil could sit a horse, and ride
him, she knew, as well as anybody; and true, Basil's face had
a high grave sweetness which was utterly unknown to the
countenance of that other; and it was also true, that if Mr.
Masters wore no air of command, he knew what the thing
meant, especially command over himself. And there the comparison failed for Evan. In the contrast, Diana, down deep in
the bottom of her heart, was not satisfied with him, not
pleased, not contented. He might know how to give orders
to his company, he had not left off himself being under orders;
he might be strong to enforce discipline among his men, but
alas! alas! he had left the reins loose upon the neck of his
passions. Basil never did that, never. Basil never would in
the like circumstances have sought a weak gratification at her
expense. That was the word; *weak*. Evan had been selfishly

weak. Basil was always, so far as she had known him, unselfishly strong. And yet, and yet!—she loved the weak one; although it pained her that he should have been weak.

Days went by. Diana lived in dreams.

'What is the matter with you?' her old friend asked her abruptly one evening.

'Nothing, I think,' said Diana, looking up from her sewing and answering in some surprise.

'Nothing the matter! Then what did you come here for?'

'I thought'—Diana hesitated in confusion for the moment—'my husband agreed with me in thinking, that it would be good for me to be away from home for awhile.'

'Wanted change, eh?' Mrs. Sutphen said dryly.

Diana did not know what to add to her words.

'Change and salt air'—the old lady went on.

'Not salt air particularly,' Diana answered, feeling that she must answer. 'I did not think of salt air. Though no change could have been so good for me.'

'*Has* it been good for you?'

'I have enjoyed it more than I can tell,' Diana said, looking up again.

'Yes, yes; but that isn't the thing. I know you enjoy it. But do you think it is making you fat?'

'I don't need that,' said Diana, smiling. 'I am fat enough.'

'You won't be, if you go on losing as you have done since you came. Now I agree with you that I don't think that is Clifton air. What is it?'

Diana could not reply. She was startled and troubled. She knew the fact was true.

'Basil won't like it if I let this go on; and I don't mean it shall. Is anything the matter between you and him?'

'What do you mean?' Diana asked, to gain time.

'You know what I mean. I spoke plain. Have you and he had any sort of a quarrel or disagreement?'

'Certainly not!'

'Certainly *not?*—then why aren't you happy?'

'Why do you ask me?' said Diana. 'Why should you question my being happy?'

'I've got eyes, child; inconvenient things, for they see. You look and act like a marble woman; only that you are not cold, and that you move about. Now, that isn't your nature. What spell has come over you?'

'You know, Mrs. Sutphen,' Diana answered with calmness, 'there are many things that come up in the world to try one and trouble one; things one cannot help, and that one must bear.'

'I know that as well as you do. But a woman with the husband you have got, ought never to be petrified by anything that comes to her. In the first place, she has no cause; and in the second place, she has no right.'

There was such an instant assent of Diana's inner nature to at least the latter of these assertions, that after a minute or two's pause she said very simply—

'Thank you. That is true.'

'He's rather fond of you, isn't he?' the old lady asked with a well-pleased look at her beautiful neighbour.

'Yes. Too much,' said Diana, sighing.

'Can't be too much, as I see, if only you are equally fond of him; it is bad to have inequality in that matter. But, my dear, whatever you do, don't turn into marble. There's fire at the heart of the earth, folks say, but it don't do us much good in winter.'

With this oracular statement Mrs. Sutphen closed her lecture. She had said enough. Diana spent half that night and all the next day in a quite new set of meditations.

And more days than one. She waked up to see what she had been doing. What business had she to be thinking of Evan, when she was Basil's wife?—what right to be, even only in imagination, spending her life with him? She knew, now that she was called to look at it, that Mrs. Sutphen had spoken true, and that a process had been going on in herself which might well be likened to the process of petrifying. Everything had been losing taste and colour lately; even her baby was not the delight she had been formerly. Her mind had been warped from its healthy condition, and was growing morbid. Conscience roused up now fully, and bade Diana stop short where she was and take another course. But there she was

Y

met by a difficulty; one that many a woman has had to meet,
and that few have ever overcome. To take another course
meant that she should cease thinking of Evan,—cease thinking
of him even at all; for it was one of those things which you
cannot do *a little*. She tried it; and she found it to be impossible. Everything and anything would set her upon the track
of thinking of him; everything led to him; everything was
bound up with him, either by sympathy or contrast. She
found that she must think of Evan, because she loved him.
She said that to herself, and pleaded it. Then do not love
him! was the instant sharp answer of conscience. And Diana
saw a battle set in array.

That day, the day when she got to this point, was one of
those which even in summer one may know on the sea-shore.
It was grey and cool, and a violent easterly wind was driving
the waters in from the Narrows. The moment Diana got a
sight of those battle forces opposed to each other in her spiritual nature, she threw on bonnet and shawl and went out.
Baby was sleeping, and she left her safely in charge of a good-
tempered servant who asked no better.

She went along the shore in the face of the wind, meeting,
breasting, overcoming it, though with the exertion of determined strength and energy. The gale was rather fierce. It
was a sight to see, the rush of that tide of waters, mighty,
sweeping, rolling and tumbling in from the great sea, restless,
endless. Diana did not stop to draw comparisons, yet I think
she felt them even then; the wild accord of the unchained
forces without and the unchained forces within. Who could
stay them, the one or the other? 'That is Nature,' said Diana
to herself; 'and this is Nature; "the troubled sea that cannot
rest." But that is spoken of the wicked; am I wicked because
I cannot help what I *cannot* help? As well put out my
tiny hand and sweep back that stormy flood of water to the
ocean where it comes from!—as hopefully, as practicably.
What am I, *I*—but a chip or a shingle tossed and chased along
on the power of the waves? The wicked are like the troubled
sea when it cannot rest; that is it, it *cannot* rest. Look at it,
and think of bidding it rest!'

She had walked a long way in the teeth of the storm, and yet, unwilling even to turn her face homewards with her mind still at war, she had crouched down to rest under the lee of an old shed which stood near the edge of the water. Diana drew her shawl closer round her and watched the wild play of the waves, which grew wilder every moment; taking a sort of gloomy comfort in the thought that they were not more irresistible or unopposable than the tempest in her own heart. Then came in the thought—it stole in—'There was One who could bid it be still—and the sea heard him and was quiet. If he could do that, could he not still this other storm? A worse storm, yes; but could not the hand that did one thing do the other?' Diana knew on the instant that it could; but with that came another consciousness—that she wished it could not. She did not want the storm laid. Better the raging forces than the calm that would follow the death of her love for Evan Knowlton. 'But it could never die!' was the impatient objection of her heart; and then came the whisper of conscience, 'It ought; you know it ought; and the Lord never bade you do a thing he would not help you to do, or do for you if you are willing.' And she remembered: 'If ye shall say to this mountain, Be thou removed.'—Could she be willing? that was all. Would she say it?

The Lord said, there are some sorts of devils that are only cast out by prayer and fasting; and I suppose that means, by very great and determinate laying hold of the offered strength and fullest surrender to all its dispositions.

This was a battle before which Waterloo sinks to a play of fire-crackers and Gravelotte to a great wrestling match. There was a struggle on those fields, and bitter determination, and death faced and death met; and yet the combatants there never went to the front with the agony which Diana's fight cost her. And if anybody thinks I am extravagant, I will remind him on what authority we have it, that 'he that ruleth his spirit is greater than he that taketh a city.' Let no one suppose the battle in Diana's instance was soon fought and over. It was death to give up Evan; not the death of the body, which lived on and was strong though she grew visibly thin, but the death of the will; and that is a death harder by far than the other. Diana was in the struggle of that fight for many a day, and, as I said, growing thin under it. She was not willing; if she could be delivered from this passion which was like her life, she was not willing to be delivered. Yet duty was plain; conscience was inexorable. Diana struggled and fought till she could fight no longer, and then she dragged herself as it were to the feet of the Stiller of the waves, with the cry of the Syro-Phenician woman on her lips and in her heart: 'Lord, help me!' But the help, Diana knew by this time, meant that he should do all the work himself, not come in aid of her efforts, which were like ropes of straw in a flame. Let no one think, either, that the first struggle to have faith was faith itself, or that the first endeavour to submit was surrender. There is a wide difference, and often a wide distance. But there came a time—it was slow in coming, but it came—when like a wearied child Diana ceased from her own efforts, and like a helpless child threw herself upon strength that she knew. And then the work was done.

Let no one say, either, that what I have described is an impossibility. 'If ye have faith,'—the Master said,—'nothing shall be impossible to you.' And nothing is. 'He is a Rock; his work is perfect.' And he who overcame all our enemies for us can overcome them in us. They are conquered foes. Only, the Lord will not do the work for those who are trusting in themselves.

CHAPTER XXXIII.

BUDS AND BLOSSOMS.

It was the end of September. Nearing a time of storms again in the air and on the sea; but an absolute calm had settled down upon Diana. Not at all the calm of death; for after death in this warfare, comes not only victory, but new life. It was very strange, even to herself. She had ceased to think of Captain Knowlton; if she thought of him, it was with the recognition that his power over her was gone. She felt like a person delivered from helpless bondage. There was some lameness, there were some bruises yet from the fight gone by; but Diana was every day recovering from these, and elasticity and warmth were coming back to the members that had been but lately rigid and cold. The sun shone again for her, and the sky was blue, and the arch of it grew every day loftier and brighter to her sense. At first coming to Clifton, Diana had perceived the beauties and novelties of her new surroundings; now she began to enjoy them. The salt air was delicious; the light morning mist over the bay, as she saw it when she went to take her morning bath, held a whole day of sunlit promise within its mysterious folds; the soft low hum of the distant city, which she could hear when the waves were still, made the solitude and the freshness and the purity of the island seem doubly rare and sweet. And her baby began to be now to Diana the most wonderful of delights; more than ever it had been at any previous time.

All this while she had had letters from Basil; not very long letters, such as a man can write to a woman whose whole sympathy he knows he has; but good letters, such as a man can write to a woman to whom his own heart and soul have

given all they have. Not that he ever spoke of that fact, or
alluded to it. Basil was no maudlin, and no fool to ask for a
gift which cannot be yielded by an effort of will; and besides,
he had never entirely lost hope; so that, though things were
dark enough for him certainly, he could write manly, strong,
sensible letters, which, in their very lack of all allusion to his
own feelings, spoke whole volumes to the woman who knew
him and could interpret them. The thought of him grieved
her; it was getting to be now the only grief she had. Her
own letters to him were brief and rare. Diana had a nervous
fear of letting the Clifton postmark be seen on a letter of hers
at home, knowing what sort of play sometimes went on in the
Pleasant Valley post office; so she never sent a letter except
when she had a chance to despatch it from New York. These
epistles were very abstract; they spoke of the baby, told of
Mrs. Sutphen, gave details of things seen and experienced;
but of Diana's inner life, the fight and the victory, not a whit.
She could not write about them to Basil; for, glad as he would
be of what she could tell him, she could not say enough. In
getting deliverance from a love it was wrong to indulge, in
becoming able to forget Evan, she had not thereby come nearer
to her husband, or in the least fonder of thinking of him; and
so Diana shrank from the whole subject when she found herself
with pen in hand and paper before her.

When September was gone and October had begun its
course, a letter came from Basil in which he desired to know
about Diana's plans. There were no hindrances any longer in
the way of her coming home, he told her. Diana had known
that such a notification would come, must come, and yet it
gave her an unwelcome start. Mrs. Sutphen had handed it to
her as they came in from their morning dip in the salt water;
the coachman had brought it late last evening from the post
office, she said. Diana had dressed before reading it; and when
she had read it, she sat down upon the threshold of her glass
door to think and examine herself.

It was October, yet still and mild as June. Haze lay lingering about the horizon, softened the shore of Long Island, hid
with a thick curtain the place of the busy city, the roar of

which Diana could plainly enough hear in the stillness; a strange, indistinct, mysterious, significant murmur of distant unrest. All before and around her was rest; the flowing waters were too quiet to-day to suggest anything disquieting; only life, without which rest is nought. The air was inexpressibly sweet and fresh; the young light of the day dancing as it were upon every cloud edge and sail edge, in jocund triumph beginning the work which the day would see done. Diana sat down and looked out into it all, and tried to hold communion with herself. She was sorry to leave this place. Yes, why not? She was sorry to exchange her present life for the old one. Quiet and solitary it had been, this life at Clifton, for Mrs. Sutphen scarcely made her feel less alone with her than without her; and she had held herself back from society. Quiet and solitary, and lately healing; and Pleasant Valley was full of painful memories and associations, her mother, and—her husband. Diana felt as if she could have welcomed everything else, if only Basil had not been there. The sight of the lovely bay with its misty shores and its springing light hurt her at last, because she must leave it; she sank her face in her hands and began to call herself to account. Duty was waiting before her; was she not willing to take it up? She had surrendered her will utterly to God in the matter of her love to Evan, and she had been delivered from the torture and the bondage of it; quite delivered; she could bear to live without Evan now, she could bear to live without thinking of him; he would always be in a certain sense dear, but the spell of passion was broken for ever. That did not make her love her husband. No; but would not the same strength that had freed her from temptation on the one hand, help her to go forward and do her duty on the other? And in love and gratitude for the deliverance vouchsafed her, should she not do it? 'I will do it, if I die!' was her inward conclusion. 'And I shall not die, but by the Lord's help I shall do it.'

So she wrote to her husband that she was ready, and he came to fetch her.

The Pleasant Valley maples were flaunting in orange and

crimson when the home journey was made. The fairest month
of the year was in the prime of its beauty; the air had that
wonderful clearness and calm which bids the spirit of the
beholder be still and be glad, saying that there is peace and
victory somewhere, and rest, when the harvest of life is
gathered. Diana felt the speech, but thought nevertheless
that for *her*, peace and victory were a good way off. She
believed they would come, when life was done; the present
thing was to live, and carry the burden and do the work.
The great elms hung still green and sheltering over the lean-to
door. The house was enlarged and improved, and greatly
beautified with a coat of paint. Diana saw it all; and she
saw the marvellous beauty of the meadows and their bordering hills; she felt as if she were coming to her prison and
place of hard labour.

'How do you like the looks of things?' her husband asked.

'Nice as can be.'

'You like it?'

'Very much. I am glad you did not make the house
white.'

'I remembered you said it ought to be brown.'

'But would *you* have liked it white?'

'I would have liked it no way but your way,' he said with a
slight smile and look at her, which Diana could not answer,
and which cut her sharply. She had noticed, she thought,
that Basil was more sober than he used to be. She thought
she knew why; and she wanted to tell him part of what had
gone on in her mind of late, and how free she was of the
feelings he supposed were troubling her; but a great shyness
of the subject had seized Diana. She was afraid to broach it
at all, lest going on from one thing to another, Basil might ask
a question she could not answer. She was very sorry for him,
so much that she almost forgot to be sorry for herself, as she
went into the house.

Mrs. Flandin was sitting with Mrs. Starling in the lean-to
kitchen.

'So you made up your mind to come home,' was her
mother's greeting. 'I almost wonder you did.'

'If you knew how good the salt water was to me, you might wonder,' Diana answered cheerfully.

'Well, I never could see what there was in salt water!' said Mrs. Flandin, 'that folks should be so crazy to go into it! If I was drownin', 'seems to me I'd rather have my mouth full o' sun'thin' sweet.'

'But I was not drowning,' said Diana.'

'Well, I want to know what you've got by stayin' away from your place all summer'—her mother went on.

'Her place was there,' said the minister, who followed Diana in.

'Now, Dominie,' said Mrs. Flandin, 'you say that jes' 'cause she's your wife. Hain't her place been empty all these months? Where is a wife's place? I should like to hear you say.'

'Don't you think it is where her husband wants her to be?'

'And you wanted her to be away from you down there? Do you mean that?'

'If he had not, I should not have gone, Mrs. Flandin,' Diana said, and with a smile.

'Well now, du tell! what good did salt water do ye? The minister said you was gone to salt water somewheres.'

'It did me more good than I could ever make you understand.'

'I don't believe it!' said Mrs. Starling harshly. 'You mean, it was a clever thing to play lady and sit with your hands before you all summer. It was good there was somebody at home to do the work.'

'Not your work, Di,' said her husband good-humouredly; 'nor my work. *I* did that. Come along and see what I have done.'

He drew her off, into the little front hall or entry; from there, through a side door into the new part of the building. There was a roomy, cool, bright room, lined with the minister's books; curtained and furnished, not expensively, indeed, yet with a thorough air of comfort. Taking the baby from her arms, Basil led the way from this room, up a short stairway, to chambers above which were charmingly neat, light, and cheerful, all in order; everything was done, everything was there that ought to be there. He laid the sleeping child down in its crib, and turned to his wife with a serious face.

'How will you stand it, Diana?'

'Basil, I was just thinking, how will you?'

'We can do what ought to be done,' said he, looking into her face.

'I know you can. I think I can too—in this. And I think it is right to take care of mother. I am sure it is.'

'Diana, by the Lord's help we can do right in everything.'

'Yes, Basil; I know it!' she said, meeting his eyes with a steady look.

He turned away, very grave, but with a deep ejaculation of thankfulness. Diana's eyes filled; but she, too, turned away. She could add no more. It was not words, but living, that must speak for her now.

And it did—even that same evening. Mrs. Flandin would not go away; it was too good an opportunity of gathering information about various points on which the 'town' had been curious and divided. She kept her place till after supper. But all she could see was a fair, quiet demeanour; an unruffled, beautiful face; and an unconscious dignity of carriage which was somewhat provokingly imposing. She saw that Diana was at home, and likely to be mistress in her own sphere; held in too much honour by her husband, and holding him in too much honour, for that a pin's point of malicious curiosity might find an entering place between them. She reported afterwards that the minister was a fool and his wife another, and so they fitted. Mrs. Starling was inclined to be of the same opinion.

The two most nearly concerned knew better. *Fit* they did not, though they were the only ones of all the world that knew it. While Diana had been away at Clifton, the minister had managed to make one of the company at Elmfield rather often, moved by various reasons. One effect, however, of this plan of action had been unfavourable to his own peace of mind. He saw Evan and came to know him; he *would* know him, though the young man would much rather have kept aloof from contact with Diana's husband. Basil's simplicity of manner and straightforwardness were too much for him. And while an unwilling and enormous respect for the minister grew up in Captain Knowlton's mind, the minister on his part saw and felt, and perhaps exaggerated, the attractiveness of the young army officer. Basil was not at all given to self-depreciation ; in fact, he did not think of himself enough for such a mischievous mental transaction ; however, he perceived the grace of figure and bearing, the air of command and the beauty of feature, which he thought might well take a woman's eye. 'My poor Diana!' he said to himself; 'her fancy has caught the stamp of all this—and will hold it. Naturally. She is not a woman to like and unlike. What chance for me!'

Which meditations, unwholesome as they were, did not prevent Basil's attaching himself to Captain Knowlton's society, making a friend of him, in spite of both their selves, as it were. The captain's mental nature, he suspected and found, was by no means in order to correspond with his physical; and if a friend could help him, he would be that friend. And Basil did not see that the young officer's evident respect for himself, and succumbing to his friendly advances, were a very significant tribute to his own personal and other qualities. It was a little matter to him, indeed, such tribute, if he could not have it from his wife.

He had everything else in her that a man's heart could desire! He saw that, soon after her return from Clifton. Diana's demeanour had been gracious and sweet before, always, although with a shadow upon it. Now the shadow was gone, or changed; he could not tell which. She was not gay-spirited, as he had once known her; but she went about her house with a gentle grace which never failed. Mrs. Starling was at times exceedingly trying and irritating. Diana met and received it all as blandly as she would give her face to the west wind; at the same time, no rough wind could move her from the way of her duty. Mrs. Starling was able neither to provoke her nor prevail with her. She was the sweetest of ruling spirits within her house; without it, she was the most indefatigable and tender of fellow-workers to her husband.

Tender, not to him, that is, but to all those for whom he and she ministered. A nurse to the sick, a provider to the very poor, a counsellor to the vexed,—for such would come to her, especially among the younger women,—a comforter to those in trouble. Such a comforter ! 'Lips of healing,' her husband said of her once; 'wise, rare; sweet as honey, but with the savour of the wind blowing over wild thyme.' If a little of that sweetness could have come to him ! But while her life was full of observance for him, gentle and submissive as a child to every expressed wish of his, and watchful to meet his unexpressed wish, it was the grief of Diana's life that she did not love this man. In the reserve of her New England nature, I think what she felt for him was hidden even from herself.

That is, I mean, as days and months went on. At Diana's first coming home from Clifton, no doubt her opinion of her own feelings, and Basil's opinion of them, was correct. If a change came, it came so imperceptibly that nobody knew it.

Diana's beauty at this time had taken a new phasis. It had lost the marble rigidity and calm impassiveness which had characterized it during all the time of her married life hitherto; and it had not regained the careless lightness of the days before she knew Evan. It was something lovelier than either; so lovely that Basil wondered, and Mrs. Starling sometimes stared, and every lip 'in town' came to have nothing but utterances of respect, more often utterances of devotion, for the minister's wife, —I am afraid I cannot give you a just impression of it. For Diana's face had come curiously near the expression on the face of her own little child. Innocent, tender, pure,—something like that. Grave, but with no clouds at all; strong and purposeful, yet with an utter absence of self-will or self-consciousness. It had always been, to a certain degree, innocent and pure, but that was negative; and this was positive,—the refined gold that had been through the fire. And no baby's face is sweeter than Diana's was now, all blossoming as it were with love and humility. If her husband had loved her before, the feeling of longing and despair that came over him when he looked at this rarefied beauty would be hard to tell. He had ruined her life, he reproached himself; and she was lost to him for ever. Yet, as I said, though Diana's face was grave, it was a gravity wholly without clouds; the gravity of the summer dawn, when the stars are shining and the light in the East tells of the coming day.

But mental changes work slowly and insensibly ofttimes; and day after day and week after week went by, each with its fulness of business and cares; and no one in the little family knew exactly what forces were silently busy. So a year rolled round, and another year began its course, and ran it; and June came for the second time since Diana had returned from the seaside. Elmfield in all this time had not been revisited by its owners.

June had come again. Windows were open, and the breath of roses filled the minister's study; for Diana had developed lately a passion for flowers and for gardening, and her husband had given her with full hands all she wanted, and much more. Mrs. Starling had grumbled and been very sarcastic about it. However, Basil had ordered in plants and seeds and tools and books of instruction; he had become instructor himself; and the result was, the parsonage, as people began to call it, was encompassed with a little wilderness of floral beauty which was growing to be the wonder of Pleasant Valley. 'It will do them good!' the minister said, when Diana called his attention to the fact that the country farmers passing by were falling into the habit of reining in their horses and stopping for a good long look. For instead of the patch of marigolds and hollyhocks in front of the house, all the wing inhabited by the minister and his family was surrounded with flowers. Roses bloomed in the beds and out of the grass, and climbed up on the walls of the house; white Annunciation lilies shone like stars here and there; whole beds of heliotrope were preparing their perfume; geraniums held up their elegant heads of every colour; verbenas and mignonette and honeysuckle and red lilies and yellow lilies and hardy gladiolus were either just beginning or in full beauty; with many more, too many to tell; and the old-fashioned guelder rose had shaken out its white balls of snow, and one or two laburnums were hung

thick with their clusters of 'dropping gold.' The garden was
growing large, and, as I said, become a wilderness of beauty.
Nevertheless the roses kept their own, and this afternoon
the breath of them, rising above all the other sweet breaths
that were abroad, came in and filled the minister's study.
Diana was there alone sitting by one of the open windows,
busy with some work; not so busy but that she smelt the
roses, and felt the glory of light and colour that was outside,
and heard the hum of bees and the twitter of birds and the
soft indistinguishable chirrup of insects, which filled the air.
Diana sewed on, till another slight sound mingled with those—
the tread of the foot on the gravel walk down below; then
she lifted her head suddenly, and with that her hands and her
work fell into her lap. It was long past mid-afternoon, and
the lovely slant light striking over the roses and coming
through the crown of a young elm fell upon Basil, who was
slowly sauntering along the garden walk with his little girl in
his arms. Very slowly, and often standing still to exchange
love passages and indulge mutual admiration with her. They
were partly talking of the flowers, Diana could see; but her
own eyes had no vision but for those two, the baby and the
baby's father. One little fair fat arm was round Basil's neck,
the other tiny hand was sometimes stretched out towards the
lilies or the laburnums in critical or delighted notice-taking,
the word accompaniment to which Diana could not hear but
could well guess; at other times it was brought round ecsta-
tically to join its companion round her father's neck, or lifted
to his face with fingers of caressing, or thrust in among the
locks of his hair, which last seemed to be a favourite pleasure.
Basil would stand still at such times and talk to her, or wait,
Diana knew with just what a smile in his eyes, to take the soft
touches and return them. Diana's work was forgotten, and her
eyes were riveted; why did the scene in the garden give her
such pain? She would have said, if she had been asked, that it
was self-reproach and sorrow for the inevitable. How came it
that she held not as near a place to Basil as her child did? She
ought, but it was not so. She thought, she wished she loved
him! She ought to be as free to put her hand on the soft

" Basil was slowly sauntering along the garden walk with his little girl
in his arms."

Page 350.

curls of Basil's hair as her baby was, but they stood too far apart from each other, and she would as soon have dared anything. And Basil never looked at *her* so now-a-days; he had found out how she felt, and knew she did not care for his looks; and kind, and gentle, and unselfish as he was, yes, and strong in self-command and self-renunciation, he had resigned his life-hope and left her to her life-sorrow. Yet Diana knew, with every smile and kiss to the little one, what a cry of Basil's heart went out towards the child's mother. Only, he would never give that cry utterance again. 'What can I do?' thought Diana. 'I cannot bear it. And he thinks I am a great deal more unhappy than I am. Unhappy?—I am not unhappy—if only *he* were not unhappy.'

She could not explain her feelings to herself, she had no notion that she was jealous of her own child; but the pain bit her, and she could not endure to sit up there at the window and look on. Rising hastily, she dropped her work out of her hand, and was about to go down into the garden to join them, when another glance showed her that Basil had turned and was coming back into the house. Diana listened to them as they mounted the stairs, Basil's feet and the baby's voice sounding together, with a curious unrest at her heart, and her eyes met the pair eagerly as they entered the room. From what impulse she could not have told, she advanced to meet them, and stretched out her hands to take the child, which, however, with a little confident cry of delight, turned from her and clasped both little arms again round her father's neck. Basil smiled; Diana tried to follow suit.

'She would rather be with you than with me,' she remarked, however.

'I wonder at her bad taste!' said Basil. But he turned his face to the baby, and laid it gently against her soft cheek.

'It is because you are stronger,' Diana went on.

'Is it?'

'That is one thing. You may notice children always like strong arms.'

'Her mother's arms are not weak.'

'No—but I am not so strong as you, Basil, bodily or mentally.'

And I think that is more yet—mental strength, I mean. Children recognise that, and love to rest on it.'

'You do not think such discrimination is confined to children?' said Basil, with a dry, quiet humorousness at which Diana could not help smiling, though she felt quite as much like a very different demonstration. She watched the two, as Basil walked on to his study-table and sat down, with the child on his knee; she saw the upturned eye of love with which the little one regarded him as he did this, and then how, with a long breath of satisfaction, she settled herself in her place, smoothed down her frock, and laid the little hands contentedly together in her lap. Basil drew his portfolio towards him and began to write a letter. Diana went to her work again in the window, feeling restless. She felt she must say something more, and in a different key, and as she worked she watched the two at the table. This was not the way things ought to be. Her husband must be told at least something of the change that had taken place in her; he ought to know that she was no longer miserable; he would be glad to know that. Diana thought he might have seen it without her telling; but if he did not, then she must speak. He had a right to so much comfort as she could give him, and he ought to be told that she was not now wishing to be in another presence and society than his. If she could tell him without his thinking too much —she watched till the letter was written and he was folding it up. And then Diana's tongue hesitated unaccountably.

'Basil,' she began, obliging herself to speak,—'I can smell the roses again.'

He looked up instantly with keen eyes.

'You know—there was a long while—a long while—in which I could not feel that anything was sweet.'

'And now?'—

'Now I can. I knew you ought to know. You would be glad. I am like a person who has been in a brain fever—or dead—and awaked to life and soundness again. You cannot think what it is to me to see the sky.' Diana's eyes filled.

'What did you use to see?'

'The vault of my prison. What signified whether it were blue or brazen? But now '—

'Well?—Now, Diana?'

'I can see through.'

Perhaps this was not very intelligible, for manifestly it was not easy for Diana to explain herself; but Basil this time did not speak, and she presently began again.

'I mean,—there is no prison vault, nor any prison any more; the walls that seemed to shut me in are dissolved, and I am free again.'

'And you can see through?'—Basil repeated.

'Yes. Where my eyes were met by something harder than fate,—it is all broken up, and light, and clear, and I can see through.'

'I never used to think you were a fanciful woman,' said the minister, eyeing her intently, 'but this time I do not quite follow you, Di. I am afraid to take your words for all they may mean.'

'But you may.'

'What may I?'

'They mean all I say.'

'I am sure of that,' said he, smiling, though he looked anxious; 'but, you see, there is the very point of my difficulty.'

'I mean, Basil, that I am out of my bondage,—which I thought never could be broken in this world.'

'Out of what bondage, my love?'

Diana paused.

'When I went down to Clifton, to Mrs. Sutphen's, do you know, I could think of nothing but—Evan Knowlton?'

Diana's colour stirred, but she looked her husband steadily in the face.

'I suspected it.'

'For a long time I could not, Basil. Night and day I could think of nothing else. Wasn't that bondage?'

'Depends on how you take it,' said the minister.

'But it was *wrong*, Basil.'

'I found excuses for you, Diana.'

'Did you?' she said humbly. 'I daresay you did. It is

z

like you. But it was wrong, and I knew it was wrong, and I could not help it. Is not that bondage of the worst sort? O, you don't know, Basil! *you* never knew such a fight between wrong and right; between your wish and your will. But for a long time I did not see that it was wrong; I thought it was of necessity.'

'How came your view to change?'

'I don't know. All of a sudden. Something Mrs. Sutphen said one morning started my thoughts, and I saw at once that I was doing very wrong. Still it seemed as if I could not help it.'

'How did you help it?'

'*I* didn't, Basil. I fought and fought—O, what a fight! It seemed like death, and worse, to give up Evan; and to stop thinking of him meant to give him up. I could not gain the victory. But don't you remember telling me often that Christ would do everything for me if I would trust him?'

'Yes.'

'Basil, he did. It wasn't I. At last I got utterly desperate, and I threw myself at his feet and claimed the promise. I was as helpless as I could be. And then, Basil, presently,—I cannot tell how,—the work was done. The battle was fought and the victory was won, and I was free. And ever since I have been singing songs in my heart.'

Basil did not flush with pleasure. Diana thought he grew pale, rather; but he bowed his head upon the head of the little one on his lap with a deep low utterance of thanksgiving. She thought he would have shown his pleasure differently. She did not know how to go on.

'It was not I, Basil'—she said after a pause.

'It never is I or you,' answered the minister without looking up. 'It is always Christ if anything is done.'

'Since then, you see, I have felt like a freedwoman.'

'Which you are.'

'And then you cannot think what it was to me, and what it is, to smell the roses again. There were not many roses about Clifton at that time in September; but it was the bay, and the shores, and the vessels, and the sky. I seemed to have got new eyes, and everything was so beautiful.'

Basil repeated his ejaculation of thanksgiving, but he said nothing more, and Diana felt somehow disappointed. Did he not understand that she was free? He bowed his head close down upon the head of his little daughter, and was silent.

'I knew you ought to know'—Diana repeated.

'Thank you,' he said.

'And yet I couldn't tell you—though I knew you would be so glad for me and with me.'

'I am unutterably glad for you.'

And not with me? she said to herself. Why not? Isn't it enough, if I don't love anybody else? if I give him all I have to give? even though that be not what he gives to me. I wish Basil would be reasonable.

It was certainly the first time it had ever occurred to her to make him the subject of such a wish. But Diana did not speak out her thought, and of course her husband did not answer it.

CHAPTER XXXIV.

DAIRY AND PARISH WORK.

ACCORDING to her custom, Diana was up early the next morning, and down in her dairy while yet the sun was only just getting above the horizon. The dairy window stood open night and day; and the cool dewy freshness which was upon the roses and lilies outside was in there too among the pans of cream; the fragrance of those mingled with the different but very pure sweetness of these. Diana was skimming pan after pan; the thick yellow cream wrinkled up in rich folds under her skimmer; the skimming-shelf was just before the window, and outside of the window were the roses and honey-suckles. Diana's sleeves were rolled up above her elbows; her hands were disposing of their business with quick skill; yet now and then, even with a pan under her hand, she paused, leaned on the window sill, and looked out into the garden. She felt glad about something, and yet an unsatisfied query was in her heart; she was glad that she had at last told her husband how the spell was broken that had bound her to Evan and kept her apart from himself. 'But he did not seem so glad as I expected!' Then she recalled the deep tone of his thanksgiving for her, and Diana's eyes took a yearning look which certainly saw no roses. 'It was all for me; it was not for his own share; he did not think he had any share in it. He has a notion that I hate him; and I do not; I never did.' It occurred to her here dimly that she had once felt a horror of him; and who would not rather have hatred than horror? She went on skimming her cream. What should she do? 'I cannot speak about it again,' she said to herself; 'I cannot say any more to him. I cannot say—I don't know what I ought to say! but I wish he knew that I do not dislike him. He is keen enough; surely he will find it out.'

Pan after pan was set aside; the churn was filled; and Diana began to churn. Presently in came Mrs. Starling.

'Hain't Josh brought the milk yet?'

'Not yet.'

'It's time he did. That fellow's got a lazy streak in him somewhere.'

'It's only just half-past five, mother.'

'The butter ought to be come by now, I should think.'— Mrs. Starling was passing in and out, setting the table in the lean-to kitchen. She would have no 'help' in her dominions, so it was only in Diana's part of the house that the little servant officiated, whom Basil insisted upon keeping for his wife's ease and comfort and leisure. Diana herself attended as of old to her particular sphere, the dairy. 'How do you know it's just half-past five?' her mother went on presently.

'I looked.'

'Watches!' exclaimed Mrs. Starling with much disgust. 'Your husband is ridiculous about you.'

But Diana could bear that.

'In your dairy is a queer place to wear a watch.'

'Why, mother, it's for use, not for show.'

'Make me believe that! There's a good deal of show about it, anyhow, with such a chain hanging to it.'

'My husband gave it to me, you know, chain and all; I must wear it,' Diana said with a face as sweet as the roses.

'O yes! your husband!' Mrs. Starling answered insultingly. 'That will do to say to other people. Much you care what your husband does!'

Diana got up here, left her churn, came up to her mother, and put a hand upon her arm. The action and air of the woman were so commanding, that even Mrs. Starling stood still with a certain involuntary deference. Diana's face and voice, however, were as clear and calm as they were commanding.

'Mother,'—she said,—'you are mistaken. I care with all there is of me; heart and soul and life.'

Mrs. Starling's eye shrank away. 'Since when?' she asked incredulously.

'It does not matter since when. Whatever I have ever felt for other people, there is only one person in the world that I care for now; and that is, my husband.'

'You'd better tell him so,' sneered Mrs. Starling. 'When do you expect your butter is going to come, if you stand there?'

'The butter is come,' said Diana gently. She knew the sneer was meant to cover uneasy feeling; and if it had not, still she would not have resented it. She never resented anything now that was done to herself. In came Josh with the foaming pails. Diana's hands were in the butter, and her mother came to strain the milk.

'There had ought to be three quarts more, that ain't here,' she grumbled.

'They ain't nowheres else, then,' answered her factotum.

'Josh, you don't strip the cows clean.'

'Who does, then?' said Josh, grinning. 'If 'tain't me, I don' know who 'tis. That 'ere red heifer is losin' on her milk, though, Mis' Starlin'. She had ought to be fed sun'thin'.'

'Well, feed her, then,' cried the mistress. 'You know enough for that. You must keep up the milk this month, Josh; the grass is first-rate.'

Diana escaped away.

A while later the family was assembled at breakfast.

'Where's the child?' inquired Mrs. Starling.

'I believe she is out in the garden, mother.'

'She oughtn't to be out before she has had her breakfast. 'Tain't good for her.'

'O, she has had her breakfast,' said Diana. This was nothing new. Diana as well as her husband was glad to keep the little one from Mrs. Starling's table, where, unless they wanted her to be fed on pork and pickles and the like, it was difficult to have a harmonious meal. It was often difficult at any rate!

' Who's with her ? ' Mrs. Starling went on.

' Her father was with her. Now Prudence is looking after her.'

' Prudence ! You want to keep a girl about as much as I want to keep a boat. You have no use for her.'

' She is useful just now,' put in the Dominie.

' Why can't Diana take care of her own child, and feed her when she takes her own meals ?—as I used to do, and as everybody else does.'

' You think that is a convenient arrangement for all parties ? said the minister.

' I hate to have danglers about ! ' said Mrs. Starling. ' If there's anything I abominate, it's shiftlessness. I always found my ten fingers was servants enough for me ; and what they couldn't do I could go without. And I don't like to see a daughter o' mine sit with her hands before her and livin' off other people's strength ! '

Diana laughed, a low, sweet laugh, that was enough to smooth away the wrinkles out of anybody's mood.

' She has to do as she's told,' said the minister sententiously.

' That's because she's a fool.'

' Do you think so ? ' Basil answered with unchanged good humour.

' I never took my lessons from anybody.'

' Perhaps it would have been better if you had.'

' And you are spoiling her,' Mrs. Starling added inconsistently.

' I wonder you haven't.'

Mrs. Starling paused to consider what the minister meant. Before she came to speech again, he rose from the table.

' Will you come to my study, Diana, after breakfast ? '

' Who's goin' to make my cake, then ? ' cried the mistress of the house. ' Society's to meet here again this afternoon.'

' I'll make it, mother—a mountain cake, if you like,' said Diana, also rising. ' Basil won't want me all the morning.' But she was eager to hear what he had to say to her, and hurried after him. He had seemed to her more than usually preoccupied.

'I do think,' she remarked as she reached the study, ' the Society eat more cake than—their work is worth.'

'Heresy,' said Basil, smiling.

'They don't do much sewing, Basil.'

'They do something else. Never mind; let them come and have a good time. It won't hurt anybody much.'

Diana looked at him and smiled, and then waited anxiously. She longed for some words from Basil different from those he had spoken last night. Could he not see, that if her passion for Evan was broken, there was nothing left for him to look grave about? And ought he not to be jubilant over the confession she had just made to her mother? Diana was jubilant over it herself; she had set that matter clear at last. It is true, Basil had not heard the confession, but ought he not to divine it, when it was the truth? 'If I do not just *love* him,' said Diana to herself, 'at least he is the only one I care for in all the world. That would have made him glad once. And he don't look glad. Does he expect me to speak out and tell *him* all that?'

Basil did not look as if he expected her to do any such thing. He was rather graver than usual, and did not at once say anything. Through the open window came the air, still damp with dew, laden with the scent of honeysuckle and roses, jocund with the shouts of birds; and for one instant Diana's thoughts swept back away to years ago, with a wondering recognition of the change in herself since *those* June days. Then her husband began to speak.

'I have had a call, Diana.'

'A call? You have a good many of them always, Basil. What was this?'

'Of a different sort. A call for me—not a call upon me.'

'Well, there have always been calls *for* you too, in plenty, ever since I have known you. What do you mean?'

'This is a call to me to leave Pleasant Valley,' said Basil, watching her, yet without seeming to do so. Diana looked bewildered.

'To leave Pleasant Valley? Why? And where would you go, Basil?'

'I am called, because the people want somebody and have pitched upon me. The place is a manufacturing town, not very far from Boston.'

'Are you going?'

'That is the point upon which I desire to have your opinion.'

'But, Basil, the people here want you too.'

'Grant that.'

'Then what does it signify, whether other people want you?'

'Insomuch as the "other people" are more in numbers and far more needy in condition.'

'Want you more'—said Diana wistfully.

'That is the plain English of it.'

'And will you go?'

'What do you counsel?'

'I do not know the people'—said Diana, breathless.

'Nor I, as yet. The church that calls me is itself a rich little church, which has been accustomed, I am afraid, for some time, to a dead level in religion.'

'They must want you then, badly,' said Diana. 'That was how Pleasant Valley was five years ago.'

'But round the church lies on every hand the mill population, for whom hardly any one cares. They need not one man, but many. Nothing is done for them. They are almost heathen, in the midst of a land called Christian.'

'Then you will go?' said Diana, looking at Mr. Masters, and wishing that he would speak to her with a different expression of face. It was calm, sweet, and high, as always; but she knew he thought his wife was lost to him for ever. 'And yet, I told him last night!' she said to herself. Really, she was thinking more of that than of this other subject Basil had unfolded to her.

'I do not know,' he answered. 'How would you like to run over there with me and take a look at the place? I have a very friendly invitation to come and to bring you,—for the very purpose.'

'Run over? Why, it must be more than one day's journey?'

'One runs by railway,' said Basil simply. 'What do you think? Will you go?'

'O yes, indeed! if you will let me. And Rosy?'

'We will go nowhere without Rosy.'

Diana made her cake like one in a dream.

CHAPTER XXXV.

BABYLON.

THE journey to Mainbridge, the manufacturing town in question, took place within a few days. With eager cordiality the minister and his family were welcomed in the house of one of the chief men of the church and of the place, and made very much at home. It was a phasis of social life which Diana had hardly touched ever before. Wealth was abounding and super-abounding; the house was large, the luxury of furnishing and fitting, of service and equipage, was on a scale she had never seen. Basil was amused to observe that she did not seem to see it now; she took it as a matter of course, and fitted in these new surroundings as though her life had been lived in them. The dress of the minister's wife was very plain, certainly; her muslins were not costly, and they were simply made; yet nobody in the room looked so much dressed as she. It was the dignity of her beauty that so attired her; it was beauty of mind and body both; and both made the grace of her movements and the grace of her quiet so exquisite as it was. Basil smiled—and sighed.

But there was no doubt Diana saw the mill people. The minister and his wife were taken to see the mills, of course, divers and various—silk mills, cotton mills, iron mills. The machinery, and the work done by it, were fascinating to Diana and delightful; the mill people, men, women, and children, were more fascinating by far, though in a different way. She watched them in the mills, she watched them when she met them in the street, going to or from work.

'Do they go to church?' she asked once of Mr. Brandt, their entertainer. He shook his head.

'They are tired with their week's work when Saturday night comes, and want to rest. Sunday was given for rest,' he said, looking into Diana's face, which was a study to him.

'Don't you think,' she said, 'rest of body is a poor thing without rest of mind?'

'*My* mind cannot rest unless my body does,' he answered, laughing.

'Take it the other way—don't you know what it is to have rest of mind make you forget weariness of body?'

'No—nor you either,' said he.

'Then I am sorry for you; and I wish I could get at the mill people.'

'Why?'

'To tell them what I know about it.'

'But you could not get at them, Mrs. Masters. They are in the mills from seven till seven—or eight, and come out tired and dirty; and Sunday, as I told you, they like to stay at home and rest, and perhaps clean up.'

'If there is no help for that,' said Diana, 'there ought to be no mills.'

'And no manufacturers?'

'What are silk and iron, to the bodies and souls of men? Basil, does that passage in the Revelation mean *that?*'

'What passage?' said Mr. Brandt. 'Here is a Bible, Mrs. Masters; perhaps you will be so good as to find the place. I am afraid, from your expression, it is not a flattering passage for us millowners. What are the words you refer to?'

I think he wanted to draw out Diana much more than the meaning of Scripture. She took the Bible a little doubtfully and glanced at Basil. He was smiling at her in a reassuring way, but did not at all offer to help. Diana's thoughts wandered somewhat, and she turned the leaves of the Bible unsuccessfully. 'Where is it, Basil?'

'You are thinking of the account of the destruction of Babylon. It is in the eighteenth chapter.'

'But Babylon!' said the host. 'We have nothing to do with Babylon. That means Rome, doesn't it?'

'Here's the chapter,' said Diana. 'No, it cannot mean

Rome, Mr. Brandt; though Dean Stanley seems to assume that it does, in spite of the fact which he naively points out, that the description don't fit.'

'What then?'

'Basil, won't you explain?'

'It is merely an assumption of Old Testament imagery,' said Basil. 'At a time when lineal Israel stood for the church of God upon earth, Babylon represented the head and culmination of the world-power, the church's deadly opponent and foe. Babylon in the Apocalypse but means that of which Nebuchadnezzar's old Babylon was the type.'

'And what is that?'

'The power of this world, of which Satan is said to be the prince.'

'But what do you mean by the *world*, Mr. Masters? We cannot get out of the world—it is a pretty good world, too, I think, take it for all in all. People talk of being worldly and not worldly;—but they do not know what they are talking about.'

'Why not?' Diana asked.

'Well, now, ask my wife,' Mr. Brandt answered, laughing. 'She thinks it is "worldly" to have a cockade on your coachman's hat; it is not worldly to have the coachman, or the carriage, and she don't object to a coat with buttons. Then it is not worldly to give a party,—but it is worldly to dance; it is very worldly to play cards. There's hair-splitting somewhere, and my eyes are not sharp enough to see the lines.'

Diana sat with her book in her hand, looking up at the speaker; a look so fair and clear and grave that Mr. Brandt was again moved by curiosity, and tempted to try to make her speak.

'Can you make it out?' he said, smiling.

'Why, yes!' said Diana; 'but there is no hair-splitting. It is very simple. There are just two kingdoms in the world, Mr. Brandt; and whatever does not belong to the one. belongs to the other. Whatever is not for God, is for the world.'

'Then your definition of the "world" is?'—

'All that is not God's.'

'But I am not clear yet. I don't see how you draw the line. Take my mills, for example; they belong to this profane, work-a-day world; yet I must run them. Is that worldly?'

'Yes, if you do not run them for God.'

Mr. Brandt stared a little.

'I confess I do not see how that is to be done,' he owned.

'The business that you cannot do for God, you had better not do at all,' said Diana gently.

'But spinning cotton?'—

'Spinning cotton, or anything else that employs men and makes money.'

'How?'

'You can do it for God, cannot you?' said Diana in the same way. 'You can employ the men and make the money for his sake, and in his service.'

'But that is coming pretty close,' said the millowner. 'Suppose I want a little of the money for myself and my family?'

'I am speaking too much!' said Diana, with a lovely flush on her cheek, and looking up to her husband. 'I wish you would take the word, Basil.'

'I hope Mr. Masters is going to be a little more merciful to the weaknesses of ordinary humanity,' said Mr. Brandt, half lightly. 'So tremendous a preacher have I never heard yet.'

Basil was silent, and Diana looked down at the volume in her hand.

'Won't you go on, Mrs. Masters?' said her host. 'What do you find for me there?'

'I was looking for my quotation,' said Diana; 'I had not got it quite right.'

'How is it?'

'Here is a list of the luxuries in which Babylon traded :—"The merchandise of gold, and silver, and precious stones, and of pearls, and fine linen, and purple, and silk, and scarlet, and all thyine wood, and all manner vessels of ivory, and all manner vessels of most precious wood, and of brass, and iron, and marble, and cinnamon, and odours, and ointments, and frankincense, and wine, and oil, and fine flour, and wheat, and beasts, and sheep, and horses, and chariots, *and slaves, and souls of men.*"'

'Sounds for all the world like an inventory of the things in my house,' said Mr. Brandt. 'Pray what of all that? Don't you like all those things?'

'"—For in one hour so great riches is come to nought."'

'But what harm in these things, or most of them, Mrs. Masters?'

Diana glanced up at Basil and did not answer. He answered.

'No harm—so long as business and the fruits of business are kept within the line we were speaking of; so long as all is for God and to God. If it is not for him, it is for the "world."'

'O my dear Mrs. Masters!' cried Mrs. Brandt, running in, —'here you are. I was looking for you.—I came to ask— shall I order the landau for five o'clock, to drive to the lake?'

Diana was glad to have the conversation broken up. When the hour for the drive came, and she sank into the luxurious, satiny depths of the landau, her thoughts involuntarily recurred to it. The carriage was so very comfortable! It rolled smoothly along, over good roads, drawn by well-trotting horses; the motion was delightful. Diana's thoughts rolled on too. Suddenly Mr. Brandt leaned over towards her.

'Is this carriage a "worldly" indulgence, Mrs. Masters?'

Diana started. 'I don't know,' she said.

'Ah,' said the other, laughing at her startled face,—'I am glad to see that even you may have a doubt on that subject. You cannot blame less etherealized persons, like my wife and me, if we go on contentedly, with no doubts.'

'But you mistake me,'—said Diana.

'You said you did not know.'

'Because I don't know you.'

'What has that to do with it?'

'If I knew you well, Mr. Brandt, I should know whether this carriage is the Lord's or not.'

The expression of the gentleman's face upon this was hardly agreeable; he sat back in his seat and looked at the prospect; and so Diana tried to do, but for a time the landscape to her was indistinguishable. Her thoughts went back to the mills and the mill people; pale, apathetic, reserved, sometimes stern, they had struck her painfully as a set of people who did not own kindred with other classes of their fellow-creatures; apart, alone, without instruction, without sympathy; not enjoying this life, nor on the way to enjoy the next. The marks of poverty were on them too, abundantly. Diana's mind was too full of these people to allow her leisure for the beauties of nature; or if she felt these, to let her feel them without a great sense of contrast. Then she did not know whether she had spoken wisely. Alone in her room at night with Basil she began to talk about it. She wished that he would begin; but he did not, so she must.

'Basil,—did I say too much to Mr. Brandt to-day?'

'I guess not.'

Diana knew by the tone of these words that her husband was on this subject contented.

'What do you think of the mill people?'

'I am very curious to find out what impression they make on you.'

'Basil,' said Diana, her voice trembling, 'they break my heart!'

'What's to be done in that case?'

'I don't know. Nothing follows upon that. But how do you feel?'

'Very much as if I would like to prove the realizing of that old prophecy—"To whom he was not spoken of, they shall see; and they that have not heard shall understand."'

'That is just how I feel, Basil. But they do not go to church, people say; how could you get at them?'

'We could look them up at their own homes; we could arrange meetings for them that they would like; we could work ourselves into their affections, by degrees, and *then* the door would be open for us to bring Christ in. We could give them help too, where help is needed.'

'*We*, Basil?'

'Don't you feel as I do? You said so,' he answered with a grave smile.

'O, I do!' said Diana. 'I cannot think of anything lovelier than to see those faces change with the knowledge of Christ.'

'Then you would be willing to leave our present field of work?'

'It does not seem to want us as this does—not by many fold.'

'Would your mother leave Pleasant Valley?'

'No.'

'How, then, Di, about you?'

'The first question is duty, Basil.'

'I think mine is to come here.'

'Then it must be mine,' said Diana, with a sort of disappointment upon her that he should speak in that way.

'And would it be your pleasure too?'

'Why, certainly. Basil, I cannot *imagine* pleasure to be apart from duty.'

'Thank you,' he said gently. 'And I thank God, who has brought you so far in your lesson-learning as to know that.'

Diana said no more. She was ready to cry, with the feeling that her husband thought himself to have so little to do with her pleasure. Tears, however, were not much in her way, and she did not shed any, but she speculated. *Had* he really to do with her pleasure? It was different certainly once. She had craved to be at a distance from him; she could remember the time well; but the time was past. Was it reasonable to expect him to know that fact? He had thoroughly learned the bitter truth that her heart was not his, and could never be his; what should tell him that the conditions of things were changed? *Were* they changed? Diana was in great confusion. She began to think she did not know herself. She did not hate Mr. Masters any more; nay, she declared to herself she never had hated him; she always had liked him; only then she had loved Evan Knowlton, and now that was gone. She did not love anybody. There was no reason in the world why Mr. Masters should not be contented. 'I think,' said Diana to herself, 'I give him enough of my heart to content him. I wonder what would content him? I do not care two straws for anybody else in all the world. He would say, if I

2 A

told him that, he would say it is a negative proposition.   Suppose I could go further '—and Diana's cheeks began to burn —' suppose I could, I could not possibly stand up and tell him so.   I cannot.   He ought to see it for himself.   But he does not.   He ought to be contented—I think he might be contented—with what I give him, if it isn't just '—

Diana broke off with her thoughts very much disturbed. She thought she did not love her husband, but things were no longer clear; except that Basil's persistent ignorance of the fact that they had changed, chafed and distressed her.

CHAPTER XXXVI.

THE PARTY.

THE morning of the next day was spent in still further visits to still more mills. Mr. Brandt was much struck with the direction his guests' attention seemed to take.

'You are very fond of machinery,' he remarked to Diana.

'Yes—I don't know much about it,' she answered.

'Surely that is not true after these two or three days' work?'

'I knew *nothing* about it before. Yes, I do enjoy it, Mr. Brandt, with you and Mr. Masters to explain things to me; but it is the people that interest me most.'

'The people!'—

'The mill hands?' Mrs. Brandt asked.

'Yes; the mill hands.'

'What *can* you find interesting in them? I am half afraid of them, for my part.'

'They look as if they wanted friends so much.'

'Friends?' repeated Mrs. Brandt. 'I suppose they have friends among themselves. Why should not they? Well, it is time you had a change of society, I think. My husband has taken you among the mill people for two days; now to-night I will introduce you to a different set; some of your church people. I want you to take rest this afternoon, my dear Mrs. Masters—now won't you!—so as to be able to enjoy the evening. I am sure Brandt has fatigued you to death. I never can stand going up and down those stairs in the mills, and standing about; it kills me.'

'I wonder how they bear standing at the looms or the other machines all day?'

'They? O, they are accustomed to it, I suppose. An hour or two of it breaks *me* down. Now rest, will you? It's quite a great occasion to-night. One of our greatest men among the millowners, and one of the pillars of the church you and Mr. Masters are coming to take care of, gives an entertainment to his daughter to-night; a bride—married lately—just come home and just going away again. You'll see all our best people. Now please go and rest.'

Diana went to her room and rested, outwardly. In her mind thoughts were very busy. And when it was time to dress, they were hardly diverted from their subjects. It was with a sort of unconscious instinct that Diana threw her beautiful hair into the wavy masses and coils which were more graceful than she knew and crowned her so royally; and in the like manner that she put on a dress of soft white muslin. It had no adornment other than the lace which finished it at throat and wrists; she looked most like a bride herself. So Basil thought, when he came to fetch her; though he did not say his thought, fearing lest he might graze something in her mind which would pain her. He often withheld words for such a reason.

'Will it do?' said Diana, seeing him look at her.

'Too good for the occasion!' said Basil, shaking his head.

'Too much dressed?' said Diana. 'I thought I must dress as much as I could. Is it too much, Basil?'

'Nobody else will think so,' said the minister with a queer smile.

'Do you think so?'

'You are just as you ought to be. All the same, it is beyond the company. Never mind. Come!'

Down-stairs another sort of criticism.

'My dear Mrs. Masters! Not a bit of colour! You will be taken for the bride yourself. All in white, except your beautiful hair! Wait, that won't do; let me try if I can't improve things a little—do you mind?—Just let me see how this will look.' Diana submitted patiently, and Mrs. Brandt officiously fastened a knot of blue ribbon in her bright hair. She was greatly pleased with the effect, which Diana could not see.

However, when they had reached the house they were going to, and leaving the dressing-room Diana took her husband's arm to go down to the company, he detained her to let Mr. and Mrs. Brandt pass on before, and then with a quick and quiet touch of his fingers removed the blue bow and put it in his pocket.

'Basil!' said Diana, smiling,—'she will miss it.'

'So shall I. It commonized the whole thing.'

There was nothing common left, as every one instantly recognised who saw Diana that evening. A presence of such dignified grace, a face of such lofty and yet innocent beauty, so sweet a movement and manner, nobody there knew anything like it in Mainbridge. On the other hand, it was Diana's first experience of a party beyond the style and degree of Pleasant Valley parties. She found immediately that she was by much the plainest dressed woman in the company; but she forgot to think of the dresses, the people struck her with so much surprise.

Of course everybody was introduced to her; and everybody said the same things.

They hoped she liked Mainbridge; they hoped she was coming to live among them; Mr. Masters was coming to the church, wasn't he? and how did he like the looks of the place?

'You see the best part of the church here to-night,' remarked one stout elderly lady in a black silk and with flowers in her cap; a very well-to-do, puffy old lady;—'you see just the best of them, and *all* the best!'

'What do you call the best part of a church?' Diana asked, looking round the room.

'Well, you see them before you. There is Mr. Waters standing by the piano—he's the wealthiest man in Mainbridge; a very wealthy man. The one with his head a little bald, speaking just now to Mrs. Brandt, is one of our elders; he's pretty comfortable too; a beautiful place he has—have you seen it? No? You ought to have gone there to see his flowers; the grounds are beautiful, laid out with so much taste. But if you are fond of flowers, you should go to see Mr. Tillery's

greenhouses. That is Mr. Tillery in the corner, between the
two young ladies in white. Mr. Tillery's greenhouses extend
half a mile, or would, if they were set in a line, you know.'

' Are there any poor people in the church?'

'Poor people?' The article called for seemed to be rare.
' Poor people? There are a few, I believe. Not many; the
poor people go to the mission chapel. O, we support a
mission; that's down in the mill quarter, where the hands live,
I mean '—

'And O, Mrs. Masters,' a young lady struck in here, ' you
are coming, aren't you? I have fallen in love with you, and I
want you to come. And O, I want you to tell me one thing—
is Mr. Masters very strict?'

' About what?' said Diana, smiling.

' About anything.'

' Yes; he is very strict about telling the truth.'

' O, of course; but I mean about other things; what one
may do or mayn't do. Is he strict?'

' Not any stricter than his Master.'

' His master? who's that? But I mean,—does he make a
fuss about dancing?'

' I never saw Mr. Masters make a fuss about anything.'

' O, delightful! then he don't mind? You know, Mrs.
Masters, the Bible says David danced.'

' The Bible tells why he danced, too,' said Diana, wholly
unable to keep her gravity.

' Does it? I don't recollect. And O, Mrs. Masters, I want
to know another thing; does Mr. Masters use the Episcopal
form in marrying people?'

' You are concerned in the question?'

' O yes. I might be, you know, one of these days; and I
always think the Episcopal form is so dignified and graceful;
the ring and all that; the Presbyterian form is so *tucky* and
ugly. O, Mrs. Masters, don't you like a form for everything?'

Before Diana could return an answer to this somewhat com-
prehensive question, a slight sound caused her to forget both
question and speaker and the place where she was, as utterly
as if they all had been swept from the sphere of the actual.

It belonged to the sweet poise and calm of her heart and life that she was able to keep still as she was and make no movement and give no sign. The sound she had heard was a little running laugh; she thought it came from the next room; yet she did not turn her head to look that way, though it could have been uttered, she knew, from no throat but one. The young lady friend reiterated the question in which she was interested, and Diana answered; I do not know how, nor did she; while she was at the same time collecting her forces and reviewing them for the coming skirmish with circumstances. Evan Knowlton was here at Mainbridge. How could it possibly be? And even as the thought went through her, came that laugh again.

Diana's mind began to be in a great state of confusion, which presently concentrated itself upon the one point of keeping a calm and unmoved exterior. And to her surprise, this became easy. The confusion subsided, like the vibrations of harp-strings which have been brushed by a harsh hand; only her heart beat a little, waiting for the coming encounter.

'Shall I take you in to see the bride?' Mr. Brandt here presented himself, offering his services. And Diana rose without hesitation and put her arm in his. She was glad, however, that their progress through the company was slow; she hoped Evan would see before he had to speak to her. She herself felt ready for anything.

It was with a strange feeling, nevertheless, that she went through the introduction to the pale lady of fashion who was Evan's second choice. Beyond white silk and diamonds and a rather delicate appearance, Diana could in that moment discern nothing. Her senses did not seem to serve her well. The lady was very much in request besides, amid her old friends and acquaintances, and there was no chance to talk to her. Then followed the introduction to the bridegroom. He was going to content himself with a bow, but Diana stretched out her hand and gave his a warm grasp. 'I have seen Captain Knowlton before,'—she said simply. She was perfectly quiet now, but she saw that he was not; and that he was willing to take refuge with other claimants upon his attention to escape any particular words with her. She stepped back, and gradually got behind people, where the sight of her could not distress him. It had distressed him, she had seen that. Was it on her account? or on his own? Gradually, watching her chances, she was able to work her way back into the other room, which was comparatively empty; and there she sat down at a table covered with photographs. She would go away, she thought, as soon as it could gracefully be done. And yet, she would have liked to speak a few words with Evan, this last time they might ever be together. What made him embarrassed in meeting her? With his bride just beside him, that ought not to be, she thought.

The company had almost all crowded into the other room about the bride, and were fully occupied with her; and Diana was alone. She turned over the photographs and reviewed the kings and queens of Europe, with no sort of intelligence as to their families or nationalities, mechanically, just to cover her abstraction, and to seem to be doing something. Then suddenly she knew that Evan was beside her. He had come round and entered by the door from the hall; and now they both stood together for a moment, shielded by a corner of the partition wall between the rooms. Diana had risen.

'This is a very painful meeting'—Captain Knowlton said, after a silence which would have been longer if he had dared to let it be so.

'No'—said Diana, looking at him with as clear and fair a brow as if she had been the moon goddess whose name she bore; and her voice was very sweet. 'Not painful, Evan; why should it be? I am glad to see you again.'

'I didn't know you were here'—he went on hurriedly, in evident great perturbation.

'And we did not know you were here. I had no notion of it—till I heard your voice in the next room. I knew it instantly.'

'I would have spared you this, if I could have foreseen it.'

'Spared me what?'

'All this,—this pain,—I know it must be pain to you.—I did not anticipate it.'

'Why should it be pain to me?' inquired Diana steadily.

'I know your feeling—I would not have brought Clara into your presence '—

'I am very glad to have seen her,' said Diana in the same quiet way, looking at Evan fixedly. 'I should have been glad to see more of her, and learn to know her. I could scarcely speak to her for the crowd around.'

'Yes, she is a great favourite, and everybody is eager to see her before she goes.'

'You are.going away soon?'

'O yes!—to my post.'

'I hope she will make you happy, Evan,' Diana said gently and cordially.

'You are very good, I am sure. I don't want you to think, Diana, that I—that I, in fact, have forgotten anything '—

'You cannot forget too soon,' she answered, smiling, 'everything that Clara would not wish you to remember.'

'A fellow is so awfully lonely out there on the frontiers '— he said, mumbling his words through his moustache in a peculiar way.

'You will not be lonely now, I hope.'

'You see, Di, you were lost to me. If I could only think of you as happy '—

'You may.'

'Happy?' he repeated, looking at her. He had avoided her eyes until now.

'Yes.'

'Then *you* have forgotten?'

'One does not forget,' said Diana, with again a grave smile. 'But I have ceased to look back sorrowfully.'

'But—you are married '—

Then light flushed into Diana's face. She understood Evan's allusion.

'Yes,' she said,—'to somebody who has my whole heart.'

'But—you are married to Mr. Masters?'—he went on incredulously.

'Certainly. And I love my husband with all the strength there is in me to love. I hope your wife will love you as well,' she added with another smile, a different one, which was exceedingly aggravating to the young man. No other lips could wreathe so with such a mingling of softness and strength, love and—yes, happiness. Captain Knowlton had seen smiles like that upon those lips once, long ago; never a brighter or more confident one. He.felt unaccountably injured.

'You did not speak so when I saw you last,' he remarked.

'No. I was a fool,' said Diana, with somewhat unreasonable perverseness. 'Or, if I was not a fool, I was weak.'

'I see you are strong now,' said the young officer bitterly.

'I was never strong; and I am weak still. I have not forgotten, Diana.'

'You ought to forget, Evan,' she said gently.

'It's impossible!' said he, hastily turning over photographs on the table.

Diana would have answered, but the opportunity was gone. Other people came near; the two fell apart from each other, and no more words were interchanged between them.

It grieved but did not astonish Basil to perceive, when he joined Diana in their own room that night, that she had been weeping; and it only grieved him to know that the weeping was renewed in the night. He gave no sign that he knew it, and Diana thought he was asleep through it all. Tears were by no means a favourite indulgence with her; this night the spring of them seemed to be suddenly unsealed, and they flowed fast and free, and were not to be checked. Neither did Diana quite clearly know what moved them. She was very sorry for Evan; yes, but these tears she was shedding were not painful tears. It came home to her, all the sorrowful waiting months and years that Basil had endured on her account; but sympathy was not a spring large enough to supply such a flow. She was glad those months were ended; yet they were not ended, for Basil did not know the facts she had stated with so much clearness to his whilome rival; she had not told himself, and he did not guess them. 'He might,' said Diana to herself,—'he ought,'—at the same time she knew now there was something for her to do. How she should do it, she did not know.

CHAPTER XXXVII.

AT ONE.

THEY returned to Pleasant Valley that day, and Basil was immediately plunged in arrears of business. For the present Diana had to attend to her mother, whose conversation was anything but agreeable after she learned that her son-in-law had accepted the call to Mainbridge.

'Ministers are made of stuff very like common people,' she declared. 'Every one goes where he can get the most.'

'You know Mr. Masters has plenty already, mother; plenty of his own.'

'Those that have most already are always the ones that want more. I've seen that a thousand times. If a man's property lies in an onion, he'll likely give you half of it if you want it; if he's got all Pleasant Valley, the odds are he won't give you an onion.'

Diana would have turned the conversation, but Mrs. Starling came back to the subject.

'What do you suppose you are going to do with me?'

'Mother, that is for you to choose. You know, wherever we are, there's a home for you if you will have it.'

'It's a pleasure to your husband to have me, too, ain't it?'

'It is always a pleasure to him to do what is right.'

'Complimentary! You have grown very fond of him, haven't you, all of a sudden?'

But this subject Diana would not touch. Not to her mother. Not to any one, till the person most concerned knew the truth; and most certainly after that not to any one else. Evan had been told; there had been a reason; she was glad she had told him.

'What do you suppose I'd do in Mainbridge?' Mrs. Starling went on.

'There is plenty to do, mother. It is because there is so much to do that we are going.'

'Dressing and giving parties. I always knew your husband held himself above our folks. He'll be suited there.'

This tried Diana, it was so very far from the truth. She fled the field. It was often the safest way. But she was very sorry for her mother. She went to Basil's study, where now no one was, and sat down by the window that looked into the garden. There Rosy presently caught sight of her; came to her, and climbed up into her lap; and for a good while the two entertained one another; the child going on in wandering sweet prattle, while the mother's thoughts, though she answered her, kept a deeper current of their own all the while. She was pondering as she sat there and smelled the roses in the garden and talked to the small Rose in her lap,—she was pondering what she should do to let her husband know what she now knew about herself. One would say, the simplest way would be to tell him! But Diana, with all her simplicity and sweetness, had a New England nature; and though she could speak frankly enough when spoken to, on this or any other subject, she shrank from volunteering revelations that were not expected of her; revelations that were so intimate, and belonged to her very inner self; and that concerned besides so vitally her relations with another person, even though that person were her husband. At the mere thought of doing it, the colour stirred uneasily in Diana's face. Why could not Basil divine? Looking out into the garden, both mother and child, and talking very busily one of them, thinking very busily the other, neither of them heard Basil come in.

'Where's papa?' Rosy was at the moment asking, in a tone sufficiently indicating that in her view of things he had been gone long enough.

'Not very far off'—was the answer, close behind them. Rosy started and threw herself round towards her father, and Diana also started and looked up; and in her face not less than in the little one there was a flash and a flush of sudden pleasure.

Basil stooped to put his lips to Rosy's, and then, reading more than he knew in Diana's eyes, he carried the kiss to her lips also. It was many a day since he had done the like, and Diana's face flushed more and more. But Basil had taken up Rosy into his arms, and was interchanging a whole harvest of caresses with her. Diana turned her looks towards the garden, and felt ready to burst into tears. Could it be that he was proud, and intended to revenge upon her the long avoidance to which in days past she had treated him? Not like what she knew of Mr. Masters; and Diana was aware she was unreasonable; but it was sore and impatient at her heart, and she wanted to be in Rosy's place. And Basil the while was thinking whether by his unwonted caress he had grieved or distressed his wife. He touched her shoulder gently, and said,

'Forgive me!'

'Forgive you what?' said Diana, looking round.

'My taking an indulgence that perhaps I should not have taken.'

'You are very much mistaken, Basil,' said Diana, rising; and her voice trembled and her lips quivered. She thought he *was* rather cruel now.

'But I have troubled you?' he said, looking earnestly at her.

Diana hesitated, and the quiver of her lips grew more uncontrollable. 'Not in the way you think,' she answered.

'How, then?' he asked gently. 'But I *have* troubled you. How, Di?'

The last two words were spoken with a very tender, gentle accentuation, and they broke Diana down. She laid one hand on her husband's arm, and the other, with her face in it, on his shoulder, and burst into tears.

I do not know what there is in the telegraphy of touch and look and tone; but something in the grip of Diana's hand, and in her action altogether, wrought a sudden change in Basil, and brought a great revelation. He put his little girl down out of his arms and took his wife in them. And for minutes there was no word spoken; and Rosy was too much astonished at the strange motionless hush they maintained to resent at first her own dispossession and the great slight which had been done her.

There had come a honey-bee into the room by mistake, and not finding there what he expected to find, he was flying about and about, trying in vain to make his way to something more in his line than books; and the soft buzz of the creature was the only sound to be heard, till Rosy began to complain. She did not know what to make of the utter stillness of the two figures beside her, who stood like statues; was furthermore not a little jealous of seeing what she considered her own prerogative usurped by another; and finally began an importunate petitioning to be taken up again. But Rosy's voice, never neglected before, was not heard to-day. Neither of them heard it. The consciousness that was nearest was overpowering, and barred out every other.

'Diana'—said Basil at last in a whisper; and she looked up, all flushed and trembling, and did not meet his eyes. Neither did she take her hand from his shoulder; they had not changed their position.

'Diana,—what are you going to say to me?'

'Haven't I said it?' she answered with a moment's glance and smile; and then between smiles and tears her head sank again.

'Why did you never tell me before?' he said with a breath that was almost a sob, and at the same time had a somewhat imperative accent of demand in it.

'I did not know myself.'

'And now?'—

'Now?'—repeated Diana, half laughing.

'Yes, now; what have you got to tell me?'

'Do you want me to tell you what you know already?'

'You have told me nothing, and I do not feel that I know anything till you have told me,' he said in a lighter tone. 'Hallo, Rosy!—what's the matter?'

For Rosy, seeing herself entirely to all appearance supplanted, had now broken out into open lamentations, too heartfelt to be longer disregarded. Diana gently released herself, and stooped down and took the child up, perhaps glad of diversion; but Rosy instantly stretched out her arms imploringly to go to her father.

'I was jealous of *her*, a little while ago,' Diana remarked as the exchange was made.

But at that word, Basil set the child, scarcely in his arms, out of them again on the floor; and folding Diana in them anew, paid her some of the long arrear of caresses so many a day withheld. Ay, it was the first time he had known he might without distressing her; and no doubt lips can do no more silently to reveal a passion of affection than these did then. If Basil had had a revelation made to him, perhaps so did Diana; but I hardly think Diana was surprised. She knew something of the depths and the contained strength in her husband's character; but it is safe to say, she would never be jealous of Rosy again! Not anything like these demonstrations had ever fallen to Rosy's share.

Anything, meanwhile, prettier than Diana's face it would be difficult to see. Flushing like a girl, her lips wreathing with smiles, tear-drops hanging on the eyelashes still, but with flashes and sparkles coming and going in the usually quiet grey eyes. Dispossessed Rosy on the floor meanwhile looked on in astonishment so great that she even forgot to protest. Basil looked down at her at last and laughed.

'Rosy has had a lesson,' he said, picking her up. 'She will know her place henceforth. Come, Di, sit down and talk to me. How came this about?'

'I don't know, Basil,' said Diana meekly.

'Where did it begin?'

'I don't know that either. O, *begin!* I think the beginning was very long ago, when I learned to honour you so thoroughly.'

'Honour is very cold work; don't talk to me about honour,' said Basil. 'I have fed and supped on honour, and felt very empty!'

'Well, you have had it,' said Diana contentedly.

'Go on. When did it change into something else?'

'It has not changed,' said Diana mischievously.

'When did you begin to give me something better?'

'Do you know, Basil, I cannot tell? I was not conscious myself of what was going on in me.'

'When?'

'Perhaps—since soon after I came home from Clifton. It *had* not begun then; how soon it began after, I cannot tell. It was so gradual.'

'When did you discover a change?'

'I *felt* it—I hardly discovered it—a good while ago, I think. But I did not in the least know what it was. I wished— Basil, it is very odd!'—and the colour rose in Diana's cheeks, —'I *wished* that I could love you.'.

The minister smiled, and there was a suspicious drop in his eyes, which I think to hide, he stooped and kissed Rosy.

'Go on. When did you come to a better understanding?'

'I don't think I recognised it until—I told mother, not a great while ago, that I cared for nobody in the world but you; but that was different; I meant something different; I do not think I recognised it fully, until—you will think me very strange—until I saw—Evan Knowlton.'

'And then?' said Basil with a quick look at his wife. Diana's eyes were dreamily gazing out of the window, and her lips wore the rare smile which had vexed Evan, and which he himself had never seen on them before that day.

'Then,—he ventured to remind me that—once—it was not true.'

'What?' said Basil, laughing. 'Your mother makes very confused statements, Rosy.'

'He was mortified, I think, that I did not seem to feel more at seeing him; and then he dared to remind me that I had married a man I did not'— Diana left the word unspoken.

'And then?'

'Then I knew all of a sudden that he was mistaken; that if it had been true once, it was true no longer. I told him so.'

'Told him!' echoed her husband.

'I told him. He will make that mistake no more.'

'Then, pray, why did you not tell the person most concerned?'

'I could not. I thought you must find it out of yourself.'

'How did he take your communication?'

'Basil—human nature is a very strange thing! I think, do you know?—I think he was sorry.'

'Poor fellow!' said Basil.

'Can you understand it?'

'I am afraid I can.'

'You may say "poor fellow!"—but I was displeased with him. He had no right to care; at least, to be anything but glad. It was wrong. He had no *right*.'

'No; but you have fought a fight, my child, which few fight and come off with victory.'

'It was not I, Basil,' said Diana softly. 'It was the power that bade the sea be still. *I* never could have conquered. Never.'

'Let us thank him!'

'And it was you that led me to trust in him, Basil. You told me, that anything I trusted Christ to do for me, he would do it; and I saw how you lived, and I believed first because you believed.'

Basil was silent. His face was very grave and very sweet.

'I am rather disappointed in Evan,' said Diana after a pause. 'I shall always feel an interest in him; but, do you know, Basil, he seems to me *weak?*'

'I knew that a long while ago.'

'I knew it two years ago—but I would not recognise it.' Then leaving her place she knelt down beside her husband and laid her head on his breast. 'O Basil,—if I can ever make up to you!'—

'Hush!' said he. 'We will go and make things up to those millworkers in Mainbridge.'

There was a long pause, and then Diana spoke again; spoke slowly.

'Do you know, Basil, the millowners in Mainbridge seemed to me to want something done for them, quite as much as the millworkers?'

'I make the charge of that over to you.'

'Me!' said Diana.

'Why not?'

2 B

'What do you want me to do for them?'

'What do you think they need?'

'Basil, they do not seem to me to have the least idea—not an *idea*—of what true religion is.'

'They would be very much astonished to hear you say so.'

'But is it not true?'

'You would find every wealthy community more or less like Mainbridge.'

'Would I? That does not alter the case, Basil.'

'No. Do you think things are different here in Pleasant Valley?'

Diana pondered. 'I think they do not *seem* the same,' she said. 'People at least would not be shocked if you told them here what Christian living is. And there are some who know it by experience.'

'No doubt, so there are in the Mainbridge church, though it may be we shall find them most among the poor people.'

'But what is it you want me to do, Basil?'

'Show them what a life lived for Christ is. We will both show them; but in my case people lay it off largely on the bond of my profession. Then, when we have shown them for awhile what it is, we can speak of it with some hope of being understood.'

————

'Has anything special come to the Dominie?' Mrs. Starling asked that evening, when after prayers the minister had gone to his study.

'Why, mother?'

'He seems to have a great deal of thanksgiving on his mind!'

'That's nothing very uncommon in him,' said Diana, smiling.

'What's happened to *you*?' inquired her mother next, eyeing her daughter with curious eyes.

'Why do you ask?'

'I don't do things commonly without a reason. When folks roll their words out like butter, I like to know what's to pay.'

'I cannot imagine what manner of speech that can be,' said Diana, amused.

'Well—it was your'n just now. And it was your husband's half an hour ago.'

'I suppose,' said Diana, gravely now, 'that when people feel happy, it makes their speech flow smoothly.'

'And you feel happy?' said Mrs. Starling with a look as sharp as an arrow.

'Yes, mother. I do.'

'What about?'

Diana hesitated, and then answered with a kind of sweet solemnity,—'All earth, and all heaven.'

Mrs. Starling was silenced for a minute.

'By "all earth" I suppose you mean me to understand things in the future?'

'And things in the past. Everything that ever happened to me, mother, has turned out for good.'

Mrs. Starling looked at her daughter, and saw that she meant it.

'The ways o' the world,' she muttered scornfully, 'are too queer for anything!' But Diana let the imputation lie.

———

They went to Mainbridge. Not Mrs. Starling, but the others. And you may think of them as happy, with both hands full of work. They live in a house just a little bit out of the town, where there is plenty of ground for gardens, and the air is not poisoned with smoke or vapour. Roses and honeysuckles flourish as well here as in Pleasant Valley; laburnums are here too, dropping fresh gold every year; and there are banks of violets and beds of lilies, and in the spring-time crocuses and primroses and hyacinths and snowdrops; and chrysanthemums, and asters, and all sorts of splendours and sweetnesses in the fall. For even Diana's flowers are not for herself alone, nor even for her children alone, whose special pleasure in connection with them is to make nosegays for sick and poor people, and to cultivate garden plots in order to have the more to give away. And not Diana's roses and honeysuckles are sweeter than the fragrance of her life which goes through all Mainbridge. Rich and poor look to that house as a point of light and centre of strength; to the poor it is, besides, a treasury of comfort. There is no telling the change that has been wrought already in the place. It is as Basil meant it should be, and knew it would be. It is as it always is; when the box is broken at Christ's feet, the house is filled with the odour of the ointment.

THE END.

MURRAY AND GIBB, EDINBURGH,
PRINTERS TO HER MAJESTY'S STATIONERY OFFICE.

Printed in the United Kingdom
by Lightning Source UK Ltd.
123014UK00001B/315/A